WOLF'S HEAD

Book 1 in *The Forest Lord* trilogy

By Steven A. McKay

For my daughter, Freya
With Love.

CHAPTER ONE

"Robin! Look out!"

The cry came from close behind him, and he dropped to the ground, rolling to his left and coming up in one fluid motion ready for the attack he knew would come.

"Hah. Nice move!" The man was laughing, but a meaty hand swung round viciously, aiming for Robin's neck.

He swayed backwards, feeling the massive fist of the miller brushing his shoulder, and, adrenaline coursing through his veins, lunged forward, arms outstretched. He caught the heavier, older man round the midriff, his momentum taking them both to the ground. Robin landed on top, his forearm pressing down on his opponent's windpipe.

"Yield, miller!"

The miller tried to laugh again, gasping as his round face turned purple. "You win...Get off, you daft bastard!"

Robin jumped up and spread his arms charismatically, grinning as he looked around at the cheering spectators.

"The winner of this bout: Robin Hood!" The adjudicator raised Robin's arm as the people of the village shouted and laughed in congratulations. The big miller, Thomas, smiled through gritted teeth, slapping his young opponent on the back, much harder than was needed. "You did well, lad. You've a natural gift for fighting. Maybe one day I'll test you properly. Better watch that temper though." He walked off, grimacing at his opponent, as the older village men mocked him cheerfully over his defeat.

Robert Hood, or Robin, as everyone knew him, was tall, and, even at just seventeen years old, had

1

incredible upper body strength, with enormous arms and shoulder muscles thanks to his training with the longbow since childhood. His honest brown eyes and easy smile made him a popular character in the small village of Wakefield.

"You did it!" Robin's friend Much slapped him on the back, a broad smile on his open face. "I never thought you'd be able to beat my da, he's strong as an ox!"

It was a fine spring day, the trees just about filled out with their green covering again, and the May Games were well under way. Everyone in the village was dancing, singing, competing in something or other, or simply enjoying the ale and meat the local lord, Thomas, Earl of Lancaster, had provided. The sounds of revelry and smells of food cooking filled the air, as the few skinny local dogs that hadn't been eaten during the recent hard winters mooched around hoping to find some scraps on the ground.

Robin grasped Much's arm, laughing as he looked at his friend. "You're right; I never thought I'd beat him either! One good punch and he'd have had me; his arms are like tree trunks." He shook his head sheepishly. "I panicked when he almost got me; that's why I just threw myself on him."

Despite his modesty, Robin had the speed, agility and quick thinking to make him more than a match for most of the men in Wakefield.

"Aye, that was a wild move; my da wasn't expecting it. Don't think anyone was! Let's go an' get a drink." Much dragged Robin along and they headed for the ale sellers. "Look, the May Queen's coming."

Robin looked up eagerly; they both knew who would be Queen this year: Matilda, daughter of Henry the fletcher. Robin thought she must be the loveliest girl in all of England, and hoped, one day not too far off, to make her his wife. They had lain together occasionally over the past year, and promised themselves to each other, but Robin hadn't worked up the courage to ask her for her hand yet. For all his swagger he was still rather a shy young man, not entirely confident in himself.

Matilda appeared, walking slowly towards the village green, smiling happily. She wore a plain white dress which accentuated her slim figure, a garland of colourful spring flowers in her strawberry blonde hair, and, when her gaze rested on Robin for a second or two, he felt a small thrill run through him. She was followed by a great black bull, led by three Jacks-in-the-Green: village men in dark-brown cloaks, with ornate leaf masks covering their faces.

The Sword Dance began as the small procession reached the centre of the village. Swords were laid on the ground in a six-pointed star shape, then the villagers, Matilda included, laughed and whooped as they spun around the steel hexagram holding hands and swapping partners.

The bull was brought forward haltingly, as if knowing its fate, its hooves dragging in the damp spring grass, nostrils flaring and eyes bulging. It was an older beast, near the end of its life, but to most of the revellers it looked a magnificent animal.

As it reached the centre of the whirling Dance, a Jack-in-the-Green moved alongside and grasped the animal's great head, bringing a long knife out from underneath his cloak. The dancers slowed to a stop and watched in grim fascination as its neck was slashed open, the younger villagers gasping, wide eyed, as the blood flowed on to the grass below.

"Praise be to Herne!" The villagers cheered and clapped in appreciation as the great bull's life-force slowly ebbed away and it dropped ponderously to the grass with a gentle thud. Some of the blood was allowed to seep into the earth, in the spirit of the sacrifice, but one of the men soon placed a large wooden bowl under the incision to catch the valuable crimson liquid.

"That was a big bull eh?" Much shook his head admiringly. "Do you think it'll mean a good crop this year? Even my da struggled last year with the hard winter. You know what it was like, the whole village nearly starved."

Robin nodded, sharing his friend's hopes. His own family had gone short of food during many of the previous winters. He didn't want to feel the pain of a hunger-swollen belly again. The dying bull was the villagers' plea to God – any god: *In return for this mighty bull, let the year bring good weather for our crops.*

Although the people of Wakefield were Christian, the old gods and their ways had not been completely forgotten. While the Church didn't approve, it generally let the people get on with it, as long as they kept going to Mass.

With the black bull now dead, the crowd began to drift away to other amusements. An archery contest was about to start, and more people were dancing, as a travelling minstrel appeared and began cajoling the crowd to join in with his crude songs of love and lust, fighting and flatulence.

"Look, shooting. We'll win that!" Robin wandered through the crowd towards the archery competition, Much following in his wake.

Both young men, like most yeomen in England, had been practicing with bow and arrow since they were seven years old, and although it was illegal to hunt deer in the forest, Robin had found it necessary during the previous harsh winters to help feed his family. Bringing down unsuspecting game with a longbow had made Robin a crack shot.

Much usually had enough food to eat, being the son of the miller, but venison was always a welcome change from bread and pottage at the table in his house too, so he had become almost as good with a bow as Robin.

They would do well in the archery competition.

"Robin! Wouldn't you like to dance with me?" Matilda, the May Queen, came up behind Robin and grasped his hand. Her blue eyes flashed in the sun as she swirled away, somehow still grasping his hand. She pulled herself in close again, pressing her face, and her body, close to his. "Hmmm? Dance?"

Robin felt his face turn red as he gazed lustfully at the girl, and Much began to laugh. "He'd love to Lady May Queen, but the archery competition's just starting. He'll be back for that dance shortly!"

Matilda pouted suggestively at Robin as Much tried to drag him away. "You'd rather play with your longbow than dance with me? Lots of other men want to dance with the May Queen; I won't wait on you forever."

Robin grinned sheepishly, sensing the implied criticism in her words and, squeezing the girl's hand, promised he'd be back shortly.

The two young men swaggered off, Robin's eyes lingering on Matilda's lithe figure as she spun around into the dancing again. "Aye, she's got a nice arse, but forget about her until I've beaten you in the shooting." Much grinned, and pointed towards the wooden figures set up in the clearing, as Robin playfully smacked the back of his friend's head.

Today, he told himself. Today, I'll ask her to marry me, I've waited too long as it is . . .

Many of the local men had entered the archery contest, being well trained in the use of the longbow. Their lord expected those of able body to practise with the weapon, should he need a force of armed men in times of trouble, and, since carrying a sword was illegal for most villagers, the longbow was the main weapon for yeomen, villein and peasant alike.

As the contest progressed the number of competitors was whittled down until only the two friends and four other men remained, but as Much raised his bow for his next shot, there was a disturbance near the dancers in the centre of the village green, and the archers turned to look.

A loud voice could be heard, castigating everyone in the vicinity.

"What's going on?" asked Much, craning his neck to try and get a better view.

Robin, unlike his smaller friend, could see over most of the people in the crowd and shook his head darkly. "Looks like that prior from down south. Shouting about something. The bailiff's with him too."

Much glanced warily at Robin, knowing his friend had a great dislike for churchmen in general, and the wealthier ones in particular. Most of the villagers harboured resentment and bitterness towards the clergy – struggling to find bread to fill your family's bellies during a long, cold winter, while the prior paraded around the country wearing a small fortune in gold and silver jewellery tended to create ill feeling.

Robin had two younger sisters, Rebekah and Marjorie, but Rebekah, always the smallest of the smallest of the siblings, had been too weak from hunger to survive the harsh winter of 1315, some six years ago. Torrential rain had fallen on England constantly that year, ruining the harvest. The wheat that remained had to be dried out in ovens before it could be used, and even then it offered little nutrition when baked into bread. Many died of hunger, while travellers in the countryside were murdered by brigands desperate for the food they carried.

Wheat rose to eight times its normal price, while barley, peas, salt and other essential ingredients were also, suddenly, too expensive for most people.

Then the Scots came.

Buoyed by their success at the battle of Bannockburn, they raided deep into Yorkshire, stealing what little food the people of northern England had left, while King Edward II did nothing to help.

Robin had been only eleven then. He had seen people in his village eating horses and dogs – even heard whispered rumours of cannibalism – and he could still remember his little sister Rebekah's tiny seven year old body, wasted away – emaciated. And even though Rebekah's twin, Marjorie, had survived, she had never

6

fully recovered her strength – her family were terrified she might go the same way as her sister if they suffered another famine like that of 1315.

The sight of an overweight, richly dressed churchman like this prior made Robin's blood boil.

"Come on; let's see what the fat bastard wants."

The pair headed over for a closer look, the archery contest forgotten.

The Prior of Lewes, John de Monte Martini, retinue in tow, was checking on those parishes he was responsible for, to make sure they were being run properly.

Today, it was Wakefield's turn.

The pleasant atmosphere of ten minutes earlier had gone, as the laughter and dancing died away under the clergyman's pious ranting, his small group of armoured guards glaring around at the villagers.

"Heathens! The lot of you!" the prior lambasted the people, forcing his way between them. "Animal sacrifice? Herne the Hunter? Green Men?" The clergyman snatched the mask made of oak leaves from the face of one of the men playing Jack-in-the-Green. The man glared back sullenly, but soon dropped his gaze to the floor. It didn't do to make an enemy of the church, and the man, Simon, a poor labourer, had no wish to get on the wrong side of the fat prior, especially with the bailiff there.

Although Wakefield was part of Thomas, Earl of Lancaster's manor holdings, his bailiff, Henry Boscastle, oversaw most of the daily business of the place. He knew everyone that lived there.

An angry voice shouted from the back of the crowd, "What's the problem, prior? We do this every year; it's just a bit of fun."

The churchman rounded in the direction of the voice, face flushing scarlet, as other villagers muttered in agreement. "I don't care what you do every year. My predecessors might not have minded this pagan...nonsense! But I do. I expected to find you

7

people at mass today, yet when I arrive at the village chapel I find the doors bolted and my flock – that's you people – out here getting drunk on cheap ale and worshipping false gods." He didn't mention the fact that the local parish priest was nowhere to be found. In fact, Father Myrc had been enjoying a few drinks with the villagers and had run off back to All Hallows when he heard the prior was coming.

The village headman, Patrick Prudhomme, pushed his way to the front of the crowd and attempted to placate the irate prior.

"Forgive us, Father. These rites mean nothing. We're all good Christians in Wakefield, the bailiff will tell you that. This is just a bit of fun to celebrate the spring coming."

The bailiff looked as if he'd rather be drinking free ale and eating some of the great bull which was surreptitiously hauled away to the butchers. A sullen man at the best of times and not averse to abusing his position for money or other favours, Henry Boscastle was not a popular figure in Wakefield.

The prior was oblivious to all this, and carried on in an even louder voice, pushing his way further into the mass of revellers, moving further and further away from his hired guards, although the bailiff kept pace, thrusting people aside forcibly. "I don't care what this is. I expect you all to go home, now, and sleep off the drink you've all taken too much of!"

There were angry groans from the villagers, but no one felt brave enough to openly disagree with the prior, especially with the half-dozen mercenaries guarding him, although they looked fed-up with the whole situation. The prior wasn't paying them much and he was a terrible travelling companion.

Much shook his head in disgust, as Robin clenched his fists and fought to keep his temper under control.

The headman raised his hands sadly. "As the prior says, everyone, let's get this stuff cleared away, and make our way to our homes."

"You can all be at church tomorrow too," cried the clergyman, "making suitable offerings, in penance for your wickedness today!"

"Shove your offerings!" someone shouted, again, from the back of the crowd, well hidden in the sea of faces. Voices were raised in agreement, emboldened by their anonymity.

"Aye, shove them up your big fat arse!"

People laughed, but the atmosphere had turned dangerous, as the angry villagers, many of them half drunk, crowded threateningly around the prior and his retinue, rather than moving away as they'd been told.

The prior's mercenaries, although they couldn't see over the mob, realised things were getting dangerous and tried to form up around the clergyman but the villagers surged forward. The lightly armoured men, unwilling to draw their weapons in such a volatile situation, found themselves being shoved further and further away from their charge.

The prior's face turned white as the bailiff, sensing the crowd's hostility, and more reckless than the mercenaries, dragged his sword from its leather sheath and pointed it at anyone he thought looked a threat. "Get back, you bastards, or I'll take this to you."

Henry was an intimidating, commanding man, and the sight of his enraged face and drawn weapon calmed most of the crowd. "Go on, get back to your homes. Now!" he roared, kicking a retreating villager in the back, sending him sprawling. The man tried to get to his feet but found the bailiff's face against his, sword blade pressing against his neck. "Go home, before I open your neck," Henry growled, nostrils flaring with the promise of violence.

The man edged backwards on the ground, wide eyes fixed on the bailiff's sword, before he stumbled up and shoved his way into the mob, looking over his shoulder every few seconds to make sure Henry wasn't following him.

"Come on," Much said, looking on in disgust from their position near the back of the crowd. "No sense in hanging around here with all this going on. Let's go and get that drink from the alehouse – we never got one earlier."

Robin stood rooted to the spot though, staring over the other villagers' heads at the clergyman, as Much, oblivious to his friend's black mood, walked off in the opposite direction.

Just then, Matilda, the May Queen, head bowed, moved past the prior and bailiff. "You – idiot girl. Get that filth off you!" The prior grabbed Matilda's arm roughly and tore off the garland of flowers she was wearing in her hair, throwing it, and, inadvertently, Matilda, to the ground.

Before he knew what he was doing, Robin found himself, in a cold fury, striding towards the prior and the girl he'd loved since childhood.

While the prior's guards found themselves hemmed in by the baying throng, unable to move towards their master, the host of people seemed to part for Robin as he stormed towards the sneering clergyman.

"Keep your hands off her, you fat bastard . . . !"

The villagers still angrily crowding the village green stopped as one, open mouthed, staring in disbelief at the enraged young man striding through their ranks towards the prior.

Much, finally realising his friend was about to do something rash, pushed back into the crowd to try and restrain him, while Henry the bailiff, his sword back in its sheath, glared at the big yeoman, wondering if he'd imagined the outburst.

"What did you just say to me?" the prior demanded in shock, then, regaining his composure slightly, he stepped towards Robin and said quietly, "I'll have you in chains and thrown in jail for that."

"Robin, leave this, please, let's just do as the prior says." Matilda's voice was shaking with anger, but the fear in her eyes was clear as she climbed back to her feet and grasped Robin's wrist.

"Oh no, girl. You'll be going to the jail too." The prior moved even closer, dropping his voice again, so only Robin, Matilda and the bailiff could hear what he said next. "Maybe the sheriff's men will find some...use...for you there. Maybe I'll even come visit you myself to see you on your knees...begging the Lord's forgiveness."

Robin understood exactly what the prior was getting at. He knew many of the wealthier clergymen owned brothels in the big cities, and Prior John de Monte Martini was said to have a stake in several, even using their services himself regularly. The bailiff looked amused but didn't say a word, simply enjoying the entertainment, while Matilda regarded the clergyman in confusion.

"You piece of filth," Robin spat, shaking with nerves, but too angry to back away. "You touch her and I'll kill you."

The prior grimaced and ran a podgy hand along Matilda's arm, staring into her blue eyes. "Oh yes, after a few nights with nothing to eat I'm sure you'll be a lot more...open...to a humble prior like me. In fact, I'm sure I could find you employment in a local establishment, I own myself – the 'Maiden's Head' in Nottingham." He nodded towards Henry. "Take them into custody bailiff. My men will help, once they remove this mob." He glared around himself, trying to locate his guards, who were still too far away to know what was happening.

Henry, nodding his head with a grim smile, began to draw his sword again, shouting for assistance from the locals around him. No one seemed greatly inclined to help.

Robin heard nothing after that, as a roaring noise filled his ears and time seemed to slow to a crawl. His right fist shot forward, smashing into the prior's nose which exploded in a burst of scarlet. As the churchman fell backwards onto the ground the shocked bailiff finally dragged his sword out, but before he could use it, Robin kicked him brutally between the legs. With a scream of agony, Henry doubled over, and, as he dropped to his knees, sword forgotten, Robin grabbed the bailiff's head and smashed his knee into the man's face.

Henry collapsed, bloodied and senseless, beside the downed clergyman.

"You fucking…peasant!" the prior looked up, and screamed through hands clutching his ruined nose. "I'll see you hanged for this!"

Robin, adrenaline pumping, feeling utterly invincible, moved forward to finish off the clergyman, teeth bared in a wild grin, but the brawny miller, Thomas, Much's father, managed to grab him, pinning his arms to his side. "Stop this, you fool, calm that temper of yours! He means what he says. His guards will have you once they realise what's going on – you need to get away."

"He's right, you have to run!" Matilda pleaded, eyes flickering nervously between Robin and the crowd, half expecting a soldier to run her big friend through any second.

Thomas and Much, who had finally pushed his way through the throng, pulled Robin away from the cursing prior and unmoving bailiff. They moved in the opposite direction to the mercenaries, who only now understood something had happened to their master and were forcing their way aggressively through the villagers.

The people parted to let the miller and the younger men through – some folk even cheered and slapped Robin on the back as he passed by, happy to see the prior bloodied, and glad it wasn't them who would suffer punishment for it.

The crowd closed in protectively behind them, although not all the villagers were pleased by Robin's actions.

"You're an idiot, Hood!" The village headman Patrick appeared beside them as they hurried away. "Do you realise the trouble you've brought on yourself? And the village too? That prior isn't one to forget this – he'll make all our lives miserable now. Christ, you've probably killed the bailiff too! What the hell were you thinking?"

Robin shook his head, his anger fading as he started to realise the danger he was in. "He was saying things about Matilda, threatening her...I just exploded, Patrick."

"I don't know what he said, but you have to get away from here, fast. Get to your house and take whatever you need, the people will delay the mercenaries. Say your goodbyes; you won't be seeing anyone around here again for a while."

That finally hammered home to Robin what he'd done, and he wanted to puke. Or cry.

"Peace, Patrick, he's still young – hasn't learned to control his temper yet. Let's help him get away for now – he can worry about what he's done later." The miller grasped Robin's shoulder sympathetically. He may not have heard what the prior said, but he knew Robin. Knew he wasn't one to lie.

The headman nodded, shaking his head regretfully. "Get your stuff together, son. Good luck – you'll be needing it. Don't worry too much about your ma and da, or young Marjorie – the prior might be powerful, but the villagers won't let him take out his anger on an innocent family. He'll be off back down to Lewes soon anyway."

Robin's head whirled. None of this had crossed his mind when he'd exploded into violence at the prior's whispered promises. Could he have held himself in check if he'd realised the consequences of his actions? He honestly couldn't say.

It mattered little now. He let Much lead him home at a sprint, mind in turmoil. John and Martha, Robin's parents, were out somewhere, enjoying the day with Marjorie, oblivious, for now, to what their son had just done.

He hastily gathered his longbow, a loaf of bread, some dried fish and his cloak, and then dragged a box out from under his bed. In it was an old sword – not the finest steel in England, but it had been well maintained and had a decent edge to it. It had a threadbare leather scabbard, so he looped it around his belt and pushed half a dozen arrows in beside it.

Much, watching from the door for any signs of pursuit shook his head, eyes brimming with tears of frustration as he contemplated the life his friend would have from this day forward. Unless Robin was pardoned, which seemed impossible for a lowly yeoman with no money, he would need to live his life as an outlaw in the depths of Barnsdale Forest – a "wolf's head", as those outside the law were known. Deprived of all legal rights, any man could kill a wolf's head on sight, as if he were nothing but an animal.

Less than an animal, in fact. The king's Charter of the Forest made it illegal for commoners to hunt deer. But any man could hunt down a wolf. Or a wolf's head.

"Get going. Hide in the forest for a day or two until this all blows over. I'll leave you food and things at the old well. You know the place."

"Of course I do!" Robin tried to smile, although it came out as more of a gimace. "We used to spend hours there as children, playing."

"Aye," Much agreed sadly. "So we did – playing games, pretending to be mighty Saxon warriors killing the evil Norman invaders".

Now, though, real warriors would be hunting for his friend, with real steel.

The time for play was over.

"Shit!" Much gasped, eyes wide. "The soldiers are coming!"

14

Robin pushed past his friend out the door and saw four of the prior's men jogging through the village, looking for him.

"You there!" one of them roared, pointing his drawn sword towards the two young friends. "Hold!"

Much pressed himself against the door frame and raised his hands to show he wasn't a threat, and yelled at his friend to make for the forest.

The soldiers broke into a run, yelling for him to stop, as Robin sprinted off towards the outskirts of the village and the safety of the trees.

Three of the pursuers, older men in their forties, were blowing hard after a short distance, but, looking back over his shoulder, Robin could see one of the soldiers was keeping pace with him, his eyes fixed determinedly ahead on his quarry. This man didn't waste his breath shouting, and Robin felt the beginnings of panic building up inside him as he contemplated the possibility that he might have to make a stand.

He had never fought with a sword before – never even really practised with one. The bow was his weapon, like the rest of the young men in the village. But the man chasing him made his living with a blade in his hand. Robin knew he couldn't beat him, and the trees were still some way off.

Trying to push his body even harder, pulling in great lungfuls of air, he risked another glance behind and cursed in fear as he realised the soldier was gaining on him. He would not make it to the trees before the man's sword took him in the back.

With a sob of desperation, Robin spun round, facing his pursuer. The man's eyes widened in surprise as Robin hastily pulled an arrow from his belt, drew back his great longbow, and desperately let fly.

The shot was a poor one; Robin's whole body was quaking with the exertion of the run, and his arms felt leaden, but the arrow hammered home with a sickening damp thud into the soldier's thigh. The man spun backwards onto the ground with a scream of agony, his leg flailing behind him.

The remaining pursuers, some distance back, cried with outrage at the sight of their fallen comrade, as Robin shakily rose to his feet and stumbled off towards the forest, gasping with exertion, the downed soldier's cries of agony ringing in his ears.

CHAPTER TWO

True to his word, Much, helped by Matilda, had left food and blankets near the old disused well in the forest, close to the neighbouring village of Bichill.

Although Robin was hardly used to living life in luxury, it was a new and frightening hardship having to sleep outdoors, in the dark, lonely, night of the forest.

Much would have stayed by Robin's side, at least on some evenings, but he was fearful that the bailiff had paid some of the villagers to spy on his movements, in the hope of tracking down his outlawed friend.

The sheriff's men had arrived the day after Robin had attacked the churchman, but they hadn't been overly keen on searching the greenwood for a violent wolf's head. They knew the forest, which covered many square miles, harboured many outlaws, all of them more than willing to stick an arrow into a lawman's back.

The prior had been taken back down south to Lewes to recuperate – his incompetent mercenaries paid off by the furious clergyman. Henry the bailiff, almost recovered, but with badly swollen bollocks and a broken nose to match the prior's, had questioned Robin's parents on where their son might have gone to hide. While the bailiff liked an easy life, Robin Hood had utterly humiliated him before the people of Wakefield. He was eager to see the young man in a dungeon, or swinging from a rope. Or, even better, on the end of his sword.

The villagers, led by the headman, Patrick, had been polite, but un-cooperative with the hunt for Robin, and banded together to make sure no one suffered unduly over what had happened. The bailiff had been made to leave by the locals when it became clear his questions were upsetting an already distraught John and Martha Hood. And more violence had been threatened when the bailiff and his foresters had tried half-heartedly to take Matilda into custody.

Eventually, when it became clear information on Robin's whereabouts would not be forthcoming, the villagers were left in relative peace.

The bailiff and the prior might have been enraged over what had happened to them, but they knew it would do neither of them any good if they pushed the close-knit community of Wakefield too far. The Earl of Lancaster was an absentee landlord, leaving the running of Wakefield to his appointed steward and the bailiff, but he still expected the village to be productive. Civil unrest would not be looked upon kindly by the earl – the second most powerful man in England – as it often led to a drop in rents and the earl needed as much money as he could get, being locked, as he had been for years, in a power struggle with his cousin, King Edward II.

As a result, the bailiff reluctantly allowed the villagers to go about their lives as normal. He knew he would find some way to make them all pay, eventually.

Robin was not forgotten altogether by the authorities, though. Publicly declared an outlaw, it was made clear he would be arrested and likely hanged if he was ever captured. Assuming one of the foresters didn't get a chance to shoot him first.

Luckily for the young outlaw, spring was in full bloom when he found himself sleeping rough in the forest. The weather was warm, the days were long, and there was enough food to eat. With nothing to lose any more, Robin, sometimes joined by Much, hunted the king's deer and rabbit, fished, and collected those berries which grew at this time of year. The pair would regularly have too much for Robin to eat himself; so Much would take the extra back to Wakefield and share it among those families that needed it most.

But Robin knew he couldn't live like this forever. Summer would fade into autumn and that into winter. Life on the run, in a makeshift shelter in the forest, with food much scarcer, would not be as easy as it was just now.

"You're going to have to leave the area and try to find a life somewhere, away from the prior and the law." Much told him. "Hiding from the foresters is simple enough when you've thick trees to lose yourself in, but come winter there'll be no shelter here."

Robin stared into the crackling fire the pair were cooking a spitted brown trout on, his belly rumbling as the delicious smell filled the little clearing they were hiding in. At any other time, this would have been a wonderful late spring day – two young friends, surrounded by the lush green foliage of beech and oak, sunlight filtering softly through the leaves, violets and bluebells carpeting much of the ground, a small waterfall burbling quietly somewhere nearby, and a couple of fat fish to share between them.

"Robin?" Much prompted.

"I know," Robin sighed heavily. "It hasn't been a terrible life as an outlaw so far. But I need help."

"Help? You need to get away!"

Robin shook his head. "I can't just leave, Much. My family is here in Wakefield. You."

"Matilda?"

"Aye, Matilda," Robin agreed, softly, before his voice rose, becoming loud and angry. "Why should I be forced to leave my home because of that fat priest? He was out of order – just because he's rich he thinks he can do whatever he likes!" He jumped up and pulled the trout from its spit, biting off a great chunk viciously. "I was going to ask her to marry me . . ." he mumbled sadly, sitting back on the ground in dejection.

Much remained silent, letting his friend vent his emotions on the food for a while.

The sounds of insects, and birds singing merrily, filled the forest as the pair sat in thought.

Then a dry twig, a remnant from the previous autumn, cracked somewhere close to their right.

Robin sat bolt upright, his eyes seeking out his bow on the ground next to him. Much looked over at his friend, wide-eyed, questioning, frightened.

The sounds of men moving none too quietly through the undergrowth came to them, and Robin silently hefted his bow over his shoulder and grabbed his bag of arrows.

"Wait! You smell that? Fish cooking!" A voice, too close for comfort, reached them, as Robin stealthily gathered his blankets and tied them to his back, motioning Much to follow him as he moved into the trees in the opposite direction to the voice.

Suddenly, a man, his green and brown attire marking him as a forester, appeared through the foliage right next to Robin and the young man started back in shock. The undergrowth, most of it fresh and damp, had masked the sounds of the forester's approach, and Robin mentally kicked himself for his lack of woodcraft.

The forester roared a warning to his fellows in the bushes nearby and dropped a hand to his sword hilt, dragging the weapon from its sheath. Robin, startled, and frightened by the sounds of at least four or five other foresters converging on them, let his longbow slip down his arm and, grasping it two-handed, swung it as hard as he could into his opponent's face.

The man screamed, and fell on the forest floor, writhing in pain, his cries panicking Robin and Much even more.

"This way!" Robin gasped, grabbing his friend by the arm and dragging him into the deeper bushes, the sounds of pursuit close behind them.

The foresters must have stopped to check on their injured companion, as the two young men ran for a long time, as fast as they could through the trees, tripping over roots and low branches numerous times, before at last, utterly breathless, they collapsed on the hard brown soil beneath an ancient oak.

There was no elation at their escape. The adrenaline coursing through their veins gave them no pleasure as they sat, backs against the rough bark of the oak, throats and chests burning, dragging in great lungfuls of air, eyes darting around for signs of other pursuers.

"Shit!" Much sobbed, slamming his palm against the tree in frustration, knowing they had been literally seconds from death or at least capture. "Shit, Shit, Shit!" His head dropped and he hugged his knees. "How can you live like this?" he groaned. "Knowing those bastards can appear at any time and kill you? How can you even sleep at night for fear of one of them sneaking up and running his sword through you?"

Robin had no answer to his friend's questions, so he sat in silence, catching his breath, too exhausted to even manage a shrug of his huge shoulders.

After a while, their hearts' stopped racing and the sense of immediate danger passed.

"You know," Robin grunted, "last week when I visited my family, my ma mentioned a group of outlaws who had been reported in the forest."

"Aye, I heard about them," Much replied. "But I heard they're a bloodthirsty lot too. Rapists and murderers."

Robin laughed bitterly, spreading his hands wide and looking around at the trees. "Bloodthirsty? They'd need to be – how the hell else would they survive, living their lives as outlaws in this godforsaken forest?"

Much looked away, understanding the point, but not liking where the conversation was heading.

"I can't do this on my own," Robin muttered. "I won't leave Yorkshire. I need to find people who can help me."

"But Robin, there's stories about these outlaws. Killing people for fun – killing children. Eating children . . . !" He shook his head in disbelief.

"Don't be bloody stupid!" Robin retorted angrily. "Who do you think's spreading those stories? The nobles! They don't want people to help the outlaws, so they spread ridiculous lies about them."

Much shrugged his shoulders. "You may be right, at least in part. But there's no smoke without fire. My da says the leader of this group's been an outlaw for years, and he's done a lot of bad things to a lot of people. Adam Bell, that's his name."

"I have no choice." Robin was almost pleading, hoping to gain some understanding from his oldest friend; hoping to gain some reassurance that this was, genuinely, the only option for him.

"How would you find this gang?"

Robin answered instantly, having thought this over repeatedly for the past three days. "They have to hunt, which means they need to buy arrows, right? Matilda's da is the fletcher in our village, so they probably get supplies from him sometimes. He might be able to send word that I want to join them."

The two friends sat for a while longer, still listening nervously for sounds of pursuing foresters, neither speaking as they contemplated how this idea of Robin's might turn out.

But the path was set. Robin travelled back to Wakefield with Much the next morning, to try and arrange a meeting with the band of outlaws.

* * *

"The king must be dealt with!" Thomas, Earl of Lancaster, slammed his palms on the hard stone bench in frustration, the noise echoing off the walls, and glared around at the other men in the chapter-house who were, mostly, nodding their heads in agreement at his proclamation.

The earl, a tall, slim man with thinning salt-and-pepper hair and heavy bags under his green eyes, had called an assembly in Pontefract priory, inviting many of the most powerful men in England to attend. In dribs and drabs they had arrived with their retainers and entered the imposing building hastily, as a heavy downpour drenched their fine clothes and a powerful gale whistled along the old stone corridors.

They were gathered in the chapter-house, a relatively cosy part of the building with a well-stoked fire burning brightly in a great hearth. Stone benches lined the elaborately carved walls, with columns and arcading all painted brightly, making the great octagonal room seem quite snug despite its high vaulted roof.

Thomas had paid the monks well to pile a table with Rhennish, Gascon and Spanish wines, and a selection of fine foods. The sight of expensive bread, fried herring, peacock and pork in breadcrumbs cheered the soaked magnates while they shrugged off their wet garments and tried to warm the damp from their bones. The wind and rain buffeted the spectacular stained-glass windows set high into the walls as the earl continued.

"Our tenants need help. There's no point in demanding taxes or grain from them when the crops have failed and they have no bread for themselves; nothing to sell to make money; and the constant threat of raids from the barbarians over the border!"

"Not to mention those damn Despensers!" Roger Mortimer, Baron of Wigmore shouted angrily. He, and some of the other Marcher lords who held lands around the Welsh borders, had travelled to this meeting after launching a devastating attack on castles belonging to the Despensers, who were loved by the king, but despised and feared, with good reason, by the other lords in the country.

Sir Richard-at-Lee listened, a slice of freshly baked, buttered *manchet* in his hand, as he gazed around appreciatively at the magnificent building, noticing with interest a grotesque, and disturbingly lifelike, leering satanic head carved into the wall far above the altar.

Sir Richard was the fifty-year old preceptor, or commander, of a modest estate in Kirklees, and had come to the gathering despite having misgivings. A knight of the Order of Hospitallers, with two fine sons, he was not too badly off under King Edward II. He knew throwing his lot in with the Earl of Lancaster and the lords from the Welsh Marches, could turn out to be a suicidal move.

Still, it was true that the king could be doing more to protect the north's interests, rather than allowing himself to be swayed by greedy, selfish and incompetent advisors such as the Despensers, which is why the proud Hospitaller had answered the earl's summons.

"The king sits in London demanding we tax our starving, impoverished tenants, but doing nothing to help while the Scots prepare again to ravage our lands!" The earl glared around at the magnates. "Stealing food from the peasants, killing our tenants – weakening *us*, gentlemen, for what are we without the income our tenants provide us?" He leaned back and crossed his arms over his chest, glaring round at the assembled nobles. "Meanwhile, the king is in the south, safe, while his greedy friends the Despensers fill his mind with poison . . . It cannot continue!"

There were grumbles of agreement again at that – the Despensers, both called Hugh, were determinedly ambitious and, with the support of the king, had managed to gain a great deal of power in the past few years. Many in England and Wales feared the Despensers ruthless greed, particularly the Marcher lords Humphrey de Bohun, the Earl of Hereford and Mortimer who had decided to take matters into their own hands, seizing castles and lands, including Newport, Glamorgan and Caerphilly, belonging to the Despensers.

Sir Richard helped himself to another cup of wine and looked around the chapter-house thoughtfully. Although there were a lot of powerful men in the room Richard wondered how many of them would back down if war was threatened by the king. Still, Edward would no doubt hear of this gathering and hopefully take it as a sign that he must do more for the northern and Marcher lords before things got that far.

"You have it right, Earl Thomas," Lord Furnival of Sheffield growled, chewing a baked spiced apple.

"The king should be doing more to help those of us on his borders, as his noble father did."

A small, bald man with an immaculately trimmed moustache Sir Richard recognized as Multon of Gilsland, shouted in angry agreement from near the back of the room, his voice echoing across the distance. "His father, God rest his soul, was a real man – a real king. If he was still alive we'd have wiped out the threat from the Scots by now and be better off for it! I've been near enough ruined these past few years!"

The Earl of Lancaster kept his expression severe, but Richard guessed he was pleased by the glint in his eyes. Years of neglect by King Edward II had turned many of his subjects against him. The gathered magnates knew the time was coming when they might be forced to take steps to remove the weak monarch and make the country great again. With Thomas of Lancaster at the helm, of course, Richard thought – he was the king's cousin after all, the wealthiest earl in the land, and hereditary steward of England, a title granted him years earlier by Edward himself. The big Hospitaller had no problem with that idea – the earl seemed a capable, if haughty man, who had tried repeatedly over the years to keep his cousin, the king, in check. Although Sir Richard was a Hospitaller – an Order which remained outwith petty local politics –he had come late in life to the order and, with two sons to provide an inheritance for, secretly retained ownership of lands adjoining his Hospitaller commandery in Kirklees.

The meeting carried on in similar fashion for a while longer, Richard and the other lords gladly eating and drinking their fill while airing a list of other grievances against the king such as his poor choice of advisors, his fondness for wine and his rumoured homosexual relations with former favourite Piers Gaveston, beheaded by Lancaster and his supporters almost ten years earlier.

Mostly, though, the Marchers demanded action against the Despensers, although the northern lords were more interested in knowing how Edward expected them to hold back the Scots should they attack again.

The Despensers greed and influence over the king was grave cause for concern amongst the noblemen throughout England, but to those in the north, such as Sir Richard, the threat of rampaging Scots was all too real, and seemed, at this stage, more immediate.

Eventually, a monk came in, head bowed, and silently lit the torches set around the walls, and Sir Richard realised it would be getting dark soon. He hoped the meeting would end before much longer, considering he had only travelled here today with his sergeant-at-arms, and the forests around these parts were thick with robbers and other outlaws. *Damn waste of good fighting men*, he thought, *someone could make a decent private army out of them.*

The Earl of Lancaster must have realised it was getting late too, as he stood and held his hands clasped before him until the gathered nobles noticed and fell silent.

"I'm glad to know we are all of the same mind, my lords," he smiled, meeting the gaze of those he knew held the most power and influence. "For now, though, I would counsel caution – we cannot afford to act recklessly, especially regarding the Despensers. Edward is still our king after all and he is very fond of those two." There were angry mutterings again; Richard was impressed at how well the earl was working his audience. "I, myself, will pledge to support the Baron of Wigmore and the other Marcher lords in their dispute with the Despensers, but I realise many of you gathered here do not agree with me on that point...yet." He glared at his audience, then shrugged his shoulder as if saddened by the magnates failure to make a stand against the king's favourites and, by extension, King Edward himself. "So, for now, I would simply ask you all to join me in swearing an oath to defend one another's lands against the Scots. If the king will not aid us, we must aid one another – we can't allow those savages to ravage our lands again."

Lancaster's plan was unanimously accepted, and Sir Richard knew the earl had made an important step. There was still some way to go though, before he had enough support to force the king to do anything about the Despensers.

"Very well, my friends," the earl smiled at everyone, meeting every eye. "I thank you for coming. Together – united! – we *will* repel any raids from north of the border." He spread his hands, looking around earnestly at the men he had gathered. "With your blessing, I will now write to bishop de Beaumont of Durham, bishop de Halton of Carlisle, and archbishop Melton of York, asking for their advice. If they are agreeable, I will invite them to meet with us on the 28th of June, one month from now. I hope to see you all there. Perhaps by then we may even be able to do something about the Despensers."

"Assuming the Marcher lords haven't already killed the bastards!" Multon of Gilsland shouted to laughs and cheers as the magnates pulled on their still damp cloaks and filed from the room, drunk with power and ambition as well as expensive imported wine.

The Earl of Lancaster had successfully enlisted the support of some of the most powerful men in northern England, if perhaps not as many, and not as unequivocally as he would have liked. Next, though, he would reach out to those nobles in the midlands and the south he felt would rally to his cause.

The earl grasped Sir Richard's hand as he filed from the room. They had met each other, in passing, various times over the years and had a mutual respect for each other.

"I'm glad you came," Thomas said. "We need men like you with us – good, patriotic men who only want the best for England. How are those boys of yours doing? Edward and Simon is that right?"

Richard was flattered that such a powerful man would remember his sons' names, and he nodded happily. "Doing well, my lord, Edward followed me and joined the Hospitallers in Rhodes. Simon, my youngest, he's off to a tournament in Wales as we speak – his first!"

The earl smiled and slapped the big knight on the arm. "I hope he does well. And I hope you'll come to the next meeting in a month's time. Too many landowners have been dispossessed recently, Sir Richard, as a result of the Despenser's and the king's actions. You and your son have as much to lose as any of us here."

The Hospitaller met the earl's eyes, wondering how the man knew about the lands he privately owned, but saw only honest concern there.

Still, a lot could happen in a month and he remained unsure whether Thomas and the Marcher lords would be able to sway the King to their cause, so he simply smiled and nodded as the earl moved on to say his farewells to the next departing magnate.

Sir Richard was impressed by the Earl of Lancaster. He would give the idea of attending the meeting at Sherburn-in-Elmet next month serious thought, as he knew the rest of the northern lords would.

Unknown to any of the assembled magnates though, Thomas, earl of Lancaster, steward of England, had sent a messenger seeking another alliance to an inconceivable place:

Scotland.

* * *

Joining Adam Bell's outlaw gang proved simpler than Robin had hoped. As Much and Robin learned, to their surprise, many of their fellow villagers often did business, covertly, with Adam Bell – selling him and his men food and other supplies.

28

Obviously, the outlaws had to get these things – arrows, clothing, ale, bread, rope etc, from somewhere. Robin just hadn't suspected that so many of their friends and neighbours helped outlaws. Either the bailiff also never knew, or he turned a blind eye to make his own life easier.

Matilda's father, Henry, repaired Adam Bell's men's old arrows, and sold them new ones when they needed them.

Henry had, a little reluctantly, asked Adam Bell to help Robin. Although the fletcher was content to do business with the outlaws, he too had heard the gruesome stories about Bell and his gang and, while not believing everything he'd been told, he knew the outlaw leader was a violent and uncompromising man. But, like Robin, Henry accepted the fact that the young man needed help and this was the only available source.

So Robin was introduced to Adam Bell; a tall, well built, yet strangely refined man, with thinning hair, intelligent green eyes, and a hooked nose. The outlaw leader was accompanied by two vicious-looking men, who, despite their size and hard demeanour, were strangely deferential to Bell.

"Don't think it's an easy life, boy," Bell growled at Robin, handing over a small bag of silver to Henry the fletcher, in return for a bundle of fresh arrows. "You pull your weight in my gang, and you do as I tell you, understand? No matter what."

Robin nodded nervously under Bell's glare, knowing this intense, forbidding man basically held the power of life and death over him. "I'm a good fighter, and I can shoot well. I won't be a burden to you."

Adam's two men grunted in amusement at that, but Robin ignored them, his face flushing. His temper had got him in enough trouble already.

They set off an hour later, after Bell had completed his business in the village, and Robin had said a final goodbye to his parents and Much. Matilda had met Robin on the village outskirts, safely hidden by thick trees and bushes, as Bell and his two men waited impatiently.

"I don't know when I'll be able to come back to see you," Robin had said, holding the young girl's hand earnestly. "I don't really know how Adam's group works. They travel around a lot, to keep ahead of the law."

"Why did this have to happen? Why couldn't that prior just leave us alone?" Matilda wiped angrily at her eyes. "God curse him, I hate that man!"

Robin hugged her close. "I know; me too. But the nobles and clergy do as they like, there's no one to stop them. I'll be back though. This'll all blow over, you'll see. And then…"

"Aye, then…what?" Matilda looked pointedly at Robin.

"Then I'll marry you of course!"

Matilda laughed gently. "Maybe. I've waited long enough for you to ask." She became suddenly earnest. "But I can't marry an outlaw, Robin. It'd be no life for us. When – if – we marry, you have to be a free man again."

Robin accepted this, knowing it was true, no matter how depressing. For all his talk of things "blowing over", he knew it would never happen. Outlaws *were* pardoned all the time in England, but it could take years, were it to occur at all. Matilda might be content to wait for now, but a girl in a village like Wakefield couldn't stay unwed for very long. Life was too hard in these times – family security was vital.

"I have to go," he told her, glancing round at the path into the forest as Adam Bell shouted at him to hurry up.

The couple shared a hurried kiss; their tongues exploring each other's mouths, before Matilda breathlessly pushed Robin away, giving his swollen manhood a playful squeeze through his trousers. "Come back to me when you're not an outlaw," she told him.

He gazed at her for a second, grinning, his body burning with desire, then, with a wave, hurried off to his new master.

Aye, you're the one for me, Robin, Matilda thought sadly as the young man ran off into the trees, tears filling her eyes again. *But I can't wait on you forever.*

CHAPTER THREE

There was a ringing crack as the quarterstaff rapped Robin's knuckles, and he yelped with the pain, almost dropping his own staff. Too late, he tried to raise it again, as his opponent continued his attacking move and thumped the weapon against Robin's shoulder, hurling him sideways into the shallow stream.

The outlaws cheered and laughed as the new young recruit splashed around, gasping in the water, before he managed to scramble back onto the grass again, cursing. He glared at his opponent, an older man called Matt Groves, all the while rubbing his bruised shoulder and blowing on his stinging fingers.

Life in Adam Bell's group was hard. There were sixteen men, not including Robin – all outlaws with nowhere else to go. The men trained nearly every day, with their great longbows, but also other weapons, such as swords, or as today, the quarterstaff.

It was a cool day, the forest filled with the sounds of loud bird song and the spring sun trying to break through fluffy white clouds in a light blue sky as the men sparred under trees filled with dark green new foliage.

"You're getting better, *boy*," Matt Groves nodded, his thinning blonde hair, arrow straight, bouncing in front of his cold eyes as he stared at the young outlaw. "You still fight like a fucking woman though."

Matt seemed to take some sadistic pleasure in besting Robin, perhaps trying to break his spirit, perhaps simply because Groves was a nasty bastard.

While he had been one of the toughest young men in his own village, these were hard, experienced fighting men Robin was with now. He regularly found himself lying on the forest floor, looking up at the trees with a throbbing shin bone, cracked ribs or aching kidneys, while the outlaw he'd been sparring with looked down at him gleefully.

"If you're finished your swim, Hood; how about catching us some breakfast?" Adam Bell tossed Robin a hunting bow, which he caught with a grimace as his painful knuckles tightened around it.

"An' don't be long, boy; I'm starving," Matt Groves smirked, lying down on the warm grass beside the other men.

Robin shook his head, his face red with embarrassment – at his defeat, and his being treated like a serf. But he held his tongue and strode from the camp into the thicker trees, promising himself he'd give Matt a good beating one day.

There was a vague hierarchy in the outlaw gang – Bell at the top, his most trusted men next, and everyone else around the bottom. As a newcomer, Robin found himself the lowest of the lot.

But his prowess with the bow, and resultant success hunting food the past few weeks had helped most of the men recognise him as a valuable asset.

Adam Bell himself rarely noticed Robin, nodding a greeting or barking an order at him occasionally, but never sharing more than a couple of words with him. Some of the other outlaws had begun to strike up friendships with Robin though, which made his new life less lonely and, in fact, the young man had started to accept his new life.

Suddenly spotting a family of grey hares relaxing in the sun near a clump of brambles he dropped onto one knee and silently fitted an arrow to the hunting bow, sticking another point first into the ground. He aimed at the largest of the little group and let fly. The other animals scattered instinctively as his arrow took the hare in the neck with a dull thump, but Robin smoothly pulled his second arrow from the ground and in a heartbeat had shot another. Smiling in satisfaction he collected the dead beasts and retrieved his arrows, his thoughts turning again to his new life as an outlaw.

A handful of merchants and well-off noblemen had passed through the forest since Robin had joined the gang, and Adam Bell had relieved them of their goods and purses. But Robin had not taken part in those robberies. Only a handful of men went along each time and Robin wasn't yet trusted enough to join in. Which suited him fine – he was quite content to stay in the background, out of harm's way.

Besides, many travellers hired bodyguards, and Robin didn't like the idea of using a sword against a man he didn't even know. Although he knew the day would come sooner rather than later, he was content to stick to sparring for as long as possible.

Sometimes Bell and his men would come back from those robberies with blood on their clothes, and wounds of their own. Robin would tell himself there was no other way – either the group got money somehow, or they would all die. Living off the land was only possible up to a point – his two hares wouldn't feed seventeen men for long. Money was still needed to buy clothes, salt, bread, arrows and other necessities from places like Wakefield and the other villages around Barnsdale.

He continued hunting for a while, catching a couple of blackbirds and a plump dove to go with his hares. They'd help make a tasty enough meal for the men tonight.

He made his way back to the camp, where one of the men had already filled their great iron pot with stream water and whatever vegetables they had lying around. Robin took out his knife and prepared the animals he'd caught. Skinning, gutting and plucking weren't his favourite jobs but no one offered to help, so he got on with it in silence.

When he was done, he added the meat to the pot and washed his bloodied hands in the stream. The other men were drinking ale round the fire, telling ghost stories, so Robin joined them, sitting near the edge of the group.

As the sun slowly started to set one of the other outlaws cheerfully handed him a wooden mug brimming with dark brown ale, which he accepted gratefully and, as the delicious meaty smell of the simmering soup filled the camp, Robin smiled in satisfaction.

It wasn't an ideal life, but it could be a hell of a lot worse.

* * *

"Morning, Hood," Adam Bell greeted him the next morning. It was a miserable, wet summer day, and Robin was planning on finding a nice big tree to shelter under where he could spend the day fishing. "We're going after a rich churchman today," his leader told him. "Get your weapons."

Robin was surprised, and found he was more than a little anxious. "You want me to come with you Adam?"

"That's right, lad. Your skill with a blade has improved a lot since you first joined us. It's time you put it to good use. There's a friar going down to visit the Prior of Lewes, and we know he's going to be carrying a fair bit of money. A friend of ours in Boroughbridge overheard the churchman talking in a tavern and passed word to us. He's probably hired a couple of guards to see him through the forest, but that'll be it. Move it now, get your gear."

Robin scrambled to obey. When it came to the military side of things, Adam Bell had an unmistakeable aura of command about him. Clearly he hadn't been a common outlaw all his life, but none of the other men trusted Robin enough yet to let him know what Bell's story was. Assuming they even knew it themselves.

He collected his longbow, along with the old sword he had brought from home, now with its edge nicely sharpened, and stuck a dozen arrows into his belt.

He strapped on his gambeson as he ran to join the other men in the raiding party. This padded green fabric body armour was a gift from Bell, and, like his sword, had seen better days, but it came down to just above his knees and would turn many blows, short of a direct sword thrust. There was a patched hole in the back, from where such a thrust had killed the armour's previous owner. Robin tried not to think of that too much as he fastened it in place.

"Ah, you're coming with us today?" One of Adam Bell's most trusted men, John Little, slapped Robin on the back, almost knocking the younger man to his knees. John was a huge man, over six and a half feet tall, with the build of a wrestler, and a wild brown beard which made him look like a great bear, although at twenty four he wasn't much older than Robin. The outlaws jokingly called him Little John.

Robin liked the enormous man immensely, although he could be terrifying if enraged. Robin had rapped him painfully on the knuckles during a quarterstaff practice the previous week and had run off into the trees rather than stand up to the roaring giant. The other outlaws had found it hilarious, as had John when he calmed down and Robin returned sheepishly from his flight with a peace offering of a rabbit he'd shot for the big man's dinner.

"Feeling nervous?" John asked as the ten-strong group headed out of the camp to the main road through the forest, a spot just over a mile and a half away from their camp.

Robin swallowed, nodding gently. "I'll be fine though."

"I was shitting myself the first time I went out with Adam on a raid," the big man admitted. "Worried I'd freeze if any fighting started."

Robin was genuinely surprised – the thought of Little John being scared of anything seemed incredible.

John laughed, reading the look on Robin's face correctly. "Listen, my life may not be worth anything to the sheriff, but it means a lot to me! It doesn't matter how big you are if an arrow takes you in the back, or a soldier stabs you in the guts. There's no shame in being scared, lad, as long as you don't let it control you."

The conversation did Robin good, calming his nerves a little, but he knew he'd always be afraid of how he'd react in a real life-or-death fight until the day he proved to himself he could handle it. He still hoped today wouldn't be that day though– most of these robberies were simple, non-violent affairs. Bell's well-armed, hard men simply threatened whoever they'd targeted, and the money and goods were handed over. It would be suicide for a merchant or churchman, normally only accompanied by, at best, a handful of guards, to stand up to the well-drilled outlaws.

And yet it did happen from time to time, when they targeted someone as aggressive and proud as John or Bell himself. Robin hoped this friar they went to rob didn't have guards like Little John with him.

It didn't take long for the group to reach the chosen ambush point, and Bell began issuing orders. Robin was surprised again, when he realised Adam didn't just have the men hide behind trees until the target appeared, then jump out waving swords and demanding gold. On the contrary, Bell appeared to know this area of the forest well, and positioned the men in handily placed trees and bushes, encircling the vicinity. The road at this point narrowed, and both sides were fenced in – a rock wall on one side, and a dense grouping of bushes on the other. The only way out of the trap was ahead, or back the way the target had come, but the outlaws laid ropes before and after the ambush site, ready to be pulled up into position, effectively penning in the unfortunate friar and his party.

Bell had sent Robin off with Little John, to the young man's relief. If it did get violent, John was the best person to be with. They settled down to wait, taking up position in the thick summer undergrowth, at the rear of the ambush spot.

John took a piece of bread from his pocket, tearing half off for Robin. He began to chew contentedly, although his gaze never left the road.

"How can you eat at a time like this?" Robin wondered, looking at the bread he'd been handed.

John laughed gently. "Don't worry. We'll have plenty warning when the friar's near. D'you think Adam didn't bother sending out a scout?" He tore off another huge chunk of the thick loaf, his eyes twinkling with amusement. "Will Scaflock's gone on to see where the bastard is."

Robin grunted sheepishly, and tried his best to chew some of the bread, but his appetite was gone for now. He handed the food back to John and set an arrow to his bowstring, just in case. John laughed again, louder this time, shaking his head and chewing noisily.

Robin was relieved to find John had been right though, when, a short time later, there was a bird call from along the road and the big man got to his feet, grunting to Robin, "That's Will's signal. They're coming."

Robin stood up too, glad to find he wasn't as nervous as he'd feared he'd be. He was focused on the job at hand, without feeling too frightened.

Little John pulled an arrow from his belt, and the two outlaws stood ready, hidden by the thick tree they'd chosen as cover.

A while later they heard a horse-drawn cart creaking along the road and, as it slowly came into sight, Robin felt his pulse quicken as he realised this might not be as simple as he'd hoped.

The friar was riding a horse. In addition to the noisy cart, which carried a roughly made, but sturdy, wooden box, there were eight hard-looking riders. These men all wore gambesons like Robin's, for protection, with helmets in seemingly good repair, and long swords at their hips. Every one of them looked as dangerous as most of Adam Bell's men.

Robin looked a little nervously at John. The bearded giant looked back, shrugging his massive shoulders. "That friar must have something good in his box, to be travelling with all those guards."

As the party reached the ambush point, there was a piercing whistle from Adam Bell, hidden somewhere in the dense foliage, and the ropes at either end of the road were suddenly pulled taut, and tied to the trees, blocking the horsemen's path. Little John and the other outlaws raced forward silently to pen the friar's party in, although they stayed close by the thick tree trunks in case they needed cover. Robin followed, gripping his bow so tight he could feel it digging into his hands.

The friar sat back in his saddle, but didn't look particularly dismayed by the ambush. Robin was a little worried, though, to see the guards quietly and efficiently take up defensive positions encircling the cart.

The young outlaw looked quickly at Little John, but the big man just glared grimly at the guards. He'd clearly seen this all before, and Robin again felt himself relaxing a little. Adam Bell knew what he was doing. He must do, after all these years as a robber outlaw leader.

Just then, Bell himself walked into view, and stood facing the friar. He never looked once at the stony-faced guards who followed him with their eyes. Some of them had drawn short bows and held them aimed at Bell.

"Get those ropes out of the way. Before we cut you down." The friar's words were cool, his voice powerful and controlled, but Robin realised the churchman probably knew this was Adam Bell in front of him. And Bell's reputation was not a good one, when it came to how he treated churchmen who didn't co-operate.

The outlaw leader simply pointed to the cart. "We're taking that, friar. Those men" – he gestured to the eight soldiers –"can keep their weapons and continue along the way with you." He spread his feet and put one hand on his sword hilt, staring at the friar.

The clergyman shook his head. "There are nine of us. Get out of the way and nothing more need be said about this."

Adam Bell continued to stare impassively at the friar for another few seconds, before raising his hand and pointing at one of the soldiers. "Will!"

Bell jumped behind a tree as there was a snapping noise, and a thud. Robin was shocked to see the soldier Bell had single out thrown backwards off his horse, gasping and clawing wildly at the arrow that had hammered into his windpipe. Will Scaflock smoothly dropped his bow and pulled his sword from its scabbard, dropping into a fighting stance, an appalling animal grin on his wide face.

No one moved for a split second, until the shock passed, and the guards realised what had happened.

"Damn it, Scaflock!" John grunted, knowing Will could have easily incapacitated the guard with a shot to the arm or shoulder, rather than killing him.

"Dismount!" one of the soldiers shouted, realising they had no chance while on horseback, penned in as they were, and the rest followed, kneeling beside the cart, weapons drawn.

Adam Bell's voice could be heard from behind a tree. "There's eight of you now, friar!" He laughed coldly. "Now tell your men to drop their weapons and we'll just take that cart of yours." He stepped into view again, expertly drawing a beautifully forged sword.

Robin held his breath, as time seemed to stand still and the friar stared silently at Bell.

The stand-off was broken as the soldier who had ordered the dismount earlier decided he'd had enough. "Get the bastards!"

The seven remaining guards charged at the outlaws ringing them, and Robin found himself staring at a wiry, red-haired man, roaring wildly as he raised his sword to bring it down on the young outlaw's head.

Robin brought his own sword up, deflecting the powerful blow, as instinct and training took over and, leaning forward, he rammed a knee between his attacker's legs. The man fell to the floor groaning, as Little John's quarterstaff hammered down on the back of his head.

The two outlaws stepped over the unconscious man, looking for other targets, but it was a similar story all around. The friar's guards, hard as they may have been, were all down, injured or dead. Not one of the outlaws seemed to have taken a scratch.

Only the friar stood in the way of the cart now.

"Right, you fat, tonsured arsehole, get out of the way." Adam Bell strode forward, the outlaws close behind, ready to check the contents of the wagon. "I'm not really a religious man, but I'd rather not have to get too violent with a member of the clergy. I don't have a problem with it though, if you push me."

The friar was an overweight man, in the grey robes of the Franciscan order, with an open, honest-looking face. As Bell closed on the wagon, suddenly, from the folds of his robe, the friar produced a short wooden club, about a foot long, and, with blinding speed, blasted the breath from Bell's lungs with a thrust to the guts, and then battered him to the ground with a vicious blow to the temple.

Everyone froze in shock. Adam Bell lay unmoving on the forest floor, as the friar moved coolly into a fighting stance and, with a small smile, said, "All right then, boys. Who's next?"

The sheer violence and precision of the friar's attack seemed to hold the outlaws rooted to the spot, as they realised this was no normal churchman. Robin could just see Adam Bell's chest rising and falling gently, so, although he was still alive, he'd likely feel sick for a while when he came to. Robin was impressed with the friar's courage.

Little John must have felt the same respect for the hardy Franciscan, as he raised his great voice and ordered the outlaws to hold their positions. "That was good for a fat friar, but you know you can't fight us all."

"No?" The friar cocked an eyebrow. "Do you want to find out, my child?"

John burst out laughing at this show of bravado. "I'm sure you'd try too, father, but I don't want any more deaths today. Now put down the weapon and let us take what we came for. You can be on your way."

Will Scaflock was shaking his head impatiently during the exchange. "Come on John, what are we waiting for? I can stick an arrow in this fat bastard and we'll help ourselves. We need to get moving."

John rounded on Scaflock, his face red with anger. "Shut your fucking mouth Scarlet! You're always too quick at killing people. There was no need to shoot that guard in the throat, and there's no need to cut down this friar." He turned back to the churchman. "Now move it, you, we don't have all day and the longer this lasts the more likely he is to use you for target practice." He nodded at Will in disgust.

Will Scaflock was nominally Adam Bell's second in command, but in practice, the men followed Little John when Bell wasn't around. Scaflock was a bitter man, earning the nickname "Scarlet" amongst the outlaws as a result of his bloodthirsty temper and eagerness to use violence on anyone who got in his way. John, although a hard man, was well liked by the men, and his sheer physical presence was normally enough to cow even Will.

The friar glanced coldly at the muttering Scaflock and nodded his head in resignation. "All right, wolf's head. You win. Take your prize."

Robin let himself relax a little as the churchman dropped his club and went to check how his companions were.

A couple of the outlaws collected the ropes from the ambush site, some of the others rounded up the mercenaries horses to sell in the outlying villages, and Will Scaflock climbed nimbly into the driver's seat on the cart. John and Robin gingerly lifted Adam Bell, who was now groaning quietly, up behind Will, laying him out as comfortably as possible beside the big wooden chest.

The robbery had taken longer than Robin had realised, and, despite it being only late afternoon, the light was beginning to fail as the heavy grey rain clouds continued to hide the sun.

"It'll be too dark to check the cart properly tonight," Little John decided. "We'll search it tomorrow, once Adam's awake." With a gesture, he directed them back to camp with their prize, but he placed a big hand on Robin's arm as the other outlaws moved off.

"Wait with me for a bit, Robin," he rumbled. "I want to talk to this friar."

As the wagon, with its new, outlaw, escort moved off, John and Robin, still with weapons warily drawn, walked over to the clergyman.

"How are they?" John asked.

The friar shook his head sadly. "Eight men. Six of them dead. Two unconscious, although they should be all right." Robin was glad to see the red-haired man who had attacked him was one of the lucky ones still alive.

Little John shook his huge head. "I'm sorry about them, friar, I truly am."

The Franciscan grunted, glaring up at John. "Maybe you are, but I'm sure you won't be kept awake at night with your sorrow."

John didn't reply. The friar had it right. He didn't enjoy seeing men die, but an outlaw's life was a violent and dangerous one, and John had seen more than his share of death. He'd sleep just fine tonight, like the friar said.

"All right, Robin, let's be off." John turned with a farewell nod to the friar and began to follow the other outlaws.

"I'm coming with you."

Again, the churchman stopped John and Robin in their tracks. "What d'you mean?" Robin asked.

"I'm coming with you," the friar repeated, tucking his club back under his robe.

"Why the hell would you want to do that?" John burst out. "We're outlaws!"

The friar walked past the two men and followed the creaking cart. "You leave me no choice. I was taking that cart to the Prior of Lewes, John de Monte Martini. The prior hates me. I won't bore you with the details, but he'd use any excuse to make my life a misery. I can't turn up and tell him I was robbed and lost all his money. He'd blame me – have me locked up, the devil."

Little John was completely lost for words. Robin, genuinely liking the overweight clergyman, grinned. "He can fight, John, that's for sure. And I know myself what a bastard that prior is – it's his fault I'm even here. What harm would it do to let the friar come with us for now?"

The massive outlaw shook his head in disbelief, but with a shrug of his shoulders relented. "Very well, you can come with us. You better hope God and all his angels are smiling on you when Adam wakes up puking his guts out, though, and finds you sitting in our camp. He'll probably let Scaflock cut your balls off."

"Better men than him have tried," the friar laughed confidently, striding through the green undergrowth.

"Where did you learn to fight?" Robin wondered, hurrying after the portly clergyman, pushing branches and leaves out of the way as he went. "And what's your name?"

The friar's blue eyes glittered as he turned towards the young outlaw. "I wasn't always a man of the cloth, lad. And you can call me Tuck."

CHAPTER FOUR

"Ride!"

At the command the mounted men kicked their heels in, urging their horses forward, trying to build momentum behind the wooden lances couched under their arms.

The spectators – well-to-do men, women and children of Glamorgan – filled the benches of a wooden stand running the length of the lists. Cheering gleefully and clad in over-stated finery of wonderful colours each had their own favourite, often chosen for no better reason than the combatant's livery or place of origin.

The horses thundered down the field, sending great clumps of damp grass flying as they tried to gain as much momentum as possible.

Banners and flags of every hue were held aloft as the audience cheered and sang in support of their chosen combatant.

The blunted lance of one man hammered off the shield of his challenger and the crowd cheered at the victory. The two knights returned to their tents with nothing badly injured other than pride.

Taking the field that day in his first jousting tournament was Simon, youngest son of Sir Richard, Hospitaller Commander of Kirklees.

Simon was a big man, just twenty years old, with the same black hair and almond eyes as his father and his older brother Edward. He had never trained with a longbow or quarterstaff – as a young teenager, Simon had spent his time training on horseback, clad in chain or plate mail, and wielding a sword and shield.

Or a great lance, as he held now, looking nervously through the visor of his helmet down the lists at his opponent, Edmund Wytebelt, son of the wealthy Charles of Bodmin.

The lances were tipped with wooden blocks to make them less lethal, but Simon still felt a sense of trepidation as the sounds of the expectant crowd filled his ears.

A man stood in the middle of the list holding aloft a yellow flag, and, as he dropped his arm with a flourish, Simon gritted his teeth, raised his lance, and kicked his great white charger, Dionysus, forward.

His eyes narrowed, and the sound of the crowd faded so all he could hear in his helmet was his own gasping, excited breath, and the thunder of his horses hooves towards his adversary.

Edmund Wytebelt, clad in a livery of red and blue checks over his gleaming armour, the pure white belt that gave him his name tied gaily round his waist, filled Simon's vision and the young northerner, adrenaline coursing through him, grinned in anticipation, all his nerves and trepidation momentarily forgotten.

The spectators' cheers and whistles grew in volume, reaching fever pitch as the knights closed in on each other at a terrific speed, their horses' eyes bulging, teeth bared and legs blurring while the riders, armour clad and helmeted as they were, seemed weirdly motionless.

Driven along on his incredibly powerful equine projectile, Simon raised his lance and, fixing his eyes on his opponent, pointed the heavy wooden weapon at the target he visualised on Edmund Wytebelt's chest.

There was a tremendous bang, and the next thing Simon knew he was lying flat on his back, staring up at the wonderfully sunny sky through the small slit in his visor, stunned.

Slowly, it dawned on him he was still alive, although his head ached a little. And he was lying on the grass rather than sitting on his horse. *But at least I'm alive*, he thought, as he rolled onto his side with some difficulty, his armour being enormously heavy, and tried to see what was happening.

His squire, Alfred, a young boy of twelve from Kirklees, was already beside him, although he hadn't noticed the lad's approach.

"Where's Edmund?" Simon asked, still squinting through his visor and seeing his opponent's horse standing, rider-less, chewing the grass at the side of the tilting field contentedly.

Alfred helped the young knight remove his helmet and Simon noticed at once where his opponent was.

Like him, Edmund had been thrown from his mount onto the hard ground. Unlike him, Edmund had taken more than a glancing blow to the helmet.

"Is he alright?"

Alfred helped his master to his feet, the pair of them straining to lift the weakened and stunned armour-clad young man from the floor.

"Is he alright?" Simon repeated, louder this time, glaring at his squire.

"Not really, my lord." Alfred shook his head, looking around in consternation as armed soldiers converged on them. "He's dead. You killed him."

* * *

"Get up, boy. Hurry!"

Robin's eyes snapped open as a rough hand shook him awake. He had been on guard duty during the hours before sunrise and felt like he'd only just fallen asleep he was so tired.

"God's bollocks, what is it?"

Matt Groves gave him a sour look. "We're moving camp, get your things together, fast, and help us shift all our gear."

Looking around Robin could see the rest of the outlaws preparing to leave, and, panicking, he jumped to his feet and hastily strapped on his weapons. *What's happening? Have we been discovered?*

Matt walked off without any further explanation, but Little John wandered past just then, a huge pack of gear tied to his broad back.

"John! Why are we moving? Have we been found?"

John patted the younger man on the back with a reassuring smile. "Calm down, man, what's the panic?"

"Matt just woke me and told me to get my things, he never said why. I thought something bad had happened."

"Aye, well, he's just messing with your head again, lad," the giant grunted with a scowl in Matt's direction. "It's nothing to worry about – we move camp like this all the time. It makes it harder for the law to find us if we don't stay in the same place for too long."

Robin carried on stuffing his things inside his blanket and tied it shut before looping it around his shoulder. "No one mentioned we were going to be moving," he grumbled.

John laughed and led Robin towards the middle of the camp where the rest of the men were gathering. "Generally, none of us ever know when we'll be moving. Adam decides, but he doesn't tell anyone until the day he wants us to leave. Keeps the men on their toes, and means none of us know where we'll be from one week to the next if anyone gets captured."

"Adam?" Robin yawned and wiped grit from his eyes, feeling like he needed another couple of hours rest. "Last I saw him he was groaning and senseless on the back of that cart."

John grinned. His massive, hairy, face, which could be so incredibly intimidating when he was angry, looked almost childlike as his brown eyes sparkled at Robin good-naturedly. "He woke up during the night. Decided we'd been here long enough. He's probably expecting that box of Tuck's to be holding a lot of money. If it is, people will come looking for it, so – safer to move to a new camp."

Sure enough, Bell stood in the centre of their camp, directing the men and looking none the worse for Tuck's beating.

With a last look around to make sure nothing had been left behind, the men moved off to the east behind their leader.

* * *

As it turned out, the new camp site Adam had chosen wasn't that far from the old one – just an hour and a half's walk, the stolen cart groaning behind them the whole time. Within another hour and a half the outlaws had erected sturdy new shelters to sleep under, and found lookout points high in the trees to make sure no one stumbled upon them.

Setting up the iron cooking frame over a fresh fire-pit, Will had sent a couple of men to go and find some meat for the big pot.

The cart they had stolen from Tuck and his retinue contained many religious and historical texts, which Bell's men had no interest in, most of them being illiterate, but also in the cart was a very large sum of money.

Friar Tuck, whom Bell appeared to have forgiven for knocking him out, told the outlaws the money was to have been a gift to the prior, John de Monte Martini, from Archbishop Melton in York, ostensibly to help renovate the local churches, but Tuck guessed it would mostly be used by the prior on his personal ventures.

"Like his brothel?" Robin spat into the campfire, still seething weeks after the prior's threat to Matilda.

Tuck nodded gently. "Amongst other things I suppose, aye."

Matt Groves gave a crude laugh and rubbed his crotch suggestively. "I might just visit that brothel of his – it'd only be right. At least he'd get some of his money back."

The outlaws joined in the laughing and joking, although none of them would genuinely venture into the city on such a frivolous errand, especially Groves, one of the most wanted men in Adam Bell's group.

Robin was pleased at getting one over on the hated prior, but the men's talk had brought back memories of Matilda. He quietly slipped away from the camp, moving deep into the forest for some time alone with his thoughts.

* * *

Matilda's mother, Mary, slammed the wooden plate down on their table, making the girl jump and her father grumble irritably.

"You're sixteen now, girl. Well past time you were wed. Every other girl in the village your age has a husband, apart from that Clara."

"God have pity on the man that weds her," muttered Matilda's father. "Face like a cow's arse." He winked good-naturedly at his daughter, who stifled a laugh as he shovelled another spoonful of pottage into his mouth.

"Shut up, Henry! I'm being serious here." Mary took her own seat at the table and helped herself to a piece of bread, glaring at her husband.

"I don't want to wed any of the village boys, ma."

Through another mouthful of dinner, Henry asked, "What about that Richard lad, the one that we saw working in the fields today, arms like tree trunks?"

Matilda shook her head. "Ach, he's nice enough, but he's a big oaf. Remember, he set fire to his own house last year when he was drunk? The fire burned down two of his neighbour's houses as well before it was put it out. Anyway, he's been with half the village girls already."

"Well, you better lower your standards, soon," her mother told her. "Or there'll be no young men left for you. You want to be a spinster all your life?"

"No, Ma I don't! I'll get married when I'm ready!" The girl took a sip of ale, wiping her mouth with the back of her hand. "If that prior hadn't…"

"For God's sake girl, you can't hang around here hoping Robin Hood comes back for you! Even if he does, he's an outlaw. You run off with him and you'll be an outlaw too. You know what the tithing would do to you if they caught up with you?"

Matilda knew only too well what would happen if she was declared an outlaw, she'd gone over this a thousand times in her head, since the day she kissed Robin goodbye.

"Drown you, that's what!" Mary finished the last of her meal and sat shaking her head at Matilda, but her voice softened as she carried on. "Forget Robin. He was a good boy, would have been a good husband too. But he's as good as dead now. Right, Henry?"

The big fletcher nodded reluctantly. "Your ma does have a good point, lass." Matilda dropped her eyes to the table, but Henry could see the tears glistening there. "Maybe Robin will be pardoned though," he smiled hopefully at his beloved daughter. "It happens often enough. If that prior dies or the parish is taken on by another clergyman . . . well, Robin might be able to come back to Wakefield then."

Matilda looked up at her father and broke into a bright smile that lifted his heart. Her mother told him to shut up again.

* * *

"You're coming with me, Hood." One of the older outlaws, a wiry, grey-haired man known as Harry Half-hand on account of having a hook instead of a left hand, grunted at Robin, with a grin. "Adam's heard there's some rich lady travelling to Pontefract with a big escort,

51

so him and the rest of the lads are heading there. Me, you and Arthur here are heading for Watling Street to relieve a merchant of his – much lighter – purse."

Robin hastily shrugged on his gambeson in surprise as the main body of outlaws marched from their camp, Little John giving him a cheery wave in farewell.

"Just the three of us?"

"Aye," Harry nodded, scratching his ear with the blunt part of his hook. "It's an easy job. Merchant with a single guard, against the three of us."

Arthur laughed as he came over to join them. He was a stocky lad, not yet twenty, with greasy brown hair and most of his teeth missing. Robin liked him a lot – he always seemed to have a smile on his filthy face. "Aye, I'd rather be doing this than going after that lady. The boys are saying she's got a dozen guards with her! Fuck that!"

"Fuck that right enough," Harry Half-hand grinned in reply, and strode off towards Watling Street, which was the name for the great old Roman road that stretched from one end of England to the other.

The trio reached the main road before midday. Even though the sun hadn't yet reached its zenith, it was a scorching hot June day, and the outlaws were glad to find a sheltered spot to await their prey.

Still, Arthur had a short attention span and started to complain after a while. "How much longer are they going to be?" he grumbled. "I'm bloody roasting here."

"How long's a piece of string?" Harry growled to a blank look from the gap-toothed young outlaw. "If they left their lodgings near Ferrybridge at dawn they should be here any minute. So shut up and watch the road."

As he stopped speaking the sounds of a rider approaching reached them. "Robin, you watch the merchant. Arthur, you watch the guard on the far side of the road. I'll take the other guard, nearest me. Okay?" The two young men nodded and Harry gestured Arthur to take up a position on the opposite side of the road. Robin was sent forward ten paces to hide in a dense clump of gorse, the plants' bright yellow flowers almost glowing in the bright sunshine.

Before long their target came into sight. Sure enough, there was one rider, a small, weasel-faced man, finely dressed in colourful clothes and flanked by a couple of broad young mercenaries on foot either side of him.

Robin took little notice of the little merchant, despite Harry's orders, dismissing him out of hand and concentrating on the guards who looked much more threatening.

Both were tall – almost as tall as Robin himself. They had decent quality light armour and weapons – one wore a sword, while the other had a wicked looking mace hanging at his side. The thought of such a brutal crushing weapon making contact with his head made Robin wince.

Harry Half-hand waited until the travellers were a few paces along the road in front of him then stepped from behind the big oak, his sword drawn and brandishing his hook menacingly, knowing the sight of it often made men nervous.

"Hold!" he commanded, as Arthur and Robin, longbows aimed at the group, stepped from their hiding places in front of the merchant's party.

The merchant looked shocked at the sight of the outlaws, the mercenaries just looked angry to have been ambushed so easily as they turned to face Harry.

"You two – drop the weapons," the outlaw ordered the guards. "Let's make this nice and easy. If any of you make a wrong move, my pals there" – he gestured towards the grim faced Robin and Arthur – "will put a nice thick arrow in your guts."

The merchant glared at Harry. "You want my purse, I assume, wolf's head?"

The outlaw grinned. "Aye that I do, so toss it over here and you can be on your way, and no one gets my hook in their face. You two" – he gestured at the two mercenaries. "Drop your weapons and move on. I promise you, we won't harm you and, let's be honest, you don't have many options anyway."

The guards looked at each other, and then the eldest shrugged and dropped his mace on the ground with a heavy thud. "They could have shot us already if they wanted us dead," he told his companion, who nodded agreement and dropped his own weapon.

As the two men walked warily off along the road, Harry nodded in satisfaction. "Now we just need your purse, merchant."

Arthur had kept his bow trained on the mercenaries as they moved further along the path. Robin could see the merchant had tears in his eyes and dismissed him as a weakling, training his bow again on the unarmed guardsmen who were, by now, a good thirty paces away.

"Here!" From the corner of his eye Robin saw the merchant reach into his belt for his purse and relaxed his aim. This had been even easier than he'd expected. Adam would be pleased with them…hopefully the others had been as lucky in their robbery of the rich lady in Pontefract.

Distracted, he saw Arthur's eyes grow wide in horror, and turned to look at Harry Half-hand.

The older man was lying in the dirt of the forest floor, blood bubbling from his mouth, a small dagger in his windpipe.

Still, Robin didn't see the merchant as a threat, his eyes searching the trees for the source of the dagger, until the horseman suddenly kicked his mount and bolted along the road towards the startled mercenaries.

Arthur loosed his arrow, the shaft, as thick as a man's thumb, slamming into the merchant's back just under his neck, throwing the rider onto the ground. The horse ran on for a few seconds before it came to a halt and stood, head bowed, oblivious or uninterested in its master's death.

"What the hell?" Robin cried, his bow still trained on the confused mercenaries who continued to back away along the trail. "What happened?" he demanded, looking at Arthur.

"You were supposed to be watching the merchant!" Arthur retorted. "Harry told you! The little bastard had a throwing dagger in his belt! He got Harry with it!"

The two guardsmen, desperate just to get away from this alive, had reached a turn in the road and suddenly sprinted away, much to Robin's relief.

"Oh shit," he gasped, rushing over to the downed outlaw. "He's dead!"

"Of course he's fucking dead!" Arthur shouted. "He's got a dagger in his throat – makes it hard to breathe! Come on."

The young man took the weapons from Harry's corpse then jogged over to the merchant he'd shot.

"Grab the horse," he told Robin, who, dazed, moved to do as he was told while Arthur used his dagger to cut the merchant's purse from his belt. "Right, let's go."

"What about Harry?" Robin asked.

"Unless you want to carry him – or dig him a grave" – Arthur growled – "leave him for the wildlife. And next time you're told to watch someone – bloody watch them!"

CHAPTER FIVE

"Robert the Bruce? Fuck off!"

"I'm telling you," Friar Tuck nodded his tonsured head solemnly, despite Will Scarlet's disbelieving laughter. "That's what people are saying: the earl of Lancaster has been seeking an alliance with the Scots."

It was a warm, humid night in the second week of June. The forest was pitch black and silent for miles around apart from the sounds of insects and laughing outlaws. Harry Half-hand's death was mostly forgotten by everyone except Robin already. Life was cheap when you were an outlaw.

Robin knew the man's death was his fault though – his lack of experience had made him focus on the two mercenaries, rather than seeing *everyone* as a threat, even the apparently harmless merchant. He wouldn't make the same mistake again.

The campfire blazed merrily in the middle of the small clearing, for light rather than heat, and Adam Bell shrugged his shoulders, looking at Tuck seriously.

"I wouldn't blame him if he's been talking to the Bruce."

Scarlet leaned forward on tree stump he was sitting on, his laughter replaced by indignation. "You wouldn't blame him? He's supposed to be defending our people from those bastard Scots, not forming alliances with them!"

Robin watched as Adam took a drink from his ale. He was surprised to see his leader glaring at Will – one of his most trusted confidants – with a look of utter disdain, but the expression only lasted a moment before it was replaced with a smooth smile, and no one else seemed to notice.

"Perhaps," Adam grunted, "the earl of Lancaster thought enlisting the aid of the Scots an acceptable price to pay in order to remove England's worthless King? Sometimes a leader has to work with people he knows are beneath him."

Robin was watching closely again as Bell's eyes lingered on Will scornfully, but Friar Tuck's booming voice drew everyone's eyes to him.

"That sounds like Prior de Monte Martini trusting me with his wagon," he laughed, "the good lord knows he saw me as being far beneath him."

"He was right an' all," Little John grinned.

Robin and the rest of the outlaws smiled at that as Tuck continued.

"I wonder what happened when those two guards got back down to Lewes and told the bastard his cart had been stolen."

* * *

After the raid on the prior's money cart the two surviving guards decided it might be safer if they returned to where they started their journey, in York, rather than going on , empty handed, to de Monte Martini away down in Lewes with the bad news. So, it took some time before news reached the prior of the theft. When he discovered it was Adam Bell and his gang who had stolen all his money he was enraged even further.

"Adam Bell! Bell has my money! Do you know how much money there was in that cart?" de Monte Martini roared at his bottler, Ralph, throwing the letter from York onto his desk. "Two hundred marks! That's how much!" He began pacing the chamber furiously, wringing his hands as he did so.

Ralph was astonished at the figure. Two hundred marks was a substantial amount of money, even by the prior's standards. He simply nodded dumbly, trying his best not to irritate the irate de Monte Martini.

Ever since the prior had been attacked by Robin, he had felt a burning, and thoroughly un-Christian desire, for revenge. It had taken weeks for his shattered nose to heal well enough for him to breathe properly, and even now, he knew he would bear the disfigurement for the rest of his life.

"Do you know what makes it worse, Ralph? When that bastard Robin Hood disappeared, the rumours in Wakefield said he had joined Adam Bell's gang. So that young piece of scum breaks my nose, then escapes justice and now he's sitting enjoying my money!" The prior picked up a silver goblet, which Ralph had just filled with wine for him, and smashed it against the wall. "Summon that bailiff from Wakefield! If he won't put in the effort to catch those outlaws on his own, maybe I should offer him a reward to do it!"

The bottler needed no more persuading to flee the room.

* * *

The weather grew even hotter as summer fully settled on Barnsdale, the trees and bushes becoming thick with foliage and flowers to hide in, and many ripe, juicy berries to eat.

Like the flora, Robin had also grown and matured during his weeks in the greenwood.

The time he spent every day, sparring with John, Will and the other men, and firing the great longbow at straw targets hung from trees had changed Robin in ways he had never foreseen. Physically, his body had become a hard, fighting machine: he had enormously powerful arms and shoulders from a young age, thanks to his practice with the bow, but now the rest of his body had filled out with muscle too, yet he retained the grace and speed he had always been blessed with. He could outfight, and outshoot, most of the other outlaws in practice now.

He had also taken to questioning Adam about military tactics. It was never mentioned explicitly, but

Adam accepted that the outlaws knew he had been a soldier at some point in his past, and he was open to discussing the strategic aspects of it with any who had an interest. Until Robin had joined the group, only Will had really had the desire, or aptitude, to understand cavalry formations, use of terrain, siege warfare or any number of other martial topics. While Will had been a mercenary previously, so already had an idea of things like how to use higher ground, Robin had never thought about such things until he'd become an outlaw.

Adam took Will Scarlet aside one warm afternoon as the men were practising. Robin was sparring with Little John, both men using wooden swords, and Bell watched with interest.

"What do you make of our new recruit?"

Will looked in Robin's direction, as the young man expertly deflected a thrust from John and stepped inside the bigger man's guard with a "killing" blow of his own.

"He's improved a lot since he joined us a few weeks ago," Will shrugged. "But you could see from the day he first came here that he had something about him none of these other lads have."

Bell nodded agreement. "And yet, don't you find it remarkable just how *much* he's improved in such a short space of time?"

The sounds of Robin and John sparring ferociously, the grunting of exertion and the clicking and thumping of wood upon wood filled the air. Most of the other outlaws had stopped their own practising to watch, as the giant and the newcomer traded blow after blow, neither managing to land a clean strike for a long time.

"What are you getting at?" Will wondered. "You think he's not the innocent little villager he says he is?"

Bell crossed his arms, fascinated by the sparring match before them. "I don't know," he admitted. "His story checks out, as far as I can tell. And yet . . . give him a few months and he'll be a better swordsman, or archer, than anyone else in this group."

There was a loud cheer as Little John, tiring, suddenly dropped his practice sword and rushed forward, grinning madly, to grab Robin in a great bear hug.

"Yield!" the giant roared with breathless laughter, as his opponent's face turned crimson and he gasped in surrender.

"You alright, there, Hood?" Matt Groves cackled, looking around at the laughing outlaws. "Maybe we should start calling *you* Scarlet, instead of Will. Your face looks like it's about to explode!"

Robin collapsed onto the grass beside John, panting like a thirsty dog. "Fuck…off…Groves…!"

"Aye, fuck off Matt," Little John roared with a massive grin, slapping Robin on the back defensively. "You sour faced little twat."

Will looked at Adam with a small smile. "Who knows? Maybe he's King Arthur reincarnated and that's why he's got all this potential. I'll tell you something though: he's not just going to be a good fighter – he's going to be a leader one day too. The men have all taken to him like an old friend."

"All except Matt," Adam grunted, gesturing towards the surly Groves as the men lost interest and returned to their own sparring matches.

Will nodded agreement. "Aye . . . but Matt doesn't like *anyone*."

"Time I reminded them all who's in charge then, eh?" Bell grunted and walked over to Groves, taking his wooden sword from him and turning to face Robin who still lay on the ground catching his breath with a smile on his face.

Adam Bell never sparred with the other men, instead practising in private with Will or John. Robin assumed this was so no one could ever publicly best Adam, which would perhaps undermine his authority.

"Right, Robin, time I tested you myself. Grab your weapon, lad."

Robin looked up in surprise, before scrambling to his feet and lifting his heavy practice sword from the grass. He had started sparring with a wooden sword that was nearly double the weight of his steel sword. Will had shown him this trick, telling him the invading Roman legionaries used to train with similar weapons a thousand years ago. Once your body got used to using such a heavy sword in practice, fighting with a lighter steel sword in the heat of a real battle was much easier.

Not all of the outlaws practised with the heavy wooden swords though – Will and Adam were the only other two who bothered. Little John tended to stick to his enormous quarterstaff, young Gareth didn't have the strength, and Tuck simply said it was too much effort since he was a man of peace with a group of strong outlaws around to defend him in a fight.

Robin had struggled greatly with the heavy weapon at first, despite his thickly muscled arms, but Will assured him it would be worth it in the long run, so he persevered with it, suffering defeat after defeat in his bouts with the other men. Eventually, though, he became used to the heavy practice sword, wielding it almost as easily as he could one of normal weight.

As their leader walked into the practice area, rolling his shoulders and swinging his arms to warm the muscles up, the other men looked at each other in surprise. Of all the people Adam could have sparred with, they didn't expect him to pick Robin Hood – simply because they thought Robin might win.

Will shrugged as Little John threw him a questioning look, while Robin, also looking perplexed, moved across, set his feet in a defensive stance and prepared to take on his captain.

The young man knew that Adam was not using one of the heavier practice swords, as he was – Matt Groves never did. Robin was also out of breath and tired from his efforts of the past hour or so, while Bell was fresh. He realised Bell intended to send a message to the men here. At his expense.

A light rain started to fall as the two combatants began to circle one another, Bell making the odd feint or lunge to warm his muscles up, while Robin was content to move and watch, trying to get the measure of his opponent, enjoying the cooling shower after his exertions sparring with John.

Bell flicked his sword almost impossibly fast at Robin's midriff, but, in a blur, Robin parried the blow, reversed his weapon and aimed his own, blocked, attack at Bell's stomach and the two men fell apart, both breathing a little heavier.

Although Adam had watched his young recruit's progress, he found it disconcerting to finally come up against Robin's astonishingly fast reflexes. He had hoped to gain a significant advantage by using the lighter sword, but all it seemed to do was even things up somewhat.

Little John had often told Robin of Adam's skill as a swordsman. The big man had been in countless battles beside his leader, seeing at first hand how fast, agile, strong and utterly ruthless he was. But Robin could see the trepidation in Bell's eyes – his first attack had been easily rebuffed and it had shaken the man.

For a few minutes more they sparred, the anger growing in Adam's eyes as he realised he might not be able to beat the young yeoman.

Robin's adrenaline was pumping, as he fended off Bell's attacks, but he held himself in check. He felt like he could explode into a combination of moves his rival would have no defence against, but he knew beating the outlaw leader would be a huge mistake.

He wanted Adam to respect him, value him – teach him his skills.

He did not want Adam to fear him or feel Robin's presence undermined him.

His eyes took on a hunted, fearful look, as he wiped the rain from his forehead with his sleeve then, with a bellow, swung a wide blow at Bell's left side, but his right foot suddenly slipped on the wet grass. Bell easily warded off the half-completed swing and stepped forward to hammer his sword against his hapless opponent's ribs. Robin collapsed on the wet grass with a cry, his hand grasping feebly at his injured side – it felt like Bell had cracked a couple of his ribs.

The outlaws cheered, and Bell smiled at them triumphantly. Little John clapped him on the shoulder in congratulation as he walked past to kneel by Robin.

"You all right, lad? That sounded painful."

"It *was* painful!" Robin forced himself to his feet, still clutching his side, and looked at Bell. "You got me, Adam – too fast for me." He grimaced in pain, and moved out of the practice area, grasping a jug of ale someone thrust at him.

The other men began talking excitedly about the fight, recounting the best bits, embellishing things so it sounded like a much more exciting contest than it had actually been.

Adam came over and sat beside Robin. A mug of ale had been handed to him too. "That was a good fight, lad. I almost thought you were going to be too good for me there."

Robin took a huge pull of his ale, shaking his head with a grimace at the burning pain in his ribcage. "I've been practicing, and picked up a lot since I joined your group, but I knew I couldn't beat you – John's told me how tough you are in a fight."

Bell smiled graciously and took a drink himself. "Anything can happen in a fight Robin, the most important thing is to stay alert. I knew you'd make a mistake eventually – I just had to make the most of it when you did."

Robin downed the last of his ale and was thankful as the rest of the men gave up their training for the day and came over to congratulate Bell on his victory. The atmosphere had grown tense during the fight, the outlaws sensing trouble should it not go the right way. Now that Adam had won it was as if the tension had been released and the men felt like celebrating without even understanding why.

Bell himself truly believed he had bested Robin, as did Little John and the other outlaws. Only Will Scarlet looked thoughtfully at Robin, but his green eyes were unreadable, as always.

CHAPTER SIX

Matilda was in the forest, not far from the village, collecting wood for her father when she felt hands suddenly grab her around the waist. She gave a small cry and tried to elbow her attacker in the ribs desperately.

"Ow! It's me, Matilda, calm down!"

The hands lost their grip and Matilda spun round, panting. "Robin, what the hell are you doing?"

Suddenly, sneaking up on her didn't seem like such an amusing idea, and Robin raised his hands defensively. "Sorry. I was just playing."

Matilda's eyes blazed furiously and she set her fists on her hips. "Well it wasn't funny you bloody idiot. Everyone in the village has been wary since Mayday when you punched the prior – the bailiff keeps coming round hassling us. I thought you were one of his men."

Robin hadn't even thought of that, and he apologised again, taking the girl's hands in his own and drawing her into a hug.

"Fine. Don't ever do that again though." To emphasise her point, Matilda kneed him playfully in the bollocks, but smiled and hugged him tighter as he squealed. "How have you been? I've missed you; it's been weeks since I saw you."

They began to walk through the forest, hand in hand, and Robin told Matilda about his life with Adam Bell's men, assuring her the outlaws weren't all murderous rapists, and trying to convince her he was having a great time.

As the outlaws had begun to accept him, so came more responsibility and Robin had found himself leading small raiding parties as they targeted rich merchants travelling through the forests of Yorkshire. By the summer solstice, most of the outlaws had come to see Robin as third only to Adam Bell and Little John.

Although Will Scarlet had great experience, and the men trusted him, not many actually liked him as a result of his brooding, dark presence. Robin, on the other hand, was a pleasant companion, full of laughter and jokes. Granted, he could retreat into his own little, grim world on occasion, but so could all of the outlaws when they thought of their families, friends and lives left behind, often as the result of some lord's injustice.

Will seemed content to accept Robin's rise over his own social status, but Adam Bell was careful never to send the two men on a raid together.

Friar Tuck and some of the other men had gone off to Bichill for some supplies today; a warm morning, the sun high in the sky and only a gentle westerly breeze to stop the temperature becoming unbearable. The gang had plenty of food in their larder though, and nothing else to do, so Adam had allowed Robin to come to Wakefield to visit his family and friends.

"I miss you," he told Matilda. "I wish I could see you more. But if the bailiff's men are still coming round hunting for me, I'd be putting you in danger if anyone saw us together."

"Yes, yes, I know that," Matilda snapped, flashing him a wry smile. "My mother never tires of telling me about the dangers of Robin Hood. And she's right. It would be nice to see you more though." Her eyes glittered and she gave a laugh. "What about Much though? He's always sneaking around my da's fletching shop, asking if I've seen you."

Robin grinned. "I'll go an' see him later on. Adam said I could spend the day here as long as I was careful, so I visited my ma and da and Marjorie, then came to find you."

Matilda gave him a questioning look. "Adam Bell worries you might come to harm?"

Robin laughed. "Of course he does. He wouldn't want to lose one of his most deadly fighters would he?" Matilda's eyebrows arched and he continued, smiling ruefully, "Not really, he's just worried I might give them away if I'm caught."

Matilda returned his smile sardonically. "'Deadly fighter', eh? As modest as ever, then."

The two continued walking, simply enjoying each other's presence, as they realised they'd come close to the village again. The mill came into sight, and Robin nodded towards it. "Maybe we could see Much now. I'll stay here out of sight, if you could tell him to come over?"

"Or maybe we could do something more interesting, for a while?" Matilda moved in close, eyes wide, pressing her small breasts against him, and cupped his balls in her hand through his breeches.

Robin felt himself stiffen almost instantly, and he grinned, pulling the girl down onto the grass beside him.

They kissed passionately, hands frantically removing each other's clothes, until Matilda climbed on top of him and he gasped as he felt himself slide deep inside her.

Matilda arched her smooth back with a wanton smile, as Robin squeezed her breasts and thrust himself almost desperately into her. Stuck in a forest with a gang of ugly men for weeks, Robin had become more than a little frustrated, and now, with this beautiful girl grinding herself into him, he couldn't contain himself for long. With an explosive gasp of pleasure, he shot his seed inside her.

Matilda leaned down and they kissed gently for a little while, embracing happily.

"Enjoy that?" the girl asked with a grin.

"Enjoy it?" Robin laughed. "It was unbelievable! The bailiff could have turned up just then and I couldn't have stopped I was enjoying it so much."

Matilda laughed, rolling onto the grass to look contentedly up at the cloudless blue sky for a moment. "Shall we head to the mill and find Much?"

"Aye," Robin agreed, pulling his trousers back on. "Hopefully he's" –

A terrible scream of pain shattered the peaceful afternoon air and the lovers looked at each other in horror.

"It came from the mill!" the young outlaw cried, frantically buckling his sword back around his waist. "Wait here!" He sprinted off, still half naked, towards the bridge that led to Much's home.

* * *

Thomas the miller screamed again as the bailiff slammed the heavy wooden mallet down onto his hand. Much was held back by two of the bailiff's men, as he struggled to somehow help his father who was bound hand and foot to one of his own chairs.

Henry the bailiff addressed Much again. "If you don't tell me where Hood's hiding, boy, your father won't have any hands left to work this mill."

The bailiff knew the miller's wife had died ten years earlier, and, since the mill was set apart from the village, no one would hear the agonized cries and come to see what was happening.

Much, tears in his eyes as he watched his father writhe against his bonds in agony, shouted in frustration at the bailiff. "I don't know where Robin is, I haven't seen him in weeks, since he joined Adam Bell's gang! I swear it! Leave my da alone, please Henry!"

The bailiff scowled at Much's denial. After having his nose smashed, the prior had demanded Henry bring Robin Hood to justice, offering him a nice sum of money to make it happen, and this had seemed the ideal way to locate the young outlaw. But this bastard Much was no help at all. He raised the mallet again, but this time he cracked the miller on the side of the face with it.

"Stop it!" Much screamed again, arms and legs thrashing as he tried to reach his father. "I swear to you I don't know where Robin is, you need to look for Adam Bell!"

Henry had to accept Much really didn't know anything helpful. He would have given Hood up by now if he did. The bailiff dropped the mallet onto a table, and Much sobbed in relief, his father lying on the floor, bloodied and dazed, but alive at least.

"Well then, neither of you are any use to me, but I can't leave you around to cause trouble – can't have the people of Wakefield complaining about me to the earl can I? He listens to the peasants too much, that one. We'll have to make it look like outlaws broke in and killed you both…"

The bailiff drew his dagger from his belt and slammed the small blade straight into the groaning miller's heart. Leaving it there, he turned, slowly drew his sword from its fine leather sheath and rounded on the horrified Much with a wicked smile. "Your turn, boy."

The door to the mill burst open, almost torn off its hinges, as a great dark figure tore into the dimly lit room. Henry raised his sword instinctively, but the shadow man came in low, thrusting his own sword upwards into the bailiff's guts, tearing muscle and flesh as he pulled his blade free. The bailiff grabbed feebly at his torn body, and collapsed on the floor, blood pouring from his slack mouth, eyes staring helplessly up at his killer.

Much fell to his knees on the floor then too, gasping in shock and disbelief at what was happening in his home, as his captors released him so they could draw their own weapons against this unexpected attack. The two foresters moved apart and fell into a defensive stance, swords held ready to face the young man who stood with his head down, glaring menacingly at them, his massively muscled bare chest heaving with exertion, thick blood dripping from the end of his sword.

"There's two of us…" one of the men began, but Robin, moving impossibly fast, lunged forward and rammed the point of his sword under the man's face, right up through the top of his head.

As the second forester moved to engage him, Robin dragged his sword free and kicked viciously at the front of the next attacker's leg. The blow sent the man stumbling face first to the floor as his knee gave way and Robin rammed his blade into the man's side. As the forester hit the floor the young outlaw punched him in the back of the head with his left hand and, for a second, everything was still.

Matilda ran into the mill and stopped, holding a hand to her mouth, her eyes staring around in horror at the sight of the four dead men in the room.

Much began sobbing again, repeating the phrase, "Mary Mother of God," over and over, sometimes looking at his dead father, still impaled on the bailiff's dagger, sometimes looking at Robin in shocked disbelief.

"Much." Robin, starting to shake with shock himself as the adrenaline drained from his system, knelt down and placed a hand on his friend's shoulder. "You need to come with me. They're going to come back for you, with more men. The prior must have ordered this."

Much moved to sit by his dead father, sobbing uncontrollably, until Matilda came and put her arms around him.

"Robin's right," she whispered, tears of disbelief in her own eyes. "You have to leave. If the prior sent the bailiff here he won't let something like this go. He'll want to make sure you don't talk."

Much sat for a moment, then raised his head to glare at his childhood friend. "This is all your fault, none of this would have happened if you hadn't punched that fucking prior!"

Robin had no answer to his friend's accusing stare, so he stayed silent.

"Much, we don't have time for this now," Matilda told her friend gently. "Maybe it is Robin's fault, but more men will be coming looking for you now – the bailiff's dead! You have to go with Robin, or you'll be hanged for murder!"

Much nodded almost imperceptibly and, after a while, got slowly to his feet, his eyes never leaving his dead father's face. "Let me get my things, please . . ."

"Of course," Robin replied. "Take everything you can carry. Money, weapons, clothes, food. We can't come back here, ever. But hurry!"

As Much, dazed, moved to collect his things, Matilda faced Robin, confusion and disbelief plain on her lovely face. "You killed three men. I've never seen anything like it."

Robin sank to the floor, his hands shaking badly. "I know. Adam's men are good teachers. I've never killed anyone before. I just wanted to stop them from killing Much." His eyes filled with tears.

Matilda took his hand gently. "You did well Robin, you saved his life."

"Maybe." He looked over at the corpses of the men he'd killed, and hid his face in his hands. He felt like throwing up.

"I'm ready." Much came back into the room, his face bleak, and Robin stood up, wiping away his tears with his hand.

"Alright. Let's go and find Adam."

* * *

"My lords!" Sir John de Bek, a dark haired man of advancing years filled the room with his enormous baritone voice, calling the meeting to order. The gathered noblemen – barons, knights and bishops from all corners of the country, fell silent as every eye turned to de Bek, who appeared to be acting almost as a chancellor, as if this was some sort of unofficial northern 'parliament'.

71

"The Earl of Lancaster," Sir John continued, nodding towards the grim-faced earl at the head of the enormous wooden table, "has called us here to discuss a number of issues. Firstly: the issue of the Scots."

The magnates sat in silence as the earl's "chancellor" talked at some length of the threat from the Scots. "For years they have been raiding deep into our northern lands – it cannot be allowed to continue!" de Bek vowed passionately. "At the last meeting in May some of us signed a pact agreeing to defend each others' lands against the threat from Scotland. Now, the earl asks those of you who were not at that previous meeting to sign the same pact."

Sir William Deyncourt led a chorus of cheers in agreement and it was clear from the mood in the room there would be no problems with this proposal. There were some uneasy glances towards the Earl of Lancaster as rumours of his fraternizing with the Scots had been heard by everyone gathered there, but no one raised the issue. The earl was the one proposing an alliance against the Scots – why would he seek friendship with them at the same time? It seemed a ridiculous piece of gossip, probably put about by the royalists to damage Thomas's reputation.

De Bek nodded to himself in satisfaction. "Since we all seem happy enough with that, I shall move onto the next item on the agenda."

He glanced down at a sheet of parchment in front of him and read off it a list of grievances against the king, including unlawful banishments, unwise treaties signed with foreign nations and, most contentiously, the bad character of Edward's closest advisors: the Despensers.

Thomas of Lancaster watched the reactions of the gathered men as de Bek outlined the problems, noting with dismay that many of them – particularly Archbishop Melton of York, the most powerful of the prelates at the meeting – appeared uncomfortable at the accusations against the king.

He swore softly to himself – not only did he not seem to be getting the enthusiastic support he had hoped for, but some of the northern lords had failed to show up for the meeting. Sir Richard-at-Lee must have decided, like his order's Grand Prior, to side with the king, Lancaster thought, noticing the big Hospitaller's absence. It wasn't a major blow to the earl's plans: Sir Richard was only a minor noble, with small personal resources, wholly unlikely to sway the Hospitaller Order in England to stand against Edward.

Still, the more support Thomas could enlist the better, and the Crusader knight would have been an excellent man to have on-side when the fighting inevitably started. Damn him! What was wrong with these people that they wouldn't stand up against such a weak and ineffectual king?

As the magnates debated the idea of opposing the king and the Despensers the door to the room was suddenly thrown open and Sir Richard-at-Lee stormed in. The big knight was clad imposingly in a suit of chain mail, over which he wore the black mantle of his order, with its eight-pointed white cross emblazoned boldly on the chest. As he pulled off his gauntlets his grey-bearded face was scarlet with fury.

There was confusion around the table, as those men who didn't recognise the stern-faced knight panicked, wondering if the king's men had come to put a stop their 'northern parliament'.

"My lords!" Sir Richard, oblivious to the effect he'd had on the room, strode to the head of the table, nodding a greeting to the Earl of Lancaster who rose and tried to calm the nervous lords.

As it became clear the Hospitaller was not there to arrest them, the noblemen quietened down, wondering what was going on.

"My lords," Sir Richard began again, looking around the room, "some of you know me, and some of you don't. I am Sir Richard-at-Lee, Commander of Kirklees. I fought in the Holy Land and Rhodes as a knight of the Order of St John – the Hospitallers." He stood proudly before them, hands spread wide as the rage left his voice to be replaced by outraged disbelief. "Although I am a Hosptialler first and foremost, I have also been a loyal subject to King Edward, and his father before him – indeed, after the Earl of Lancaster's last meeting a month ago, I wasn't even sure I should come here to this one, for fear of displeasing the king."

There were quiet mutters of understanding at that, as many of the gathered lords had harboured similar thoughts, only turning up for this meeting as a courtesy to the wealthy earl who was, after all, Steward of England.

"However," Sir Richard went on, "in return for my loyalty, our monarch has allowed his – current – favourite, Hugh Despenser, to imprison my youngest son in Cardiff castle on a trumped up charge of murder!"

Sensing an opportunity, Lancaster roared indignantly, demanding to hear the facts of the furious Hospitaller's case against his hated enemy.

As it turned out, the father of the young knight Sir Richard's son had – accidentally – killed in the jousting tournament was a family friend of the younger Despenser. Richard's son, Simon, had been arrested and was now being held in custody by men acting in the name of the Despenser who, on hearing what had happened from his friend, Charles of Bodmin, had demanded bail monies from Sir Richard of one hundred pounds.

"How am I to pay that?" Richard demanded. "Hospitallers take a vow of poverty when they join the Order. I can't pay a ransom like that! Why is King Edward allowing this?"

Despite the knight's righteous anger, the king did not actually have anything directly to do with the imprisonment – Sir Richard just blamed him by extension of his favour for the Despensers.

"This is outrageous!" Sir John de Bek cried indignantly, while others, even the wealthiest, gasped in

74

shock at the enormous bail demands and the room was thrown into a noisy babble again.

"This is exactly why we are here today, my friends," the Earl of Lancaster shouted as the clamour calmed at last. "Sir Richard-at-Lee isn't the first innocent man to feel the illegal force of the Despensers' royally-sanctioned greed, and, unless we stop pissing about here, he won't be the last either!" He walked around the table, meeting the eyes of those he knew were undecided whether to support him or not. "Will you sit by and allow another of the king's unworthy favourites to ruin our country? I warn you now – the Scots aren't the biggest threat our people face. The Despensers are!"

There were angry shouts of agreement, some of them from men who had been undecided at the start of the meeting, and Thomas walked back to stand next to Sir Richard-at-Lee, his eyes fierce. "I will stand beside the commander of Kirklees in the fight for justice against these leeches – will you?"

Sir John de Bek called the assembly to order and asked the clergymen to retire to the rector's house to consider what they would do, while the lay lords would deliberate where they were. It was another unusual move, copying parliamentary procedure and didn't go unnoticed by the magnates, some of which were impressed while others were somewhat outraged at what they saw as Lancaster's arrogance.

When the deliberations were over, the earl was again disappointed by the reluctance of the northern and western lords to agree to his proposals. Although many of the men who had attended the meeting pledged themselves to the destruction of the Despensers, many others – some of whom suspected the rumours of Thomas's overtures to the Scots may have some truth to them – refused to follow his lead.

The prelates, led by the Archbishop of York, agreed to aid Thomas as best they could against the threat of the Scots, but they decided to reserve judgement on John de Bek's accusations against the king until the next – official – parliament.

It was not a complete failure, the earl, mused as the gathering broke up and the men made their way home again. Yes, many of the most powerful lords would probably never go against the king, but some new friends had been made today and, he knew, the more support he could muster, the more likely it was the king would take heed of them.

Sir Richard-at-Lee nodded a distracted farewell to Thomas, and the earl pulled him gently aside.

"What will you do about your son?" he wondered, apparently genuine concern written on his long face.

Sir Richard sighed, his eyes heavy with stress and exhaustion. "The abbot of St Mary's in York has offered to loan me the money to pay Simon's bail. It's a massive amount, I fear I'll never be able to repay it but...I need to get my son out of jail then, hopefully once all this is sorted, Despenser will be forced to return the money. It's extortion, nothing more!"

The earl narrowed his eyes. Abbot Ness of St Mary's had not said a word during the meeting – Thomas knew the man was a staunch Royalist, and today had only reinforced that opinion.

"I have no need to know what terms you agreed to the abbot's loan under," Lancaster clapped the big knight on the shoulder. "You should be wary of him though – I fear you may be swapping one evil debt for another."

Sir Richard shrugged and rubbed at his eyes. "What's done is done," he muttered. "I must go now to free my son. I thank you for your words in there and, you can be sure, for what little it's worth – you will have my sword at your side against these bastard Despensers!"

CHAPTER SEVEN

The outlaws were happy to take Much into their group. He was good with the longbow, knew the forest well, and his outgoing nature made him popular with the men. Despite the reasons for his joining the gang, Robin was pleased his friend was with them. Although it had taken a few days grieving, Much had finally forgiven him for his father's murder – the bailiff had killed his da, not Robin. If he hadn't turned up when he had, Much would be dead now too – Robin had saved his life.

To Robin's great relief, then, they were still friends.

"What's the story with Adam?" Much asked one afternoon while they were out hunting together.

"I'm not sure," Robin admitted. "Everyone's heard of him – he's famous. But there's more to him that he never lets on. Even Little John doesn't really know the full story. But Adam's more than just a yeoman turned outlaw. He's been a soldier at some point."

Much nodded. "Aye, and he's been a leader of soldiers too. You can see it in his bearing. All the stories of Adam Bell say he's a common outlaw, but he's a nobleman, it's obvious."

Again, Robin just shrugged. Much was right – Adam Bell carried himself like a nobleman, fought like a soldier, and was a military tactician. They also knew the stories of Bell had been told around campfires since long before they were born, which should make the outlaw leader at the very least in his sixties. Yet the man looked not much more than forty five summers.

The pair were silent for a while, as they made their way through the trees searching for game.

"Do you think that's a French accent he's got?" Much looked at Robin curiously. "He doesn't talk much, but when he does, I could swear he's got a funny accent."

Robin laughed softly, always aware, even subconsciously, of the sounds of the forest and alert against disturbing the natural rhythm needlessly. "You think Adam Bell, the Saxon outlaw hero, is actually a French nobleman?" He shrugged. "Who knows? I just assumed it was a Scottish or Welsh accent he had." Truthfully, there were so many variations in local dialects throughout the whole of the country, there was no way for most people to tell where a stranger came from, unless widely travelled themselves.

Much didn't reply. The suggestion that Adam was a noble was clearly absurd. Yet both men couldn't help wondering what Bell's real story was.

"We'll ask Will about it," said Robin. "He's closest to Adam. If anyone knows the story, Will . . . will . . . ?"

He looked at Much in mock confusion, and they grinned at each other. Just then a rabbit ran across their path but within a moment both men had pulled and released their arrows.

"That's another one for the pot!" Much hooted, as both arrows thumped home in their target.

When they returned to camp, Much and Robin found most of the outlaws had already eaten, so they prepared their catch and added it to the big stew pot over the fire.

As they settled down to eat, there was an urgent whistle and, for a split second, everyone froze.

"On your feet!" Will Scaflock hissed to the outlaws, shouldering his bow. The rest followed his example. Robin dropped his bowl of food and hushed Much who had no idea what was going on.

"Someone's come close to our camp," Robin whispered to his friend. "Grab your bow, you might need it again." He hastily kicked the campfire out, covering it to prevent any smoke, and tightened his gambeson.

Will and Little John efficiently directed men to positions around the camp.

The outlaws were silent, and well hidden amongst the thick undergrowth, the fading daylight helping to make the small clearing less noticeable, although the smells of recent cooking would lead any hunters straight to their camp.

Slowly, the sounds of a dozen or so men moving stealthily through the forest carried to the hidden outlaws. Low voices could be heard conversing and some of the men – the sheriff of Nottingham and Yorkshire's soldiers by their uniforms – stepped cautiously into the clearing, swords drawn and shields held ready.

Again, there was another whistle and the outlaws let fly a volley of arrows. Three of the soldiers collapsed to the forest floor, while a fourth screamed and grabbed at the shaft sticking from his thigh.

"Attack!" The sound of Adam Bell's voice carried loudly through the evening air and the outlaws fell upon the remaining soldiers.

Much hung back in confusion, not being a part of the well-trained fighting unit, but he watched in frightened fascination as he saw his boyhood friend Robin moving with astonishing speed and efficiency to dispatch one of the sheriff's men. Much's eyes swept over the battle, which the outlaws were winning easily, and settled on Adam Bell.

Bell had engaged the soldier's leader, a tall nobleman, with dark hair and a small, neatly trimmed moustache.

Much could see the noble mouthing the word, "You?" a shocked look on his face as Bell thrust his sword directly at his groin, seeking a quick killing blow. The man parried desperately and shouted something in a strange language; akin to that spoken by the nobles he'd seen visiting Wakefield – French? Much wasn't

79

surprised when Bell grunted something back, apparently in the same dialect.

The outlaws were finishing off the other soldiers, and Adam Bell didn't take long to find an opening in his opponent's defence, raking his sword across the man's throat and slamming an elbow into his side, knocking him to the ground. The soldier spat a final, defiant sentence at the outlaw leader and then choked, eyes bulging in pain, as Adam Bell thrust his sword into his chest.

Robin and the others were already taking the weapons and armour from the corpses of the soldiers, but Much glanced over and saw Tuck watching Adam Bell, a surprised look on his face, which he quickly masked as he met Much's gaze.

"Good work, lads!" shouted Adam Bell, wiping his sword clean on his dead opponent's clothes, and ramming it back into its scabbard. "Get 'em stripped of valuables and dumped. Much – see if you can find yourself some armour and a decent weapon on one of these corpses. Will – you and John with me. We've got a prisoner. Let's find out what these bastards wanted in our forest."

Normally the outlaws would simply dump the corpses of men they killed in the forest for scavengers to find. But since Tuck had joined their group, he had insisted they bury the dead, in accordance with Christian custom. Although the outlaws were all Christian, they didn't enjoy digging holes for people who had tried to kill them, but Tuck was insistent and his personality was such that the men found themselves complying with his wishes.

Tuck himself never lifted a spade, but stood at the side offering blessings, and promising the cursing gravediggers rewards in heaven for their piety.

By the time the sheriff's men had all been buried in very shallow graves, Adam Bell had finished interrogating the prisoner – a straggler, captured as he took a piss, by Bell himself. Adam had let the man go after questioning, to carry the news of the outlaw's triumph back to Nottingham. Every victory like this added to their legend.

"They were after you, Master Much." The outlaw leader took a long drink of ale from his cup as he spoke but it was Robin he fixed his gaze on. "And your big mate here. Seems the prior sent some men to Wakefield to question you and your family, and none of them came back."

Robin nodded. "That's right, you know that Adam, we told you what had happened."

Bell grunted. "You told me there had been a fight. The way that soldier told it, you single-handedly carved up the bailiff and two of his best fighting men. Problem is – you didn't kill all three of them like you thought. One of them lived long enough to be found, and he gave a description of you." He grinned and raised his cup high. "I doubt we've heard the last of this either – those weren't just foresters, they were the sheriff's own soldiers. You've got the prior *and* the sheriff pissed off now, lad!" The other men cheered and raised their own cups in salute to Robin.

The young outlaw smiled nervously, and took a pull of his own ale, but could take little satisfaction from his leader's apparent pride in him. He had killed another man in the fighting tonight, but it didn't feel noble, or mighty. What worried Robin was the fact that this time hadn't felt horribly wrong, as it had when he slaughtered the men attacking Much. Although he hadn't gained any pleasure from tonight's violence, neither did he feel like throwing up, as he had after he rescued his friend.

Killing was just something that had to be done. Robin was shocked as he realised he was desensitized to the brutality of the outlaw lifestyle already. He looked at Tuck and was surprised to find the friar gazing back knowingly.

The rest of the men settled down to drink and enjoy their night, knowing the soldiers would not return for at least another day or two, by which time they'd be long gone to another part of the massive Yorkshire forest.

Tuck came over and sat beside Robin, chewing noisily as he tore another chunk from the leg of roasted venison he carried.

"I thought monks were supposed to live a life of austerity, Brother Tuck." Robin was annoyed at the man for imposing himself on him, but regretted his words instantly, as he felt a genuine friendship for the clergyman.

Tuck just laughed loudly, and took a long drink from his wine cup. "As you may have noticed, Robin, I'm not exactly the most orthodox clergyman you'll meet. And I'm a friar, not a monk." He winked and patted his large stomach as he took another bite of his venison. "I am a man of God though – if you feel the need to confess any sins, or just to talk, I'm here for you my son." He squeezed Robin's wrist and the sincerity in his eyes gave the young outlaw some comfort. The men may have been forced to live as thieves and killers, but they were bound to each other by friendship.

"No confession, Tuck, thank you. I'm doing what I can to survive, like all of us. I just can't take pleasure in killing."

Tuck nodded. "That's good. When a man loses himself in blood lust, he becomes nothing more than an animal."

Robin glanced over at Will, and Tuck followed his gaze. "Don't be too quick to judge that one, Robin. Who knows what he's suffered in his life to make him embrace violence so readily? I see a loyal and, deep down, good man, in Will Scaflock."

Robin was surprised to hear the friar defending Will, but shrugged his shoulders. "Maybe you're right. He's a good man to have on your side anyway."

The two men sat quietly for a while, eating and drinking, and enjoying the banter and songs of the other outlaws round the fire. It was a cool, clear evening in the forest, and Robin felt the stress of recent days drain away until he felt as happy as he had since becoming an outlaw.

As the men finished a ribald song, Tuck crossed himself in mock disgust, and Much came over to sit beside them. He looked around to make sure no one else was listening and said to Tuck, "So, what did that soldier say to Adam?"

For the first time since joining them, Tuck looked uncomfortable. "What soldier?"

"The one he killed, the captain of the sheriff's soldiers. He shouted something at Adam in some funny language. French maybe? You can speak French can't you? You clergymen can speak all sorts of languages. That soldier looked like he knew Adam."

Friar Tuck sighed heavily, nodding. "Yes, I can speak French, Much. And yes, that's the language Adam was talking in."

Robin was just as curious as his friend now. "What did he say then?"

Making sure Bell was well out of earshot, Tuck looked at the two younger men grimly. "The captain knew Adam all right. But from where, I have no idea. Before he killed him, the nobleman told our leader he would burn in hell for his betrayal. Whatever that might have been, who knows? He called him 'Gurdon'. I assume that's his real name."

Much looked confused, but Robin was nodding his head. "This makes sense. Adam Bell should be older. In all the stories he was just a yeoman too, but this man leading us is obviously a trained soldier – a knight. This explains how he's got us all working together to fight like a unit: it's second nature to him to train and lead soldiers."

Tuck agreed, but Much still looked puzzled. "That may be so, Robin, but if he's really someone else, why's he going around the forest telling everyone he's Adam Bell? It doesn't make sense."

The rest of the outlaw band took up another loud song, ale and wine and the high of their victory over the soldiers tonight making them merry.

Tuck helped himself to another swig of his own wine and looked earnestly at Much. "It's brilliant, what Adam's done here. Think about it. If an outlawed noble –a knight – was to look for help in the villages around Yorkshire, what do you think the people would do? They'd be straight to the Sheriff. Bell, or *Gurdon*, wouldn't last a week without the help of the locals. But the people of Wakefield know who Adam Bell is. They've all heard the tales round campfires just like this one. He's a hero. People want to help a man like Adam Bell – it's one in the eye for the nobles."

"You're right." Robin nodded at Tuck. "But if this is all true, where's the real Adam Bell? And how did a knight or whatever he is, like…him-" he nodded towards Adam, "manage to get everyone to believe he was really a folk hero?"

Tuck had been thinking about the same questions ever since he heard the sheriff's soldier shouting out Gurdon's real name. "I can't tell you where the real Adam Bell is. For all I know he never existed except in folk tales. Have you ever seen Adam Bell?"

Robin and Much shook their heads.

"Do you even know what he was supposed to look like? How tall was he? Did he have a beard or clean shaven? Blue eyes or brown?"

Again, Robin and Much shook their heads. The tales of Adam Bell never went into details of his physical characteristics, only his amazing deeds.

"You see, then?" Tuck slapped his knee. "It's not so hard to pretend to be someone when no one knows what you're supposed to look like!" He smiled at the two friends and grabbed another piece of meat from his wooden bowl, wiping his chin with the sleeve of his robe as the juices dribbled down his chin. "Brilliant, it really is brilliant what he's done."

The three men sat quietly again for a while, letting the sounds of the outlaws' feasting wash over them, and wondering about what they'd learned.

"Where does this leave us?" Much asked quietly, staring into the fire.

"For now," said Robin, "nothing changes. We carry on as before. If Adam was really a knight at one point, he's lived in Barnsdale for the past few years as a wolf's head. He has a lot he can teach us – about warfare and surviving as outlaws. I don't know about you, but I mean to take whatever I can from his lessons."

CHAPTER EIGHT

A few weeks passed and things seemed to continue as normal for the outlaws. They had again moved their camp to another part of the forest, and things were quiet, but Robin knew the peace wouldn't last long. Prior de Monte Martini seemed to have given up on the idea of hiring someone to hunt down him and Adam Bell – it must have cost too much – especially if the hunter failed, as Henry had. Certainly, since Robin had killed the bailiff, there had been no sign anyone else had come into Barnsdale looking for him.

Unknown to the outlaws, though, the prior had sent a letter to the sheriff demanding he uphold the king's peace and bring the wolf's heads to justice. Which was why the soldiers had been in the forest looking for Adam's gang a fortnight earlier.

Now, Sir Henry de Faucumberg, Sheriff of Nottingham and Yorkshire couldn't let the destruction of his men go unpunished; it would send the wrong message to the people of Yorkshire. He'd try again to capture or kill the outlaws somehow. It was just a matter of time.

Robin was repairing a hole in the roof of the makeshift shelter he shared with Much when Little John approached him.

"You heard the news, yet?"

Robin put down the timber and iron nails he was using and shook his head, knowing, from the look on John's face, something unpleasant was coming.

"The sheriff's made you a wanted man."

Robin didn't understand. "We're already wanted men. We're outlaws!"

"Up until now, we've just been normal outlaws. Now the sheriff's put a price on your head."

Robin was stunned. "A price?"

John put a big hand on his friend's arm. "Anyone who helps the sheriff capture you gets twenty pounds. And if it's an outlaw that turns you in, they'll be pardoned too."

Robin's blood ran cold. This was a disaster. Twenty pounds was a huge sum of money for most people in England, and the promise of a pardon would be just as attractive to outlaws who wanted nothing more than to go home to their families and live a normal life again.

"Who told you all this?"

"I went to Locksley today to visit a friend," John told him. "The whole village is buzzing with the news, Robin. People aren't openly saying they'll turn you in – they know you're part of Adam Bell's group and are afraid of what he might do if he's crossed. But sooner or later someone will decide it's worth the risk." He leaned in close to Robin and, in a low voice, said, "You're going to have to watch your back even with some of these lads. Not all of them are as honourable as me and Tuck!" He smiled at that, and slapped Robin's back, but they both knew there was a grain of truth in what he said. Although Robin was a popular man in the outlaw band, some of the men might see this as a golden opportunity.

"I'll be careful. Thanks for warning me. I'd better have a word with Adam about this; he's not going to be too happy at the thought of all the trouble I've brought down on us. God, he might even tell me to leave."

Little John grunted. "Don't worry about that, Robin. Adam knows you've got friends here now. We'll have your back no matter what happens. We might be wolf's heads, but some of us are still good men."

They grasped arms, and Robin went off to look for Adam, casting wary glances at the rest of the men, paranoia settling over him already. *Mary, mother of God,* he vowed silently, *I will earn myself a pardon! I can't go on living like this – I will, somehow, be pardoned!*

He searched the entire camp, but couldn't find Adam Bell. While he was wandering around he bumped into Will Scarlet.

"Have you heard about the price on my head?" Robin asked, wondering how this violent, quick tempered man would view the sheriff's bounty.

"I've heard." Will grunted. "But you're one of us now, Robin. You're probably wondering about some of the lads here – wondering if they'll turn you over to the sheriff."

Robin tried to keep his face impassive as Will carried on. "Maybe one of them will, but I don't think so. You know the stories of what Adam does to traitors – he won't stand for it. If one of these men turned you in Adam would have the rest of us hunt him down. His life wouldn't be worth living, money and pardon or not. Don't you worry – I'll be having words with everyone, let 'em know this is a brotherhood. We stick together. You stood up to that prior, bust his nose – that makes you a good man to my mind."

Robin was struck by the sincerity in Will's eyes. Will Scarlet, a man Robin always stepped carefully around, was vowing to put his life on the line for him.

"Thank you. You don't know how much it means to me to know you men are there for me."

Will smiled grimly. "Well, I feel a bit responsible, to tell the truth."

"How so?" Robin asked in surprise.

"If I hadn't been teaching you how to use a sword so well for the past few months, you'd never have been able to kill the bailiff and his men!" He laughed and slapped Robin on the arm, pushing past him. "Come on, I'm going fishing, you might as well come too unless you've got anything better to do."

In the months Robin had been an outlaw, he had never had a real conversation with Will Scaflock. Maybe today he'd find out what made this man tick.

As the pair sat on the grass with their rods in the river, they shared a large skin of strong ale together. The drink seemed to make Will relax more than Robin had seen in all his time with the group.

"What's your story, Will?" he asked. "It's obvious you've been a soldier. It's even more obvious you hate our noble rulers. How did you end up a wolf's head?"

For a minute or so, Will sat in silence, staring out across the water, which sparkled like gold as a bright afternoon sun shone down from above.

Then, quietly, he began to speak.

"I was a soldier," said Will. "A mercenary. I fought in many battles, in many different countries. France, Germany, I even fought alongside the Hospitaller knights in the Holy Land. I was a good soldier. I loved the life, I loved the danger. I loved the fighting. I never loved the killing though, not then. Although I was paid well to fight, I picked my wars – I only fought for causes, and men, I felt were honourable."

"Then, when I was back at home in Nottingham for a while, I met a girl. Her name was Elaine. I'd never met a girl like her. She was beautiful, with long brown hair and dark eyes, and we could spend hours together, just talking. We never got tired of each other's company," he smiled, picturing his wife, then his customary frown fell on his face again.

Will couldn't stand the thought of being away fighting in another far off place, away from Elaine. So he took a job as a forester, in Sherwood, to be close to her. It wasn't as exciting as being a soldier, but Scaflock was happy, and, for the first time in his life, content.

"We eventually married," Will said with a grunt, casting his line into the sluggish river again. "We had a small house in Nottingham. Then we had three children: two boys, Matthew and David, and a little girl, Elizabeth. My little beautiful Beth…" he stared out at the water, his eyes dull, the expression on his face almost childlike as he thought again of his daughter.

After a while Will seemed to come out of his reverie and carried on. "But the boys were getting bigger, and Elaine kept saying we needed a bigger house. She was right, but being a forester didn't pay well enough for us to move to anywhere else."

Then Will had heard that one of the nobles living in Hathersage was looking for bodyguards, and went to see him. The man knew him – Scaflock had fought under him in Damascus a few years before. He offered Will a job, with a much higher wage than he was getting as a forester, so he jumped at the chance.

"Christ, how I wish I'd never met that man!" Will hissed. "Roger de Troyes, his name was. He probably wishes he'd never met me either now…" a dark smile lifted the corners of his lips for a moment before he continued his tale.

Everything had gone well for a few months. It became clear why the nobleman needed a bodyguard – he was forever getting drunk and treating people like filth. Will had to restrain people from killing him quite a few times.

"He was an unpleasant bastard, he really was," Will grumbled. "But me and my family had moved to a bigger house in Hathersage, away from the stinking tanner's workshops and filth of Nottingham, and I needed the money he was paying me to pay my rent. So I just got on with it. I had to.

"Then one day, me and de Troyes were back in Nottingham at a feast thrown by the sheriff. No, not the same one that's there now, this was a few years ago before de Faucumberg got the job. Anyway, de Troyes and some of the other guests were getting drunker by the minute, as I sat in a corner making sure no one tried to kill him if he got to be too much of a pain in the arse."

Again, Will paused, replaying the moments in his mind – the moments that changed his life forever, and turned Will Scaflock into Will Scarlet.

"I went off for a piss," he went on, "and when I came back to the hall, he was nowhere in sight. I found him in a side room, with a couple of others, taking it in turns with this young girl. But the girl wasn't willing; she was crying, and trying to get these so-called noblemen off her.

"I dragged them off – they were so drunk they just laughed – and sent them back out to the hall to pass out. The girl was in shock, but I didn't know what to do. I'd seen women raped before, but during wars, in the heat of battle, not like this. She was breaking her heart, so I tried to calm her, and gave her some money – I thought she was just a serving girl, see – and went back out to make sure my piece of shit employer behaved himself for the rest of the night."

Robin was appalled, but he wasn't naïve. He knew things like this happened all the time, up and down the country. "The nobles can do what they like," he muttered in disgust.

"Exactly," Will snarled angry agreement. "If a nobleman wants to hump a serving girl – he does. If anyone tries to stop him, they get killed, or outlawed, or...you know, Robin! You're lucky your girl Matilda wasn't stuck in some brothel by that bastard prior, 'cause he could do you know. He could.

"Anyway, I thought everything was sorted out. Things went on as usual for a couple of weeks. Then . . ."

Will had gone to Nottingham to buy a new dagger. He was only gone a matter of hours. But when he got home to Hathersage...

"I found Elaine." Will whispered, his head drooping, the fishing rod in his hand completely forgotten. "She was lying on the floor, holding onto my little boy Matthew. They'd both been stabbed, over and over again. My other son David, he had only a single wound in his side, but it was deep and long and his blood was everywhere...Our servants....everyone, everyone in my house had been butchered. Even our pet dog had had its back broken. My entire family, wiped out...

"I couldn't take it all in," he looked at Robin with a look of disbelief on his weather beaten face. "My mind just snapped. I couldn't bear to look at it, I had to get away. It was as if I left my body. I don't even know where I went for the next few hours. I just remember waking up in an alley, with some beggar trying to steal my fancy new dagger.

"After that, I had nothing left to live for. My whole life had been stolen from me. Even if the law were interested – which they wouldn't be – my family were gone. I had nothing. I've...*got*...nothing any more."

Will never knew who had murdered his family, but it seemed obvious he had been the main target and the murderers would still be after him. For that reason he slipped into his employer, Roger de Troyes's, house when he finally came to his senses, to see if – with his money and connections – de Troyes could help find out who had done this.

"I didn't expect his reaction," Will growled. "He was terrified when he saw me, obviously thought I would be dead. Before I could say anything he blurted out the whole story."

The girl de Troyes and his friends had raped wasn't a serving girl after all. She was another – very powerful – nobleman's daughter. When her father found out his girl had been raped at the feast, he demanded to know the story from Roger de Troyes, since he recognised de Troyes from her description.

"De Troyes said it was me!" Will exploded, jumping to his feet and hurling the fishing rod onto the grass. He turned back to Robin, his fists clenched in rage. "That noble scum blamed me for the rape! I had *stopped* the bastards from brutalizing her any more, I'd tried to comfort her . . . yet her father had come to *my* house and butchered *my* family!"

In a fury Scaflock had drawn his dagger and, seeing his death coming, de Troyes begged forgiveness. "Said he was sorry for blaming me for the rape, offered to pay me fortunes to leave, and cried that he was my friend really." Will slumped back onto the grass beside Robin and held his head in his hands, tears coursing down his face. "Of course I killed him, then and there: slit his throat with my dagger. But it didn't really make me feel much better.

"I would have gone after the man whose daughter had been raped – the man who had killed my family. But in my blind rage I'd been too hasty: I'd killed de Troyes without even asking him who the man was. He might have blurted it out when he was confessing, but I couldn't remember if he had or not. If he did, it's never come back to me."

When he left de Troyes house, Will was covered in blood, wild eyed and crying to himself like a wounded beast. Of course people saw him, and knew his face – Hathersage being a small place.

He moved from place to place for a long time, but the memory of his butchered family would never let him find peace. Visions of the bloody murder scene woke him in the night and haunted his days.

"The only thing that keeps me going is my rage," Will said matter-of-factly. "My hatred for the real scum in our society: the rich and so-called *noble-* men. I'd take my own life and pray I'd meet my family in heaven, but I plan on killing as many of those fucking "noble" parasites as I can before God judges me."

Will sat in silence for a long time after he finished his tale, staring out at the river, the tears he had shed drying slowly in the warm breeze. Robin kept his peace, knowing there was nothing he could say that would make his brooding companion feel any less empty.

Eventually, Will reached for the ale skin again and took another long pull. He forced a bleak smile. "That's my story. I might not be the most sociable outlaw in Adam's band, but you know you'll always be able to count on me if there's any noblemen after your hide."

93

Robin returned the smile. "I hope you find some peace, Will."

Scarlet just grunted, but the pair recast their fishing lines and talk drifted to more mundane matters – the quality of the fish in the river and the warm weather they had enjoyed so far this year. Little John eventually joined them with a jug of ale of his own and the intense bond of camaraderie Robin had briefly shared with the taciturn Will passed – the young outlaw wondered if he'd ever feel such a bond of friendship with the man again.

Tuck's words had proved correct though, Robin mused. There were certainly hidden depths to Will Scarlet. His rage was understandable given the horrors he had suffered, but would his anger consume him in the end?

* * *

"Move aside!" Sir Richard, dressed in his most impressive Hospitaller armour roared at the two guardsmen, who shared a nervous glance at the sight of the two riders coming towards them.

Even their huge horses wore coats of mail covered with mantles of black and white, while the men themselves seemed to be dressed ready for battle.

"Stand aside!" the knight shouted again, removing his helmet to reveal his grey-bearded face. "My name is Sir Richard-at-Lee. Your lord" – his mouth twisted in disgust as he spat the word – "is expecting me. I bring the bail monies for my son who has been unlawfully imprisoned here!"

The two guards had been told someone might come to pay the bail for the young man from up north, so they nodded respectfully at the knights and stepped aside.

Sir Richard had travelled a few days earlier to St Mary's abbey in York, where he had collected the money Abbott Ness had promised to loan him. From there, he had come to Glamorgan as fast as possible; every minute his son was imprisoned felt like an hour to the fiercely protective big knight.

Richard and his sergeant – Stephen – pulled their swords from their scabbards and handed them over to the guards, who waved them through the gatehouse.

The steward of the castle had been warned of their approach, and he appeared now to greet them, a pair of stable boys rushing over to take their horses to be fed and watered. The Hospitallers lifted heavy saddlebags from their mounts and glared at the steward, a haughty, proud looking thin man of about forty years.

"You must be the commander of Kirklees," said the man, a heavy Welsh accent making him hard to understand, squinting in the bright late-afternoon sunshine. "I bid you welcome."

"Never mind that bollocks," Sir Richard cut the man off. "I'm here to pay your lord for the return of my son. Where is he?"

The steward looked irritated by the knight's rudeness. "My lord Despenser is away with the king. I am his steward here, I act in his name. As for your son, he has been well looked after. If you will follow me to the great hall, I have sent word for him to be brought to meet us there."

The castle, of motte-and-bailey design and built on the site of an old Roman fort, was hugely impressive, in comparison to Sir Richard's own rather modest fortress. It was manned by a large garrison, in response to trouble with the locals who disliked their Despenser lord, and the guards were a highly visible presence as the three men walked along the corridors to the great hall.

"Does your lord make a habit of extortion?" the big knight demanded.

The steward never turned as he continued walking, "Your son has been accused of murder, my lord. It is entirely your choice to pay the bail fee – you can leave him here until a judge arrives from the King's

Bench and he can receive a fair trial, as the law demands."

"How long will that take?"

"Maybe a few months," the steward shrugged, pushing open the door to the hall which was empty apart from five guardsmen, armed with pikes. "Maybe much longer – who knows?" He turned and smiled. "These judges are very busy men."

Sir Richard wanted to punch the smug bastard, but he noticed his son, who looked sullen although healthy enough, standing by the long table in the centre of the enormous room. "Simon!" he cried, hurrying over, angered at the sight of the manacles on his son's wrists. "Get these damn things off him!"

"All in due time, all in due time." The steward sat in a chair on the other side of the table and opened a ledger, running a long finger down it until he found Simon's name, which took some time as the man seemed to suffer from poor eyesight. The steward never offered the visitors a seat as Richard embraced his son and they stood waiting together, facing the man as he read what was written on the parchment silently, his lips moving, nodding his head occasionally.

"I see, yes," he glanced up, squinting disapprovingly at Simon who growled at him. "A very serious matter this, your son apparently used a lance that hadn't been blunted, which is why his opponent was killed."

"That's a lie!" Simon shouted, shaking his head furiously as he looked at his father. "The lance was blunted, I remember it distinctly. It was an accident! It could just as easily have been me who was killed."

Sir Richard patted his son reassuringly on the arm as the steward continued. "That may be the case, my boy, and it could be the judge will agree with you, but the charge is so serious that your bail has been set by my lord Despenser at one hundred pounds."

The big Hospitaller snorted. "What you mean, you pompous little arsehole, is that the victim's father is a friend of your lord. Between them, they've decided to make my son and I suffer for what was nothing more than an unfortunate accident."

The steward shrugged and pressed his bleary eyes with his fingertips. "You have the money?"

Sir Richard nodded to his sergeant and they hefted the saddlebags onto the table. "It's all there, I counted it myself."

The steward smiled. "Of course, I trust you, a knight of God, but you understand my lord expects me to make sure. You can wait outside while I make sure the full amount is here." He waved dismissively to the door, ordering one of the guards to remove the manacles from Simon on the way out.

The three men stood in the dim hallway while the money was checked, Simon fidgeting nervously at the thought of walking away a free man again. At least until the trial.

"Where did you get all that money, father?" he wondered. "Our family isn't rich – you gave it all away when you became a Hospitaller. I've never seen so much silver."

"I borrowed it from an abbott," Sir Richard grunted. "Only Christ knows how I'll ever pay it back, but the main thing is to get you out of here. These bastards would let you rot in their jail for years." He stopped and fixed his son with a calm gaze. "You did have your lance blunted, didn't you?"

"I did!" Simon shouted, his voice echoing down the long stone corridor. "I swear it. I did nothing wrong. We tilted, I found myself lying on the grass, dazed, then Alfred ran over and told me I'd killed Wytebelt. It all happened so fast, I think the lance must have slid up and caught him in the face, breaking his neck. It had nothing to do with the lance being blunted or not, it was simply an accident."

Richard nodded. He knew Edmund Wytebelt had indeed died of a broken neck – when the squire, Alfred, travelled back to Kirklees with news of what had happened the boy said the dead man's head had been lying at a funny angle.

Hugh Despenser's greed was sickening – the Hospitaller knew he was as good as ruined, while Despenser sat somewhere laughing with the king, accumulating wealth illegally from good men like Sir Richard.

No wonder the Earl of Lancaster and the Marcher lords were determined to do something about the injustice that was rotting the very heart of the country. Well, Sir Richard would help any way he could.

"For now," he growled, looking at his son and his loyal sergeant, "we get the hell out of this castle and back up the road to Kirklees. Once we're safely away from here, we'll see what we can do about all this."

"I'll have to come back to stand trial, won't I?" Simon muttered fretfully.

His father never replied, but the look on his face suggested none of them would ever be coming back to this place.

The big door opened again and a page boy came out, handing a rolled up piece of parchment to Sir Richard: a receipt. "The steward says everything's in order," the lad told them in a reedy little voice. "You're free to go. He says you'll be summoned to attend a trial at some point, when you'll have to return."

The page showed them back to the courtyard and pointed to the stables. "You can retrieve your horses and leave, my lords."

Richard grunted a word of thanks and led the other two into the low building. Stephen breathed deeply and smiled – he loved horses, the smell of them brought back memories of his time with the Hospitallers in the Holy Land, and he was pleased to see his destrier had been well looked after.

The head groom saw them and came over, gesturing to the two big war-horses. "I had my boys rub 'em down and feed 'em before they were allowed to go and have their own meal," he smiled. "We take better care of our horses than we do people here."

"My thanks to you," Sir Richard nodded, tossing a small coin to the groom. "Saddle my son's horse, please and we'll be on our way."

The groom looked confused. "Your son's horse?"

"Dionysus," Simon replied, as if talking to a simpleton. He saw his own mount in a stall next to his father's and stepped over with a grin to greet the big animal which made a soft noise almost like a laugh as it spotted its master.

"No one said you were taking that one," the groom shook his head firmly. "You'll just have to get up behind your da," he told Simon. "Your horse belongs to my lord Despenser now."

Simon wasn't sure what to do, but his father was. "Stephen," he glanced at his sergeant. "Saddle Dionysus as quickly as possible please."

As the groom moved to stop him, Sir Richard grabbed the man round the throat and slammed his back, hard, into one of the wooden pillars supporting the roof. The whole building shook at the force and the man went limp as the burly knight slammed him into the pillar again. "Give me those!"

Simon grinned and lifted the stirrups his father had indicated from their hook on the wall next to him. The Hospitaller used them to bind the man's arms behind his back, and then tied another piece of leather round his mouth to stop him shouting.

"Get them outside," he ordered his two companions who led the three horses from the stable, into the courtyard, the setting sun casting long, menacing shadows from the surrounding towers onto the dusty ground.

Sir Richard dragged the semi-conscious groom into Dionysus's vacant stall and threw him onto the hay, locking the door. "Your lord Despenser has my hundred pounds of silver you little prick. If he needs something to ride, he can ride you."

He walked outside and jumped into his saddle. "Let's move!" he ordered, and, after collecting their weapons from the gatehouse, the three men rode as fast as possible out of Wales.

CHAPTER NINE

"Where the fuck is he?"

The night had worn on with no sign of their leader returning, and Robin was growing increasingly edgy.

"Probably found some willing young lass in one of the towns hereabouts," John grinned. "Don't worry yourself – we all like to have a night away from the camp now and again."

Robin accepted this with a grunt, but as it had grown dark that evening and Adam Bell hadn't returned to camp the young wolf's head felt a knot in his stomach for no reason he could put his finger on.

The outlaws had set guards, as usual, and the rest of the group relaxed around the fire. It was the middle of August and, although the weather was extremely hot during the days, on cloudless nights like this one it could get chilly.

"What if he's been captured?" Much asked. "He could lead the sheriff right to us."

"Aye, he could, lad. But we've got four lookouts posted in trees around the camp's perimeter. You'll be taking one of the watches yourself later on, right? If a load of heavily armed men try to sneak up on us in the pitch black, through the trees, I'm sure one of our guards will notice." Little John slapped Much on the back, grinning good naturedly. "Like I said – don't worry."

"Does he do this often? Disappear for days without telling anyone I mean?" Robin wondered.

John laughed at his friend's obvious concern. "Christ, if he knew you cared so much he could have just stayed here and shared his blanket with you instead of looking for an eager girl!"

Robin reddened, and John, not wanting to upset the young man, grew serious. "Relax. Adam knows how to take care of himself better than any of us, there's very little chance of him being captured."

The big man could see his reassurance hadn't quite worked yet. "Listen, if Adam's not back by mid-morning tomorrow, we'll talk about it then. Trust me" – he leaned forward earnestly, spilling much of his ale onto the grass – "there's nothing to worry about!"

John's confidence took some of the edge off the fears of the two younger men, and they began to relax and enjoy the ale and the biblical tales Tuck was telling round the fire. Adam's absence seemed to be somewhat liberating. Robin noted, with some surprise, that men who were normally quiet and shy were enjoying themselves immensely tonight, like children when their strict parents leave the room. The bright cooking fire threw flickering shadows on the trees around the camp as the men ate and drank their fill of roast venison and ale, singing and laughing late into the evening.

Much left to take his turn on guard duty, so Robin moved to sit on a log next to Will Scarlet, who seemed to still be lost in the melancholy brought on by his earlier tale.

"You alright?" Robin asked gently.

Will looked up in surprise at the big young man's sudden appearance next to him. "Christ, you can move like a ghost! I never heard you coming at all."

"Sorry," Robin replied sheepishly, feeling guilty for disturbing the tortured Scarlet. "I seem to be picking up the woodcraft skills you've all been teaching me."

Will forced a half smile then looked away, watching the rest of the men laughing and singing a short distance away. One of the men was playing a musical instrument and the others slapped their legs and stamped along with the rhythm.

"Aye, I'm fine," Will replied. "Why aren't you joining in with that lot?"

Robin shrugged. "Don't really feel like it. To be honest, I'm a bit nervous about Adam. He's been gone a while – where is he anyway?"

Will grunted. "No idea, he never told me. You'd be better asking John."

Robin leaned over and looked into Will's eyes. "Are you serious? You don't know where he is?"

"No," Scarlet replied irritably. "I just said so, didn't I? What's the big deal?"

Robin straightened, his hand moving reflexively to his sword, and he peered anxiously around at the dark trees surrounding the outlaws' camp. They seemed to take on a sinister, threatening look as the young man's imagination began to run away with itself and he forced himself to keep calm.

"I think we need to move camp, Will. Now."

Scarlet stood and faced Robin, a baffled and somewhat angry look on his face. "What the fuck are you on about? Move camp? In the middle of the night? When half the men are half drunk? Who put you in charge anyway?"

"It's not about who's in charge," Robin retorted. "You don't know where Adam is – well, neither does Little John, I asked him earlier. Don't you think that's worrying? Our leader goes off somewhere and doesn't tell either you or John where he's going or when he'll be back?"

Will listened and found himself agreeing with the younger outlaw – the fact John didn't know Adam's whereabouts was a surprise – but he was in no mood to have Robin ordering everyone around like he was in charge.

"Listen, Hood" – he growled, pointing a finger menacingly at the other man.

"What's the problem?" Little John had noticed the discussion and strode over from the campfire to stand between Will and Robin before things could get any more heated.

"He doesn't know where Adam is either," Robin replied, nodding at Scarlet. "I'm telling you, something's not right. If we don't move camp we're going to regret it."

103

Will snorted, but John looked at him seriously. "Hang on; maybe the boy's got a point. Adam always tells one of us where he's going if he thinks he might be away for a while."

"So, what then?" Scarlet demanded. "We all pack up our stuff and run off into the forest in the pitch black?"

"If Adam's been captured," John replied, "he can lead the law right to us. Aye, he can fight better than any of us, and he knows the forest like the back of his hand, but anyone can be taken by surprise."

"Adam wouldn't let himself get captured!" Will shouted. "You know him – he'd fight to the death before he let himself be taken. He's even crazier than me! I've had enough of this shit, John – I'm away to sleep."

As Scarlet stormed off, muttering to himself, Robin remembered the conversation he'd had with Much and Tuck a few days earlier and in a flash of inspiration things suddenly became clear.

"We have to move, John," he told the huge outlaw earnestly. "Adam hasn't been captured – he wants that pardon. He's going to lead the sheriff right here – and wipe us all out."

* * *

Two days earlier Adam Bell, or Gurdon, had left the outlaws' camp and made his way to Nottingham, where he had struck a deal with the sheriff.

He had shaved and dressed himself in his finest clothes once out of sight of the outlaws, and, on reaching the castle, had begged an audience with the sheriff, telling the guards he knew the location of the notorious murderer Robin Hood. The guards , after divesting him of his weapons, had ushered him into see Sir Henry de Faucumberg, Sheriff of Nottingham and Yorkshire.

"Well, well! Adam Gurdon – my former bailiff in Stamford!" De Faucumberg's eyes opened wide in surprise when he saw his visitor. "I haven't had the pleasure of your company in years! Where have you been hiding? Along with the other wolf's heads in my forest? I seem to recall you disappeared when word got around you had been a Templar knight."

Gurdon inclined his head to the sheriff, who he had indeed known, years ago, before he was declared an outlaw. He had once saved de Faucumberg's life, yet despite that, Adam suspected the sheriff may have been the cause of his ruin . . .

"Things in Stamford went to shit once I left and the king split the manor in half, eh?" de Faucumberg grinned. "Those two fools that took over from me made a right arse of things. I heard they had you enforcing marriages the brides didn't agree to just to claim tax on the dowry!" The sheriff's face grew stony. "You imprisoned people on trumped-up charges just to extort bail money. You even let rapists off as long as they bribed you well enough . . . yes?"

Gurdon remained silent. The sheriff's accusations were true – de Faucumberg had been a decent lord in Stamford – fair and mostly honest – but when he had moved on the people of Stamford had become sick of their corrupt bailiff and the two new lords, Gilbert ad Pontem and John Chapman. The king was petitioned by some of the wealthier local residents, and, in order to convict the two lords, Gurdon gave evidence against them, in return for the charges against him being dropped.

Chapman and ad Pontem were imprisoned while Gurdon simply returned to his job as bailiff in Stamford, under the care of another new lord, Edward Le Rus.

"Well, speak up, man!" the sheriff cried. "Have you been living in the forests with those outlaws or not?"

Gurdon snapped out of his reverie and stammered a reply. "You're right, Sir Henry. Somehow," he emphasised the word and met de Faucumberg's eye looking for a reaction, but the sheriff remained impassive, "the people in Stamford found out I had been a Templar and I was forced to flee into the forests. I had to take up with the scum and dregs of society: it was the only way I could survive. I had to act like them, speak like them, dress like them – become just like them. After years of this…existence, I heard of your offer of pardon to any who turns in Robin Hood of Wakefield."

Many of his former brothers in the Templars had been arrested, imprisoned, tortured, and even killed after the Papal Bull of 1307. Although King Edward II had taken his time in carrying out Pope Clement's instructions to arrest all Templars, the monarch had eventually given in and, in late 1309 effectively ended the Order. Arrests, accusations of apostasy, torture…Hundreds, perhaps thousands, of Templars, had no choice but to become outlaws and seek refuge in the forests of England, Scotland, even Ireland.

"You know where that young savage Hood is hiding?" de Faucumberg asked, leaning forward and eyeing Gurdon thoughtfully.

"I do. What's more, in return for pardon and a chance to serve in your guard, I'll lead you straight to Hood *and* the rest of his gang. Seventeen outlaws, my lord, in one fell swoop."

The sheriff crossed his legs and stroked his chin in an almost theatrical manner, as he pondered the implications of Gurdon's proposal. While it was in his power to pardon the outlaw, he knew the disgraced former lords of Stamford Gilbert ad Pontem and John Chapman. When they had been imprisoned they had sent word to de Faucumberg offering to pay for any information he might have that would help them ruin Adam Gurdon. He had gladly told them Gurdon had once been a Templar knight – de Faucumberg had been disgusted by his former bailiff's behaviour in Stamford and it galled him to know the man was walking the streets a free man after ruining so many people's lives.

Besides, ad Pontem and Chapman had paid him well for the information.

But they had been released from prison by now, de Faucumberg knew, and had been restored to positions of relative power and influence. They would not look too kindly on the man who pardoned Adam Gurdon.

Still, it was his duty as sheriff to uphold the king's law, no matter who it upset.

"This Robin Hood must be brought to justice," de Faucumberg stated firmly. "He killed a bailiff for God's sake. If you can deliver him and his friends to me it'll send a powerful signal to the rest of the outlaws around here. It might also shut up that nagging prior from Lewes. I'm sick of his whining letters." The sheriff shook his head in disgust. "You will have your pardon."

Gurdon smiled widely and thanked the sheriff with a bow. "You will not regret it, my lord."

De Faucumberg stared at him and nodded. "I hope not. Now, before you lead my men into the forest, you must meet Sir Ranulph de Craon. Normally, a man of your particular military skill would find employ as the captain of my guard. But Sir Ranulph already holds that position. You will serve under him."

A bearded, haughty-looking bear of a man stepped forward from behind the sheriff's chair and gazed at Gurdon, who felt a little dismayed as he realised he wouldn't be walking into quite as powerful a position as he had hoped.

"Of course, lord sheriff. I will serve in whatever capacity you deem fit."

"Good. De Craon will take you to the quartermaster and have you kitted out although you look surprisingly well fed for one who's been scratching an existence in the forest for years." The sheriff stared again straight at Adam, his eyes questioning. "How *do* you know so much about these outlaws anyway, Gurdon? While I can believe you had to live with those criminal scum, I *cannot* believe you allowed any of them to tell you what to do. In fact…now that I think on it, that particular area of the Yorkshire forest has been plagued by a particularly well-organised outlaw band for…well, years. About the same length of time as you were there, probably."

Gurdon opened his mouth to reply – he had expected questions like this and had concocted an elaborate story to explain how he had served under an English former noble called Adam Bell, but the sheriff raised his hand.

"Never mind. I've heard all about this Adam Bell, I expect you took orders from him."

Gurdon nodded in relief, sensing the danger pass.

"You do seem to match Adam Bell's description very closely though. You even share his Christian name…"

Sir Ranulph de Craon looked questioningly at de Faucumberg and placed a wary hand on his sword hilt, not sure where this was leading, but the sheriff gave a humourless laugh. "Ah well, that can be a story for another day, eh? Sir Ranulph, take our new sergeant and see he is kitted out. Then take thirty men into Barnsdale Forest and destroy Robin Hood and his friends."

"My lord." De Craon gave a shallow bow, and gestured Gurdon to follow him out of the hall.

"I take it you have a plan how to do this, Adam," de Faucumberg asked as the pair walked from the room. "I mean, without my men being wiped out by those blasted longbows the outlaws favour?"

Gurdon smiled grimly. "Don't worry Sir Henry. I know how the outlaws live. Thirty of your men will be more than enough to destroy these vermin once and for all."

* * *

"Wake up, Matt! Allan, get up! We have to move – everyone, up!"

Robin moved quickly around the outlaw's camp, shaking, shouting and gently kicking everyone awake.

Little John had finally, after talking to Friar Tuck and hearing what he had to say, agreed to lead the men to a new campsite – just in case Robin's theory was right. John had sought out Will to discuss it with him, but Scarlet was lying near the fire, curled under his blanket, staring at nothing, and simply waved the big man away with an angry growl when he tried to talk.

John knew they were safe during the night – only a fool would lead armed men into Barnsdale in the dark hunting outlaws, and Adam was no fool. So he had decided to let the men rest until first light, then they would pack up and be on their way.

The sun was only just beginning to crest the horizon so the outlaws had little light to see what they were doing under the thick foliage around their camp, and the thick morning dew lent the air a chilly atmosphere.

"I don't understand what the bloody hurry is." Matt Groves was in a foul mood, and didn't appreciate being told to get up and ready to move when no one had explained to him what was going on. "Has someone found us? Are there foresters about?"

"We'll explain it all once we're on the move," Robin replied, loud enough for the other men to hear, so he didn't have to keep repeating himself. "Just help us get all the gear together ready to go."

"Just because Adam ain't here, doesn't mean you're the leader now, Hood!" Groves spat, moving towards the young man "Don't you start ordering me about!"

Luckily Little John came to Robin's aid, grabbing Matt by the arm with a fierce look that warned of further argument. "Look, it doesn't matter right now why we're moving. Just get your stuff together and move. Or stay here if you like, maybe this is all a waste of time and we're leading you out of a nice comfortable campsite for nothing. Your choice, Matt, but the rest of us are going."

"You bought into it then," Will shook his head at Little John. "This is a wild goose chase."

"If you'd let me talk to you last night instead of having a tantrum you'd have heard what Robin – and Tuck – had to say," John retorted angrily. "If this is a waste of time, so be it. I'd rather waste a little time moving camp than hanging around and getting a forester's sword up my arse."

In an extreme emergency the outlaws could escape the camp in a few minutes, and fade away into the trees so anyone hunting them would have little chance of finding them. Robin was sure they had enough time to collect together all their belongings before Gurdon and the sheriff's men were upon them, so, although they were in a hurry, nothing was left behind and they were on the move within half an hour, with little trace left to show they had ever been there. Another half an hour later, the outlaw band had travelled a fair distance to the west, along the road to Kirklees, in the opposite direction to Nottingham, where Robin knew Adam Gurdon would come from.

"Right, Hood – that's us left our nice comfy camp behind us." Matt looked at Little John. "Where are we going? And what about Adam?"

"Adam is the reason we've had to leave the camp. He's betrayed us." Robin expected some extreme reaction to this news from the volatile Groves – anger, fury, threats of violence and vengeance maybe. He hadn't expected him to laugh.

"Adam's betrayed us? We left the camp because you say Adam's betrayed us? Why would he do that?"

Matt had stopped walking and, as his initial amused disbelief at Robin's claim wore off, he began to get annoyed again. The rest of the outlaws halted as well and every eye turned to Robin to hear what he had to say about their missing leader.

"He's betrayed us to the sheriff: to be pardoned. Where do you think he's been the past couple of days?"

"I don't believe I'm hearing this. Are you listening to this shit, John? You know Adam – he'd never betray us. And now this…boy, tells us Adam's turned us all in?" He looked back at Robin, "If Adam's not around any more, we'll be needing a new leader, eh? I expect you think that'll be you? If you think I'm taking orders from you…"

"Will you give it a rest for a fucking minute?" Little John rounded on Groves, his face like thunder. "Give Robin a chance to speak!"

For all Robin's leadership instincts, and Matt's accusations that he wanted to take control of the gang, Robin wasn't used to addressing all the outlaws at once. He felt his cheeks flush as he looked around at the people he had spent the last few months living and fighting alongside.

"I'm telling you, it's the truth, I'm sure of it. Adam Bell wasn't who he claimed to be. He was a disgraced knight or something, not some peasant folk hero."

Friar Tuck held up a hand as some of the men began to jeer and laugh at this. "He's right." His powerful orator's voice cut through the hubbub, and he told them all what he had heard when the sheriff's soldiers, with their Norman captain, had attacked their camp.

Will, who of all the outlaws had been closest to Adam Bell, couldn't or simply didn't want to, accept what he was hearing. "If you knew Bell was really some kind of noble why the hell didn't you tell the rest of us?" he shouted.

"Would you have believed us?" Tuck asked gently.

"No!" Will dropped his belongings on the forest floor and grabbed Robin's cloak, pinning him against a tree. "And I don't believe you now either! I've been part of this gang for three years and Adam's done right by us all that time. I don't give a fuck what you have to say about him – he wouldn't betray us! We're brothers, we look after each other – Adam more than anyone."

It was true; Adam Bell had been a good enough leader. Not exactly a friend to any of the outlaws, not even Will. Bell had always seemed aloof – superior to everyone else. But he had kept them safe from the law and kept their bellies full even in the horrendously harsh winters of recent years, when so many people all over Europe had starved.

Adam may not have been well liked by the men of the gang, but he was highly respected and, perhaps more importantly, *trusted* by them. Many of them had seen how he reacted on the couple of occasions over the years when former members had tried to betray them to the law – Adam had hunted those turncoats down and killed them without mercy.

Bell had always appeared to live by a violent code of honour that made it so hard to believe he could betray them all to the very people they had been hiding from for so long.

Robin could see the outlaws would never accept what he was telling them – in fact, their disbelief would soon turn to distrust and his position within the group would become untenable. He had to prove what he said was true.

"Damn it! I wanted us to get as far away from him as possible, but if you insist on seeing for yourselves, fine. Let's make a temporary camp here, and then we can go and watch our great leader bringing his new friends to butcher us."

CHAPTER TEN

Adam Gurdon and Sir Ranulph de Craon had left Nottingham Castle at dawn that morning, with thirty men. All were mounted on warhorses, although these weren't armoured since they were purely for transportation to and from the forest, and would not be used in any fighting. The men themselves were all seasoned fighting men, clad in good quality chain mail which would keep them fairly manoeuvrable in the tight confines of Barnsdale Forest.

In a straight fight, twenty or so lightly armoured outlaws would stand little chance against such a force. And Gurdon expected this to be far from a straight fight – this was to be a massacre. Adam would take care of the lookouts at the outlaws' camp himself – he would know roughly where they would be, since he himself had organised the protocols for choosing the positions of such lookout posts. The lookouts themselves would not see any danger in the form of "Adam Bell" approaching, making it easy for the pardoned soldier to dispatch them.

It would then be a simple matter for the sheriff's men to walk into the unsuspecting outlaws' camp and massacre every one of them before they had a chance to fight back.

It was a straightforward plan, but one that seemed infallible. Gurdon was convinced it would work, and de Craon, while not overeager to commit to a possible rival's plan, was content to see how things went. Even if the outlaws sprung the trap, there seemed little danger to de Craon's men. They were simply too well armed, too well trained, and too battle-hardened. De Craon was also no fool, and understood the outlaws had probably been made leaderless with the defection of "Adam Bell".

"You were a Templar, Gurdon?"

It was still quite dark, the thick trees running along the side of the road blocking much of the slowly rising sun's light.

Adam, hunched over his horse, cloak wrapped around him to ward off the chill glanced warily over at his new captain. "I was. For years I fought the Saracens in Armenia and Syria. I decided to come home when we lost Tortosa – it was clear to me the order was dying."

De Craon growled angrily. "They were a fine Order – it was a disgrace what happened to them."

Adam grunted agreement but didn't particularly feel like discussing something that could still see him arrested.

"How did you come to meet the sheriff?"

"I saved his life," Gurdon replied. "I'd come home to Stamford and couldn't find a decent job. I was in the local alehouse when a fight broke out and a man attacked de Faucumberg with a dagger. I smashed a chair over the man's head. De Faucumberg offered me employment as his bailiff."

De Craon rode on in thoughtful silence for a while before turning to Gurdon again.

"You've lived with these fugitives for years. Yet here you are leading a force of men to destroy them. Did you form no friendships with any of these outlaws?"

Gurdon snorted. "Friendships? No. How could I ever empathise enough with a bunch of simple peasants to the extent I'd form friendships? We were simply too different, although I managed to play my part well enough to fool them into thinking I was just another yeoman fallen on hard times." He looked frankly at de Craon. "I formed no friendships, because I'm not the type. I'm too self-centred to have made many friends in my life, never mind any of those outlaw scum. I admit I did develop a grudging respect and admiration for some of them though."

The sun started to appear above the treetops, throwing soft shadows on the old Roman road behind the armoured horsemen, and, as birdsong and the almost hypnotic, rhythmic drumming of hooves filled the cool morning air, the forest seemed a wonderfully peaceful place.

"Tell me, then. Who of these wolf's heads impressed you?" De Craon seemed genuinely interested in Gurdon's opinion of the outlaws, perhaps planning ahead in case anything went wrong with the morning's work.

"There's a friar, he joined the group not long ago. An overweight, jolly-looking man, but he's incredibly strong, and can use a sword or quarterstaff almost as well as any man I've ever met. You should have a couple of your men take care of him as soon as possible – he could cause problems otherwise."

"Go on," de Craon prompted.

"My . . ." Gurdon looked hurriedly at Sir Ranulph, realising he had given away his role as leader of the outlaw band with one careless word. But the damage was done, and he understood de Craon probably knew all about his former role as Adam Bell anyway, so he carried on, ". . . the . . . second in command, was William Scaflock, or Will Scarlet as you probably know him. Although I was closer to him than any of the other outlaws, he would skin me alive if he knew I'd betrayed him. He's a good fighter, nothing particularly special normally, but he's filled with so much rage and hatred that I sometimes feared he would even turn on us, his companions, during the night. I believe his mind has snapped to some extent – he barely holds himself together. All he seems to live for is to kill nobles and any lawmen who might try to stop him. Of all the outlaws, you should take him down first, before he's aware of what's happening. There'll be no reasoning with him."

Sir Ranulph de Craon looked thoughtful as his horse picked its way around a fallen tree, glancing all around himself, constantly alert for danger, hand on his sword hilt. "What about this Robin Hood, the one we're here for? What's so special about him?"

115

Gurdon's horse carefully followed the route de Craon's horse had taken, scattering old, partially rotted orange and brown leaves left over from the previous autumn. Gurdon felt a shiver down his spine, yet couldn't have said why. He shrugged. "I'm not sure. He's young and seems guileless in his dealings with the rest of the men. To all appearances he's just another yeoman with a temper that got him into trouble. Certainly, that's how he sees himself. Yet . . ." Gurdon shrugged. "There's more to him, but I was never sure what. He can fight with a sword far better than the training we gave him warrants. He shoots with incredible accuracy, better than any man I've ever seen – and I've seen some master marksmen, believe me. He has instinctual knowledge of battlefield tactics, without knowing himself where his understanding comes from...And he has a sixth sense for approaching danger."

Sir Ranulph looked over sharply at Gurdon, who shrugged. "He's no soothsayer. Don't worry, he won't see our approach in his crystal ball, he just seemed to sometimes have an uncanny edge over his opponents." Gurdon paused, lost in thought for a few minutes. "Given a few years, Hood could become a fighter of unsurpassed skill, and a leader to match it. He almost beat me not too long ago . . ."

Gurdon's reputation as a swordsman had preceded him, and de Craon knew his new sergeant was utterly deadly with a blade, so the admission that such a young yeoman wolf's head had almost bested him was surprisingly honest.

"You know...." Gurdon turned with an almost comical look of genuine surprise towards de Craon, "when I think back to our sparring match, I begin to wonder if the boy let me win!" He shook his head and laughed, but the uncertainty was clear in his eyes.

Sir Ranulph grunted disagreeably. "You're not filling me with confidence that this will be an easy mission! A superhuman friar, a berserker, and what sounds like the best swordsman in the country, who has a sixth sense for approaching danger?"

Gurdon laughed, but he was supremely confident that the outlaws wouldn't expect this attack. Their destruction was a formality, and he mentally kicked himself for talking too frankly to this de Craon, a man he hoped to usurp sometime in the near future. Conversing with a nobleman again after so many years – one close to his own perceived station in life – had made him relax too much, he realised irritably.

"Well?" Sir Ranulph raised an eyebrow towards him.

"Well what?"

"Is there anyone else among this band of wolf's heads we should be aware of?"

"Only one." Gurdon lifted himself in his stirrups and raised a hand. The soldiers behind him slowed to a stop as they neared the outlying reaches of the outlaws' camp.

Gurdon's eyes flicked around the forest, searching for signs of danger, then, seeing nothing, he dropped down from his mount and nervously placed a hand on the hilt of his sword.

"The bear we called Little John."

* * *

"Ow!" John squealed, as he lay on the ground and inadvertently pressed his big elbow onto a little stone.

"Keep the fucking noise down, you big girl!" Scarlet hissed as they crawled beneath a thick stand of gorse, startling a red squirrel which loped off as it heard the giant outlaw's pained cursing.

The rest of the outlaws had stayed hidden at their new campsite while Robin had gone back with Will and Little John to see if his claims of Adam's betrayal were true. It would be much easier to hide from any soldiers if there were only three of them – seventeen men would make a lot more noise and be a lot more visible. The others hadn't been too happy at being left behind, but they knew it made sense.

The sun had almost crested the horizon and the waiting outlaws were getting restless when, finally, the sound of riders approaching reached them.

Their hiding place in the bushes was less than a mile from their now deserted old campsite and, as the soldiers came into view, with Adam Bell at their head, Will swore softly in rage, watching their former leader as he dropped smoothly to the ground.

His voice carried to the concealed outlaws, telling the sheriff's men to tie their horses to the trees off the road and to follow him on foot. Two men were ordered to stay behind and watch the horses.

Robin could clearly see the pain of betrayal written on Little John's honest face.

"That bastard," the giant growled. "I'll fucking kill him." He started to fit an arrow to his bow but Robin held him back, not wanting a chase from a party of well-armed soldiers led by a man who knew the forest at least as well as any of them.

Will stared numbly at the men below. "How do we know he's betrayed us? All I see is Adam and a group of soldiers. Maybe he's their prisoner."

Robin looked at Will in disbelief, while John, exasperated said, "Oh come on, Will! Do you see any chains on his ankles? He's even got his sword with him!"

"Who's that?" said Robin, pointing.

They all looked at the tall, very heavily built, but older man who was clearly in charge of the soldiers.

"Sir Ranulph de Craon," said John. "I remember seeing him with the sheriff once when I was in Bichill. He's never come after us personally before. He's the Sheriff's right-hand man and not a bad character from what I've heard. Well," he grunted, "as lawmen go."

118

Robin nodded thoughtfully. "At least the Sheriff didn't give Adam control of the soldiers. If there's one man we don't want in charge of hunting us down it's Adam. I can't see this fellow de Craon taking too kindly to being told what to do by a former outlaw. Hopefully they'll find our abandoned camp and Adam will be discredited. The Sheriff won't be too pleased when they go home empty handed."

Will began to move forward, following the line of soldiers. "We'll track them and see what happens when they realise we're not where they expect us to be. I still don't believe Adam's betrayed us all, even if he" – Will stabbed an angry finger towards Robin – "says so."

Robin nodded. "Fine, we'll follow."

"Well keep it quiet then," Little John murmured as he moved quietly after Will. "I'd rather not get into a fight with that lot."

* * *

"Right, men, fan out," Adam Gurdon ordered. "I want ten of you left, ten right and the remaining ten centre with me and Sir Ranulph, that way – "

"Gurdon!" De Craon's sharp tone brought everyone up short. "I'm in charge here, Gurdon, I'll decide how we proceed. You're only here to advise me, please don't forget that."

Adam flushed at the rebuke, knowing the soldiers were watching the exchange with amusement.

"Your pardon, my lord," he said, bowing slightly, in deference to the older man. "I'm so used to being in command of men I forgot myself."

"In command of a bunch of peasant outlaws, eh, *Adam Bell*?" De Craon snorted mirthlessly, making Gurdon flush again, anger burning in his brown eyes.

"Nonetheless," de Craon went on, oblivious to the Englishman's ire, "Gurdon's plan seems sound so" – he pointed with his sword – "you men, go left, you lot, right. The rest come with me and the wolf's head. When

I blow the horn, we all move in and attack the camp. They'll hopefully all still be asleep and we'll have an easy morning's work."

As the soldiers moved to take up their new positions Sir Ranulph murmured to Adam, "I would have expected there to be sentries posted, Gurdon. Are you planning on taking care of them before they rouse the entire forest?"

The former outlaw leader looked uncomfortable. "I checked ahead earlier when your men stopped to water their horses. I never found any sentries where I expected them to be."

De Craon stared at him. "What do you think that means?"

Gurdon shrugged. "They must have relaxed their routine since I've not been there the past two days to organise them."

"Let's hope so, that should make our job even easier." De Craon ordered the party to begin moving forward carefully towards the site Adam Gurdon claimed was the outlaws' camp.

When he was sure the men flanking left and right must be in position the sun had only just begun to show itself, but the thick foliage in this part of the forest meant little light was cast on the target area. No one was visible, but the flickering shadows played tricks on the eyes.

The captain turned to his men. "It's all quiet in there, they must all be asleep. The lazy peasants haven't even set sentries so all we have to do is gut them while they sleep. Ready?"

The soldiers nodded, knowing what to do. Anyone unarmed was to be captured for a public trial, while those who resisted arrest were to be shown no quarter.

Gurdon slowly eased his sword from its leather scabbard as de Craon raised his hunting horn to his lips and blew one long blast.

With a roar, the soldiers charged into the clearing, weapons held ready before them. The two flanking parties charged at the same time until all of de Craon's men stood, staring around themselves into the gloom in confusion.

"There's no one here, Gurdon!" shouted the captain, turning on the former outlaw leader. His adrenaline was pumping and he was ready for a fight.

Gurdon looked around in consternation. "They must have moved camp."

"You said they would remain in this place for three days, you fool! This is only the second!" Sir Ranulph roared, shaking his sword in a fury.

Gurdon sheathed his own weapon and looked around at the deserted campsite, baffled. "I've no idea why they moved camp. They should have waited on me returning... I would suggest we are wary though...they may have set traps."

De Craon looked astonished. "Traps? Why would they do that? They never knew we were coming, did they? Men! Let's get back to Nottingham, this has been a waste of time. We're going to look like fools when this gets out, and you, Gurdon"- the angry soldier moved his horse in and shoved his face into Adam's – "will look the biggest fool of us all. I'll see the sheriff sends you back into these godforsaken woods where you belong!"

Gurdon's plans were coming to nothing. In despair he dragged his sword from its sheath again as de Craon turned his back on him. He was ruined anyway; it would make no difference if he rammed his blade into this arrogant bastard's spine. He might even be able to escape into the forest and find Will and the rest of the outlaws.

As the bitter thoughts spun around his head, something out of place, a noise perhaps, a tiny movement in the air, made Gurdon drop to the ground as de Craon spun round and stared at him in astonishment. A split second later a single arrow blasted through the leaves, passing through where Gurdon had been standing a fraction of a second earlier, and lodged itself in Sir Ranulph de Craon's throat.

Almost instantly, the sheriff's soldiers' training took over and one of them barked an order. The men formed a shield wall around their fallen captain, while Gurdon remained prone on the forest floor, eyes darting around him warily.

No more arrows came from the trees though, and after a few moments Adam rose to his feet. His calculating mind was inwardly cheering at this unexpected turn of events and he knew his situation had improved dramatically.

"You two: lift Sir Ranulph. The rest of you: tight formation round them. Let's move, back to our horses, and Nottingham!"

Gurdon's voice and bearing, so naturally used to command, was enough to still any doubts the soldiers might have had about following his orders. They were just glad to have someone with them who seemed to have an idea what to do.

The hunting party warily set off back home to Nottingham, empty-handed.

* * *

Robin, Little John and Will Scarlet had watched the soldiers bluster into their former campsite from a well-hidden vantage point. John had found the whole scene amusing, while Robin looked more apprehensive as he wondered what might happen next.

Will hadn't said a word since the so-called attack on the camp began. He simply stared coldly at Adam Gurdon, the leader who had betrayed them.

As de Craon had raged at Gurdon, the other two outlaws had exchanged smiles – this was the end for Adam Gurdon, surely. No matter what Adam said, the sheriff would take de Craon's advice and, at the very least, send Gurdon on his way. He would not be leading any more searches for them, and life for the outlaws could go back to normal. They had all known they probably wouldn't last long if Adam were to lead any sustained hunt for them on behalf of the sheriff. His knowledge of the forest, and their methods, combined with such well-drilled manpower, would make life extremely difficult for any outlaws.

Now, though, it seemed they were safe.

As relief washed over him, Robin heard the snap of a bowstring and watched in horror as the arrow missed Adam Gurdon and tore into the big captain.

"No," the young outlaw gasped in horror. "No!"

Little John turned on Will who was busy fitting another shaft to his bow. "Enough, Will! They'll be after us now, we have to move." The big man grabbed Will's shoulder and dragged him onto his feet. "Come on Robin, move!"

The three outlaws ran back into the forest, John leading them a circuitous route as they headed for the sanctuary of their new camp. They never noticed the sheriff's soldiers, now led by a pleased looking Adam Gurdon, had lost interest in them . . .

* * *

"How very fortunate for you . . ." The sheriff of Nottingham, Sir Henry de Faucumberg, poured himself another cup of wine and took a long pull as he looked knowingly at the recently returned Gurdon.

"My lord?" Adam looked innocently at the sheriff, who had failed to offer him any of the wine – an expensive French red.

"Don't be coy with me, man. The soldiers have told me de Craon was going to recommend I chase you from my castle with your tail between your legs. Apparently my now deceased captain thought you were a blundering fool. I expect I would have taken his advice: he was a very good judge of character."

The former outlaw leader held his tongue as the sheriff continued.

"He was a fine captain you know. The men liked him, probably because he tended to be rather soft on them. He was getting on in years and didn't have the same ruthless vigour for soldiering as he once had."

Seeing an opportunity, Gurdon spoke up. "I could see that, my lord. He was overly cautious as we tracked the outlaws, as if he couldn't really care less whether we caught them or not."

The sheriff nodded, tapping his fingers absently on the side of his cup. "You care a great deal though, eh, Adam?"

"I do, Sir Henry. They are vermin: scum without honour. They need to be purged from our lands."

The sheriff smiled coldly. "You were the leader of those vermin not so long ago, Gurdon – an outlaw just like them. In fact, you never did help us capture Robin Hood or any of the rest of them, as was our agreement when I pardoned you."

Adam looked away, knowing his life was once again in the hands of the sheriff.

"I don't understand why you feel quite so bitter towards your former comrades – perhaps they're a reminder of your own fall from grace. A reminder of when you had to steal to eat – to survive. A reminder of the fact that you were nothing." The sheriff leaned forward suddenly, his eyes hard. "You are still nothing, Gurdon, unless the king – or myself, as his representative in this – decides otherwise."

De Faucumberg seemed determined to humiliate him, to make sure he knew exactly who held all the power in their relationship. Yet, Gurdon noticed, his dressing down didn't come in front of an audience. The soldiers who had returned from the failed mission with him had all been dismissed. Hope flared in him again, as the sheriff drained his cup and rose from his ornately carved seat.

124

"You're on probation," said de Faucumberg, brushing past Gurdon as he headed for the door that led out of his great hall. As he reached it he turned and continued in a grim voice. "The Earl of Lancaster needs a bailiff in Wakefield, since Robin Hood killed the last one. I've been asked to find a replacement. Despite today's farce, you've proven yourself a capable man in the past, so I'm sending you to Wakefield. If you can do a good job as bailiff there until I find a suitable replacement, you will take over from de Craon as captain of my personal guard. I expect you to do at least as good a job as he was doing until today. Better! But first – bring me Robin Hood and the rest of those outlaws."

Gurdon breathed a sigh of relief, and nodded in agreement. "My word on it, Lord Sheriff!"

De Faucumberg stopped and looked back darkly as he left the room. "Adam, I warn you: do not mistreat the villagers in Wakefield. There's been enough unrest and nonsense there in the past few weeks. You treat the people fairly or you'll have me to answer to."

CHAPTER ELEVEN

For the next four weeks, as summer began to give way to autumn, and the green leaves turned to brown, red and orange, the outlaws moved their camp much more often than previously, as Adam Gurdon and his foresters tried to track them down.

The outlaws managed to stay one step ahead of their pursuers, but it was close on more than one occasion. Gurdon's knowledge of the forest, and of the outlaws' tactics, allowed the lawmen to get closer to capturing them than ever before.

Little John had, unofficially, taken over as leader of the group. Some amongst them felt resentment towards Robin, seeing him as the source of their present troubles.

"Life was never this hard until he joined us," Matt Groves muttered to Little John one evening, as the men sat drinking and telling tales round the campfire. "Adam would never have betrayed us to the law if it wasn't for Hood. Now we're hunted like dogs by the man that was our own leader just a few weeks ago!"

John understood the fear and frustration of Groves and the handful of others who felt the same way. When winter drew in the food would become scarcer. The thick foliage that the group was able to hide in had already started to fall from the trees and bushes, and the warm comfortable nights would very soon be replaced by harsh, biting snow, wind and ice.

If Gurdon and the Sheriff decided to continue their hunt for the outlaws during a hard winter, John knew his men wouldn't see the bluebells herald another spring.

Will Scarlet had also changed since Adam's betrayal. Always an intense, moody character, Will had become even more withdrawn and the other outlaws had begun to fear he might explode violently at any moment.

Little John, seeing him sitting alone by the river one chilly sunset, crouched down and, with a small smile, asked if he was alright.

"No, not really," Scarlet replied with a grimace, seemingly oblivious to the icy wind that was blowing across the water. "Me and Adam were never what you'd call mates, but I thought we respected each other. I can't believe he's betrayed us – betrayed me!" He had felt like there was little to live for after his family's destruction, but he had a place high in the outlaws' hierarchy with a leader who, apparently admired, trusted and respected him. That had kept Will going in the mornings, when it didn't seem worth it to get off the forest floor.

Now, Gurdon had become his persecutor – thrown his lot in with the hated nobles who hunted them like animals! And, like Matt Groves, Will seemed to think it was mostly down to Robin.

The young outlaw had hoped to share more quiet moments with Will, as they had that sunny day fishing by the riverbank, but Will barely spoke a word to anyone anymore.

John decided he had to speak to Robin, to see if they could find some solution to their problems, so he stood up, patting Will awkwardly on the shoulder and headed off to look for the young man from Wakefield.

He found him soon enough, working with Much to place animal skins over their small shelters to keep the worst of the autumn winds out.

"We can't go on like this, Robin," the bearded giant muttered without preamble. "Some of the men feel resentful about what's happened and Will acting like he has a death wish is putting everyone on edge. We have to do something."

Robin sighed, shrugging his shoulders resignedly and dropped the tatty old sheepskin he was holding. "I know. I seem to have brought nothing but bad luck since I joined you men. If we could find some way to reach Will – brighten his mood, give him something to live for – maybe everyone would feel better."

John nodded his massive head as Robin sat down next to him. "But what? Will's lost everything – his wife, children and now, even his pride. He trusted Adam."

"If we're to survive the winter, we need Will, you know that," Robin frowned. "Will has skills none of the rest of us have now Adam's gone. We need to help him."

"I know," the big bearded outlaw agreed. "I've spoken to people who knew Will years ago, before he became an outlaw. They all say he was a happy, friendly lad, but with a hint of steel in him. After everything he's been through, all that's left is the steel. His humanity's been torn out of him."

The sat in silence for a time, the drunken revelry of the other men doing nothing to lighten their mood, and then Robin pushed himself to his feet. "I'm going to try and help him. I'll take Allan with me in the morning; his experience should come in useful. We'll be gone no more than a few days, hopefully. Maybe with me out of sight for a bit some of the men might cheer up!"

Little John smiled mirthlessly. "What are you going to do?"

"Find Will's humanity."

* * *

Robin and Allan-a-Dale, a broad shouldered, confident young man who had been a minstrel before he was declared an outlaw gathered some food, money and concealed weapons about themselves before setting off.

"Where are we going, Robin?" Allan asked for the tenth time, having been given no answer yet from his grim-faced friend.

128

"Hathersage," came the reply, at last. "We need to see if we can find some information that might bring Will back from the purgatory he's living in."

Allan snorted, shaking his wiry brown hair gently. "Purgatory? Hell more like."

The two young men knew the way well enough to Hathersage, it was only about fifteen miles southwest from their camp, and they made good progress before the sun began to dip below the horizon, when they decided to make camp for the night.

After a short search of the area they found a suitable place, well off the main track and lit a fire to cook a little supper and take the chill from the air. Allan took first watch, Robin the second. With Bell's extra patrols hunting the outlaws, it didn't do to be unwary although the night passed without any trouble.

Robin's dreams were vivid during the night and he slept fitfully, but all he could remember on waking was a girl's face, unhappy and dejected.

They arrived at Hathersage just after midday. Neither of them had been into the village before, always waiting on the outskirts when the outlaws came to buy or trade for supplies, so there was little chance of their being recognized as wolf's heads. As strangers they would naturally be viewed with suspicion, but that was to be expected.

"Will told me he lived in a nice house near the mill; we should start around there, see if anyone has any information about what happened to his family."

Allan shrugged. "What is it you think we're going to find here? Will told you: his family were all killed. Everyone knows that."

Robin looked thoughtfully at the path ahead, trying to answer the question himself. It did seem like nothing more than a wild-goose chase, but he was hopeful something good would come from this trip to Hathersage.

"I honestly don't know what we'll find here, if anything," he admitted. "It can't hurt to ask around though."

The mill was easy to find, simply by following the river. The miller's wife was in the garden, tending to some carrots she was growing there, probably the last crop of the season and not a particularly good one judging from the occasional curses the woman was grunting.

"God give you good day, lady," Robin smiled, openly.

The miller's wife glanced up warily and returned the greeting before returning to her work.

"We're just looking for an old friend of ours, used to live around here. William Scaflock was his name. Do you know him?"

The miller's wife looked up again, a cautious look in her eyes. "He's been gone from here for a few years, boys. Upset some of the nobles and he suffered for it."

The outlaws feigned surprise at the news. "But he had a family – what happened to them?"

The woman clearly didn't feel too comfortable talking to two strangers, but her natural desire to gossip won out. "The soldiers killed them all. Although, when our men came to clear the mess that was left, they said there were only five bodies. Should have been six, but the little girl was missing."

Robin's eyes flared eagerly but he tried to act calm. "What happened to her?" he asked.

The woman leaned in closer, looking around as if someone hidden might be listening, which was absurd, given their open location. "No one knows for sure, but some of the villagers go to the manor house up on the hill to trade or do work for the lord, and some of them swear Scaflock's daughter is up there. A kitchen maid she is. So they say…I've been there to pay my rents, and for feasts, but I've never seen the girl myself."

Robin and Allan, although buoyed by the possibility that the little girl might still be alive, were outraged.

"You mean the local lord took an English girl and made her a slave?" Robin demanded.

The woman shrugged. "It's probably just a tale – some other girl that looks like Scaflock's daughter. I don't know, but if it is true, well, at least they never killed her like they did the rest of her family. Here, you two can do me a favour in return for all that information: take these two bags of flour to the baker in the village. Ask him about the girl when you're there – he's seen her, and he was a friend of Scaflock's."

The two young men grinned as they were loaded up by the helpful woman and set off to the baker's with a renewed sense of purpose.

* * *

The baker, Wilfred, took the delivery from Robin and Allan with a gruff word of thanks, inviting them into his shop and offering them a jug of ale each in return for their help. He joined them for it, his rosy red face, purpling nose and run-down premises suggesting he often took a break from work for an ale or two.

"Aye, Will was a friend," he admitted in reply to Robin's query. "We used to drink together sometimes when he wasn't off fighting Saracens or whoever."

Robin watched the baker's face closely as he asked about Will's daughter and what the miller's wife had said.

"Bah, that woman's tongue is too bloody loose, she needs to learn to keep her mouth shut. Talk like that can get people into trouble."

The ale had begun to warm the three men by now though, and Wilfred gazed thoughtfully at nothing until Robin tried again. "It's true though? The girl is at the manor house? She's a kitchen maid, or some kind of servant?"

The baker stared at Robin, then Allan, trying to decide how much he should trust these two dangerous-looking young men.

"I promise you, Wilfred, we are friends of Scaflock," said Robin gently. "He's in a bad way – he cares for nothing any more, other than revenge against the rich nobles. We'd like to help him. Give him something to live for again."

Wilfred took another long pull of his ale, and refilled his mug before fixing the two men with a stare and replying. "He's a wolf's head now, so I suppose you two are as well."

Robin and Allan shared an uncomfortable glance, well aware of the danger they could be placing themselves in by trusting in this gruff baker.

"I knew the girl well," said Wilfred. "She was a lively thing, full of energy and mischief. I see her at that manor house now and she's like a wraith. Never smiles, head always down – and what will happen to her when she's older? If it hasn't already?" An anguished look crossed his face, and he sipped his drink again, wiping his eyes angrily, as well as his mouth.

The outlaws grimaced at the implications of the baker's words, knowing they were true. Will's daughter had no life to look forward to if she stayed at the lord's house.

"What I don't understand . . ." the baker muttered, "why did Will never come back for the girl? I'd have expected him to come looking for revenge, same as he did with Roger de Troyes."

"He doesn't know Beth's alive," Robin replied. "He saw the rest of his family, brutally murdered, and he lost his mind with it – anyone would. Then, in a rage, he killed de Troyes before he found out who'd done it."

Wilfred shook his head. "Christ, poor Will. When you tell him it was Lord de Bray that destroyed his family and took his daughter...He'll get himself killed trying to fight his way into de Bray's manor house."

Allan grunted. "Robin has a better idea: you'll like this."

"We need your help, Wilfred"- Robin nodded, looking directly into the baker's eyes – "to get into that manor house, so we can take the girl. You'll be saving two lives – neither Will or Beth have any future if we don't do this."

The baker stared into his empty ale mug for long moments and then whispered, "I saw what those butchers did to that family. It was a massacre. I'll never, ever forget it. I don't know why they spared little Beth's life" – he looked up at Robin, a determined look on his face – "but if I can make some of this right for Will, I'll do whatever I can."

* * *

Matilda had stopped for a break from working at her father's fletching shop. The sun was high in the early afternoon sky and it was unseasonably warm today. She drew herself a cup of water from the well in the centre of the village and savoured its coolness as she tipped it into her mouth.

Just then, a man reeled from the alehouse, obviously worse for strong drink and the effects of the heat.

Matilda groaned inwardly as the drunk spotted her and began weaving his way over. Simon Woolemonger was an older man, nearly forty years old, and an unpleasant character even when sober. Rumours spoke of him informing on neighbours and generally causing trouble for the villagers.

"Hello, Matilda," he leered, sitting unsteadily beside her by the well, his eyes glassy. "Fancy a walk down by the riverside? It's nice at this time of the year with the leaves all orange and stuff."

Matilda was horrified at the thought of being alone with Woolemonger, but politely tried to hide her discomfort.

"No thank you, Simon. The recent warm weather has turned the Calder sluggish. I'm thinking it won't be too nice down there today." She stood up and replaced the wooden cup beside the well. "I better get back to work. God give you good day."

"Don't you want a man, girl? That fool Robin's not coming back for you and you'll be too old for anyone else soon." Simon leaned forward and ran his hand along Matilda's thigh, pressing it against her crotch. "Come on, girl; let's go down to the riverside where it's nice and quiet."

Matilda was so shocked she froze, but then her revulsion and outrage took over as she furiously slapped him hard on the side of his face. "Don't you ever touch me, you disgusting old sot! I'd sooner die than have your filthy hands on me!"

There were a handful of other villagers nearby and they stopped what they were doing to watch what was happening. Some shook their heads at the reeling Woolemonger, while others laughed and shouted insults at him. The drunk staggered to his feet, face flushing scarlet with both embarrassment and Matilda's slap. He burned with humiliation, but, even in his inebriated state he knew he couldn't physically attack Matilda in public – she was a popular girl in Wakefield.

"You think you're better than us, don't you, you little bitch?" His eyes bulged and he spat as he spoke. "Well, you'll pay for that. No woman hits me, you'll see…"

"You're worse than that new prior, Woolemonger, you dirty bastard!" someone howled, as the crowd laughed and jeered at the unpopular drunk again, and he staggered off shouting obscenities at the onlookers.

Matilda shook her head in disgust and walked back, shaking, to her father's shop. If only Robin were here, she thought, fools like Simon Woolemonger wouldn't dare bother me!

* * *

Wilfred the baker had a twice-weekly standing order from Lord de Bray's manor house, for bread and savoury pastries so he readied the delivery to be made the next day, telling Robin and Allan they could travel with him, disguised as travelling minstrels.

Allan, who had performed many times before falling foul of the law, had his gittern, a small stringed instrument, which he carried everywhere, while Robin had borrowed the baker's own citole, with its holly-leaf shaped body and short neck. Robin was a passable player, and he, along with the much more accomplished Allan, would often entertain the other outlaws at their camp. The inhabitants of the lord's manor house would undoubtedly be used to finer entertainment than a couple of scruffy-looking young men playing borrowed instruments, but Wilfred assured them the lord would be happy to hear music in his hall and that he would give them a meal and a night's shelter in return.

Somehow, they would have to persuade the girl, Beth, to hide in Wilfred's wagon before they left the manor house the next morning.

It was an absurdly simple plan, but, since the lord and his underlings were expecting no trouble, the outlaws hoped it would work well enough.

"What if we're discovered though, Wilfred?" Robin asked the baker, who shrugged.

"I'm almost fifty now, I'm an old man. My wife died fifteen years ago and we had no children. I spend my days making cakes and my nights drinking ale. If it comes to a fight I have little to lose. But, I'll tell you...I haven't felt this alive in years! A chance to stick it up those bastards, and help my old friend?" His big red face broke into a huge grin. "Come on lads, let's go make this delivery."

So they set off, Wilfred's cart fully laden with his boxes of bread and pastries along with some barrels of beer he'd offered to deliver for one of the village brewers. Barrels big enough for a small person to hide in…

Allan and Robin practised their minstrel act on the road to the manor house, and Wilfred declared himself impressed. They may not have found employment at King Edward's court, but they were good enough not to be kicked out of John de Bray's hall after their first tune.

It was an overcast day, and windy, orange leaves blowing off the trees all around them, but the three men were in good spirits, especially the old baker who saw the whole business as a noble adventure. He had fought in battles himself as a young man, but had thought that was all behind him. He had, in truth, hoped it was all behind him, having seen up close the horrors of war and its dire aftermath. But now, travelling with his bright, confident young outlaw companions, Wilfred felt more excited than he had in twenty years.

"I can see you lads are still young enough to feel like you're arrow-proof" – the baker smiled – "invincible almost." His face became deadly serious. "But you're not – if we're caught we'll be killed. Don't take this lightly, especially once you get a few ales down you in the lord's hall."

Robin nodded solemnly and whispered a prayer to the Blessed Virgin Mary as the manor house slowly came into sight.

While not as impressive as most of the other lords' residences in England, it was still an imposing and, to Robin and Allan, worrying sight. It looked more like a small castle than a house, despite the fact Lord John de Bray was only a minor noble, of Norman descent, who counted Hathersage as his only manor.

A three storey building, built from stone, with heavy oak doors and, Wilfred told them, an undercroft where the food and drink was stored. There were numerous windows, all with glass in them, and even a drawbridge, although the moat was empty of water. There was a single lightly armoured guard at the entrance, who knew the baker from his regular visits to the house.

"Morning, Wilfred!" shouted the guard, grinning broadly as the old cart rumbled up to the gatehouse. "You got any cakes on that cart for me?"

The baker smiled and reached into the cart, pulling out a large pork pie. "Here you go, Thomas. Just for you."

The guardsman's eyes lit up and he took a bite of the pie, glancing at Allan and Robin. "Who's these two, Wilfred?"

"I met them on the road, Thomas, travelling minstrels they are, on their way to London to make their fortune."

The guard laughed sardonically at that.

"I told them, Tom, wasting their time going to that dump -" the baker smiled – "but I thought Lord de Bray would probably be glad of a couple of minstrels to entertain his hall on a dreary autumn night."

Wilfred took out his dagger and handed it over to the guardsman. Robin and Allan did the same with their longbows and bags of arrows, although they both had blades concealed in their clothes.

The guard, Thomas, still cramming pork pie into his mouth gave the two young men a quick look, and, seeing no other obvious weapons, just the gittern and citole, he waved the cart on through, shouting his thanks again for the pie.

Wilfred waved merrily as they passed into the courtyard and the two outlaws breathed a sigh of relief. They were in.

The square courtyard was a large, busy place, with liveried servants rushing to and fro between the whitewashed buildings, carrying firewood, water and foodstuffs. The lord's coat of arms – a magnificent yellow peacock – was displayed on a scarlet flag that blew wildly in the strong wind.

Wilfred drove the cart over to the wide doorway that led to the undercroft and food stores. The three men climbed down and, under the baker's direction, began to unload the cart.

A groom appeared, the gatekeeper having alerted him to their presence.

"You two are minstrels? Well, I hope you're better than the last troop we had, lost control of their dancing bear, wrecked half the hall and three of their own performers before they cut the beast down."

Allan and Robin exchanged glances. "Well, we don't have any bears with us, sir, so unless people enjoy our playing so much they become bewitched, there shouldn't be any trouble." Allan winked at the bored-looking groom.

"Anyway," replied the man, "you're not hanging around here idle all day, you can earn your keep until dinner time by helping the baker unload his wagon."

The two young outlaws nodded obediently, and went back to helping Wilfred with his load.

Everything was going perfectly.

CHAPTER TWELVE

After Matilda's unpleasant experience with Simon Woolemonger, she had been relieved to have seen or heard nothing from him around the village for the next couple of days.

She had put the incident to the back of her mind, with the hope he had sobered up and forgotten what had happened or, with any luck, he'd gone down to the River Calder himself and fallen in.

Some of the villagers had teased her about it for a while, but interest had died down as other, fresher, pieces of gossip had come along.

Matilda and her parents were sitting down to breakfast just before dawn on the Wednesday morning, her mother, Mary, laughing at a story she'd heard about some local boy caught by the butcher trying to steal a leg of beef bigger than the lad himself.

Matilda's father was quiet. He'd been upset when he heard what had happened with Woolemonger and took the chance to tell Matilda, again, to give up waiting on Robin Hood and find herself a suitable husband.

Mary ladled pottage onto their plates from the steaming cauldron over the fire, and set a mug of weak home-brewed ale at each of their places. She had cooked their meal outside, since it was a chilly but nice, clear morning and cooking indoors in a little house such as theirs was an unpleasant smoky job. The family, like most of the villagers, rarely ate breakfast, but the pottage was close to being spoiled so Mary had insisted they eat it while they could – food was too precious to waste, especially with winter so close.

As the family began to eat, the noise of an excited commotion reached them, and they turned to see what was happening.

"Oh, Christ," Matilda's father muttered, earning a pious rebuke from his wife.

Coming towards them, through a throng of sleepy villagers, was the new bailiff, Adam Gurdon, mounted on an impressive-looking horse. More than twenty of his men were with him, most of them on foot. All were grim-faced, except Gurdon, who smiled as he caught sight of Matilda.

"What's he want, lass?" asked Henry. "Tell us now – if you've done something, so we can sort it out."

Matilda shook her head. "I haven't done anything, Da. I don't know why he's here."

As Gurdon and his men came to the Fletchers' gate, Matilda caught sight of a figure near the back of the clamouring villagers. Simon Woolemonger. Her heart gave a lurch and she felt the strength leave her legs as the drunkard grinned maliciously and gave her a wave.

"He's told them I was talking to Little John," Matilda mumbled through tight lips. "John came to the village a few days ago to buy supplies. You were out so I sold him some arrows. Simon must have seen us."

Her mother groaned, but her father put a reassuring hand on her shoulder and smiled. "Plenty people talk to John Little and no one arrests them. We'll sort this, don't fret." His smile turned to a grimace as he fixed his eyes on the leering Woolemonger. "And that little bastard will rue the day he crossed my family. If John doesn't do for him, I will!"

Adam dismounted expertly from his horse, handing the reins to one of his foresters, and let himself in through the gate. His men took up positions outside on the road behind their leader, who smiled again.

"Ah, this must be Matilda: I've heard so much about you. My old acquaintance, that notorious wolf's head, Robin Hood, was always telling me about you. You're even prettier than I imagined – no wonder you caught the prior's eye!"

The fletcher moved to stand in front of his daughter. "What do you want here at this time of day, bailiff? My girl's done nothing wrong – none of us have."

Gurdon's smile fell from his face and his eyes turned towards Matilda's father. "Hello, Henry. Still doing good trade selling arrows to outlaws?"

"Aye, and I supplied you with plenty when you were their leader, 'Bell'!" Henry's face had turned red with rage at the fletcher's impudence and the foresters moved closer to the bailiff defensively, hands threateningly on the short cudgels they had tucked into their belts.

"No matter, Fletcher, I'm not here for you today," Gurdon growled, visibly restraining himself. "Perhaps another day. For now…" He looked at Matilda and raised his voice to carry over the watching villagers. "I am here to arrest Matilda Fletcher, for providing aid to the outlaw known as Little John. We have a witness, and you will come with me to Nottingham where you will await trial for this accusation."

"Witness?" Matilda spat. "You mean that filthy drunk Simon Woolemonger!"

Gurdon nodded. "You are aware of who saw you with the outlaw then. That seems a clear admission of guilt to me. Take her."

One of the foresters moved in and tied Matilda's hands. Her father could take no more and lunged towards the bailiff, who moved with lightning speed to deflect the fletcher's blow, tripping the big man as Matilda yelped in dismay. One of the foresters brought his cudgel down on Henry's head, and the fletcher lay still on the ground as Matilda tearfully struggled to free herself.

The villagers were outraged. Loud shouts of protest went up, but Gurdon vowed reprisals if anyone else raised their hands to stop them, and the angry shouts turned to angry muttering.

"Let's go," said the former outlaw, nodding his head in the direction of the main road, the rising sun casting long shadows on the ground, and the men, pushing Matilda in front of them, moved through the gate. They half helped, half pushed the girl up to sit on one of the horses. A burly forester climbed up behind her and grinned at her irate expression.

Matilda's mother, Mary, knelt beside her husband, who still breathed, but was out cold. She cradled his head lovingly, tears staining her cheeks. "Don't worry Matilda! We'll not let them harm you!" she shouted reassuringly, but in her heart she feared the worst.

Gurdon placed a foot in his mount's stirrup and jumped smoothly onto the beast. "Let it be known," he shouted, "Simon Woolemonger is a witness to a crime. If any of you people decide to harm him, you will be declared outlaws yourselves. And I will hunt you down, as I will hunt down Robin Hood and his men. Woolemonger is under the King's – and my – protection!"

With that, the foresters moved off onto the main road through the greenwood, heading to Nottingham with their prisoner.

Simon Woolemonger, with two friends of his, also known in the village as idlers, stood grinning around himself. He wore a fine new white cloak, no doubt paid for by Gurdon in return for his information about Matilda.

"Let's go get a drink, boys," he laughed. "I'm feeling flush today."

Adam Gurdon's reputation as "Adam Bell" was enough to stop any of the villagers raising a hand against Woolemonger, but the atmosphere was venomous.

Patrick, the village headman, came into the garden to talk to Mary and Henry, who was beginning to come around.

"We must get word to Little John and Robin, Patrick," groaned the fletcher. "They're the only ones that can help Matilda."

Patrick nodded reassuringly. "I'll send one of the local boys to take word to the outlaws, Henry. You take care of yourself and…when all this is over with, have no fear: that scum Woolemonger will be run out of the village!"

* * *

"I know this isn't what you want," Sir Richard-at-Lee told his son. "But there's no other choice."

"Rhodes, though!" Simon muttered. "It's so far away."

Richard nodded sadly. "I know, son. You'll be fine though, your brother will make sure you settle in, and the Hospitaller lifestyle will suit you. The weather in Cyprus is better than in England too!" He smiled encouragingly, but he was depressed at having to take this course of action just to avoid Despenser's 'justice'. They knew Sir Hugh would send his men from Cardiff castle with a summons to trial for Simon, and there would be no reasoning with those men. Richard also knew there was no chance his son would be found innocent of murdering that Wytebelt fellow – Despenser wouldn't give up his hundred pounds bail monies.

Simon would hang, Sir Richard would be ruined, and there would be nothing left for his firstborn, Edward, to inherit. It would mean the end for their family.

Although he loved both his sons equally, Richard felt more protective of Simon. The elder son, Edward, had always been tough – clearly cut out to be a knight from a very young age, always willing and able to take care of himself.

Simon on the other hand had been much less warlike – more interested in reading and riding his big horse Dionysus than fighting.

When Edward had left to join his father's Order in Cyprus, and his wife had died just a year later, Sir Richard became even more protective of his beloved youngest son.

So, the Hospitaller had decided, with a heavy heart, to send Simon overseas, to join his brother, Edward, and the Hospitallers at their base in Rhodes. Once his son was safely out of the country, far from the grasp of Hugh Despenser, Sir Richard and his sergeant would try to raise money to pay off the new debt to Abbott Ness of St Mary's by seeking loans from other local lords. And then they would help the Earl of Lancaster in any way they could in his struggle against the corruption that was bringing the country to the brink of civil war.

Things were looking up in that respect, as the king had recently agreed to exile the Despensers and issued pardons to the Earl of Lancaster and hundreds of his supporters. And yet, although they were supposed to be banished, the Despensers continued to exert great influence over the country, as Sir Richard was discovering now.

The Hospitaller and his son Simon, accompanied by the gruff sergeant-at-arms Stephen, had ridden out that morning for the docks at Hull, a journey of two days, where the young man could find passage to Cyprus. The letter of introduction his father had written, and his elder brother's presence on the island, would see Simon inducted as a Hospitaller sergeant-at-arms without any problems. It would be up to him how far he progressed in the Order from then on.

They wore no mantles, or identifying marks of any kind – their usual Hospitaller eight-pointed white cross against a black background would be a dead giveaway to any hostile pursuers.

Stephen had hung back on the road, to allow father and son time alone before their parting, but the loyal sergeant was alert for any sign of pursuers. He was disgusted at what had befallen his lord. A Hospitaller

144

knight, basically robbed by their own king's best friend, and now forced to part from his own child, while looking over his shoulder like a common peasant chased by the tithing for stealing a loaf of bread!

Thankfully, it was a pleasant autumn day, with a gentle wind behind them, and the road was quiet, with few other travellers. Those they did meet moved deferentially aside, lowering their eyes at the sight of the three mounted and well-armed men.

They ate a small lunch of blackberries, boiled eggs and bread from their packs, eating while in the saddle to try and get to the port as soon as possible.

Sir Richard and Simon were sharing a joke together when Stephen suddenly hissed at them to be quiet, turning in his saddle to stare back along the road.

"What is it?"

Stephen grunted, his eyes still scanning the horizon. "Thought I heard a shout. Probably nothing. You two mere making so much bloody noise laughing like little girls, makes it hard to hear anything else."

Simon grinned. "Christ, man, what did eat for your lunch? Blackberries or lemons?"

"Ah fuck off"- the sergeant grumbled, then swung back suddenly to look behind them again, pulling his horse to a halt. This time there was no mistake, as the sight of half a dozen mounted men came into view, cantering over the horizon towards them.

"What d'you think?" Stephen wondered, glancing at his lord and fingering the handle of the mace he had brought along in case they did meet heavily armoured resistance. The crushing power of a mace was much more useful against plate mail than a sword. It looked like it may come in handy now.

"I don't know, they're too far away," Sir Richard replied, looking to his son in case his younger eyes could see any sign of markings or a livery that would identify the approaching riders but Simon shook his head.

"We're outnumbered so it makes sense not to hang around waiting to see if they're friend or foe," the Hospitaller decided. "Ride!"

They kicked their mounts and galloped off, noting with dismay the men behind them were keeping pace. "Shit, they must be after us," Simon cursed.

His father shouted in agreement. "We'll keep up this pace for a while – whoever it is back there must have been pushing their horses to have caught up with us even though we had a head start. They'll drop back before we do."

They rode hell-for-leather a while longer, then allowed their tired horses to slow. Sir Richard's words proved right, as their pursuers had fallen back and, despite the straight, flat section of road they were on, there was no sign of anyone behind them.

"At least we know the bastards are after us now," Stephen muttered. "All we have to do is keep ahead of them until we reach Hull."

Sir Richard rode in silence, wondering if his sergeant was right and they should just continue to the port as fast as possible, or try some different strategy to evade their pursuers. Set up an ambush? Pay some locals in the next village they passed to throw Despenser's men off the scent and in another direction?

He rejected the ideas – their followers must know their plan to get Simon on a ship out of the country, they wouldn't be easily diverted, and the idea of the three of them trying to ambush six mounted knights was an unappealing one.

Stephen was right. Their best bet was simply to reach Hull before Despensers men.

With a last glance over his shoulder, he spurred his horse again, giving a shout of encouragement.

"Let's move!"

* * *

The day before Matilda was arrested Robin and Allan-a-Dale ate an exotic (by their standards) meal, in Lord John de Bray's great hall.

They had unloaded Wilfred's cart at a leisurely pace; then, despite the groom's earlier admonishment, they had spent a restful afternoon practising their minstrel's act and surreptitiously watching the house's inhabitants bustle about their business.

They had not seen the girl they prayed was Will's daughter, Beth, but Wilfred hoped if the hall was busy enough tonight the girl would be serving tables along with the older servants.

So, after eating a lavish dinner of salted beef, cabbage and bread, grudgingly served to them by a sullen page boy, Robin and Allan were full and content, although nervousness began to settle on them at the thought of their next few hours work.

They knew they would have to perform their music well, to avoid being thrown out of the manor house as beggars, but that was almost a minor worry. Now that they were actually here, and realised how many hands would be raised against them should their plan to kidnap Beth go awry, they began to feel a little fear knot their stomachs.

"Just try to relax," Robin told his grim-faced friend. "We'll play for these people, who'll all, no doubt, wake in the morning with thundering hangovers. They won't be in the mood to keep an eye on the minstrels from the night before – all we have to do then is bundle Beth aboard the cart and roll out the door."

"The *guards* won't all be drinking tonight, Robin. They'll be fresh enough in the morning and they're the ones I'm worried about!"

Robin laughed. "We'll deal with that if it happens. There won't be guards watching us load the cart tomorrow, and that will be the dangerous part."

Allan nodded, but his knuckles were white as he played his gittern. After a few minutes he stopped and said quietly, "What if the girl doesn't want to come with us?"

Robin sighed at his friend's continued black mood. "We're here now; we have to go through with this right? So stop worrying about it. We need to talk to the girl first and take it from there. For now, just concentrate on playing that gittern for a while so we can give these people something to dance to later on."

Wilfred had spent the afternoon talking to some of the other merchants and tradesmen who were delivering goods to the lord's house, but the big baker joined his outlaw friends now.

"It's to be a fine busy feast tonight, boys. They'll need every available servant to keep the food and drink flowing. You'll get your chance to talk to Beth then, I'm sure. Just don't make it too obvious, or we'll arouse suspicion – she's still just a wee girl, mind."

Eventually, the sun began to go down and pages scurried to light the torches set around the walls of the hall. The enormous room looked hugely impressive to the young outlaws, who had never seen such a big room before. There were fresh reeds on the floor, fine expensive tapestries depicting heroic scenes from history and mythology decorated the walls and the guttering orange flames from the torches cast long shadows over everything. It was a fine place for two minstrels to perform.

The more distinguished wealthy and noble visitors began to file in from their rooms, joining, although not mingling with, the lower classes like Wilfred and the rest who were lucky enough to be there that night enjoying the lord's hospitality.

The volume began to increase as the ale and wine was served, then finally, Lord John de Bray himself appeared, accompanied by his wife. She may have been a real beauty in her youth, but her severe features bore a look of such boredom and disdain for everything around her that she was now rather unpleasant to look at.

"My friends!" Lord de Bray, a fat, jowly man who looked as though he could probably still wield a sword well enough, clapped his hands and the room slowly fell silent. He smiled and spread his arms to encompass the two long tables where the nobles were sitting. He ignored completely the benches and small tables on the corners and around the walls of the great hall, where the commoners, including Robin and Allan, sat. These people were clearly of no interest to the portly lord, only being there out of necessity and etiquette.

"Please, enjoy the humble feast I have had prepared for you," he continued. "Drink your fill of the finest wines my cellar has to offer, imported from France and Italy. And," he smiled widely again as his noble guests cheered loudly at his promise of alcohol, "we are lucky enough to have entertainment this night. Some of you will know my own pet fool, Rahere. A more amusing man could not be found in all the courts of Europe!"

An old but painfully enthusiastic jester stood and bowed, exaggeratedly, somehow managing to break wind loudly as he bent, which brought more laughter from the already half-inebriated guests.

"We also happened upon these two strolling players," de Bray continued, as the jester sat back down on his chair which collapsed theatrically.

The lord waved into the shadows as Robin and Allan stood, giving smiles and waves around the room.

"They promise to keep us amused! And if they don't, well…we'll set the dogs on them, eh?"

The guests thumped their mugs on the tables at this, roaring and cheering loudly.

Lord de Bray smiled wickedly at the two "minstrels", who had started to feel even more nervous about their night's work. "Now! Let the feast begin, friends!"

* * *

149

Beth Scaflock had been just five years old when her family were cut down by Lord de Bray's soldiers. On finding the little girl hiding, terrified out of her wits in a cupboard, the lord had decided to take her home since his wife was always on at him to hire more servants for the kitchen. To all intents and purposes, Beth had become his property, for who could stop him, the Lord of Hathersage?

She had been given a pallet in the kitchen, in a tiny cupboard like the one she had hidden in while her family was murdered. She slept and spent most of the little free time she had in this tiny space, when she wasn't doing chores around the kitchen for the cook, a cold middle-aged woman called Joan.

Beth and Joan were the only two females who lived in the lord's household, apart from his own wife. Like the rest of the manor houses in England, the vast majority of residents were male. Joan had cut her hair short, like the boys, so most people never even noticed she was a little girl.

Beth was thankfully left alone for the most part. Lord de Bray had never taken any notice of her again and, once she had learned to do her kitchen duties quickly and efficiently, Joan had stopped beating her so often.

It was, though, a horrible existence for the now eight-year-old child. Although many of her memories of her previous life had begun to fade, she still sometimes cried herself to sleep when she thought of her mother cuddling her after she'd fallen, or playing with her brother and their pet dog, Sam. She would also cry when she thought of her doting father, Will.

Although Beth was too young, even now, to understand what a mercenary was, she knew her father could be a violent, terrifying man. Yet he never acted like that around her – he had always made time to play with her when he was home, and her memory of his smiling face, full of joy as they had climbed in trees together and ran through the little stream by their house with her on his back twisted her heart until she felt she would never get over it.

She had wished for a long time that her father would come and take her home from this terrible house. But he never had, and her tears had, mostly, dried up as the hopelessness of her existence had begun to crush her spirit.

Tonight, there was a feast, as there often was at the manor house. This night Lord de Bray was entertaining more guests than normal though, and Joan had told her to serve ale at the tables of the commoners.

The sounds of men and women laughing filtered through the kitchen door – a sound she never shared in any more.

She joined the serving boys, shoved to the back of the line, being by far the smallest, and waited humbly to carry drinks to the men in the shadowy corners of the hall.

"Here, you!" A tray was thrust towards her, loaded with wooden mugs of watered-down ale, and Beth took it without a word, turning with practised ease, and went out into the great hall, where the noise of revelry was almost overpowering, even at this early stage of the feast.

She took her tray into the farthest corner of the room and set it down on a table, as her arms were too small to hold it while handing out the drinks as the other servers could do.

She saw two young men, both holding musical instruments, watching her as she worked, so she carried her tray to them before they started roaring at her as everyone always did when thirsty for ale.

"Hello, lass," said one of the young men. "I'm Robin. This is my friend, Allan, and this is Wilfred, the baker from Hathersage; you've probably seen him before."

Beth dipped her eyes; she knew not to get into conversations with the people she served, or Joan would have words, or worse, with her, for wasting time.

151

"There you go, sirs," the girl said, eyes still downcast as she placed a mug of ale before each of their places.

"What's your name, girl? We've given you ours, it's only polite to tell us yours." The big man, Robin, smiled warmly as he lifted his mug and took a small sip.

"Elizabeth, sir. I must be on with my work now or I'll get in trouble."

The three men shared a glance, and the one who had spoken looked around the room warily before saying to the girl, "We're friends of your da, Beth. Carry on with your work as normal, but be sure to serve us later on." He winked at her and looked away towards the jester, Rahere, who was cavorting ridiculously around the Lord's Table to much amusement.

The little girl's heart skipped a beat and she felt too weak to lift her half full tray for a moment, but she sensed the need not to draw attention to herself or these two minstrels and their baker companion, so she pulled herself together, gave a small curtsey and moved on to the next table.

She emptied the tray, filled it with empty mugs and carried them back to the kitchen to be refilled. Her eyes flickered over the three men. The two minstrels seemed relaxed, practising their instruments, presumably in anticipation of performing at the feast tonight. The baker, who she had indeed seen before making deliveries to the kitchen, was happily stuffing his round face with sweetmeats and ale. His eyes turned and met hers, and a memory came rushing back to her, of her father, Will, and this baker, standing together in the local tavern drinking and laughing together as she played happily on the floor.

A lump filled her throat and she hurried through the door into the kitchen, the sounds of laughter chasing her as the jester cavorted around the room.

The jokes were ribald, childish, filthy and misogynistic, and Rahere's audience were in stitches at every fart and punch line. Often the punch line *was* a fart. Robin took it as a good sign when he saw one man, a noble too, fall right off his chair he was laughing so hard.

"The crowd are pretty drunk and in a good mood, Allan. We just need to sing a few songs as if we were back at the camp with our mates, and we'll be fine."

Allan nodded gloomily despite Robin's ever-present grin. In fairness, Allan had little to worry about, having performed professionally as a minstrel many times in his past. He could play tonight's planned repertoire in his sleep. Robin, who, as a youth, had spent much more time practising with the bow or a wooden sword, had more reason to worry about their forthcoming performance. But Robin had a natural flair and charisma that was ideally suited to the role of a minstrel. Allan took comfort from the thought and, as he finished his ale and the time to play approached he felt a calm resolve settle over him.

"That's better, Allan!" Robin laughed as he saw his friend finger a fast run on the strings of his instrument.

Allan smiled. He was actually looking forward to their "show" now. He loved to play for an audience, and this would make a fine story to tell the rest of the outlaws when they got back to camp.

Just then, Rahere, the jester, his act exhausted, gave a bow and, to hearty applause and cheering, walked off the floor, belching loudly in time with every step.

There was a short break then, for everyone to get another ale or wine, and to laugh about the funniest parts of Rahere's act. The steward caught Robin's eye and signalled the two minstrels to start their performance.

"This is it, Allan. A few songs, another ale, then back to camp in the morning with a surprise for Will."

"Good luck, lads!" Wilfred cheered, supping a fresh ale, and smiling blearily at them.

"Thanks, Wilf! Just you make sure you're able to drive that cart tomorrow eh? Take it easy on the drink!" Robin laughed, but his look was serious, and the baker nodded sheepishly, placing his mug back on the table.

The two outlaws walked confidently onto the middle of the floor, near the lord's own table, where the torches burned brightest, and began to play.

CHAPTER THIRTEEN

The other outlaws had gone on with their usual routine in the absence of Allan and Robin, until the young boy from Wakefield, sent by Patrick, the village headman, found them. Or rather, the outlaws found him, wandering around the forest shouting for Little John.

"What are you playing at, lad? You trying to get yourself arrested by the bailiff's men, for consorting with criminals?"

The boy started in shock as he suddenly realised he was surrounded by half a dozen burly outlaws. He had heard or seen no sign of them until John suddenly spoke, almost right in his ear.

"You have to help," he stammered. "Matilda's been arrested!"

Some of the outlaws knew, and liked, Matilda. Not just because she was Robin's girl, but they had met her when buying arrows from her father Henry, and her pretty smile won most men over. Even the stone-faced Will Scarlet.

"What are you babbling about, boy?" Will demanded. "Arrested by who? For what?"

"Aye, I saw her just a few days ago, she sold me some arrows," added Little John. "She never mentioned being in any trouble."

"That's the problem," said the boy, Andrew. "You were seen with Matilda, John, and Simon Woolemonger went an' told the new bailiff, Adam Gurdon, about it. He came and arrested her right from her own house. Battered the fletcher and warned everyone off going after Woolemonger."

The outlaws had heard about their former leader being appointed bailiff of Wakefield but they hadn't expected him to make a move like this.

"Who's this Woolemonger?" Will asked, still looking confused. "What's his problem?"

"He's one of the village drunks," Much replied in disgust. "Waste of bloody space, someone should have thrown him in the river years ago."

The boy nodded agreement. "The bailiff must have paid him for his information about Matilda; he's going around the village like he's the lord of the place, paying for his mates and him to drink themselves stupid."

"We've got to do something about this, John," said Will, to a chorus of agreement from the rest of the outlaws. Even Tuck nodded his head coldly.

"He's right, John," said the stocky Franciscan friar. "If we don't do something about this everyone will think they can get away with informing on the people who give us aid. Our supplies will dry up, no one will trade with us in case they have the foresters after them because someone like this Simon informed on them."

John nodded his huge head. "I know, lads. This time of year we'll be needing all the help we can get too." He looked at Andrew. "Simon Woolemonger needs to be taught a damn lesson. But we need to get Matilda back too, or that bastard Adam will use her as a tool to get at us. Do you know where he was taking her?"

Andrew nodded. "He told everyone he was taking her to Nottingham. He left a few hours ago."

"Were they on foot, boy?" Will asked.

"Some were, but the bailiff and a couple of others had horses. They put Matilda on one of them with a forester."

"Shit!" Will hissed. "How are we going to catch them on foot?"

There was silence for a few moments as everyone thought about the situation.

"The ford at Hampole Dyke?" Much wondered, half to himself. "If some are on horseback they'll have to stick to the main road. If we cut through the forest we should be able to head them off."

Will grunted unhappily. "We'll have to move some if we're to get there before them, Much."

The miller's son shrugged. "We better get a move on then!"

"Right. I'll take the men and we'll get Matilda back from Adam," said Will, moving to gather up his weapons. "I've a score to settle with the bastard, and this is my chance. You and Much can go pay this Simon a visit."

John was reluctant to let the volatile Will Scarlet take charge of something like this, with Matilda's life at stake, but he knew refusing Will's suggestion would only lead to an argument in front of the rest of the men. There was nothing for it but to agree.

"You mind and be careful then, Will. Don't just rush in waving your sword over your head like a maniac. We want Matilda to come out of this safely. Be as stealthy as possible."

Will simply grunted something about not being stupid, and moved off with the rest of the men to start the run to Hampole Dyke.

"I'll keep an eye on him, John," Tuck reassured his giant friend, as he stuffed a handful of arrows into the already straining cord he used as a belt round his grey friar's robe. "I won't let him put Matilda in any unnecessary danger."

Little John slapped the jovial clergyman on the arm and thanked him. "Come back here when you have her. Me and Much will be back by then anyway – sorting this informer won't take long. Hopefully Robin and Allan will be back by then too, wherever they are."

He grabbed his huge quarterstaff, a foot longer than most men's staffs; slung his similarly oversized longbow over one shoulder, and stuffed a piece of bread from his pack into his mouth. "Right, Andrew, lad!" he shouted, spitting crumbs at the boy. "Let's go sort this bastard!"

* * *

When Robin and Allan began their act the audience had taken little notice, but after a song or two most people were watching, with more than a few tapping their feet and humming the melodies to old favourites like "As I Lay upon a Night" and "Man in the Moon".

The pair had played a selection of upbeat, merry songs, mainly about girls, drinking and fighting, before slowing things down and performing "Alison", a ballad in a minor key.

Their voices worked well in harmony, with Allan taking the higher vocal and, as the last chord faded, the lord's hall erupted in loud applause, with more than a few of the women, and even some men, wiping a tear from their eyes.

The outlaws stood and enjoyed their moment, bowing to all, and grinning widely at each other.

The crowd reaction was almost certainly down to the free flowing alcohol and generally happy atmosphere in the hall that night, rather than any musical genius on the part of the two performers, but it hardly mattered. Their ruse had clearly worked. Even Lord de Bray handed them a few marks each with a grand flourish, and, as they returned to their seats in the shadowy corner of the room, well wishers thumped them on the back and praised their skill.

Robin laughed and smiled at the compliments, while the normally reserved Allan was on a high. It felt to him like this was one of the best performances of his life, and the grin stayed on his face for the next half an hour.

Then young Beth appeared at their places carrying two more ales for them, and the outlaws suddenly remembered the real purpose of their visit here.

"Beth," Robin began, but the girl cut him off, her face twisting.

"Why hasn't my da come looking for me?"

Both outlaws looked at the ground, embarrassed, feeling the little girl's obvious pain.

"Your da thought you were killed along with the rest of your family, lass," Robin told her, glancing around the room to make sure no one had noticed their conversation with the upset serving girl. No one seemed to be paying any attention.

"Listen to me. You have to pull yourself together. Don't attract any attention to us or yourself. We're going to get you out of here and take you back to Will."

The girl placed a mug in front of Allan. "How?"

"In the morning, we'll hide you in one of the baker's barrels, load it on his cart and take you straight out the gate. Will you be missed?"

Beth shook her head, her greasy brown hair falling around her dirty face. "The kitchen staff will be up early, but the housekeeper, Joan, will be up late drinking and won't be out her bed 'til later in the morning. If we leave early I won't be missed for a while."

Robin and Allan nodded and Wilf promised to have the cart loaded and ready to go not long after sunrise.

"Carry on as normal then, Beth," said Robin. "But be ready to leave in the morning. We won't have time to come and find you if you're not around."

A flicker of a smile came to the little girl's lips and a glimmer of hope flared in her eyes for the first time in months. "Thank you, sirs!" she whispered to them, and walked off to the next table to serve the rest of the mugs on her tray.

"A strong wee lass, Robin," Allan said approvingly.

"She's had to be, to survive what she's been through..." replied Robin, shaking his head at the thought of the hopelessness and fear Beth had suffered for the past three years.

Wilf laid a meaty hand on Robin's arm and locked eyes with him. "Tomorrow, we set this evil right."

Although the outlaw's camp was a fair distance away from Wakefield, it didn't take Little John, Much and the youngster, Andrew, long to reach the village outskirts.

"All right, lad, thanks for coming to get us. We'll sort this out now; you take word to Henry everything will be fine." He ruffled the boy's hair and handed him a small silver coin, which Andrew took with a grin and loped off towards the fletcher's house.

Much thought the best place to find Simon Woolemonger would be the local alehouse. This belonged to Alexander Gilbert and was literally more of a house than a tavern or inn.

The outlaws wandered up and peered in the side window. Sure enough, Woolemonger was inside, a mug of ale before him and two friends at the table with him. They were the only people drinking in the alehouse at that time.

The three were joking noisily as if they hadn't a care in the world, their drunken laughter filtering through the unglazed window loudly, while Gilbert threw them dark looks every so often.

There seemed little point in wasting time. John wanted to get back to camp as soon as possible in case Robin and Allan returned from wherever they'd gone and wondered where everyone was.

He pushed open the door and strode over to the table Woolemonger sat at. The three drinkers looked up indignantly.

"What do you want?" one asked, just before John's massive fist slammed into his nose, throwing him backwards off his chair in a spray of crimson. The man lay on the ground groaning.

The second of Woolemonger's friends fumbled at his belt, presumably for some weapon, but Much moved faster and kicked him hard in the face. The combination of excessive ale and the blow to the head was too much for the man, and he collapsed on the floor vomiting noisily. Much gave him another kick and leaned down to growl in his face. "Stay the fuck down, or we'll come back for you." Woolemonger knew many tales about Little John and, while his friends had instinctively tried to defend themselves against the outlaws, Woolemonger had simply frozen in fear as he recognised the giant.

"What do you want with me?" he squealed, eyes wide with fright.

John grabbed him by the throat and hauled him out the front door, where a crowd had gathered on hearing the commotion.

Woolemonger tried to free himself, flailing his legs wildly, but Little John punched him hard in the stomach, blasting the breath from the man, before throwing him into the road where he lay, crying and gasping.

There were cheers from the villagers, but John raised his hands for silence.

"You all know why I'm here," he said loudly. "This piece of shit here has been telling tales about me, to the bailiff. Everyone knows what we do to people who inform on us."

Woolemonger spluttered a denial, but John wasn't listening. He looked around the crowd slowly.

"People that cause me, and my outlaw brothers', trouble…regret it." With that he pulled his sword from its leather sheath and pointed it at the man on the ground.

"Wait!" Woolemonger cried. "I can help you. The bailiff knows you and your friends will try to rescue the girl. He's setting a trap for you!"

John and Much exchanged a worried glance at this, and the big outlaw lowered his sword a fraction.

"Where?"

"The ford at Hampole Dyke," whimpered the informer, clutching his guts in pain. "Adam expects an attack there, because the bridge has collapsed and it's an

161

ideal place for an ambush when your friends are struggling through the ford. The bailiff's going to station his men all around the place and wipe the lot of you out. He won't even be there; he's going to continue on the road to Nottingham where he'll hand over the girl to one of Prior de Monte Martini's men at his brothel."

"The prior?" John demanded in confusion. "What's he got to do with it? I thought Adam was working for the sheriff?"

"The sheriff isn't interested in the girl; he just wants you outlaws dead or captured, this is nothing to do with him. The prior paid the bailiff to arrest the girl – she's to be put to work in the prior's brothel. Gurdon's expecting to make some money *and* wipe out your friends when they try to rescue the girl."

Matilda's father had pushed his way to the front of the crowd and he spat at Woolemonger now. "This is all your fault, you bastard! None of this would have happened if you'd kept your drunk nose out of it!"

Much grasped Little John's arm. "Finish this! We need to warn Will and the rest, now."

The big man nodded, a look of disgust on his normally jovial face. "The fletcher's right – this is all your fault." He leaned over and rammed his blade into the drunkard's heart, impaling the man on the ground. Woolemonger stiffened in shock, staring first at John, then down at the blade impaling him.

There were gasps of shock and fright from some of the villagers, many of whom knew Little John as a gentle giant. This was a side to him they had heard stories of but had never seen before. Some of the children in the crowd began to cry, and their mothers pulled them in close to comfort them.

"That's what happens to people who betray me or my friends!" John roared as he pulled the sword free, wiped it on Woolemonger's fancy new coat.

"I thank you all, who trade with us and sell us provisions. We'll always look after those who help us –

but let this be an example. If anyone betrays us, we *will* hunt them down and kill them."

John knelt and used his dagger to cut the purse from Woolemonger's belt. He walked over to Patrick, the village headman, and handed the money to him. "The sot might have already drunk half of the payment he got from the bailiff, but use the rest of it for whatever the village needs."

Patrick nodded his thanks to John and Much, as Henry Fletcher clapped them on the back. "You two better get moving, and warn your mates. I don't want any more good men to die because of that scum. You can borrow a couple of our horses – they're no *destriers* but they'll get you where you need to go a lot quicker than on foot."

Much grimaced; he wasn't much of a rider, but there was nothing else for it. "He's right, John, it makes sense. And don't worry, Henry, we'll get Matilda back safely, I promise you."

Patrick gave a shout at one of the villagers and the man hurried off, returning a few minutes later leading two horses saddled and ready to go. "Don't be beating them," the man warned, handing the reins to Much and Little John with a glare. "Treat them right and they'll treat you right."

The fletcher smiled weakly at the outlaws as they warily eyed their mounts. "God go with you, lads. Help my wee girl."

They climbed awkwardly onto the palfreys and, with a nod of farewell, kicked them forwards through the crowd of villagers, many of whom shouted thanks up to them for dealing with the hated Woolemonger.

As they urged the horses into a run through the forest, John told Much they would head back to the camp first, in case Robin and Allan had returned. "We're going to need every man we can get if Adam's laid a trap at Hampole Dyke."

Much didn't reply as he gripped the reins fearfully, praying fervently they would be able to outwit Adam Gurdon.

Behind them in Wakefield the villagers buried Simon Woolemonger in an unmarked pauper's grave.

* * *

Morning came quickly for Robin and Allan-a-Dale. Wilfred the baker, despite vowing to drink little at the feast, was nursing a hangover, and was jumpy and irritable as a result.

The two outlaws were annoyed at Wilfred but could do nothing about it.

Having no previous experience of a morning in a lord's house, Robin and Allan had hoped the place would be quiet before dawn, but many servants were up early, quietly tidying things from the night before. They stepped over sleeping revellers, sometimes carefully, sometimes not so much, depending on whether the revellers had been nice to them during the previous evening's drunkenness.

More than a few were woken by a servant "accidentally" standing on them. Or kicking them in the bollocks, before dodging out of sight.

"This isn't going to be as simple as we'd hoped, Robin," Allan grumbled.

"None of these servants will be paying us any attention. Calm down," Robin muttered. "Come on, we'll start loading Wilfred's cart, and slip Beth on board once we're nearly done."

Wilfred had found a couple of ales left over from the feast, and declared himself ready for anything after swallowing them. The two young outlaws almost puked watching the old baker drinking the stale beer so early in the day, but it genuinely seemed to liven the man up, and the three moved into the kitchens to set about loading the wagon.

John de Bray's steward hurried over as he saw them approach. The irritating little man seemed to have spent the night in his bed rather than drinking and feasting, as he was bright and alert.

"You two. Minstrels!" he shouted. "I want that cart of his" – he jabbed a finger at Wilfred – "loaded up and gone within the next hour, got it?"

The outlaws nodded.

"Will do, sir!" Robin replied deferentially. "Our thanks to you for having us."

The steward grunted, somewhat mollified by Robin's servile attitude.

"By all accounts you were passably entertaining last night, but Lord de Bray wants his house cleared by mid-morning, so get a move on. And don't even think of lifting anything that doesn't belong to you. We have half a dozen guardsmen here who'll quickly sort you out. I know your type, and I'll be watching you like a hawk."

Allan's blood ran cold at the steward's vow, but neither outlaw replied, they simply nodded again and set about loading the cart.

As the wagon slowly filled up with the empty crates and barrels, it became clear they would never smuggle Beth on board without being spotted. There were too many people about, and the steward hovered around the place constantly.

"How the hell are we going to do this, Robin? That bastard steward checks up on us, and everyone else, every few minutes!"

"I know Allan," Robin hissed. "We're stuck unless we can get him out of the way. When you see Beth ask her if she can create a diversion. Time's running out."

But Beth never appeared. Wilfred overheard two of the serving girls talking, and it seemed Beth had been vomiting that morning and was lying terribly ill in her bed.

The three conspirators began to panic. This was the only chance they would ever get to rescue the little girl and take her back to her father, Will.

"Right, we have to get the steward out of the way and Beth, sick or not, into one of these barrels. Allan, you find the girl. Wilfred, carry on loading the wagon. I'll take care of the rest."

Allan groaned, while Wilfred looked queasy.

"Don't make a commotion, Robin," said the big baker, "or we're done for."

Robin nodded, his hand dropping reflexively to his waist, where his dagger was concealed.

"Let's go."

Allan-a-Dale wandered further into the kitchens, looking for open doors, trying to appear as innocent as possible. The place was busy, and everyone had jobs to attend to, so no one paid him any attention.

Robin went through the door the steward had taken a minute earlier. It led to a deserted hallway, with storerooms on each side and the courtyard at the far end.

The young outlaw moved slowly along the corridor, wondering where the steward was, when the man suddenly appeared at the far entrance.

Robin quickly asked for directions to the latrine.

"Latrine?" roared the steward. "It's not likely to be along here beside the food stores is it? You idiot, get back out there and finish loading that wagon. You can piss when you get on the road to London!"

The steward put his hand on Robin's arm to shove him back towards the kitchens, but the young outlaw grabbed the man's wrist and twisted it behind his back while slapping his other hand over the man's mouth to stifle any cry.

"Struggle, and I break your fucking arm," Robin whispered, pushing his captive into one of the unlit, fusty smelling storerooms. Warily looking to see no one had noticed them go in, he shoved the steward forward and shut the door behind them.

"If you shout or try to escape, you die." It was almost pitch black in the cool room, but as Robin drew out his knife the little sunlight that filtered under the doorway was enough to throw the wicked looking length of steel into sharp relief. "Trust me. Now, where does the girl, Beth, sleep?"

The steward looked bewildered, but his eyes flared angrily as he gave directions to the little girl's sleeping area.

"Thank you," said Robin, but the furious steward, outraged at being treated like this by a simple peasant, opened his mouth and roared for help.

Robin panicked and without thinking, rammed the point of his dagger into the steward's belly, more than once. Slowly, he lowered the dying man to the ground.

"I'm sorry. I truly am," the outlaw whispered in anguish, thankful for the darkness so he couldn't see the life draining from his victim's eyes. "But we need to escape and I can't have you raising the alarm."

He quickly wiped his blade with shaking hands and piled some sacks of fruit over the steward's corpse, then made his way back to Wilfred's wagon as fast as he could, thankful that no one seemed to have heard the steward's cry for help.

He was relieved to see Allan waiting for him, a small smile on his face as the servants hurried around the kitchen busily, the steward's absence obviously unnoticed.

"Got her!" Allan hissed. "She was pretending to be ill and watching out for us from her bedroll. Where's the steward?"

Robin looked miserably at his friend, feeling nauseous and guilty after murdering the nosy official, even though he knew it was the only way they would escape without pursuit.

"Dead. Is the girl on board?"

Allan nodded. They had hidden the girl in a barrel behind the wagon, where no one could see, and loaded it on along with the rest of the empty load.

"We're ready to go," Wilfred told them, his red face anxious. "All we have to do now is get past the guard at the gates before anyone raises the alarm."

The baker climbed onto the driver's seat and the two outlaws clambered up behind him. They lifted their instruments from the top of a crate where Allan had loaded them, and began to strum a simple tune – more to conceal their nerves than from any desire to play.

Wilfred gave a hoarse "Yah!" and cracked the reins over his two old oxen. As the wagon moved off with a lurch, Robin felt the bile rise in his throat and a cold sensation like pins and needles crawled up his hands and arms.

He put down his citole and prayed.

CHAPTER FOURTEEN

Hampole Dyke was miles away from the outlaws' camp. Will Scarlet knew the place well enough – they had robbed a few rich merchants and churchmen here over the past two years or so. It was the only place to cross the river for miles, but it was surrounded by trees on either side, so there was plenty of cover to spring an ambush.

When the outlaws came close to the ford they had seen no sign of Adam Gurdon or his foresters. Will assumed he and the other outlaws were in time, so he began formulating a plan to rescue Matilda.

Tuck gently pulled Will aside and asked if Adam knew the area.

"Aye he does, "Scarlet replied. "It was him that planned any robberies we did here – I scouted the land with him myself."

Tuck looked worried. "Don't you think he might be expecting us to ambush him right here then, Will?"

Scarlet looked thoughtful for a moment, but his lust for revenge lit his eyes like a fire and he swung away from the portly friar.

"He has no reason to expect us to be here. Why the hell would we be? He only just arrested Matilda a short while ago. Why would he think we even heard about it yet?"

Tuck shook his tonsured head in consternation. "You're underestimating Adam, Will. He's not a fool – you know that!"

Scarlet began sending the men to positions within the surrounding foliage, shouting over his shoulder at Tuck as he went. "No, he's not a fool – but he is a traitor, and we're going to get our revenge on the bastard today. Right lads?"

The men cheered, unaware of Tuck's misgivings, but as they began to move to their hiding places in the trees an arrow flashed through the dense undergrowth catching an outlaw in the chest, spinning him onto the ground, gasping and clutching feebly at the wooden shaft sticking out of him.

"Ambush!" Tuck cried, running for cover behind a fallen tree as more arrows whistled murderously through the air around them. "They've been waiting for us!"

* * *

It seemed to take the baker's old cart forever to reach the gatehouse, but it was the same young sentry on duty who had let them in the day before.

"Wilfred!" the guard grinned. "Those minstrels you found were all right last night; I fair enjoyed my evening off."

"Thank you, sir," Allan smiled, and Wilfred slipped the man an oatcake, glancing around and winking conspiratorially.

"Nothing too sweet or stodgy, Thomas, since you're no doubt nursing a hangover, same as me, eh?" the baker laughed ruefully. "No eating on duty, mind. I wouldn't want you getting into trouble with Lord de Bray."

The guard took the cake with a rueful smile and waved them through. "Hangover? Aye, that I have, Wilfred; too much of his lordship's watered-down ale!" He squinted up at Robin and Allan. "If you two are passing this way again, make sure you come and play for us, eh? We see too few entertainers these days." He handed their weapons back to them with a friendly nod.

The cart rumbled slowly over the entrance bridge and the outlaws waved merrily at Thomas as he surreptitiously bit into his oatcake.

They were out.

Now they just had to get far enough away from the place before the missing serving girl and dead steward were discovered.

"Even if they do find him," Allan murmured, leaning back as the cart rumbled onto the rough road, "they have no real reason to blame us. Same with Beth: why would they connect her disappearance with us?"

"They think we're heading for London anyway," Robin nodded, "not Barnsdale."

All three men began to feel a little safer, as the road brought them closer to the forest and freedom, at last, for the little girl hidden in a barrel on the cart behind them.

"You can come out now, Beth," Robin said as the groaning wagon was finally swallowed up by the thick trees, and he prised the lid off the cask with his dagger.

The little girl smiled shyly at him, blinking in the daylight, and stood up slowly, her legs stiff from hiding in such a cramped place.

"You're free, lass!" Robin gently lifted Beth out of the barrel and Allan whooped like a little boy, as Wilfred laughed and roared in delight. "We did it!"

A grin spread across Beth's grubby little face and she looked around, wide eyed, at the outside world she hadn't seen for so long.

"Now," she asked, eventually, "can I see my da?"

And she burst into tears.

* * *

Little John and Much headed back to the outlaws' camp as fast as possible, desperately hoping Robin and Allan-a-Dale would be there to help rescue their friends from Adam Gurdon's trap.

They were.

Once the road from Lord de Bray's manor house entered the forest Robin, Allan and Beth had thanked

Wilfred and headed back towards Barnsdale, while the baker made his way home to Hathersage.

The girl had struggled to keep up with the fit, hardy young men so they had taken turns to carry her on their backs or shoulders. She laughed as she swatted aside branches, the happy sound making Robin think sadly of his own little sisters – Rebekah who passed away when she was much the same age as Beth, and Marjorie, at home in Wakefield. He missed them both, and his heart ached as he thought of them, but Beth's simple joy at being free was infectious and his mood soon lifted.

John and Much returned to the camp and dismounted noisily, tying the horses to the branch of a slim young beech tree before hurrying over to see Robin and Allan.

Robin grinned as he saw his two friends approaching and, holding Beth by the hands, he spun the squealing child round in a circle.

"Who's this?" John asked, glancing at Much who shrugged his shoulders in bafflement.

"This," Robin replied, still smiling, "is Elizabeth. Will's daughter!"

John looked at the beaming little girl, his eyes wide, and puffed his cheeks out in astonishment.

Robin finally realised something wasn't right as his eyes took in the deserted outlaws' camp and the two palfreys. "Where is everyone? What's happened?"

"Bad news," Much told his boyhood companion. "Adam's arrested Matilda" –

"What?" Robin roared, making Beth flinch back in fright to stand, wide-eyed, next to Allan who patted her arm reassuringly. "Why? Where's he taking her? I'll kill the bastard!"

Little John nodded, understanding his friend's outrage. "He's taking Matilda to Nottingham, but we have another problem: we know his men are going to ambush Will and the rest of the lads at Hampole Dyke

172

while he takes another route to the city. We have to warn them."

Robin swore. "I have to go after Matilda!"

John shook his head firmly. "You can't, we need to help the others or they'll be butchered."

"You three go on and warn Will and the rest, then" – Robin started, but John cut him off with another shake of his wild brown hair.

"You can't take on Adam on your own, he'll have foresters with him; it'd be suicide. You have to come with us. We'll stop the ambush and then we can *all* go after Matilda."

Much placed a consoling hand on Robin's arm. "John's right. Adam doesn't know we've found out about his plan, so he won't be in any great hurry to get to Nottingham. We can catch him up once we help the others."

Robin cursed again, but he knew his friends spoke the truth. "Alright," he growled, "but we've walked all the way from Hathersage today. Me and Allan will take the horses if that's okay? Beth can climb up with me – we can't leave her here."

John grinned and rubbed his backside which ached even from the relatively short ride from Wakefield. "Aye, fair enough, my arse is killing me anyway."

The one thing in their favour was the fact Adam and his men would be expecting *all* the outlaws to blunder into their trap. If Robin and the others couldn't make it in time to stop the ambush, they might at least be able to help their friends fight their way out alive.

"If we can figure out exactly where they'll spring the ambush we can work our way to their rear and hit them one by one," Robin suggested.

John nodded thoughtfully as he kept pace with the trotting horses. "Aye, they won't have a clue how many of us there are behind them, so if we can take out a few of them the rest might panic."

Robin expected Adam's men would take up positions in the trees either side of Hampole Dyke and strike while the outlaws were crossing the water, out in the open with no cover and nowhere to run, where they could pick them off with their longbows.

"We'd be better splitting up" – he decided – "since we have the horses. Me and Allan can go on ahead and cross the river upstream at one of the other fords. We can work our way round behind the dyke and hit them from that side while you and Much come at the ones on this side of the water."

It was a good plan, and everyone was happy to go along with it, so Robin helped Beth climb off the horse and onto Little John's shoulders.

"How'd you like your new steed?" Robin smiled at the girl.

"Smellier than the horse," Allan grimaced. "Hairier too."

"Shut it you little prick"- John clapped a hand over his mouth as Beth burst out laughing. "Pardon my language, lass," he grinned sheepishly.

"Right, let's get a move on," Robin, impatient to get after Matilda, looked over at Allan, and they headed towards the river's edge where the horses could move faster. "See you in a while, lads!"

As Much and Little John neared the Hampole Dyke John lifted Beth down and hid her near a great old oak tree, telling her to wait there on their return.

"What if something happens to you?" the girl asked, her face screwing up anxiously, as if she were about to cry.

"Look at the size of me!" John replied, smiling reassuringly. "Do you think anyone's going to harm me?" He stood up, his massive frame towering over her, a fierce look on his face, and the girl giggled. "If no one comes for you before it starts to get dark," he laughed, ruffling her hair, "head towards the river and follow it downstream for half a mile. There's a cottage there. It's not too far and you'll be safe. Just tell them Little John sent you."

Beth nodded at the bearded giant uncertainly, and the two men set off towards the ford, only a few minutes jog away, moving silently through the undergrowth at the side of the path.

As they neared the river, the sound of men shouting filled the air and Much groaned. "Adam's men must have sprung their trap, we may be too late!"

"The noise will help us," John replied resolutely. "We can sneak up on the foresters without them hearing us coming. Let's split up. You go left, I'll take the right. No prisoners." He looked his companion in the eyes and hefted his quarterstaff grimly as Much nervously drew his sword, crossing himself for luck.

As they moved off in their separate directions Robin and Allan had worked their way across the river. After safely tying the horses and splitting up as John and Much had done, they were now creeping through the undergrowth looking for signs of Gurdon's foresters. The shouts from the battle were strangely muted and Robin wondered what was happening. Were Will and his men already dead? Had Adam Gurdon's ambush worked to such devastating effect that the outlaws had succumbed in so short a time?

He carried on through the trees, heart thumping nervously, towards the river.

As he got closer he realised Gurdon's foresters, lacking his expert leadership, must have attacked too soon, allowing Will, Tuck and the rest of the outlaws to find cover behind the old collapsed bridge. There was the ping of a longbow to his right, from under a big beech tree, its green summer foliage almost entirely lost, and he inched his way towards the noise. A forester, oblivious to the danger creeping up on him, was fitting another arrow to his string. Robin swiftly came up behind him, and thrust his sword powerfully into the man's back.

The forester fell with a cry of pain and disbelief, blood bubbling from his mouth, as Robin withdrew his blade and listened for signs of more foresters. He moved on again as he heard another bow being fired somewhere close to the left.

There were two men this time, standing side by side, and the young outlaw knew he would have to work fast.

Throwing caution to the wind he made straight for the pair, who were intent on Will Scarlet and the outlaws pinned down with seemingly no escape route. Robin could see Will, face red with rage and frustration, shouting obscenities about Adam Gurdon.

As he came up behind them, one of the foresters began to turn towards Robin, so he lunged forward, swinging his sword savagely into the man's neck, almost decapitating him.

"Attack! We're under attack!" the second man screamed, dropping his bow and fumbling for his sword, but he was too slow, and Robin much too fast.

The outlaw calmly stepped over the corpse of the man he had just killed and chopped his blade down into the arm of the shouting forester, feeling the bones crunch.

The man's shout changed from a warning to a scream of pain, until Robin slammed the pommel of his sword into his mouth, smashing teeth and bone. As the forester fell back, eyes wide in horror, Robin shoved his blade deep into the man's guts and disappeared into the trees again.

From some distance to the right another cry went up, swiftly silenced, then, a few moments later, another shout of alarm came from amongst the trees on the other side of the river. This lasted longer, a cry of terrible pain and slow death. John must have left someone half alive Robin realised, to spread fear among the foresters.

It was a brutal but effective tactic, as Gurdon's men began shouting to each other across the water, wondering what the hell was going on, and who was attacking them from within the trees.

"Will!" Robin roared towards the ford when there was a brief few moments of quiet. "It's Robin Hood! I've brought the rest of the men – we've circled the bastards! Prepare to leave your cover and attack; we'll smash them between us!"

By now, the outlying foresters had begun to panic and make their way from both sides of the river towards the clearing near the ford, giving up their hiding places, and cover, amongst the trees in order to find their captain who had positioned himself there to direct the ambush.

One forester came close to Robin so he quickly fitted an arrow to his longbow and fired it into the man's backside. His agonised roars of pain as he stumbled towards his companions only served to spread the alarm among the foresters even further.

Allan-a-Dale moved into view and Robin crept to join him.

"What now?" Allan wondered. "Looks like there's only about ten of them left, all shitting themselves."

Robin had no desire to cut down these men. The foresters weren't, for the most part, trained soldiers, just decent local men, who normally didn't find themselves caught up in a pitched battle with a squad of hardened outlaws.

"Will!" Robin shouted.

"Aye!" came the eager reply from the other side of the great fallen tree.

"Hold, for now!"

"What?" Scarlet was ready to unleash the fury that had built up inside him. He stood, grasping his sword, as Tuck tried to restrain him.

Little John jogged through the trees his eyes shining with adrenaline as he raised his enormous bow and fixed it on the frightened foresters who were milling about around the ford, clearly lacking any real concrete leadership, swords held out desperately before them. Much appeared like a ghost from the undergrowth and, aiming his own longbow, took up position beside his giant friend.

"You men! Adam Gurdon's foresters!" Robin roared. "Either we can cut you down like wheat during harvest, or you can throw down your weapons and live. I know the bailiff isn't with you. We have no quarrel with you."

The foresters, knowing they were utterly beaten, slowly began to put down their swords, as the one who appeared to be in charge, an overweight, balding middle-aged man, shouted in reply, "My name is Samuel. We surrender Hood. I only hope you men are as honourable as the villagers around here seem to think."

Robin nodded thankfully to himself. "Will! Tell the men to collect those weapons and make sure the foresters are subdued. Peacefully! We'll keep you covered until it's done."

Little John patted Robin on the back. "That was nicely done, lad. Those men are indebted to us now. Looks like we got here just in time."

As Friar Tuck and the rest of the outlaws moved onto the ford and began taking the dropped swords, staffs and longbows, Will Scarlet screamed in rage and flew towards the foresters.

"Where the fuck is that bastard Gurdon?"

The brawny forester, Samuel, seeing Will's intent, quickly retrieved his sword from the ground and started to rise, bringing the weapon up to defend himself.

The outlaws watched in horror as Will, moving too fast to stop himself, ran straight onto Samuel's blade.

"No!" Robin burst from the trees and raced forward to restrain the rest of the men. "No more killing!"

He looked forbiddingly into Samuel's eyes and the big man, a frightened look on his face, pulled the sword from Will's side. "Drop it, and you and your men can be on your way."

The forester nodded. He placed his bloodied sword back on the ground, beside the stricken Will Scarlet, who lay in the icy shallow water, eyes staring straight up at the cloudy afternoon sky.

"John, Tuck! Get Will out of the water! The rest of you, finish collecting those weapons. You foresters, sit on the bank, make no threatening moves and you have my word, no one else will raise a hand to you." He stared around at the men, eyes blazing, hand on his own sword hilt.

The power in the young man's voice was unmistakable, and everyone moved to follow his instructions.

"Will," Robin said gently, when Little John and Friar Tuck had lowered him onto the dry riverbank.

"I'm sorry, Hood. You knew my temper would kill me one day. I've lost so much in my life . . ." Will shuddered, grimacing in pain and clutching the wound in his side as a tear squeezed from between his eyelids. "All I have left is death and vengeance and . . . I won't even get my revenge on those bastards now: Adam and the bastard that took my family . . ." His eyes closed and he shook his head weakly.

Tuck knelt down and examined the wound in Will's side. "It's impossible to tell what damage has been done internally, but . . ." He looked up at Robin and shrugged his wide shoulders hopelessly.

Just then, the sound of running footsteps reached them, and little Beth burst into view through the sparse autumn foliage. She saw Robin and broke into a smile, making her way over to him, then her face crumpled as she saw Will, blood caking his side, his skin deathly pale. But his eyes fluttered open briefly, just as Beth screamed, "Daddy!"

* * *

Sir Richard-at-Lee and his two companions made good time, pushing their horses to their limits, and reaching Hull late in the afternoon the day after leaving Kirklees.

They paid for their mounts to be looked after in a stable near the town gatehouse and made their way to the harbour, which seemed loud and crowded after their journey on the near deserted road.

Shouting sailors loaded crates and barrels onto ships, fishmongers hawked their freshly caught wares from stinking stalls, blood and fish guts littered the ground in some areas making young Simon in particular feel like puking and prostitutes of all ages and nationalities showed their wares with varying degrees of enthusiasm.

Sir Richard asked a few questions and, eventually, a ship bound for Cyprus, the *la Maudelyn*, was located. They made their way aboard, meeting the captain on deck, and passage was booked for Simon. The captain told them, however, he still had much of his cargo to load, so they wouldn't be leaving until dawn the following day.

"My son has to leave tonight," the big Hospitaller told the sailor, a man similar to his own age, who shrugged and spread his hands wide.

"Sorry, my lord. I've told the men they can spend the night drinking and whoring in the town – there'd be a mutiny if I told them I'd changed my mind just so some rich boy could leave early."

Sir Richard laughed sardonically at the idea they were rich, given the debt he owed to Abbott Ness, but he pulled a small bag of silver from his pouch and emptied it on the table. "Tell your men they can drink and fuck in Cyprus. You leave tonight."

The captain glanced at the money. In truth, it wasn't all that much – the Hospitaller simply couldn't afford any more – but it was still a substantial amount and his men had already spent a few days in the town anyway, frittering away their pay. Besides, this big knight with the thick neck and bushy grey beard didn't look like a man to haggle with.

He smiled. "You have a deal, my lord. Once the ship is loaded, we'll leave. Take yourselves off to one of the local taverns – I can recommend the Dog and Duck, just a few yards that way – and come back in a couple of hours. We'll be ready to cast off by then."

Sir Richard grinned in relief and led his son and sergeant-at-arms back down the gangplank and onto the bustling street where they could see the gaudy green and gold sign for the Dog and Duck swinging in the autumn breeze.

"Come on," the Hospitaller shrugged. "We'll be out of sight in there at least."

"Aye," Stephen smiled as one of the prostitutes waggled her tongue at him suggestively. "And I've been choking for a drink all day!"

Simon grinned at his father's gloomy sergeant, a man he'd known almost all his life. "Who'd have thought it? All it takes to put a smile on your face is the thought of an ale and a saggy old pair of tits."

Sir Richard howled with laughter at that, as Stephen grimaced, and they made their way through the packed street to the inn.

"When you see your brother," Richard smiled at his son, "tell him I miss him, and I'm proud of him."

Simon nodded, pushing his way through the people thronging the docks.

"I'm proud of you both," Sir Richard continued. "You've been fine sons."

Despite the hour – it was almost sunset – the street was still heaving with people and, as they approached the door to the Dog and Duck with dry mouths, Simon suddenly stumbled, the people around him buffeting him as he fell forward.

Stephen grabbed his right arm and made to help him up, but the young man felt like a lead weight and, as Sir Richard grasped his other arm, Simon collapsed, face first onto the ground.

"What's wrong" – the Hospitaller demanded as he looked at his son and saw the red stains spreading over his back.

"Stephen!" he roared, trying to pull his sword from its scabbard. "He's been stabbed!"

The crowd, which had been pressing so close until then, suddenly parted, leaving the three men in a circle of their own as the burly knight drew his blade and held it defensively over his fallen son. Stephen had his own weapon drawn by now and the two men searched the mass of people for threats.

A man was pushing his way, forcibly through the people on the street and, when he looked back, Stephen gave a cry of rage and raced after him, waving his sword over his head to try and clear the way.

Sir Richard, fearing the worst as the small red wounds on his son's back had spread to form one great crimson stain, knelt down and grasped Simon by the shoulder, turning him over.

The young man's eyes were glazed, staring straight up, unseeing.

Lifeless.

Despenser's men had managed to catch up with them.

The commander of Kirklees screamed in despair. His beloved son was dead.

CHAPTER FIFTEEN

Friar Tuck bandaged Will's wound, but the outlaws knew it was hopeless.

Robin felt a great sense of helpless frustration. To have rescued Scarlet's daughter, only for the hot headed fool to impale himself on a sword in a moment of madness before he could be reunited . . .

Little Beth was inconsolable, having to be dragged off her father in despair, while Tuck tended to him.

"We need to move fast, Robin," Little John said to his young friend. "If we're to stop Gurdon locking Matilda away in some Nottingham dungeon, we have to catch up with him."

"What about Will, though?" Allan-a-Dale asked. "We can't just leave him here to die."

John expression was dark as he turned to Allan. "Will only has himself to blame for what's happened. He let his temper get the best of him and he's paid the price. We need to help Matilda while we still have the chance. If Adam gets her into the city she's as good as dead – we would never be able to rescue her from there. If we can catch them on the open road in time though…"

Beth had stopped crying by now, and she gazed at Robin forlornly. "Please help my da," she sniffed. "I have no one else."

Robin leaned down and clasped Beth's small hand in his own.

"I won't lie to you…your da took a terrible injury. It doesn't look good for him. But we won't leave him here. And whatever happens, lass, you won't be alone. We have friends and family in the all the villages around Yorkshire. We will find you a home, with good people."

He smiled reassuringly at Beth, and she nodded in return, but her eyes flickered to Will again, which brought a fresh bout of sobbing.

Robin patted her awkwardly on the arm and stood up. "Tuck. You, Allan and young Gareth there make a stretcher and carry Will back to our camp. Make him comfortable and…just do what you can for him Tuck."

The friar met Robin's eyes and both men knew what the young leader meant – Will would need the Last Rites before the day was out.

"Come on, Beth, help us find some straight branches to make a stretcher for your da," said Allan, leading the girl into the trees. Gareth, a fifteen-year-old outlaw from Wrangbrook, followed them, eyes roving across the ground searching for sturdy sticks.

Robin turned away sadly. "You foresters can be on your way, as I promised."

The captives stood up gratefully, relief plain on their face. Most of the outlaws around the great forests of England would not have been so merciful.

"Just remember this day," Robin told them, "should we ever find ourselves in a situation like this again, with the roles reversed."

The foresters nodded and moved gratefully off along the road towards Nottingham. Their big leader, Samuel, grasped Robin's hand firmly.

"I thank you for our freedom, Hood. If ever the day comes when I can aid you in return, know that I will do all I can for your men."

Robin clapped him on the arm, nodding, although he knew it was unlikely Samuel would find himself in charge of men often, after his rout at the hands of the outlaws. It was plain the middle-aged forester was no gifted leader of men. But he was another friend to the outlaws, and they needed every one they could get. Robin waved the grateful man off and checked his weapons were firmly secured.

"Make ready to move lads!" he roared at his men. "Adam must still be on the road to Nottingham. We might have time to catch up with him if we cut through the forest. He must only have a couple of men in his party now, so, as long as we move fast enough, we can stop the bastard and repay him for everything he's done."

"Let's move!" Little John's huge voice shook the trees, and the outlaws moved into the hidden pathways of the forest that they knew so well, yet which would have been invisible to any outsider.

Friar Tuck, Allan-a-Dale and Gareth quickly fashioned a crude but sturdy stretcher and eased Will onto it. Then they, along with Beth, struck off towards their camp.

"How do we know Gurdon is on the Great North Road?" Matt Groves demanded as the main party of outlaws hurried through the forest. They had collected the two horses and brought them along, in case Gurdon saw them coming and tried to get away, but no one was riding them just now. Robin wanted them as fresh as possible, should they be needed for a chase.

"I found out his plans from Henry Woolemonger, before I ran him through," Little John replied to Matt. "Adam's plan was to crush us at Hampole Dyke while he escaped unchallenged with Matilda."

"If it had worked he would have wiped us out in one blow," the teenager, Arthur, grunted. "Just as well you four came along when you did."

Little John nodded. "Aye. Now *we* have the element of surprise with us. The turncoat bastard thinks we're all dead. He'll be in no great hurry to deliver Matilda to the prior."

"That's my fear…" Robin admitted.

"What do you mean? Surely if they take their time it gives us more of a chance to catch them?" Much glanced over in surprise at his boyhood friend.

Robin stared ahead of him, face set in determination, as he picked up the pace, forcing the rest of the outlaws to speed up to avoid falling behind.

"Aye, Much, but Adam and his men…left alone with Matilda; in no great hurry…they might just decide to make a whore of her before the prior gets her into that brothel of his."

Adam Gurdon was a brutal man. Much expected he would enjoy using Matilda – whether she consented or not. Much had known the girl as long as Robin; she had been a good friend of his in Wakefield too.

"Come on lads," he shouted, pulling alongside Robin. "Time for the bastard to pay for his betrayal!"

* * *

"All right boys, let's take a rest and have something to eat." Adam Gurdon reined in his horse and his two companions followed suit gladly.

The late summer sun was still warm and the three lawmen were thirsty, as was Matilda who had been forced to endure a steady stream of inane and often filthy chatter from Gurdon and his men as they made their way along the well-worn road.

The bailiff dismounted smoothly and, none too gently, helped Matilda down.

"Sit." He pointed her towards a large boulder, on to which she gratefully slumped. The girl was not used to riding, and even after a short period on horseback her whole body, particularly her buttocks, felt stiff and sore.

Gurdon's two foresters made themselves comfortable on a rotten old log, and drank their fill from their ale skins, murmuring contentedly as they relaxed in the warm sun.

"I'd love to know how you managed to fool the outlaws into thinking you were Adam Bell," one of them suddenly asked the bailiff, shaking his head wonderingly.

186

Gurdon laughed and shrugged his shoulders, wiping wine from the side of his wet lips.

Almost everyone in England knew the folk tales about the outlaw Adam Bell, a Saxon hero, who hailed from the town of Inglewood. Bell, with his friends Adam Cloudesley and Clim of the Clough, had great adventures, outwitting the sheriffs and lords of whichever county the tale happened to be told in.

"What did Adam Bell look like, lad?" Gurdon asked the forester.

The man racked his brains for a while and looked to his grizzled companion for support, but neither of them could answer the question.

"Exactly," Gurdon smiled. "The stories don't say. All I had to do was find a small group of outlaws, tell them I was Adam Bell and, before long everyone believed it was true." He dropped his ale skin and pulled an apple from his pack, eyes sparkling merrily as he bit into it. "If he ever lived," Gurdon went on, spitting juicy flecks of fruit from his mouth, "Adam Bell and his mates must have died years ago. Who could say I wasn't him?"

The foresters nodded in admiration at their new bailiff's ingenuity.

"Here, girl." Gurdon, having half drained it, passed his own ale skin to Matilda. She took a sip, but found it was much more bitter, and stronger, than she was used to.

"You like that?" Gurdon watched her drink, his eyes roving across her body unashamedly.

Matilda squirmed under his gaze and handed the ale back to him defiantly. "No, I don't. It tastes like piss."

The three men laughed at that.

"I can see why young Hood covets you so much, girl," the bailiff told her, wiping the thick sheen of sweat from his forehead. "You've got a fine body on you, eh lads?"

The other two made lewd replies, grinning like young boys, but their eyes were humourless. Matilda felt a cold shiver run down her spine.

"You can forget about Hood," Adam continued, taking another drink of his ale. "He'll be dead by now. Him, and the rest of those fools I used to lead will have chased off after you, right into the ambush my men prepared at Hampole Dyke."

Matilda felt her blood turn to ice, but her captor continued, walking over to stand before her, triumphantly.

"Those idiots will walk right into a storm of arrows, and any that survive the first volley will be cut down where they stand by my foresters."

Matilda remained silent as Gurdon carried on, a self-satisfied smile playing around the corners of his mouth.

"There's no one left to help you, girl." He leaned down to look into her eyes, grinning savagely. "The prior will make sure you're tried, and found guilty of aiding the outlaws. Then…"

His hand moved slowly down to cup Matilda's left breast. "Then the prior will put that body of yours to work in his brothel – the 'Maiden's Head'. It's a nice place; you'll have a lot of fun there."

The two foresters grunted. "I'll be in to visit you a lot, girl," one of them promised, staring at her malevolently. Matilda felt the panic begin to build in her. Tears filled her eyes as Adam pulled her top down to expose her nipples, drawing more grunts and gasps from the two foresters.

She desperately wanted to fight the bailiff off, but her arms wouldn't respond as she screamed inside and tried to block out what was happening to her.

Gurdon leaned down further and roughly bit her breast, pushing her legs apart, and the girl felt a wave of black despair wash over her. She and Robin would never be together now.

She thought of all the good things in her life: her loving parents and her friends in Wakefield, her home. She went limp with grief as she thought of Robin, shot through and broken by the arrows of Adam Gurdon's men.

"There boys, she's starting to relax. She's a natural!" the bailiff laughed and stood up, undoing his trousers as Matilda watched numbly.

"Now, girl. Open that pretty mouth of yours…"

* * *

There was no time for anyone to plan or prepare. Robin had taken the lead, his men struggling to keep pace with him as he pushed himself on, tortured by visions of Adam abusing Matilda.

They were beside the river again, which followed the course of the road at this point, and the water gurgled noisily over a small waterfall, so neither party heard the other until Robin jogged around a small rise and almost ran into Gurdon, his breeches at his ankles, Matilda sitting in front of him and his two henchmen laughing gleefully. Their faces fell as they caught sight of the outlaw just two yards away, but the bailiff had his back turned, and neither of the foresters had ever seen Robin before, so they were slow to draw their weapons.

The young outlaw stopped dead in his tracks, frozen to the spot, as Matilda squirmed, tearfully trying to keep Gurdon's cock away from her mouth.

Then she saw Robin appearing like an avenging angel, and felt a surge of elation. He wasn't dead! As her lover's hand moved to his sword hilt, Matilda looked up at Adam Gurdon with a look of fierce triumph and opened her mouth.

Robin swiftly drew his blade and rammed it into the nearest forester's guts before the man realised what was happening. He dropped to his knees like a stone, and

Robin savagely ripped the blade free, spilling the man's intestines onto the grass.

Too fast for the eye to follow, the outlaw spun completely around and hacked into the side of the second man's sword arm. The forester collapsed, bellowing, clutching at his near-severed limb.

When she'd seen Robin attacking, Matilda had taken Adam's manhood in her mouth…and bit down as hard as she could.

The bailiff screamed in agony as half his cock was completely severed, blood pumping thickly from the horrendous wound. Matilda spat it onto the grass in front of his disbelieving eyes.

"You fucking bitch!" he screamed in shock, feebly clasping his hands over his bleeding crotch, the shock at his mutilation rendering him oblivious to the fate of his two companions. "I'll kill you, I'll fucking kill you!"

His cries were cut off suddenly, as the point of a sword erupted out the front of his chest.

Robin leaned in behind his former mentor and whispered in his ear. "You won't be killing anyone. I'm going to take your carcass to Nottingham and leave you there for everyone to see."

He pulled his sword free with a wet, sucking, sound and kicked the sagging Gurdon sideways onto the grass, where he clutched at his terrible wounds, whimpering pitifully.

Matilda, adrenaline pounding in her veins, picked up Gurdon's severed penis, and rammed it into his weakly protesting mouth furiously.

"There, you can suck it yourself now, you evil bastard!" she shouted hysterically, forcing him to gag on it.

The second forester had tried to make a run for it, his sword arm almost hacked off by Robin, but Little John and the rest of the outlaws had caught up with him. They pushed him back into the clearing, crying like a child and clutching his arm in terror.

John took in the carnage before him, eyes wide in disbelief. "What do we do with this one, Robin?"

Hood turned, his face frozen in a grimace of rage, and calmly drove his sword into the man's belly.

"Leave those two animals," he said, pointing with his sword to the two foresters. "Gurdon we take with us."

No one argued, as Robin lifted Matilda to her feet and took her in his arms. She was shaking uncontrollably now, as the adrenaline faded and shock took its place.

"He said you were all dead," she sobbed.

Robin held her fiercely, his own hands starting to shake as he stroked her long brown hair. "Aye, that was his plan, but we beat him Matilda. We're fine. And you're safe now."

They stood like that for a while, everyone silent in the face of the awful violence they'd just witnessed, before Little John spoke to two of the outlaws.

"Lift Adam. We should get moving."

Robin nodded. "Me and Much will take his body to Nottingham, and make sure Prior de Monte Martini and everyone else in the town finds out what happened to him. That'll send a message to anyone else that might decide to come hunting us."

It seemed an extreme gesture to Little John, but right now, in this mood, Robin was in charge, so the giant simply nodded his head and promised to take Matilda safely back to their camp with the rest of the men.

"We'll meet you back there when we're done," Robin said, his gaze still vacant, his sword still drawn, dripping blood onto the pale green grass.

"All right, we're done lads. At last. Let's get back to camp and celebrate!" John smiled half-heartedly, and some of the men cheered as they began the journey home.

Although they had beaten Adam and gained their revenge for his betrayal, most of the outlaws felt it was a hollow victory. They knew they would still be wolf's heads when they woke up the next day, and the day after that. No matter how many of their pursuers they killed, they would never be able to go back to their families and a normal life again.

Adam Gurdon's body was loaded onto his horse, while Robin and Much inexpertly mounted the two horses the foresters had been riding.

"Be careful, Robin," said Matilda, quietly.

He nodded. "We won't be long. Then tomorrow we'll take you home to your ma and da."

The girl's eyes filled with tears again and she forced a smile as Robin and Much rode off towards Nottingham, the bailiff's mutilated body strapped tightly to the horse he had ridden so proudly into Wakefield earlier that day.

* * *

Although Robin had told Tuck to take Will back to the outlaws' camp, the friar knew that was a death sentence for the wounded Scarlet. They only had rudimentary medical supplies at camp and, although Tuck was fairly certain Will would not survive no matter what aid he received, he felt it his duty – to Beth if nothing else – to seek out the best help possible.

Allan-a-Dale and the youngster Gareth, outlawed for stealing food from a chapel for his sick mother, carried Will's stretcher through the forest, with Tuck taking turns to relieve one of the other periodically.

"Obviously, this isn't leading to our camp, Tuck," Allan noted after a couple of miles. "Where are we going?"

"Kirklees Priory," Tuck replied, wiping sweat from his tonsured head with the sleeve of his grey robe. "The nuns there have a better chance of saving Will than we do. The convent has skilled surgeons, and medicines that will help him."

The friar felt guilty as Beth looked towards him, her face alive with hope. He had seen too many sword wounds over the years, and never had he seen a man survive one as grievous as that which Will had sustained.

He mouthed a silent prayer to St Francis, and gave the little girl's shoulder a reassuring squeeze.

"How much further?" Beth asked him.

"We'll reach there just after sunset, lass," Tuck replied. "Do you need a rest?"

Her small face grew determined and she straightened her shoulders. "No. Let's get there as fast as we can."

Tuck nodded and gave her an encouraging smile. It was obvious Will's daughter was struggling – she'd spent the past three years cooped up in a house. True, she had worked hard every day, but long distance travelling, indeed *any* travelling, other than between rooms in the manor house, hadn't been part of her routine. Tuck was glad she was still little – he knew she would need carried soon.

It was going to be a long hard journey to Kirklees Priory for them all.

* * *

It was sometime after the sun had set, and the constellation of the dragon looked down on the small party, when they finally reached Kirklees. Tuck had carried Beth through the dark forest for the last mile, her short legs and undernourished body having in the end given out. She had fallen asleep in his arms. Although he was a portly man, who ate and drank too much, the friar was as strong as an ox. Still, his arms ached terribly as they hammered on the door of the priory.

Allan-a-Dale and Gareth were as exhausted as Tuck. They were hard, fit lads, used to physical exertion and forced marches, but the fast pace they had set, along with the burden they carried, meant aching backs, arms and legs. They were glad when a young nun opened the great wooden door and invited them in once Tuck had explained – after a fashion – their predicament.

She had looked at Will, pale on the stretcher, then Beth, exhausted in the large friar's arms, and waved them inside, promising to fetch the abbess.

When the abbess came, she led them to a small room and bade them place Will on the bed there. Beth drowsily insisted on staying with her father, so the nuns brought her a blanket and the little girl fell asleep again in a chair by Will's bedside.

The men were shown to a sparsely furnished chamber with four beds and little else inside its grey stone walls. It was cool and, to men used to sleeping on the forest floor, hugely comfortable. They were brought a little bread and cheese each, with cool water to wash it down.

Allan and Gareth, having carried the stretcher for most of the way, ate their small meal gratefully and quickly fell asleep, completely drained.

Tuck sat a while in the small chapel, saying another prayer for Will's well being. The abbess came and questioned him there, about Will and how he came to be so horribly wounded, but she seemed to care little for the answers, or the truth of them. She knew very well they were probably not entirely true.

Tuck simply claimed bandits had attacked Will and his daughter in the forest, and he and his two friends had found them as they made their way along the road to Nottingham.

"You don't expect him to survive do you?" she asked.

Tuck shook his head sadly. "I'm surprised he isn't dead already, truth be told."

The abbess agreed. "We have cleaned the wound but I have no doubt he has internal damage which we cannot heal. What will happen to the girl when he dies? Where is her mother?"

"She told us her mother was dead, but she has an uncle in Wakefield. We will take here there when…if…her father dies."

The nun nodded. "I won't keep you any longer, you should get some rest yourself – you must be worn out. It was very good of you and your friends to carry them all this way…" She gave him a calculating look, and he burst out laughing.

"I expect a reward!" he smiled. "In *heaven*…Although, if you have any spare communion wine around, that would be pleasant indeed."

"You're pushing your luck, friar, you shouldn't even be in here," the nun snorted, surprising him with her knowledge. "It's against the Rule of your own Franciscan order: 'Brothers should not enter the convents of nuns.'"

She wandered off, shaking her head sternly but when Tuck returned to the chamber Allan and Gareth were asleep in he found a jug of poor quality, yet strong wine next to his own bed.

As he felt the bitter liquid begin to relax him, he mouthed another prayer: Mary, mother of our Lord, help Will, and little Beth, whatever happens during this night…

Then at last, he fell asleep.

* * *

Will Scaflock was dying. Indeed, he should have been dead already – *would* have been dead already if not for one thing.

In some dark, hidden corner of his subconscious mind Will knew he had heard his daughter's voice before he had blacked out at Hampole Dyke.

Before today he would have embraced death as a release at last from his tormented life, but now, his little girl's face filled his soul. His body would not give in to death so easily.

195

The nuns had known Will was dying, from the evil smell coming from his wound. They had cleaned it as best they could, and stitched it up with a healing poultice, but they knew that smell. They knew the little girl clutching the man's hand would, in a few hours, maybe less, be left without her father, despite their prayers.

Beth knew none of this. Her da looked quite peaceful lying in the bed. She was sure he would be fine: he was strong, a fierce warrior; nothing ever hurt her da!

Then he began to turn blue, and his hand started to feel cold and clammy, and Beth began to wail, fresh tears streaming from her brilliant blue eyes.

Consciously, Will Scaflock knew nothing of this. Yet, as his ruined body lay comatose within the great stone walls of the priory, he dreamt – a more vivid dream than he had ever had before.

His wife, Elaine, came to him. She looked as she had in life, but she carried a lantern which only served to light her dimly. All around her was darkness.

"You're a fool Will Scaflock!" she chided him with a smile. He had no strength to argue, and knew she was right anyway. "But you have a part to play in this yet. You mustn't give in to death just yet. Fight it, Will, fight it for Beth!"

His wife seemed to come closer to him and she placed her hand on his side. Without looking down, Will knew there was a terrible gaping hole in him, yet as Elaine touched the wound he felt something…a strength, or force, coursing through him.

He grinned as the power filled his soul and he raised his eyes to look at the woman he had loved since the day he had first met her.

But it wasn't Elaine looking back at him. As he watched, her face seemed to shift and change in the darkness, until another face Will knew was staring back at him: Robin Hood, his face set in stony determination, gazed into his eyes. Yet it wasn't quite the Robin he knew: the face was somehow older, somehow different, somehow more…commanding, Will thought.

By his bedside, two nuns had come running when Beth started screaming in despair, and they watched in wonder as Will's blue lips slowly began to turn red again, and his grey flesh became a healthy pink.

In his fever dream, Scaflock stared at 'Robin'. "Leave me alone, Hood. I've nothing to live for. I can go and be with my family, with Elaine. I want to die!"

His skin slowly turned blue again.

Beth had not noticed the change in him and continued to cry the whole time, heart broken. As she laid her head down against Will's face, her tears rolled onto his pale cheeks. "Daddy!" she cried. "Please don't leave me again!"

Will's body gave a spasm, and he gasped for air, his eyes snapping open in shock, seeing his daughter's little face for the first time in three years.

"Beth . . !" he breathed. Then his eyes closed again and his body went limp. But this time there was a smile on his lips and he only slept. His daughter *was* alive! And, for now, so was he.

CHAPTER SIXTEEN

"Bastard!" Sir Richard-at-Lee roared with anger, kicking his chair and sending it flying despite its weight.

Stephen grimaced but remained silent as his lord vented some of his frustration.

"This is all because 'Sir' Hugh Despenser, in his greed, wanted to extort some money from a decent man!" the Hospitaller shouted, the hurt he was feeling evident in his voice. "The bastard's supposed to be in exile, yet he continues to bring his black influence to us!"

After his son had been murdered, Sir Richard had brought his body back to Kirklees and buried him by the priory, his heart close to breaking with rage and despair. Stephen had been unable to catch the assailant in Hull, so they had no legal redress – not that it would have counted for much anyway. The Despensers appeared to be above the law, even in exile.

Sir Richard, in his grief, had wanted to ride to Cardiff and attack the castle with his own small garrison, but Stephen had stopped him. The Marcher lords would take care of Despenser – indeed, serious trouble was brewing for both the king and the Despensers, as Leeds castle had been besieged by Edward in the past few days, with the Marcher lords Mortimer and Hereford riding to the aid of their ally Lord Badlesmere against the king's forces.

The country was truly on the point of civil war as a result of the Despensers evil influence over the king.

Half an hour earlier, Sir Richard had gathered the staff in his castle at Kirklees and given them the bad news.

"I know, it's coming into winter – the worst time I could do this to you," he told them sadly. "But I have no money left to retain your services – my personal income will have to go towards my debt to Abbott Ness, until I can secure more loans to cover that debt."

His staff cried out in shock – how would they look after their families without a job? Food was almost too costly even with a regular wage coming in, what would they do now?

The Hospitaller could only spread his hands wide and beg their understanding.

To ruin so many lives, after his own son being murdered…it was too much.

* * *

Robin awoke with a gasp, drenched in sweat, his head pounding.

"What's wrong?" Matilda asked, sitting up beside him under their shared blanket.

Robin and Much had reached Nottingham in the afternoon. They had made sure Adam Gurdon's cock was firmly stuffed in his mouth, tying it there with a piece of torn linen so it couldn't fall out, then gave his horse a slap on the rump. It had raced off, through the gates of the town, chased by the surprised gate guards.

Robin knew everyone in Nottingham would have heard about the bailiff returning tied to his horse, mutilated and humiliated in death. The note Friar Tuck had written before they split up, they had pinned to Adam's body. It would serve as a warning to any who might think to come after them in future.

This is Adam Gurdon, Bailiff of Wakefield, formerly known as Adam Bell – traitor! it read. This is what happens to lawmen in Barnsdale. The forest is ours!

Although only a small handful of people would see the note, tongues would wag, and, in a big town like Nottingham, within a few days everyone in the place would know what it said.

Robin and Much had made their way back to the camp in the Yorkshire forest where John, Matilda, and the rest of the gang waited.

Tuck's party were, of course, nowhere to be seen, but one of the men, Arthur, the nineteen-year-old from Bichill, had noticed the stretcher-bearers' trail had changed direction on the path to camp and it was assumed the canny friar had decided to look for aid at Kirklees Priory.

Despite rescuing Matilda, and destroying their despised former leader, the mood in the outlaws' camp was somewhat sombre, since no one knew whether Will Scarlet lived or not. He may not have been the most pleasant of companions, but he was one of their own, and had saved many of their lives at one point or another.

Ale had been drunk, they sang a song or two, but no one really felt like enjoying themselves. Robin had led Matilda to his pallet when night fell, the camp fire burned low, and the outlaws, after setting the watch, had turned in.

Matilda shed tears of relief as she made love to Robin in the darkness. Will may have been mortally wounded, but Matilda had never met him. Robin though, *her Robin,* was here, and in her arms. For that, she cried and said silent prayers of thanks.

A short while later, she was surprised to hear sobbing coming from beside her. It was a moonless night, and the campfire had burned low, so she could hardly make out Robin's face in the shadows as he turned and buried his face in her shoulder.

"What's wrong?" Matilda whispered, shocked and a little frightened by Robin's unexpected show of emotion.

He didn't reply for a while, just held her tighter. "It's all too much," he wept. "I'm only seventeen, yet I'm practically leading a gang of outlaws. I've killed men; my mate Will's dying after being run through in front of his little girl; it's my fault Harry Half-hand's dead…and still, the law will be after us tomorrow. Just as they always will be."

His voice cracked and he buried his face deeper into Matilda's shoulder as she stroked his hair comfortingly. "It feels like the weight of the whole world is on me!"

They held each other tightly in the darkness. Matilda was lost for words so she simply whispered comforting noises as if to a frightened child, and eventually they fell back asleep.

Until Robin started awake, again, not long before dawn.

"It's Will," he gasped, sitting up wide-eyed. "Something's wrong. Seriously wrong."

Matilda put a hand on his shoulder, frightened by his tone.

Robin shook his head. He had dreamt of Will, he was trying to help him get better, but…Will didn't *want* to get better, and Robin had woken then, despairing for his friend. He looked at Matilda in the darkness, her face beautiful in the dim orange glow from the embers of the campfire, and forced a smile.

"What will be, will be. Let's go back to sleep."

When the dawn sun rose, Robin took Little John and set out for Kirklees Priory.

"The men will be brooding about Will," Robin had said to Matilda as they prepared to leave. "So we've told them to spend the day in combat training to take their minds off it. You can go pair off with Much – if you're going to be staying here with us for a while you need to learn how to defend yourself."

Matilda nodded. She had never been in a true physical fight in her life, not even as a child, but, since the foresters would be hunting her now, she had to learn how to live as an outlaw. And that meant fighting.

"Don't worry." Robin grasped her hands and gazed at her, the previous night's self-pity gone as fierce determination filled his eyes. "Somehow I'll get a pardon for us. For all of us. Adam managed it, we can too! I won't live like a hunted animal for the rest of my life, I swear it."

She forced a smile and Much handed her one of the lighter wooden practice swords with an encouraging grin. Robin gave her a last lingering kiss goodbye before he and John headed off towards the priory.

After only an hour or so they were met by Allan-a-Dale and Gareth, who Tuck had sent back to camp to take the news of Will's recovery to the rest of the outlaws.

"He lives, Robin!" Allan cried, a grin lighting up his handsome face.

"A miracle, truly!" put in young Gareth.

Robin and John looked at each other in disbelief.

"How?" John asked. "That wound he took was mortal, we could all see it!"

Allan shrugged, laughing. "I told you: a miracle. One minute he was dead, and little Beth was crying her heart out, the next his eyes opened and he spoke to her. Just for a moment, though. He's been sleeping ever since, but the nuns say his wound's clean and the smell from it's gone."

John shook his great head in wonder. "Aye, a miracle right enough. God be praised!"

Robin smiled, but felt Beth had been the one who had brought Will back from the dead, rather than the nuns' prayers.

"All right, you two head back to camp and let the others know. Me and John will go and see how he fares, and what Tuck would have us do next."

Allan and Gareth nodded, and whooped as John promised a proper celebration feast for them all tonight.

* * *

The great stone walls seemed to crowd in on Robin, as a pretty young nun led him and John to Will's sickroom in the priory.

The outlaws were used to the open skies and the leafy canopies of the greenwood, occasionally the low thatched roof of a village alehouse. These great high ceilings, tiled floors and cold, grey stone walls made both men nervous, but the nun had smiled happily at them when they had knocked on the door, asking after Will.

"Your friend has made a miraculous recovery," the girl said. "Truly God was at work in our priory last night!"

John smiled back, admiring the gentle curves of the young woman's body, which the dark habit couldn't hide. Robin nodded distractedly as the big man nudged him, smiling lecherously behind the nun's back.

Despite the girl's enthusiasm, both Robin and John were stunned to see Will sitting up in bed, wolfing down a large bowl of apple stew. He smiled sheepishly at them, and Beth leapt up from her chair to rush over and hug Robin's legs.

"He's all right! I knew he'd be all right!" she laughed happily.

"So I see, lass," Robin replied, ruffling her hair as he looked down at Will who finished off the last of his meal and closed his eyes, grimacing slightly as a shiver of pain ran through his side.

"I'm alive, but it still bloody hurts," he grunted.

"How's the wound?" Little John asked. "Allan said it had healed over – surely that's not true?"

"The nuns stitched it up, they say it's clean and will heal up nicely soon enough. As for it healing over, well, Allan's a bloody minstrel isn't he? He likes to exaggerate. Still...we all know I should have died yesterday, so I can't complain." He smiled weakly.

"You can't stay here for long," Robin told him. "Someone's bound to find out who you are and the sheriff's men will come for you. We need to get you back to the forest as soon as you're able to travel."

Will nodded. "What about Beth? The forests are no place for a child."

"I've spoken with Matilda about Beth," Robin replied. "She says her ma and da will be happy to take care of her. They'll have the extra space now, since Matilda will be living with us for a while…"

Will grinned in relief. "That sounds good my friend. And…" He lowered his eyes, as they filled with tears. "I don't know how to thank you and Allan for getting my little girl back for me." He pulled Beth to him and hugged her tightly. "I never believed she was still alive. I feel guilty now for never looking for her myself. I thought the soldiers had killed them all." His body shook as he sobbed gently, stroking his daughter's long brown hair. "I'm so sorry, Beth."

"Well, she's safe now," Robin replied awkwardly. "You two can start again."

"Aye," John laughed loudly. "And maybe now since you have something to live for you won't be so bloody miserable all the time?"

Everyone smiled at that.

"Aye, you're right. I know I've been hard to be around. But now, well, like you say I've got something – someone – to live for. Thanks to you Robin."

Friar Tuck wandered into the room, chewing a piece of black bread. His eyes lit up as he saw his friends. "Truly a miracle, lads," he cried, crumbs spilling from his mouth. "The Virgin Mary gave us our brother Will back – she must have a purpose for him here."

"Oh I have a purpose all right, Tuck." Will's smile turned to a steely glare. "I want to be up and about as soon as I can. Because once I'm better, I'm going after the bastard that took Beth from me!"

* * *

"The king must be dealt with!"

The magnates gathered by Thomas, Earl of Lancaster in another of his "parliaments" rumbled agreement at his assertion, although some looked uncomfortable at such a treasonous statement.

"The younger Despenser – with Edward's connivance – has embarked on a career of piracy!" Lancaster, his face red with anger, slammed a fist onto the long table before him. "The Despensers have been banished, yet the younger of them continues to act as he pleases, while the king does nothing. In fact, the king *aids* Despenser in his criminal activities!"

"At least his father has accepted his fate and gone abroad," Sir John de Bek growled.

"Many of us," Lancaster roared, "pledged ourselves when we last met in June to secure the destruction of the Despensers. Both of them. Yet the younger is allowed to live the life of a murderous pirate, waylaying many English merchant ships on the Channel, while I have heard strong rumours that the king has been in contact with him and plans to recall both father and son before the end of the year."

There were cries of outrage at this.

"Surely Edward would not be so foolish?" Sir Richard-at-Lee demanded in disbelief. "He knows the depth of feeling against the Despensers. If that piece of murdering filth ever sets foot in the country again I will hunt him down myself!"

"The king cares nothing for our feelings!" Lord Mowbray spat. "Do my lords forget the other...*favourites*...the king has kept over the years? The Despensers have manipulated him for years – and will continue to do so – just as Piers Gaveston did."

The Earl of Lancaster nodded in agreement. "My cousin is not fit to rule I'm afraid, gentlemen. When I was made Steward of England I naively thought I could influence him. I hoped to curb the influence of men like Gaveston and the Despensers, but Edward is blind to the faults of these...friends...of his."

Lord Clifford shook his head despairingly. "It grieves me greatly to say it, my lords, but I fear the time has come that we take matters into our own hands, before the king ruins us all, as he has recently ruined Lord Badlesmere."

There was a silence in the room at this pronouncement, as each of the assembled magnates contemplated the terrible fate of Badlesmere, who had sided with the Marchers against the king.

Edward's wife, Queen Isabella, had sought lodging for the night at Leeds Castle, of which, Badlesmere was constable. Although he was away at the time, his wife, Margaret, had refused the royal party access, going so far as to have her archers shoot down half a dozen of the queen's retainers. The king had, understandably, been incensed at this, and had laid siege to Leeds castle.

Some of the Marchers, including Mortimer and Hereford, had travelled to Lady Badlesmere's aid, they had arrived too late and the castle had fallen to the king.

Although Lord Badlesmere had not been captured, his wife, their children and other immediate family had been imprisoned in Dover Castle, while many of his supporters were hanged.

The king had shown a new side to his character: decisive, ruthless and merciless. His actions had shocked Sir Richard-at-Lee and most of the other lords gathered here at Pontefract who were used to seeing an indecisive, weak and inept Edward.

The Marchers, and the Earl of Lancaster, were particularly worried. If they did not act soon, the king's newfound sense of purpose would be the end of them.

Time was not on their side.

"The king has shown by his unlawful treatment of Lord Badlsemere, who has been found guilty without due legal process, that he will do as he pleases even to his most devoted subjects. He has gone insane with power – he has become a tyrant!"

Sir Richard noted a few frowns around the room, but the loud roars of outraged agreement from the Marchers and their friends filled the room.

"The time to act is almost upon us, gentlemen," Thomas stated. "Or any one of us will be the king's next target. Would you sit twiddling your thumbs while

Edward strips you of your lands?" He glared at the men seated before him. "Will you wait, like lambs to the slaughter, hoping our beloved monarch and his friends will not imprison or even murder *your* children, as the king has done to Badlesmere, and Despenser did to Sir Richard-at-Lee?"

Again the Marchers shouted angry demands for action, and Sir Richard could tell Lancaster's speech was having the desired effect as many of the lords who had appeared undecided at the start of the meeting were now joining in with the cries of outrage.

The commander of Kirklees grinned savagely. He had paid the ransom to the younger Despenser and freed his son, but, despite that, his son was dead and Sir Richard was as good as ruined. His private estate was small; it didn't provide the sort of income he needed to repay his debt to the Abbott Ness. The situation enraged him and he had vowed to stand with the Earl of Lancaster against the Despensers and, by extension, the king.

He had lost almost everything anyway.

All he wanted now was revenge.

The meeting ended with most of the magnates signing a petition warning the king of their intent to defend themselves by force of arms, should his attitude not change.

It was all the justification King Edward needed to move, once and for all, against his rebellious lords.

There would be war.

CHAPTER SEVENTEEN

Divine assistance or not, Will was well enough to travel within a week and rejoined Robin and the other outlaws at their camp with grins all round.

The nuns at the priory had informed Archbishop Melton in York of their miracle patient, and he had travelled to Kirklees to see for himself. Will and Beth had sneaked out the evening before he was due to arrive. Will was not ungrateful for their help, but he knew the more people that saw him, and the more fuss made, the more likely someone would recognise him for the outlaw he was.

Little John had told him he was a fool for returning to the camp.

"What the hell are you talking about, you big oaf?" Will growled. "Where was I supposed to go?"

"You're a walking miracle!" John grinned, slapping him on the shoulder. "The priests would have made the King pardon you. You could have lived like a lord."

Will laughed. "Until the next miracle came along, and they lost interest in me. Then the sheriff would have come along and hanged me for a wolf's head."

Despite the fact he was able to travel, Will was still not fully healed, so, as summer finally gave way to autumn and the leaves that hid them so handily started to fall off the trees, there had been no more mention of hunting down Lord John de Bray for enslaving Beth. Robin was glad. He had hoped that the return of his daughter might have softened Will's outlook on life – dimmed his never-ending need to kill powerful noblemen.

While he understood the desire to avenge Beth's cruel imprisonment for so long, Robin still wished Scarlet would forget about it.

The little girl had settled in well with Matilda's parents, Henry and Mary. They were upset at their daughter having to take up with the outlaws of the greenwood, but looking after Beth tempered the blow. Considering what she had endured in her short life, Henry told them the girl was as bright as a button and Mary was pleased to have a willing helper around the house.

Since they had destroyed Adam Gurdon and his foresters no one else had made an effort to hunt them down. It would have been a happy time for the outlaws, if food wasn't so scarce. They managed to hunt just enough venison, rabbit, birds and fish to survive, buying milk, eggs, salt, bread and other foods when they were available from the surrounding Yorkshire villages for exorbitant prices. But, like Robin's family in Wakefield, people all over the country could barely get enough food to survive. It was a source of worry for many of the outlaws, who had family and friends living in the villages surrounding the forests of Barnsdale.

Robin had been accepted by all the men, if only grudgingly by Matt Groves, as their leader by now, despite his youth – he had just turned eighteen in October – and lack of experience. Little John, Friar Tuck and Will Scarlet were always available for advice, if and when he needed it.

"You know, things are going to get even harder than this?" John said one frosty morning as they skinned a pair of small rabbits they'd trapped.

"Harder?" Robin looked at his big mate in disbelief. "Are you taking the piss?"

"You joined us in the spring," John replied, peeling back the fur from one little animal's carcass. "You've been an outlaw only during the easy weather, when there's plenty of game and fruit to eat, plenty of rich travellers to rob and plenty of leaves on the trees to hide us. But it's coming into November now – winter. And it's been a shit year for growing food, as you know yourself."

Robin sighed in frustration. "I know. My little sister Marjorie's probably going to suffer. I've been trying my best to help my family with food and money but…" His voice tailed off and he stared at the trees disconsolately. "What can we do?"

Little John finished skinning his rabbit before he rinsed off his hands and knife in the swiftly flowing stream next to them, then he stood up and looked down at his young leader with a sly smile. "I know a certain local we might be able to rob – it'd please Will too."

Robin sat for a moment, wondering what John meant, then he realised. "You're having a laugh, right? Are you seriously saying we should attack John de Bray's manor house?"

John nodded his head vigorously, and walked over to sit facing Robin, his hazel eyes gleaming earnestly. "The people in Hathersage say de Bray's got a great pile of food stored away in that undercroft of his."

"What?" Robin demanded, his face twisted in fury. "He's hoarding food, while folk like my sister Marjorie are starving to fucking death?"

"So they say," John shrugged. "Smoked or salted meat and fish, pickled vegetables, dried fruit. It's perfect. Scarlet wants his revenge on the bastard – and we know the layout of the place thanks to you and Allan. Beth could probably help us plan it as well. She must have a good idea of the kitchens and undercroft. Think about it! How much money and food has that little prick got lying around in his fancy manor house? Winter clothes? Weapons? Armour? If we go in during midwinter, we'll come out with enough food and money to feed and clothe the whole of Yorkshire 'til next spring!"

Of all the manors in the surrounding areas, John de Bray's in Hathersage was one of the smallest. Some powerful English nobles, like Thomas of Lancaster or the Earl of Warenne counted scores of villages among their holdings, but John de Bray was Lord of Hathersage alone. De Bray was still a wealthy man though, and, as Robin knew from personal experience, his manor house wasn't that well defended.

It was an ideal target for a small gang of outlaws, especially if the wicked bastard had been hoarding food so he could stay fat while the villagers starved through the winter.

Robin was lost in thought, wondering if John's plan was feasible, when a shout came from near their camp.

"Robin! John!" Much appeared from the trees, eyes scanning the forest.

"What is it, Much?" Robin got to his feet, helping John up with him.

The miller's son hurried over to them, excitedly.

"Men – coming this way. Gareth spotted them. From his description, Tuck and Will say it sounds like Hospitallers."

Robin and John shared an uneasy glance as they all started back towards the camp. The Knights of St John – Hospitallers – were an immensely powerful and wealthy order of warrior monks who had grown even stronger with the demise of the Templars. A hostile force of Hospitallers would pose a huge threat to the outlaws.

"How many are there?" Robin demanded.

"Only two of them," Much replied. "Well armed and armoured though, and on big warhorses too."

"They can't be hunting us, then." Little John heaved a sigh of relief. "They must simply be travellers, passing through."

Robin nodded, winking at his giant friend. "*Rich* travellers…"

They reached the camp and found the rest of the outlaws waiting on them, already armed and ready to move.

As John and Robin strapped on their own light armour they, with Will and Tuck, discussed what to do.

"These aren't a couple of soft, fat priests," Will cautioned. "No offence, Tuck."

"None taken," laughed the friar.

"Looks like a Hospitaller knight and his sergeant," Will went on. "They'll be dangerous, and could be damn hard to bring down if they decide to fight."

The outlaws headed for the main road, where they would ambush the Hospitallers. They had chosen a heavily wooded area, which would hinder the mounted men greatly, should a fight break out.

"We'll have a handful of the men in plain sight, high up, with their bows ready and aimed at these Crusaders," Robin said. "The rest of you take up positions close to me, by the roadside. I'll talk to them, see if we can avoid any bloodshed."

Matilda was told to hang back with Much.

They reached the road at midday, and the sound of a distant church bell could be heard tolling mournfully in one of the surrounding villages.

Will and Little John ordered the outlaws into their positions, and they settled down to wait for the knight and his man-at-arms.

A short while later, the sound of heavy horses could be heard coming through the trees towards them. Harnesses jingled, the animals snorted softly and their great hooves made distinct thuds on the hard ground.

The riders were silent, and, as they came into sight, both men looked gloomy and downcast. They were indeed heavily armoured, with black tunics, and bore black shields with white crosses painted on them. Hospitallers right enough.

Robin let them come closer and, when they were around twenty yards away, he stepped out from behind the oak tree he had been hiding behind.

"Good day, sir knights!" he smiled, folding his arms across his chest, and leaning against the tree, his blue eyes glinting cheerfully.

The men pulled up their horses, and both moved their hands instinctively to their sword hilts, eyes scanning the woods around them.

Now that the outlaws could see them clearly, it was plain these two soldiers had fallen on hard times. Their armour and clothes were shabby, and their horses looked poorly fed.

"What do you want?" said the largest, and slightly better dressed, of the two knights, a thick-necked, grey-bearded, commanding looking man.

"To invite you to dinner," replied Robin.

The men looked at each other in bemusement, but both drew their swords, sensing the danger they were in.

Robin gestured up at the high verges on either side of the road. The knights looked and saw a dozen men pointing longbows directly at them.

Will Scarlet, Friar Tuck and the great figure of Little John emerged from the trees to the front and rear of the two mounted men.

"I ask again: what is it you want?" said the big Hospitaller. "I assume you mean to rob us. I can assure you we have no money, that's why we're even on this damn road. So you're wasting your time." Despite the overwhelming numbers arrayed against him and his sergeant he seemed fed-up, rather than frightened.

Robin smiled. "You take us for common outlaws, Sir Richard. We see few visitors in the forest, and simply wanted you to share dinner with us. You can tell us the tale of why you're in this damn forest."

The second Hospitaller growled. "They're only peasants, my lord. Let's just kill them and be on our way. Look." He pointed into the trees at Matilda. "They even have women fighting with them!"

Sir Richard-at-Lee looked again at the bowmen around him, and the other armed men on the road. He had dealt with highwaymen before. Generally, such men were poorly disciplined, poorly trained and poorly

213

armed. They would normally shout and make insults at their victims, their bravado often masking their own fear.

These men were not like that. They stared at the Hospitallers in confident, and unnerving, silence. They had the look of well-trained soldiers. The bowmen, Sir Richard felt certain, could each put an arrow through even the Hospitallers' thick plate mail. If he were to take his sergeant's advice and attack these wolf's heads, he wasn't convinced they would be able to kill even one of them before they were cut down themselves.

"Put your sword away, Stephen," said the grey-bearded knight with a sigh, sheathing his own weapon. "It seems we shall dine with these men. We could do with a decent meal anyway."

* * *

Back at their camp, the outlaws relieved the Hospitallers of their weapons. The sergeant had protested, but, as Robin said with a wink, "You would surrender your weapons when you enter a lord's manor house, wouldn't you? Well, this" – and he spread his arms wide, to encompass the greenwood around them – "is *our* house."

The sergeant bristled at Robin's arrogance, while the outlaws laughed, and even Sir Richard smiled a little. He liked this exuberant young man with the pretty girl by his side. He reminded him of his murdered son.

He just hoped the wolf's heads' would allow them to leave their camp alive…

There was a big cauldron of pottage bubbling over their campfire. Whatever the outlaws had available that day had been tossed into the pot. The rabbits Robin and John had caught, some old cabbages that were turning to black and almost spoiled, a few leeks, some mouldy bread, even a couple of old apples.

It was simple fare, but better than many people enjoyed at this time of year, and Friar Tuck knew how to

214

add a touch of salt, parsley or garlic so that it tasted much nicer than it should have.

Robin himself filled a couple of bowls and handed them to Sir Richard and his grimacing sergeant, Stephen, along with some dark barley and rye bread. He gave them ale as well, and accepted Richard's thanks with a grin, before sitting down and getting stuck into his own food.

"So," Robin began, shoving a slice of meat into his mouth, "you look like you've fallen on hard times." He chewed as he looked at the big Hospitaller. "What happened?"

Richard's sergeant put his bowl down angrily. "Sir Richard's business has fuck all to do with you, wolf's head."

The outlaws ignored the man, and Robin continued to eat, looking at Sir Richard, eyebrows raised curiously.

"Peace, Stephen. Finish your pottage," said the knight. His man swore, but picked up his bowl and began to eat again, the rage plain on his face.

"It's no secret," Richard-at-Lee went on, smiling sadly as he swallowed some of his ale. His face dropped again though, as he continued. "My son, God rest him, was in trouble, and, as a result, I owe a great deal of money to the abbot of St Mary's in York. I've just been visiting Lord John de Bray in Hathersage to ask him for a loan so I can repay the abbot, but de Bray laughed in my face. The bastard wants to buy some of my lands from the abbot, to increase his own manor. I should have known he wouldn't help me. My loss will be his gain."

Friar Tuck laughed humourlessly. "If you owe Abbot Ness money, you had better pray to Our Lord for help. That one will bleed you dry."

Sir Richard nodded grimly at the friar. "You have it right, brother. I mortgaged my lands to Ness so I could pay bail for my son, who killed a man – accidentally – in a jousting tournament. He was arrested purely to extort money from me. The abbot's demanding

215

repayment now or he'll seize my lands and I'll lose everything. Of course, the church has strict laws against usury, but no one seems to care. Anyway…that's why I was passing through 'your' forest." He smiled sadly at Robin. "I've been to every lord within a hundred miles trying to borrow the money to repay my debt. That bastard abbot – or the king – must have warned them all not to help me. I haven't managed to raise so much as a shilling." His voice trailed off and he stared into the fire sadly. "Hugh Despenser had my son murdered. I'm paying a debt for nothing."

"You must have noble friends that could help you," Little John said, but the knight shook his head.

"The only one who could help me repay such a huge debt is the Earl of Lancaster, but he has troubles of his own just now – I haven't had the effrontery to approach him for money."

The outlaws had all heard of the earl – a noble lord who actually stood up for the poorest people in his manors. He had petitioned King Edward II for aid on behalf of his tenants whose crops had failed for the past couple of years. As lords went, the earl of Lancaster was a popular one with the lower classes, including the people of Wakefield. Robin had heard his mother and father talking well of the earl many times when he was growing up, as had Much and Matilda.

However, it was common knowledge in the villages around Barnsdale that the king had ignored the earl's petition and relations were strained between the two powerful men. Sir Richard also knew Lancaster needed all his coin to pay for the army he would need to stand against the king.

"What about your Order?" Tuck wondered. "The Hospitallers have more money than they know what to do with, especially these days, since the Templars were disbanded and much of their wealth was passed to you."

Sir Richard shook his head in consternation again. "You haven't been keeping up with things in the wider world, have you, friar? The English Prior of the

Hospitallers – Thomas L'Archer – is a senile old fool. He's ruined us, financially, in this country. I'd have more luck making a pact with the devil!"

The men sat in silence for a moment, eating and drinking, before Matilda asked, "How much do you owe this abbot of St Mary's?"

"One hundred pounds," Sir Richard replied, to gasps and whistles from the outlaws.

"That's a lot of money," Will grunted sympathetically.

"State the fucking obvious," Stephen muttered sarcastically.

"Oh give it a rest," Sir Richard told his sergeant. "These men have fed us and been good hosts. Have some courtesy."

"Good hosts?" Stephen replied. "They'll be robbing us as soon as we're finished this food."

Robin looked at the man, then nodded to Much and the youngster Gareth.

"Search their packs."

"See!"

Sir Richard laughed. "Stephen, what are they going to steal from us? We have nothing!"

Much and Gareth went through the Hospitallers' packs, but turned up only a few small silver coins.

"They're telling the truth, Robin," said Much, after he counted it all. "There's only a few marks here."

The young outlaw leader finished off the last of his ale and smiled at the Hospitaller. "I think we may be able to help each other, Sir Richard-at-Lee."

The knight raised his eyes to the sky and, with a hopeful smile, made the sign of the cross.

* * *

After discussions with Richard and his sergeant, plans were made and preparations begun to rob Lord de Bray's manor house.

Sir Richard and Stephen had helped the outlaws draw up a more complete map of the building, as they had spent time in the areas reserved for noble guests. Along with what Robin and Allan were able to recall from their short time there, they had a fairly detailed plan of de Bray's house to work from.

Sir Richard would make another visit to the manor house, ostensibly to plead again for a loan from de Bray. He and Stephen would wait until the dead of night, and then open the gates for the outlaws to come in and ransack the place.

Will Scarlet was desperate to get moving.

"I'm going to skin that bastard de Bray alive, for what he did to me and my family," he said to Robin, after the other outlaws, and Sir Richard, had gone to sleep.

Robin shook his head.

"No you're not – not yet. If we kill him, the king and all the lords in England will come for us. We'll never survive the winter with so many people hunting us. We're simply going to steal his money and whatever supplies we can carry."

Will looked angrily at his young leader, but it was a sign of his new found respect for Robin that he didn't start a heated argument.

"You seem to know what you're doing." Scarlet sighed. "Rescuing Beth and saving us from Adam proved that. So I'll accept what you're saying for now. But I want revenge on that piece of shit. I *will* have it."

Robin laid a hand on his friend's arm. "You'll have it, Will. But we can't just murder him. That much is obvious. Murdering a lord would bring the king's attention on us. If we think we have it hard now, it would be ten times worse if we just wander in and kill de Bray."

Scarlet shrugged, but looked away in defeat – Robin was right, they had to think of the bigger picture. "I suppose not."

"It's almost Christmas," Robin said, with a sly smile.

"So what?"

"Lord de Bray relies on his tenants' good will and hard work to keep him as wealthy as he is. One of the things he does to keep those tenants loyal is to provide a Christmas feast for them."

Scarlet nodded, but still looked confused. "Aye, I know, I remember being at his Christmas feasts with my family. Before he murdered them…"

"How are the people of Hathersage going to react when they hear their Lord won't be providing their feast this Christmas? Many of them are almost starving as it is – the lord's Christmas meal might be the only chance of a filling meal they'll have all winter."

Will thought about that and smiled. "They'll be pissed off. De Bray won't be popular. It's not like he is anyway – everyone in the village knows he's an evil bastard."

Robin nodded with a sly smile. "We'll take all his food so he can't provide a feast, and all his money so he can't pay his guards. Then we'll stir up trouble in the village, and the people will turn against him. John de Bray will be ruined."

"He'll lose his lands!" Will laughed wickedly. "He'll find himself in a worse place than Sir Richard is in just now, but without us outlaws to help him."

Robin grinned back at Scarlet. "And *then*, when he's landless and penniless, and a nobody…"

Will's face became hard again. "Then, I can kill him."

"Aye, and afterwards we'll provide the villagers with some of the food we steal so they see us as heroes," Robin smiled.

Will glanced at his young companion thoughtfully. It would never have occurred to him to use the situation to impress the people of Hathersage. Clearly the young yeoman from Wakefield had picked up the skill of self-promotion from Adam Gurdon, along with so much of his military expertise.

"I'm glad you're on my side, Hood," he laughed. "You're a devious bastard."

CHAPTER EIGHTEEN

Two days later, in the middle of November, the outlaws gathered up their weapons, put on whatever armour they had cobbled together, and headed for Hathersage. Robin took Will Scaflock, Little John, Matt Groves, Allan-a-Dale, Much and four other men he felt were trustworthy – and skilled – enough to pull off such a dangerous raid. Matilda stayed at the camp with the rest of the men.

The Hospitaller knight Sir Richard, and his sergeant, Stephen, had gone on ahead and gained entry into Lord de Bray's manor house, to beg again for aid from the lord.

Robin had gone with Will Scarlet into Hathersage village to speak to Wilfred the baker, who was overjoyed to see his old friend again. The outlaws needed a wagon to remove de Bray's valuables and food, and Wilf's was as good as any, assuming they could get him to agree to their plan. Robin didn't see a problem in that, and sure enough, Wilf was more than happy to help out.

Little John and the rest of the outlaws had found a place near de Bray's house, well hidden amongst the trees, and far enough from the road that no unwary traveller would stumble across them.

There, they waited for night to fall. Some of the men played dice, some of them drank ale to bolster their nerve, although Little John made sure no one drank too much and still had their wits about them. Tonight called for balls and bravery, not drunken over-confidence.

"Right men," Robin said quietly, appearing with Will from the darkened road to Hathersage. "Gather round."

He pulled a rolled-up piece of parchment from his pack, and spread it out on an old tree stump.

"Wilfred the Baker has agreed to bring his cart along for us to fill with de Bray's stuff. And Sir Richard and Stephen helped us draw a map of the manor house. They've been in the guests' quarters. Me and Allan have also been here before, in the servants' areas. So, with all our knowledge combined, we have a pretty comprehensive plan of the place. It's not complete, obviously. There's parts of this manor house that none of us have ever seen – the upper floor, for example, where Lord de Bray's bed chamber is. But we know roughly how big the house is, and we know roughly how many guards there will be in the place at this time of year."

"How many?" Matt Groves asked.

"We doubt there will be any more than five armed guards," Robin replied. "We don't expect them to be hardened soldiers for the most part. If they have been soldiers, they're probably older men, past their prime."

The outlaws nodded.

"Don't think it's going to be a stroll along the Calder, though, lads," Will cautioned. "We have no idea where the guards might be stationed when we get into the place, and an old soldier can be as dangerous as a young one if he knows how to use his weapons. John de Bray's been a soldier too, so he can handle himself. Remember too, we're not going to be fighting in the open: we'll be inside. Be ready to use your daggers if there's no room to swing a sword."

"There are also more people in this place than just the guards," Robin continued. "The cook, the grooms, the servants in general might not take kindly to a bunch of dirty outlaws running riot in their lord's home. We need to incapacitate *everyone*, women and children included."

"That don't mean killing them!" Little John growled. "We take out the armed men first, but anyone that doesn't fight back we lock in one of the storerooms. If you look at the map, you can see where they are."

"The servants aren't likely to feel any great love for Lord de Bray," Robin said. "Some of them might even want to join with us to ransack the house. Don't let them. We can't have an unknown factor like that roaming around the place until we're finished. Like John says, lock them all away. They can get out afterwards."

"What if they fight back?" Groves wondered.

"Do what you have to do, Matt," Robin said. "Just remember these people aren't our enemies. If they fight back it's probably because they think you're there to slit their throats or rape them."

Robin knew the men he had picked would not slaughter the servants purely because of blood-lust. That was one of the reasons he had chosen these particular men. It was one less thing to have to worry about – if they went around killing their own people, the villagers around Yorkshire would soon turn against them.

"Right," the young leader grunted. "Everyone take a good long look at this map. Learn it as best you can. Any questions about it, ask *before* we go in. Then, if you need it, grab some sleep.

"Sir Richard will, all being well, take out the guard at the gatehouse sometime after midnight, and open the doors for us."

Will smiled wickedly. "Then all we have to do is take the place. And that bastard de Bray is mine."

* * *

"Get much sleep?"

The stocky red-haired guard, Gilbert, shook his head. "No, it's too bloody cold to sleep, even during the day, since his bloody lordship won't keep the fire banked. Miserable fucker."

Thomas grunted agreement and clapped his relief on the back sympathetically.

"All quiet out here?" asked the red-haired guardsman.

Thomas nodded. "Aye, fine. That Hospitaller, Sir Richard-at-Lee, turned up again, with his torn-faced sergeant. He must be fucking desperate to come here again looking for help from de Bray. The noble lord will laugh him out the door after watching him squirm a bit. I feel sorry for him – he seems a decent sort and his son was murdered not long ago."

Gilbert stamped his feet and blew on his hands with a bored expression. "All quiet in there too; everyone seems to be in their beds."

Thomas grunted. "Aye, I think I'll head to bed as well, after I grab some bread and cheese. I'm starving."

With that he wandered off indoors to seek warmth and his supper, as Gilbert yawned and rubbed his hands over the small brazier in the gatehouse.

It was midnight.

An hour later the guard, Gilbert, was asleep at his post.

* * *

"Ready?" Sir Richard-at-Lee rose from his bed and patted his ribs where he had concealed his dagger.

Stephen grunted assent and stood up with his companion.

They would need to move quickly and quietly through the house, so both men left off their plate mail, only wearing their gambesons for protection. They had, as was the custom, surrendered their swords at the gatehouse, but Stephen, like his lord, had concealed his dagger within his clothes. Besides, these were no common soldiers: Richard and his sergeant had fought alongside the elite Hospitaller and Templar knights during the Crusades. These two men were highly trained killers.

Robin and his outlaws could have stumbled upon no better allies.

"Let's go." Sir Richard quietly pulled open the door to their chamber and slipped out into the dimly lit hallway, followed silently by his grim-faced sergeant-at-arms.

When they had arrived back at de Bray's earlier in the evening, the fat lord had not been pleased to see them, although he had been courteous enough to allow them dinner – a thin, greasy, beef broth.

"You again, Hospitaller?" the lord grimaced, spilling his soup down his chins. "What d'you want this time? You'll be expecting me to put you up for the night eh, as well as feed you."

Richard-at-Lee knew his part well, though, and begged de Bray, again, for a loan to pay off his debts. "I'll be ruined, John," he wheedled. "Please, for the love of God, all I ask is fifty pounds. I'll repay you, with interest."

John de Bray snorted derisively. "Listen, you're never going to raise the money you owe the abbot, so you might as well give up now. I've been offered some of your lands for a very fair price too," he grinned wickedly as the big Hospitaller clenched his fists in silent rage. "Once the abbot legally takes full control of your holdings, he's promised to let me have some of them – the ones adjoining my lands, at Kirklees. I'll need a bailiff to take care of them though. Maybe you would think of applying for the position? You know the area after all."

De Bray burst out laughing at that.

"You're a filthy piece of dog shit," Sir Richard growled. "I should" –

"Enough of this!" roared de Bray. "Make no threats against me in my own manor house, Hospitaller. Especially when you're here expecting a bed for the night. Your Order demands that you surrender all your property to them when you join – yet you retained your old lands against those rules. You're lucky I'm not sending a messenger to your Grand Prior telling him of your corruption."

He waved a hand dismissively.

"Get out. You can take your soup with you. My steward will show you to your beds. Be grateful I'm not kicking you back out into the night."

Sir Richard and Stephen had stalked angrily from the room with their bowls of tepid broth.

Now, in the dead of night, the Hospitaller and his man were going to teach Lord de Bray a lesson in humility.

Voices came from the great hall. It sounded like a couple of men were having a late game of dice. Stephen and Sir Richard, who was gingerly carrying his bowl of cold soup with him, clung to the shadows as they crept along the hall silently. Their passing wasn't noticed by the gamers.

"Shouldn't we deal with them just now?" Stephen whispered.

Sir Richard shook his head. "Our priority is opening the gates for the outlaws. We can't get sidetracked."

They crept along the corridor, moving silently between the shadows cast by the few dim torches de Bray allowed to be lit at night.

Sir Richard held up a hand as they reached the front door. "This door creaks a little when opened, I noticed on the way in." He poured his bowl of greasy soup onto the hinges. "Be ready to move fast. If the guard is alert he'll have the whole place awake before we can silence him."

Stephen nodded and pulled his dagger out from the sheath hidden in his thick sock. Richard drew his own weapon and, as gently as he could, raised the wooden bar that held the doors locked.

He pushed it open a touch and the two men cringed, half expecting a creaking noise to betray them, despite the lubricating broth smearing the hinges, but there was no sound from the door, and no cry of alarm from the gatehouse.

Sir Richard slipped out in a crouch and edged towards the main door and the gently glowing light of the guardsman's brazier.

Stephen remained at the inner door, to prevent anyone locking them out and undoing the entire plan.

As the big Hospitaller crept towards the gatehouse the sound of gentle snoring reached him and he shook his head. Falling asleep while on duty was a heinous crime – one that could lead to the deaths of everyone you were supposed to be helping protect. Richard smiled grimly at his own good fortune though, as he peered into the gatehouse and saw the red-haired guard slumped against the wall, completely relaxed and oblivious to the doom that was coming for him.

Sir Richard hadn't expected the man to be asleep, and, as he slid towards the snoring figure, he wondered if he could simply tie him up rather than killing him. The Hospitaller must have made a sound then, though, or perhaps Gilbert the guard finally sensed something amiss, as his eyes flickered open wildly, and he gasped in shock at the sight of the armed man right in front of him.

Sir Richard's dagger slammed straight into the slim white throat of the young guard, crimson spraying wildly, and a low, tortured gurgling filled the small gatehouse.

Richard dropped the body on the floor, and wiped his dagger on Gilbert's sleeve. "God forgive me," he murmured sorrowfully, thinking of his own murdered son, then he quickly lifted the bar on the main doors and swung them wide open.

A moment later the outlaws, all ten of them, appeared like wraiths from the gloom of the night.

"Good work!" Little John, looking even more massive and terrifying in the darkness, clapped Sir Richard on the arm.

"Any trouble?" Robin wondered, as the party moved inside. They pulled the doors closed behind them, although they left them unbarred in case they needed to escape quickly.

Sir Richard shook his head. "One guard. Sleeping, the stupid bastard. I would have spared him, but he woke up and left me no choice. Stephen's inside watching for us." He moved back into the gatehouse as they passed, emerging a moment later with his and Stephen's surrendered swords.

"Let's find de Bray," he growled.

Will grabbed him by the arm. "You leave him alive, Hospitaller!" he warned. "Whatever that bastard's done to you is nothing – *nothing* – compared to the scores I've got to settle with him. We leave him alive – his time will come soon enough."

Richard, the shame of his earlier meeting with de Bray still burning in him, opened his mouth to argue, but the intensity in Will Scarlet's green eyes made him pause.

"Fair enough," he shrugged, eventually, before his wide face broke into an evil grin. "Let's go and clean the fucker out!"

Two of the outlaws remained at the gatehouse to prevent anyone escaping into the village and raising the hue and cry. The rest of the men split into three small groups – one group for each of the storeys in the manor house.

Sir Richard and Stephen tied linen round the lower part of their faces so no one would recognise them, and went with Robin and Little John to the upper level, where the lord and his family's quarters were.

Will Scarlet took Matt Groves and the brawny young lad from Bichill, Arthur, to the middle floor, while Friar Tuck, Much and Allan-a-Dale headed for the undercroft and the servant's area.

"Remember," Robin cautioned quietly. "The guards are probably skilled enough, and they'll be decently armoured, so be careful."

"Aye," Little John nodded. "And try not to kill any of the servants!"

The house appeared silent, and was only very dimly lit by the occasional flickering torch on the grey stone walls. To the outlaws, unused to being indoors, the place gave them an eerie feeling, and enhanced the sense of danger as they all moved into the building, weapons drawn, alert to any threats.

"No talking from here on," Sir Richard told John and Robin, automatically assuming command of his small group. The two outlaws were happy to accept his guidance – he did, after all, know a lot more about manor houses and, indeed, leadership of soldiers. They nodded in agreement and the two Hospitallers led the way silently upstairs.

As they reached the landing, Robin, the lightest on his feet of the four, placed a hand on Sir Richard's arm and moved past him into the long hallway from which the bedrooms led off. The other three waited as the young outlaw leader scouted ahead, taking note of the glow from the occasional guttering torch to make sure he remained hidden by the shadows.

"Huh?" a deep voice grunted in surprise and the sound of a man getting to his feet came to Robin as he passed a dim alcove. The outlaw spun back to his right and slammed the pommel of his dagger into the guard's face. The noise of bone and cartilage breaking seemed deafeningly loud, and the man gave a squeal as Robin moved in and battered the weapon against his temple, knocking him to the floor, blood beginning to cake his broken nose and face. Robin bent down and, taking out some rope, hurriedly tied the unconscious guard's hands and feet together.

He waited, breathlessly, half expecting someone to raise the alarm, but the hallway remained silent.

Robin moved quickly back to his waiting companions and motioned them forward.

"The guard won't bother us. Which room is de Bray's?"

Sir Richard pushed ahead and waved the others after him as he made his way to a door in the middle of the hallway. "You two," the knight whispered, "deal with de Bray and his wife. Me and Stephen will deal with anyone that comes out of these rooms. Since we're going to leave the bastard alive, it'd be best if he doesn't see me, right?"

Robin and John nodded as Richard extinguished all but one of the torches, making the hallway even more foreboding, but also harder for anyone to make out what was going on, should they stumble out of their room in alarm. Richard handed the final torch to Little John and moved off to the end of the hallway, while his sergeant took up a position at the opposite end of the hall.

John placed his hand on de Bray's chamber door and lifted the iron latch slowly, then pushed the door open. A horrendous creaking filled the hallway, and Robin hurried into the bedroom as John's torch flooded the room with a hellish orange glow.

Lord de Bray was a light sleeper and was half out of his luxurious bed when Robin's fist slammed into his face. He roared in surprise but the young outlaw continued his attack, using his elbows and knees to bring de Bray to the ground, whimpering.

Little John had followed his friend into the room and, as de Bray's sour-faced wife opened her mouth to scream, John placed a giant hand round her throat and squeezed gently, cutting off the sound. He shook his head in warning and she shrank back into her pillow, eyes bulging in terror at the enormous bearded man carrying a flaming torch into her bedroom.

Robin moved fast, quickly using the rope in his pack to tie and gag the lord and his wife. He and Little John looked out into the hallway to make sure Sir Richard and his sergeant had dealt with any other threats. All was well. The Hospitallers had quietly dealt with a couple of guests who had peered out of their doors to see what was happening.

Now they began to move into each room to tie up whoever they found.

"Help them," Robin growled to Little John, before he headed to the stairs and made his way to the middle floor.

Arthur stood nervously, fingering his dagger, but his eyes lit up when he saw Robin. The botched robbery with Harry Half-hand seemed a lifetime ago now –

Robin had certainly learned a lot since then, Arthur realised.

"Everything all right?" Hood asked.

Arthur nodded. "Aye, fine. There was a guard, but Will took care of him. They're clearing the other rooms now."

Robin smiled encouragingly at the young man and squeezed his shoulder. "Good work! You keep guard here until Will and Matt are done. De Bray's tied up, the upper floor's clear. I'll check on the undercroft." He flashed a grin and moved quickly back to the stairwell.

As he headed down to the lower floor, Robin was dismayed to hear shouts and the clatter of weapons. They had expected the undercroft to be the easiest part of the building to subdue, it being occupied by servants. What the hell had gone wrong?

He burst through the door into the undercroft and was met with the sight of his men trying to hold off an attack by a gang of servants wielding kitchen utensils. Much and Allan-a-Dale, marshalled by a sweating Friar Tuck, were using their staffs desperately, backs to the wall, clearly trying not to hurt anyone.

Robin shook his head and drew his sword.

"Enough!" he roared, and moved into the room.

The servants warily stopped their attack, eyes moving to watch this new threat, while the three outlaws kept their staffs raised defensively.

"Your lord is tied up, with his wife, in their bed chamber," Robin shouted, glaring at the servants. "I'm Robin Hood. My men have taken the house; the upper floors are subdued. The only reason you people are still alive is the fact you're peasants and yeomen, like us, and we don't kill our own kind." The outlaw leader pointed his sword at the biggest servant, a man almost as tall as Little John although nowhere near as brawny. "Now drop your fucking weapons and get into that storeroom there. All of you!"

231

The servants all looked to the big man leading them, unsure what to do. They'd all heard of Robin Hood. He was a murderer. Merciless, the stories said, he'd killed the bailiff of Wakefield and half a dozen of his men without blinking. Yet here he was being merciful. Was it a trick? The young man seemed earnest enough.

"What do we do, Harold?" one of the servants asked the big man Robin had addressed.

Harold, adrenaline rushing through him, saw glory beckoning. If he could stop these raiders, Lord de Bray would surely reward him. Maybe promote him to the position of steward. He raised the thick wooden broom handle he carried and flew towards Robin, a maniacal grin on his face. "Kill them!" he screamed, swinging the pole down towards the outlaw with terrible force.

Robin bent his knees and rolled to his left as the lanky servant flew past him, broom handle cracking off the stone floor and snapping in the middle.

The other servants remained undecided, as they stood watching the confrontation. Robin knew he had to finish it quickly, before the rest found their courage, or there would be a bloodbath down here.

He came up swinging his sword and felt it bite into the side of Harold's knee. A terrible scream filled the cold, dimly lit room, and the servants shrank back in horror.

Robin stepped forward, ready to smash the hilt of his sword into the servant's temple, but the big man on the ground was desperate and his snapped wooden pole shot out desperately, slicing deeply into Robin's thigh.

The young outlaw gave a cry of rage and, instinctively, brought his sword down on the tall servant's skull, cracking it wide open. Blood and brain matter spilled on the floor, as the watching servants cried out, and Robin dropped to one knee, his injured leg giving way beneath him.

"Fucking deal with them, Tuck!" he roared, squeezing the wound on his leg.

The big friar, with Much and Allan at his side, moved forward forbiddingly, shepherding the servants towards one of the store rooms. The servants were really frightened now – none of them had ever seen a man killed before, especially not so violently, and they moved willingly enough, most of them crying, or gagging at the sight of their broken comrade.

Tuck slammed the door shut, dropping the heavy latch into place once the prisoners were all safely inside, and hurried over to Robin. Much and Allan piled some heavy sacks of food against the door to stop anyone escaping for a while.

"Are you all right?" Tuck asked, checking the nasty wound on his leader's leg.

Robin grunted. "Aye, it's not that deep, but it hurts like hell. Help me up."

Much and Allan grasped an arm each and lifted Robin to his feet.

Tuck found a piece of linen used for cleaning dishes and tied it round Robin's thigh tightly. The friar had also found a few wineskins and he handed one to his young friend now.

"Right, check the storerooms for anything valuable," Robin ordered, taking a long pull of the strong wine. "And open the doors" – he grimaced, as the vinegary taste hit his throat – "so Wilfred can get his wagon in. It looks like we've had a successful night's work, lads!"

A muffled voice came from the locked storeroom where the servants were imprisoned. "You'd better get out of here, Hood! One of our men made a run for it when we saw your lot coming – he'll be in Hathersage soon, bringing the tithing up here after you!"

Robin swore colourfully. He had two men stationed at the gates to stop anyone escaping, so he knew any runaways wouldn't be getting through to raise the hue and cry, but he hoped his men had managed to subdue the servant without killing him.

"Damn it," he grunted as he moved back to the stairwell. "Let's move quickly now lads, before anyone else tries to be a hero."

He slowly climbed the stairs back up to the first floor, where Arthur was helping Will Scarlet and Matt Groves to pile valuables in the hall, ready to be carried downstairs to Wilfred's waiting wagon.

Robin nodded in satisfaction and made his way back up to the top floor. The pain in his wounded leg had lessened a little thanks to the tight bandage Tuck had applied, and the strong wine.

As he hobbled back towards Lord de Bray's bedroom he heard Little John's great baritone voice raised threateningly. Sir Richard-at-Lee and his sergeant, Stephen, were, like Will and Matt a floor beneath, collecting any valuables they could find in the hallway.

Robin limped into de Bray's room. The lord's wife was lying, bound hand and foot, on their bed. The fear had gone from her eyes and she looked at Robin contemptuously as he came through the door.

John had tied the lord's fat hands to the arms of a chair, and was questioning him angrily about the location of his money. Bruising was beginning to show on his face, where John had tried more forcibly to extract some information.

"What's happening?" Robin asked, quietly, in the silence between one of John's shouted questions.

The huge outlaw glared at his young friend in annoyance. "The bastard won't tell me where his money's stashed."

As he looked at the smug-faced noble, the knowledge of what this man had done to little Beth and her family filled Robin's mind. In a cold rage he drew his dagger and moved to stand in front of de Bray, who smiled dismally. "You won't harm me, I've -"

Robin placed his blade on de Bray's right pinkie and pressed down hard. Blood pulsed wetly and there was an almost imperceptible little thud as the severed digit landed on the lavishly carpeted floor. De Bray screamed like an animal, and thrashed against the chair.

Little John looked at Robin in surprise, then shrugged and punched de Bray in the guts again, silencing the roaring man.

"Don't fuck me about!" Robin shouted, pressing his face against the whimpering nobleman's. "That's nothing compared to what'll happen if I let Will Scaflock in here! Now – where's the money?"

De Bray struggled against his bonds, but his feet were also tied to the chair and his efforts simply wasted energy. His eyes bulged fearfully at the long-forgotten name of Scaflock, but he spat a mouthful of blood at Robin and muttered an oath in French.

Robin looked out into the hallway, and nodded in satisfaction as he saw Sir Richard and his sergeant had cleared all the valuables down to the undercroft. They were ready to leave – all they needed was the lord's money.

"Last chance," Robin told de Bray, as he stood over the bruised and bound Lord of Hathersage. "I don't have all night, and you won't have any fingers, or toes, or a cock, or a tongue, left, unless you tell us where the money is." The young outlaw placed his dagger over the remaining three fingers of de Bray's right hand, and pressed gently, drawing more blood from the fat digits.

"It's hidden over there!" de Bray screamed, his mouth foaming with fear. "Behind the wardrobe, there's a concealed door, the money's all in there!"

His wife mumbled, and tried to shout through her gag, but it was her husband she was raging at, furious at the fact he had given up their wealth to these outlaws.

"Oh shut up, you sour old bitch!" de Bray shouted back at her, which only made her grunt into the gag even more ferociously.

Little John laughed cheerfully over at Robin. "Young love, eh?"

He shoved the heavy oak wardrobe out of the way effortlessly. In the gloomy lighting there was no sign of any obvious hidden doorway, so he and Robin tapped on the wall systematically, looking for hollow spots.

It didn't take long to find the cupboard, and Robin prised it open with his dagger. Inside was a large pile of silver coins of all sizes.

Little John growled happily, like a great mastiff having his ears rubbed. "How much do you think's in there, Robin?"

The outlaw leader shrugged, and began scooping the cash into a sack. "We'll find out back in the greenwood when we count it."

De Bray and his wife had given up on their one-sided conversation, and stared furiously at the two outlaws.

"They don't look angry enough," Robin said, thoughtfully, rubbing his injured leg. "Search the room for more hidden compartments." He watched the nobleman closely, and was rewarded with a look of desperation as John began tapping the other walls in the room.

There was more still to be found here.

Before the night was out, they would effectively ruin this man. Robin would be sure of that before they made their way back to the forests of Barnsdale.

CHAPTER NINETEEN

"She's dying!"

John Hood shook his head in exasperation, waving a hand at his wife to silence her. "No, she's not, woman!" He stroked his daughter's pale forehead gently, as tears blurred his vision. "She'll be fine," he muttered.

They sat in their little house in Wakefield, smoky from the fire they had banked high to try and keep the winter chill from their poorly daughter Marjorie's bones.

A cauldron of pottage was cooking over the hearth, but it was a thin concoction – mostly water and oatmeal, with no vegetables and little nutritional value. John and Martha kept their strength up by eating lots of bread, but Marjorie had found it difficult to digest the solid food recently, so had been eating little but the watery broth her mother made.

Martha sobbed at the sight of her little girl – thin at the best of times, but now weak and bedridden as winter closed in and good, nutritious, food became ever scarcer. "She's ill, John. We haven't been feeding her well enough."

John nodded disconsolately. "Christ knows how Robin turned out so big and strong," he muttered, "while Rebekah and Marjorie have always been so weak."

"Robin!" Martha breathed, staring at her husband.

"What about him?"

"He can help! He might be able to find food from somewhere – buy it from one of the other villages! Steal it from someone!"

"Christ almighty, woman," John growled. "Now you want your son to steal food from starving people?"

237

"I never said from starving people," his wife retorted. "Some people must have more than they need. Maybe Robin can get fruit and vegetables from them."

They sat in silence then, lost in thought, watching their daughter breathing shallowly, and wondering if their outlaw son could help save his little sister's life.

* * *

The outlaws had piled Wilfred the baker's wagon high with all the money and food they found in Lord de Bray's house. John had discovered another two hidden compartments in the noble's bedroom and Robin felt fairly sure they had found everything there was to find. The livid, then pleading, reaction of the lord and his lady gave Robin confidence in the complete success of their evening's efforts.

Robin and his men had completely emptied the manor house of anything of value. If they could get the lot back to Sir Richard's castle in Kirklees de Bray would be ruined, and the Hospitaller would be able to pay off the grasping Abbot Ness of St. Mary's.

It had been a good night's work.

"All right, Will?" Robin grinned and slapped Scarlet on the back contentedly.

Will nodded, but didn't share Robin's smile. "This is all very good, Robin, we've done well here. But I won't be happy until that bastard is forced out of his house and ruined. Then I'll hunt him down and really make him pay for what he did to Beth and the rest of my family."

Robin promised they'd exact their revenge on de Bray soon, and gave a shout for the wagon to get moving. The inhabitants of the house were all locked in storerooms or cupboards – the outlaws had only been forced to kill two of the guards. The rest, including Thomas, Robin was pleased to see, had thrown down their weapons and allowed themselves to be imprisoned.

The captives were left with enough food and water to last a couple of days until someone discovered them or they managed to break the doors down. By that time the outlaws would be safely away with their plunder.

De Bray and his wife were locked in their own bedroom, screaming at each other, which at least made Will crack a small, grim, smile.

As the cart trundled ponderously out through the gatehouse and onto the road towards Kirklees, Robin sent Matt Groves and Allan-a-Dale to scout the road ahead, just in case anyone tried to stop them. It was the middle of the night, though, and there should be no travellers around at this time.

Sure enough, they met no one during their nocturnal journey, and were safely inside Sir Richard's castle in Kirklees before daybreak.

The Hospitaller was looking forward to a good night's sleep before paying off his debt to the abbot...

* * *

Abbot Ness, seated on the misericord of St Mary's Abbey, took a sip of his wine, a very fine red imported from Gascony, and took another mouthful of his dinner. The majority of the monks were eating fish in the refectory, where meat eating was not allowed, but the abbot stuffed himself on beef, pork and bacon in the misericord every day except Wednesday, Friday and Saturday, assuming it wasn't Lent or Advent. Today, a Tuesday, the abbot was gorging himself on umbles, a great favourite of his: sheep entrails cooked in dark ale, with breadcrumbs and imported spices.

Outside, frost coated the stained glass windows and thick snow carpeted many parts of the country, but in the misericord of St Mary's a roaring fire filled the room with heat and light and Abbot Ness leaned back in his chair, grinning contentedly.

He was entertaining a guest, and was in a very good mood. Today was the deadline for Sir Richard-at-Lee to repay his debt to the abbot. If the Hospitaller knight did not show up with one hundred pounds of silver, the abbot would become the owner of much of the lands adjoining Kirklees. He had already agreed to sell most of it to Lord John de Bray, a neighbour of Richard-at-Lee.

His guest was Sir Henry de Faucumberg, High Sheriff of Nottingham and Yorkshire. The abbot needed a representative of King Edward's justice to make his seizure of Sir Richard's lands legal. Abbot Ness had wined and dined the sheriff all day to gain his good favour, and had given him a substantial bribe of twenty pounds to make sure he was on his side.

"Enjoying the wine, Henry?" Abbot Ness asked, swilling a mouthful of his own, eyes already red and bleary from too much of the stuff.

"Very much, abbot," De Faucumberg smiled, raising his silver goblet in salute to the Gascony's quality. "I've enjoyed your hospitality today." He placed the cup back on the table and looked seriously at the clergyman. "Don't mistake me though. I may have accepted your bribe"-

"It was merely a contribution from the church towards the running of the king's estates"- Abbot Ness replied hastily, trying to look shocked.

"As I say," the sheriff continued as though he hadn't heard the abbot, "I accepted your bribe. We're men of the world, you and I. We understand how things are done. If we can help each other out while profiting ourselves, it's all to the good. Please be aware though, I will help you only so long as what you're doing is entirely legal."

Ness nodded enthusiastically. "Legal. Of course – you can be certain of it! I hope this can be the first of many such visits, sheriff. I'm a very ambitious man, and it's always good to have someone like you onside."

De Faucumberg smiled, and spooned some of his meal into his mouth with a grunt of agreement as a freezing winter wind howled against the windows, the sound of whistling coming from various parts of the room as the draught forced its icy way in. "It's rumoured that this Sir Richard-at-Lee has been conspiring with the Earl of Lancaster to undermine the king," the sheriff went on, hunching his shoulders against the cold. "As you know, I'm the king's man, so if you can bring down the Hospitaller legally, you will find me helpful in future."

"Abbot," a young monk came quietly over the small round table where the abbot and his guest were eating. "The Hospitaller is here to see you."

Ness grinned. "At last, he's finally turned up. This will be fun."

The sheriff finished the last of his dinner and pushed the plate to one side. "You're sure he won't have your money?"

The abbot laughed wickedly. "Not a chance. He's been over the whole north of England trying to borrow money, but no one would help him. I made it known the Church wouldn't look kindly on anyone loaning money to the father of a murderer."

De Faucumberg smiled and picked at a bowl of grapes. He liked how the abbot thought, although he would know to be wary of him in future.

"Show him in, then, lad," Ness shouted at the young monk, who scurried off, to return a few seconds later with Sir Richard-at-Lee in tow. Stephen, his sergeant, had been told to wait outside.

The big Hospitaller was, as expected, poorly dressed, Abbot Ness noted with a smirk, eyeing the man up and down. His armour was dented, his clothes torn and mended numerous times, and he even looked dirty. Almost as if he was trying to look pitiful in the hope of rousing some Christian charity in the abbot. Ness almost burst out laughing at that thought, but restrained himself to a gleeful smile.

Sir Richard walked over to the small table and knelt humbly before the two nobles. His frayed leather scabbard got stuck under his legs, almost tripping him.

"Sir Richard," said the abbot, emphasising the epithet sarcastically. "You came, as agreed. Today is the deadline for repaying your debt to me."

"My lord abbot," Richard bowed his head in assent.

"Well? You have my money?" Ness leaned forward in his seat, rolling his extravagant wine goblet in his hands, the hugely expensive liquid spilling on the table almost obscenely.

Sir Richard shifted his weight to a slightly more comfortable position. The abbot had left him kneeling on the floor like a common servant, in a belittling breach of etiquette.

"My lord," Sir Richard began, addressing the two noblemen before him.

"Here it comes: the begging," Ness whispered theatrically to the sheriff, who nodded distastefully. The sight of a once proud warrior monk bowing and scraping on the cold stone floor disturbed de Faucumberg, even although he desired the ruin of a possible rebel.

The Hospitaller knight kept his eyes on the floor, ignoring the insulting treatment as he continued. "One hundred pounds is a huge amount of silver. You understand my son did not kill that man on purpose; he was wrongly accused. It was an accident."

"Not my concern," the abbot snapped. "The law set your son's bail at that amount, and I loaned it to you in good faith. Today you repay me, or I legally," he glanced at the sheriff, "seize your lands and property. It's clear to us you're a man living in poverty. You're dressed in the manner of a peasant – despite that once fine Hospitaller armour you insist on wearing."

Sir Richard's ears turned red, but he kept his face down until the churchman finished his tirade.

"Abbot Ness, you know I fought bravely in the Holy Land, in our Lord's service. Could I not repay some of my debt to you in your service, perhaps as a bailiff or steward?"

"The man's desperate." Sir Henry growled, feeling genuinely uncomfortable at what he was seeing.

The abbot roared with laughter, wine and crumbs spilling from his mouth unpleasantly, and the sheriff was almost tempted to walk out the room in disgust.

Abbot Ness wiped the spittle from his lips and, after a time, his face became hard again.

"Enough of this, nonsense, Hospitaller. Don't disgrace your knightly Order – or yourself – any further. Since you've barely a mark to your name, I'll call on my colleague here, the sheriff of Nottingham and Yorkshire, Sir Henry de Faucumberg -"

"'Henry of Hell,'" shouted Richard angrily, referencing the not entirely fair nickname the sheriff had earned for the rumoured treatment of prisoners in his dungeons. The knight raised his eyes at last to glare at his two tormentors.

"I will call on Sir Henry -of Hell – as you say," the abbot laughed loudly at that, as de Faucumberg glared back coldly, "to witness my seizure of your lands and estates."

"Fine," the sheriff growled, "let's get this over with." He finished his wine and refilled his goblet, hoping the alcohol would make this whole episode more palatable. Abbot Ness produced a small collection of legal documents from a leather bag beside his chair.

Sir Richard-at-Lee stared contemptuously at the drink sodden abbot seated before him. "You've kept me kneeling on your stone floor like a peasant-"

"You *are* a peasant, now!" the abbot sniggered, almost choking on another mouthful of wine at his joke.

Sir Richard stood up.

Despite his shabby armour and clothing, he was a powerfully built man with the unmistakeable bearing of a knight. He strode over and stood menacingly in front of the sturdy wooden table Abbot Ness and the sheriff sat at, glaring malevolently down at them, his dark eyes strangely triumphant.

The two seated men shrank back, as Sir Richard opened his lungs and roared, as if in the middle of a pitched battle somewhere in the Holy Land, "Stephen! Bring me the bag!"

His sergeant appeared on cue, carrying a clearly heavy sack, and handed it to his master, with an angry glance at Abbot Ness, who sat with a look of bewilderment on his flushed, round face.

Sir Richard took the bag and leaned forward to shove his face right up against the abbot's. "Here, you fucking leech. Your money!" and he upended the big sack onto the table. "The rest is outside in a locked chest. Your lackeys are counting it now."

The abbot and the sheriff stared open-mouthed as a great pile of silver coins of all sizes rained down onto the table, spilling onto the floor and into their laps as they instinctively grasped at them.

In total, the outlaws had managed to steal £160 in cash from Lord John de Bray's manor house, plus a quarter of that again in jewellery, weaponry, ornaments and other valuables. They also managed to carry off a sizeable amount of food which they traded or simply gifted away in the villages surrounding Barnsdale.

The Hospitaller and his sergeant were given the generous sum of £30 for their help in the robbery, while Robin Hood had agreed to lend Sir Richard the £100 he needed to repay his debt to Abbot Ness, to be repaid whenever the knight was able. The outlaws kept what remained of the spoils – still a considerable sum – in their communal fund to help see them through the winter.

Sir Richard was in the outlaws' debt, but he would no longer be in the abbot's.

"One hundred pounds!" the big Hospitaller growled. "Exactly what I owe you. If you'd been courteous and treated me with the respect due a

Hospitaller knight, you might have been rewarded with more."

The abbot looked to Sir Henry de Faucumberg for support, but the sheriff of Nottingham had quietly pushed his chair away from Ness and sat apart as if none of this was any of his business, a small smile of approval playing around his lips. The abbot opened his mouth to say something, but Sir Richard slammed his hand down on the table with a huge thud, cutting him off.

"Shut your mouth, priest!"

He reached forward and lifted the scrolls Ness had laid on the table before him: the documents needed to legally take ownership of the Hospitaller's manor.

"My lands" – Richard tore the documents in half – "remain" – he ripped them again – "mine! Your sheriff of Yorkshire and Nottingham can witness *that*!"

Sir Richard leaned forward all of a sudden and grabbed hold of the abbot's robes, pulling him halfway across the table, so their faces almost touched. The big knight took the torn papers and shoved them into the face of the clergyman, grinning in satisfaction.

"And these scrolls – you can shove these up your arse!"

He pushed the abbot backwards onto his chair, but the wine had taken its toll and the churchman lost his balance, chair and torn scrolls skittering wildly, as he sprawled on the floor, his face white in shock.

Sir Henry de Faucumberg sat and enjoyed the show. He raised an eyebrow and smiled a wry farewell to Sir Richard as the Hospitaller and his sergeant stormed from the room, fists clenched.

For a while Abbot Ness simply lay on the floor: humiliated, frightened and embarrassed. Then, he began to wonder.

"Where?" he asked, almost to himself, as he grasped the arm of his chair and dragged himself into it. "Where did he get that money?"

The sheriff refilled his wine cup and waved his hand dismissively. "What does it matter? At least you have your money back."

CHAPTER TWENTY

For a while, things in the greenwood became quiet again, as the weather worsened and December began with thick, heavy snows, stopping all but the most determined traveller from passing through the outlaws' domain.

With the weather so bad, there was little chance of the law either hunting for them or stumbling upon their camp by chance. The bailiffs and foresters in the closest towns and villages had more pressing things to attend to than a wild-goose chase in an icy forest populated by dangerous wolf's heads.

So, Will Scarlet had led them through the frozen forest to a new campsite, previously chosen by the now dead Adam Gurdon. There were a couple of good-sized caves to store their small supplies of food and drink, or shelter in for a while if the weather got really bad, and thick trees all around against which they erected sturdy lean-tos, covered in thick hides stolen from merchants. The trees here around here were mainly yew, with juniper and holly bushes also in thick clumps. So, unlike most of the trees familiar to the outlaws, such as the oak, beech, hazel or ash, they retained much of their foliage and provided excellent shelter even in the winter, dispersing the tell-tale smoke from campfires and forming a thick protective canopy against the snow, wind and freezing December rains.

Robin wondered if the evergreen trees and bushes in this part of the forest had been planted by a previous sheriff, to provide winter cover for the animals the king loved to hunt.

The outlaws had enough food and ale to survive, with plenty of money to buy more if they could find it in the local villages. Of the money left over from their raid on John de Bray's manor house, Robin kept most of it in the common fund, and split ten pounds fairly between the men, who used some of it to buy decent winter clothes and blankets.

Despite the cold, then, the small band of outlaws was comfortable. They spent the days training, and hunting the meagre game they managed to find. The nights were occupied by drinking ale round warm fires, laughing and telling tales, singing and playing dice. Some night's small groups would head off to one of the larger towns to visit the inns and brothels.

Robin was glad of this, otherwise the atmosphere around the camp could have become severely strained when Matilda joined them and began to share his bed each night. As it was, he knew some of the men muttered amongst themselves, asking why Robin should be allowed his woman around the camp when none of them had such a luxury.

As a result, Robin made sure Matilda was pushed hard during combat training. He had to show the men she was a useful member of their group, not a passenger.

Thankfully, the girl was a quick learner, and made up for her lack of strength with speed and enthusiasm. She could not pull the great longbows the men used – that took literally years of practice to build the strength required – but her accuracy with a smaller-sized hunting bow was such that the other outlaws appreciated her skill. She also learned how to use a smaller quarterstaff and the short sword Robin gave her well enough.

Matilda was no killing machine, like Will or Little John or Robin himself, and she was untried in battle, but she pushed herself to show everyone she was no giggling little girl just hanging around to share a bed with their young leader.

"Ow! In the name of Christ, lass!" Will yelped as her quarterstaff deftly deflected his, before she brought it up and cracked it against his chin. "That was sore!"

The men howled with laughter as Matilda held the tip of her staff threateningly at Scarlet's face. "That's what you get for under-estimating me," she smiled.

The gruff outlaw stooped to retrieve his dropped quarterstaff, his eyes remaining warily fixed on Matilda's weapon. "Aye, I won't be doing that again," he muttered irritably, but his eyes glittered with good humour.

Little John nudged Robin as they watched the sparring. "Your girl's fitted in well enough. I was worried she might not be much use – it wouldn't take a lot for Matt Groves to start complaining and maybe turn the men sour against her."

Robin nodded affectionately. "Aye. She can also cook a tastier rabbit stew than Tuck, which has helped keep even Matt happy enough."

During this time, Robin was genuinely happy. Like all the outlaws, he had a deep resentment of the system that had made him a social outcast – a wolf's head. But the camaraderie of his small group and the companionship of the girl he had loved since he was a boy made the onset of winter seem more pleasant than he would have expected.

One person in particular, though, frowned on Robin's relationship with Matilda.

"Are you going to marry that girl, or not?" Friar Tuck demanded one morning as the pair sat eating a small breakfast of bread and cheese washed down with ale.

Robin was surprised. As far as he was concerned, he and Matilda *were* married. They had shared a bed. They had even shared simple vows with each other in private one night in the darkness. What else was needed?

"We are married, Tuck," he replied, tearing into the end of his small dark loaf.

"Not in the eyes of the church, you're not," Tuck told him, disapprovingly. "Clandestine marriage is not recognised by Our Lord."

Robin shrugged. Hardly anyone bothered with a church ceremony when they wed, why should he, an outlaw, care about it? Matilda was his wife as far as he was concerned.

The friar knew Robin loved the young girl. More than most men loved their partners, certainly. Still, he was a religious man, and he wanted Robin and Matilda to have their union properly blessed.

Robin didn't really care, but he could see it was important to his friend, so he smiled at the friar and agreed to a formal ceremony.

Tuck grinned, his eyes gleaming happily, and the two men continued to eat their meal in companionable silence for a while.

"You know, Tuck..." Robin tailed off, not sure how to continue the conversation. Although he thought of Friar Tuck as a good friend, he never knew anything about the big clergyman. Not even his real name.

"Spit it out, lad!" Tuck demanded with a grin, knowing where this was going. The friar had expected this conversation ever since he had joined the outlaws, and was surprised it had taken so long for one of them to ask him about his past. It showed that they were all friends, who would put their lives on the line for each other, but would also allow one another their secrets.

"I don't understand why you joined us," Robin said, turning to look at the tonsured friar in puzzlement. "You had no need to, as far as I could see. Aye, we stole a lot of money from you and your friends, but...why would you join us? We killed most of the guards, I doubt the abbot would expect you to have fought us all off and brought back his money, so. . ?" Robin shook his head, eyes fixed on Tuck, hoping for an answer without explicitly asking for it.

Robin wanted to know Tuck's reasons for joining them because, like all of the other outlaws, he was curious. But Robin was also now the leader of the outlaw band, and Tuck's willingness to join them seemed curious to him. He had to clear it up, in his own mind if nothing else.

Why would a reasonably well off friar join a band of outlaws?

"I wasn't always a friar," the cheerful Franciscan told him. Neither had he always been called Tuck, which was simply a nickname for the way he wore his grey robes.

"My real name is – was – Robert Stafford, and, as a young man, I was part of a travelling jongleur group.

"The group included a variety of performers and entertainments. We had the lot: minstrels and fools, acrobats, bear baiting, cock fighting, and my own particular skill: wrestling."

There would be a large prize, dependant on the number of entrants, but generally around twenty shillings – more than a fortnight's wages to most people – offered to the winner of the wrestling competition. The local men would pay a fee to join in, and the last man standing would walk away with the money.

"I would spend the day mingling with the locals," Tuck set down his bread and moved his big, chubby fingers to and fro, mimicking a walking motion, "acting like one of them, and then I'd enter myself in the wrestling tournament."

He wasn't outlandishly tall, at a shade under six feet, or noticeably well muscled, being rather portly even back then. He was then, as now, a rather unassuming individual. He had no great charisma to draw people's attention. So his appearance never put people off entering the competition.

"What the locals never knew was that I'm much stronger than I look, and I trained long and hard as a wrestler," the friar went on, biting off a large chunk of cheese and swallowing some of his ale noisily. "I know how to use my body-weight, how to throw people, how to hurt them enough to stop them fighting back without damaging them. I was, generally, unbeatable, even with opponents much bigger than myself."

In nine towns out of ten, Stafford won the wrestling, his jongleur group made a fat profit since they never had to pay the prize to the winner, and no one was any the wiser.

"I enjoyed the life." Tuck smiled distantly. "It was easy enough – unless a town had some big hard bastard that managed to beat me – and I was well paid. I could eat and drink my fill after I'd taken care of business at each fair, and I never saw myself as a cheat. After all, if someone could beat me, they would win their twenty shillings: it was always paid out on the very few occasions it had happened."

It was, he thought, a fair fight, one-on-one, whether the entrants knew he was a ringer or not. That was important to him, because he was, essentially, a good man, with a strong moral code. He didn't like the idea of cheating people, so he frowned on some of the other members of his group, who used loaded dice, sleight of hand, and other unfair means of fleecing people out of their money.

For three years Robert Stafford travelled with his jongleur group, enjoying himself, until one afternoon, in the village of Elton, by the banks of the River Nene, he was discovered.

"It was inevitable, I suppose," Tuck sighed, his wide shoulders slumping. "I'm surprised I managed to avoid detection for so long. In Elton, though, I was spotted by a man I'd beaten a few weeks before in King's Ripton. The man realised what was going on and gathered a few of the locals together as my wrestling competition began."

A while later, after Robert had won as usual – beating a giant, red-faced, bald man in the final round – he took himself off to the local alehouse. Supposedly, the landlady had just brewed a vat, but Stafford could tell by the liberal addition of herbs and honey this was no fresh brew.

"Not that I cared much," he grinned sheepishly. "After a few mugs of it, cheap at just a shilling per gallon, I could have been handed a jug of piss and swallowed it gladly."

Robin laughed as the Franciscan took a long pull of his ale and belched in appreciation.

"I knew I'd had enough so I stumbled out the door and started making my way back to our camp. I remember weaving through a really dark part of the village, near the outskirts I think, then... I never knew what hit me," he shook his head with a wince. "I was too drunk. I just realised, suddenly, that I was lying flat on my face, in the road, with blows raining down on me from all sides."

Instinctively, he had curled himself into a ball to protect his head and stomach, too inebriated and bewildered to even think about trying to land a blow of his own.

"It went on for a long time," he winced, his breakfast forgotten as he recalled the pain and fear of that night. "Or at least it seemed to; maybe it was only a few seconds, I don't know. I was vaguely aware of voices shouting at one particular person to stop. It was the man from King's Ripton they were shouting at. He was actually crying with rage as he battered the shit out of me."

Eventually, the locals dragged him off, before they all had to face a murder charge, and the man, his fury almost spent, shrugged off the men holding him back.

"I finally managed to get it together enough to look up at him just as he spat in my face. He shouted at me, demanding to know if I remembered him." The friar looked at Robin with a sad smile. "I didn't even know what day of the week it was, never mind remember one face from the hundreds I'd seen that week. I couldn't answer, couldn't even shake my head, so I just stared at him as he screamed in my face about how I'd stolen his money in my rigged competition. Apparently he'd owed his lord the money and had been thrown out his house – along with his family – because I'd cheated it from him... He was about as pissed as me," Tuck sighed.

Even in his intoxicated, and severely beaten, state, Tuck knew his attacker's logic was severely flawed, but he couldn't say anything to refute the man's tirade, so he simply closed his eyes and wished his rapidly purpling limbs and torso weren't beginning to hurt so badly.

The attackers faded away into the night then, thankfully, dragging the man from King's Ripton with them to stop him killing the prone wrestler, and Stafford passed out. Some of the minstrels, themselves returning to camp after a few ales, found their jovial wrestler unconscious on the road and carried him back to his pallet.

"When I woke in the morning my whole body ached terribly, but I was lucky," the friar smiled and shook his tonsured head ruefully, picking up his loaf again and swallowing a mouthful. "No bones were broken and my thick skull was intact, although I'm sure a number of my ribs had been cracked. One of the minstrels brought me more of the local ale with henbane in it, which alleviated the pain a bit."

The jongleur troupe moved on the next day, to Peterborough.

Stafford never wrestled for them again. He left them a few days later, when his bruises had healed somewhat and he was able to travel on his own again.

What the King's Ripton man had said to him had hurt Stafford deeper than any of the physical blows he had received that night.

"I knew it was a foolish case he'd made against me," the friar grunted. "The man had obviously frittered away all his money gambling, drinking and whatever else. I hadn't forced him to enter the wrestling competition with the last of his wages, he made that choice himself. I was just a convenient scapegoat for his miserable weaknesses."

254

Robert Stafford knew all this. He was no fool.

"Yet...there had been an element of truth to what the man had said," the clergyman admitted miserably. "Men entered the wrestling competition for fun, expecting to be up against untrained, regular men like themselves. They felt they had a fair chance of winning the prize.

"Would they have entered the competition if they had known how skilled I was? No, most of them probably wouldn't have done."

Stafford had never looked at it from their side before, and he realised now, he *had* cheated all those men out of their very hard-earned money. "It *hadn't* been a fair fight," he muttered, "when I'd beaten all those countless farmers, labourers, peasants and yeomen in the towns and villages. Not really."

No, no one had forced those men to enter the competition, but they had done so expecting a fair chance to win, and that had never been the case. How many of them had left their families without food to eat that night, or behind with their rent, because Stafford had tricked them out of their day's wages?

"The thoughts tormented me," he confessed to his young leader. "Aye, I enjoyed fighting, and winning... but I couldn't handle the idea that I had cheated honest men."

So he gathered his belongings, and the money he had saved over the past three years, and left the troupe.

His savings had been quite sizeable, and he was reasonably comfortable for a while. But his attempts to find suitable employment all failed – he was too used to an easy life, and couldn't bring himself to do back breaking labour in a field all day for just a shilling and a meal. Without any skills other than fighting, his options for employment were limited.

He had decided, without much enthusiasm, to become a mercenary. His martial skills were not limited to wrestling: he had also been trained to use a quarterstaff and a sword, and it seemed to be the only way to support himself, using the only real talent he had.

"It wasn't my ideal career," Tuck said. "But I thought I might be hired to guard some sweet noblewoman on her travels or something like that. You know" – he looked at Robin, his eyes twinkling – "protecting a beautiful young maid from blood-thirsty outlaws like you lot. That was my hope anyway – I hadn't taken vows of chastity at that point."

"Dirty old bastard," Robin muttered in reply, shaking his head with a grin as Tuck continued his tale.

"I spoke to a man in the Stag's Head, a seedy tavern in Cambridge, and my employment was arranged. I was to work as part of a small personal militia defending Thomas Clerk, a local merchant.

"I felt dirty agreeing to the job, but the pay was good. It seemed like money was the most important thing I needed to survive then," he said, shaking his head in disbelief. "My savings were almost spent and the wages being offered were much better than what I could get as a simple labourer."

Terms of employment settled, he left the tavern and made his way along the stinking road – known locally as "Shitbrook Street", for obvious reasons – back to his lodgings. The former wrestler wondered despondently where he would eventually end up in the world. Would he ever find something to bring meaning to his life? Or was he destined to flit from one menial, depressing, poorly paid job to another until he expired, too old, or drunk, to move, in a pile of human waste in a place like Shitbrook Street?

"Then I heard someone scream," Tuck said. "It was a man, as I found out, but it sounded like a frightened woman." He smiled at the memory, and then his face grew hard. "I'd taken to carrying a cudgel since my beating in Elton, and when I heard the cry again I knew I had to do something. I couldn't ignore it, like everyone else seemed to be doing."

Two dirty-looking robbers had a well-dressed monk, or priest – Stafford couldn't tell the difference back then, he simply knew it was some kind of clergyman – pinned against the wall of a house in the alley around the corner. One of the men had a hand on the priest's throat and was squeezing hard enough to stifle any more cries for aid, while his other hand waved a tarnished old dagger in the clergyman's face.

The other thief, seeing the priest safely restrained, knelt down and began to search the pack of another, younger, clergyman clad in grey robes, who lay on the ground, blood oozing thickly from a horrendous, and certainly fatal, wound to his forehead.

"I watched it all for a few moments. I had no idea what to do," Tuck told Robin with a shrug. "I had no love for religion or the Church, so I felt no pious duty to help the priest. He meant no more to me than any other man...But, I had no love for robbers either. What I was seeing in that filthy alley disgusted me."

As quietly as he could, he slipped into the alleyway, pulling out his cudgel, and crept towards the robber kneeling on the ground.

The thief never noticed his approach, so engrossed was he in his search of the fallen priest's belongings.

Stafford slammed his weapon down on the back of the man's head with a loud thump.

The thief crumpled to the ground, but the sound of the blow had alerted his accomplice who released the asphyxiating, blue-faced priest and spun, dagger held defensively before him, to face Stafford.

The robber glanced down at his fallen accomplice and, panicking, rushed at Stafford, waving his dagger around wildly, while the priest knelt on all fours amongst the human waste on the street, coughing and gasping as he tried to suck air in through his squashed larynx.

Robert's training took over as he dodged nimbly to the left, grasped his opponent's wrist in his right hand and squeezed, hard.

"I remember it like it happened just last week," the friar said. "For all my wrestling matches, this was the first true, life-or-death fight I'd been in, I'll never forget it."

The grimy dagger dropped to the ground with a dull metallic thud, as Stafford twisted the robber's arm until it was behind his back; then the big wrestler slammed the screaming man's face hard into the wall of the house.

Once, twice, three times, he battered the would-be thief into the solid timber, then he dropped the senseless man to the floor, face broken and bloody, and his arm twisted at a sickening angle underneath him.

"I went over to check on the priest, who was still coughing his guts up on the floor. When he got his breath back he looked at me as if I was Christ himself," the Franciscan crossed himself quickly, and carried on. "His eyes rose heavenwards, and he said to me: 'The Lord sent you to save me, my son!'

"I just shrugged and slid my cudgel back into my belt. I was more worried about friends of the robbers turning up than discussing if I was an angel sent from heaven, so I lifted the priest and carried him back to my own lodgings in Shitbrook Street."

As it turned out, the "priest" Stafford had rescued was actually John Salmon, the Bishop of Norwich. He and his murdered companion, a Franciscan friar, had taken a wrong turning on their way to a meeting with other clergymen and been accosted by the robbers.

The bishop genuinely seemed to think Stafford had been divinely sent to rescue him, and his enthusiasm for that belief was infectious.

Before long Stafford began to think maybe the man was right. After all, if almost any other man had chanced along as the robbery was in progress, things would not have turned out for the best, as most other men would have simply run off or else been slain by the robbers, wouldn't they?

"'Surely it wasn't coincidence that a man like you – that can fight like you – appeared at just the right time,'" the bishop told me, and, eventually, I realised he was right. God had sent me for a purpose. I'd been trying to find my way for months and now, it seemed like it was staring me in the face."

He smiled gently, nodding his head in pious contentment. "I never fulfilled the mercenary contract to defend the rich merchant Thomas Clerk.

"Bishop Salmon helped me and I became a Franciscan friar: took the grey robes, shaved my crown and devoted the rest of my life to God.

"I had, at last, found my true calling."

For the first time, perhaps ever in his life, he was happy and full of hope for the future.

"Of course, it wasn't to last," Tuck sighed, "which is why I'm here now. But that's a tale for another day."

* * *

Sir Richard-at-Lee smiled. He felt a small sense of peace again after the tortured few weeks since his son's murder.

Thanks to his short alliance with Robin Hood and the other wolf's heads in Barnsdale he had been saved from financial ruin.

It was the start of December and his castle had felt cold and lonely since he'd been forced to sack his staff a few weeks ago.

The door to the great hall opened as he was piling logs on the fire and he glanced over his shoulder, smiling as he saw the people coming in and the blaze began to build in the hearth, warming the room and casting a merry glow on the room.

"My friends," he smiled, rising and rubbing his cold hands as he walked over to meet the newcomers. "Welcome back!"

His former staff members smiled back uncertainly, wondering why they'd been summoned to their lord's castle again.

"Cheer up," Sir Richard told them, placing his hands on his hips and gazing at them. "You can thank Robin Hood and his friends for it – I know I'll be helping them any way I can from now on. I'm re-hiring every one of you."

As the men and women realised their lord was being serious, they raised a cheer of thanks to Sir Richard and Robin Hood.

Maybe winter wouldn't be quite so desperate after all.

CHAPTER TWENTY-ONE

In the first week of December, Friar Tuck performed a small wedding ceremony for Robin and Matilda under one of the giant oak trees in the forest not too far from their camp. The outlaws feasted and, with heated mugs of ale, sang and danced long into the cold winter night, a great fire burning merrily, bringing light and warmth to the revellers.

Robin was glad Tuck had talked him into the ceremony. It didn't mean much to him, despite the fact he considered himself a decent Christian, but he could see Matilda was happy to be properly wed in the eyes of the church.

Robin was no fool. He knew this was no life for a young couple. Matilda was already past the age where most young women had begun having children.

With things as they stood now, though, every one of the outlaws knew they could not lead a normal life. Robin was just happy to give Matilda whatever happiness he could, and the joyful look on her face when he had proposed the formal wedding ceremony had given him some comfort.

Their life together was not perfect, but at least they were together.

So life went on in the freezing forest of Barnsdale. The outlaws, wealthy from their attack on Sir John de Bray, had no need to rob as many unwary travellers, which Robin saw as a good thing. It allowed them to lie low, and gave the foresters no incentive to go out of their way hunting the outlaws.

Despite the period of quiet, though, the outlaws always kept lookouts posted around their camp. All through the day the men – and Matilda – would take turns, hidden high in the branches of whatever evergreen trees grew nearest to the forest pathways, to make sure no one sneaked up on them. There was no need to set a watch at night – no attacker would be foolish enough to stumble blindly around the pitch black woods in the middle of winter. Even so, Robin insisted on it – better safe than sorry, he thought.

The lookouts had proven a wise precaution. Several times foresters had almost stumbled upon the outlaws' camp, only to be seen by the lookouts and shepherded, with shouts and other noises, away in the opposite direction.

Two weeks before Christmas, Will Scarlet sat, comfortably nestled in the branches of a (rare for Barnsdale) Scots Pine, with a thick blanket wrapped around him. The outlaws had cut away enough branches to make an opening large enough for a man to fit, and hammered in wooden boards to make a small platform to rest on. Not quite comfortable, or large, enough to fall asleep in, but tolerable enough for a couple of hours at a time.

As always, he heard the people approaching long before he saw them. The sounds of fallen, dried-out twigs cracking, as inexperienced, or simply unwary, travellers walked on them, generally gave their presence away and allowed the lookouts time to prepare for their arrival.

Will grinned as the noisy party of wayfarers came into view along Watling Street, the main road from one end of the country to the other.

Clergymen. Two of them. Will's smile became thoughtful as he noted the number of armed guards escorting the two priests. Twelve mercenaries, grim and competent-looking, every one of them.

Twelve. That was good. No one would hire such a large band of soldiers to defend them unless they were carrying something valuable.

The priests had something worth stealing then, and the slow-moving horse drawn cart Scarlet could see in the centre of the party no doubt carried it.

Will gave the travellers time to pass, then he swung down from the tree silently.

He wasn't sure who got the biggest shock, as he landed on the forest floor with a soft thump: himself or the swarthy mercenary he landed in front of.

Instinctively, Will went for his dagger first. He could draw it quicker than his sword, and, at such close quarters, it would be more useful, especially if his surprised opponent reacted as he expected and tried to draw the unwieldy long sword at his side.

The mercenary didn't try to draw his sword. The mercenary captain was clearly competent enough to realise their best chance of surviving an ambush was to have as much warning as possible, so must have told his men to make raising the alarm their first priority on being attacked. Hence the scout that Will had, literally, stumbled upon, turned his back on the stocky outlaw and began to run back towards his companions, lungs sucking in air to roar a warning.

The mercenary never got the chance to warn his fellows. Being unused to wandering around in the deep forests of northern England, he didn't notice the thin but sturdy tree root underfoot which sent him sprawling on his face, his cry of alarm dashed from him instead as a low painful grunt.

Scarlet was upon him instantly, dropping both knees onto the man's back, thrusting his dagger into the side of the fallen mercenary's neck, killing him instantly.

The outlaw quickly rose to his feet, looking warily around for any more mercenaries, but the trees around him were silent.

He knelt and wiped his dagger clean on the fallen mercenary's gambeson, checking the corpse for valuables as he did so, then hastily, but silently, hurried back to camp, hoping none of the other lookouts were surprised by more of the mercenary group's outlying scouts.

A couple of the outlaws were away collecting food and other supplies from the village of Wooley, but thankfully the rest of the men were close to the camp, and they all gathered round the small fire when they heard Scarlet arrive, sounding the birdcall they all knew meant danger.

"What's happening, Will?" Robin demanded, seeing the excited grin on the lookout's face.

"Foresters?" Matilda asked, her hands tightening around the staff she had been using to spar with Much.

Will shook his head. "Better. A couple of priests, with a horse-drawn wagon, and around a dozen men escorting them through the forest."

Friar Tuck grunted. "That's a lot of men."

Matt Groves smiled thoughtfully, and said what everyone was thinking: "A lot of guards means a lot of money . . ."

The other lookouts came hurrying back into the campsite as the outlaws discussed what they should do. They also reported twelve guards, although none of them had noticed outlying scouts. Will mentioned the one he'd run into though, as he was worried there may be more.

"Hang on," Robin cautioned. "Twelve men, at least, possibly more, presumably well armed and well trained. That many guards could mean some of us getting killed. For what? We don't need the money. Why not just let them go?"

Will snorted derisively, his eyes twinkling. "You're getting soft, Robin, sitting around here all day drinking ale, eating venison and whispering poetry into your wife's ear."

There were whoops and sniggers of agreement at that, and Robin shrugged his shoulders good-naturedly. The men clearly needed to stretch their muscles after a few weeks of relative inactivity.

"Fine, we'll rob these priests if we must then. I just don't see much point in risking our lives when we have no need to."

Friar Tuck laid a brawny hand on his young leader's arm. "A good general never throws away his men needlessly, Robin, I think you're right."

"Aye, he *is* right," agreed Little John. "But I'm bored. Let's go kick these mercenaries' arses and steal all the priests' money."

Robin laughed along with the rest of the men, and shook his head, but the matter was settled.

In truth, the young outlaw was quite happy to rob the priests, but he didn't think he should lead his men on such a dangerous hold-up when they had so much money already tucked away for the winter. Why take a chance?

For all his charisma, and his skill with a sword and a bow, Robin was still very inexperienced as a commander. He was only just learning that men, particularly soldiers – which was basically what his outlaws were – soon get bored unless they have something to do. And a camp full of bored, testosterone-filled soldiers could quickly become a volatile place unless there was some focused outlet for their aggression.

"Right, everyone, grab your weapons, and your heaviest armour. You too Matilda, let's see if you can shoot a real target as well as you can a bag of grain hanging from a branch."

His young wife thumped Robin on the backside with her staff playfully then rushed to their shelter to pick up her sword and bow, sticking a handful of arrows into her belt as she fell in with the outlaws who were already moving off.

"We'll head them off on the ridge beside the pair of old oaks, eh?" Little John suggested.

Robin thought for a moment, but shook his head. "There's not enough cover there – the trees have all lost their leaves, and there's hardly a green bush to hide behind."

John pictured his suggested ambush point in his mind's eye, and realised Robin was right.

"What about the bent beech trees, a quarter of a mile further on from the pair of oaks?" rumbled Will Scarlet, who had fallen in beside the two men at the front of the column.

There was a momentary pause as John and Robin visualised the spot Will suggested, then both nodded approval.

"There's some juniper bushes to the west *and* east of there," Robin agreed. "And some holly dotted around as well that we can hide men behind."

"Aye, and it's a bit further off than the two oaks, so we'll have more time to prepare," Will said.

Robin clapped his two lieutenants on the shoulders with a confident grin and picked up the pace, wanting to gain as much time as he could to set up their ambush.

The spot selected by Will turned out to be ideal. One third of the men, led by Scarlet, were able to hide in the undergrowth to the east of the road, while another third, with Tuck at their head, huddled amongst a great patch of juniper on the other side of the track, just a little further ahead. The rest of the men, including Robin and Little John, concealed themselves behind some thick holly, its berries bright as blood against the frost and snow covering the rest of the forest.

Robin had got into the habit of taking Little John with him whenever they robbed people on the road. When Robin stepped out in front of the victims and demanded their valuables, he knew people would be less likely to try and fight their way out when they saw the near seven-foot-tall, bearded giant standing menacingly at his back.

And he had taken Matilda in his party this time too, simply so he could protect her if anything should go wrong. She had yet to face a combat situation, and Robin worried she might not handle it. Fighting a man desperate to kill you was quite different to the sparring Matilda was used to with the outlaws.

Once the men were all in position, they waited.

After half an hour the priests' party came along the road and Robin, with his huge friend behind him, roared at them to halt.

The hard-faced, and obviously competent, mercenaries had quickly drawn up into a circular formation, small shields held before them, forming an impressive barrier around the two clergymen and their wagon.

"Come on now," Robin said. "There's no need for any bloodshed. You men know we *will* be taking all your valuables whether you try and stop us or not."

"There's only a handful of them!" one of the priests shouted at his guards. "And one of them's just a woman! Kill them, and let's be on our way before more of the scum turn up."

The guards hesitated, eyes taking in the surrounding undergrowth. Robin watched as the mercenary captain noted the juniper and holly bushes the other outlaws were hidden in.

"Aye, we have you surrounded," Robin nodded. "The clergyman might think we're a bunch of village idiots, but you know that's not the case. If you fight, every one of you will die. All we want is the money, jewellery, that sort of thing, from the two priests. You men can keep whatever you have and be on your way."

"Kill him!" the priest screamed again, not liking where this situation was going at all. "You're being well paid to protect us, so earn your wages, fools!"

"Will! Tuck!" Robin shouted calmly, turning his back on the mercenaries and looking at the ground in apparent boredom. The rest of the outlaws appeared, arrows already fitted to their bowstrings.

The two priests began to pray.

"What's it to be then, lads?" Robin asked the mercenaries, still facing in the opposite direction. "You're outnumbered. We won't bother you any more if you leave right now. It's your choice."

As always, the rest of the outlaws remained unnervingly quiet, staring calmly at their intended targets.

The captain raised his shield before him a little higher, and shouted to his men, "Use your shields to block their arrows, then engage at will. Forward!"

Robin was surprised at the mercenaries' decision to fight, but he spun round with a shouted command, "Choose your target carefully, then fire!" and drew his sword. He saw Little John at his side, bringing his great quarterstaff up defensively in front of himself.

Matilda loosed her arrow but it embedded itself harmlessly in the shield of one of the guards, so she smoothly pulled another missile from her belt and had it aimed at the same man almost instantly, her hands surprisingly steady.

The majority of the outlaws saw their arrows embed themselves in shields, or bounce uselessly off onto the forest floor. Only three found their mark: one made its way right through the defensive circle and took a guard in the back; one ricocheted off a mercenary's helmet and pierced the man to his left through the neck; the third caught an unwary man straight in the face as he lowered his shield too early to see where he was going.

Some of the outlaws did as Matilda had done, quickly fitting another arrow to their longbow, as their companions moved defensively in front of them, swords drawn. The outlaws' second volley, rushed as it was, also managed to take out three mercenaries, as the guards panicked under fire and pressed their charge recklessly.

The remaining six guards now reached the waiting outlaws, and the close combat began.

Matilda was stunned at what she saw. The mercenaries, grim-faced, hard-looking men, attacked, but the outlaws outnumbered them and worked together like a brutal killing machine, their endless days of relentless training making them utterly unstoppable.

Little John engaged the guard captain, as Robin slipped past the man and stabbed him in the side. As the mercenary cried out, twisting away in pain, John's enormous staff swung upwards into his chin and lifted the man off the floor with a sickening crack, his neck broken.

The other outlaws worked in a similar fashion, one man defending while another pressed the attack from another direction.

In only a few seconds the mercenaries were all dead. Not a single outlaw had taken a scratch.

Matilda stared at the carnage before her then dropped to her knees sobbing. Robin tried to comfort her, but she shoved him roughly away, and, rising slowly, walked over to a boulder where she sat, tears streaming down her pale face, staring into the distance.

"Check the bodies for valuables," Robin ordered Matt Groves and Much, who set to their dark task efficiently.

"Are there any more guards with you?" Will roared, pointing his still bloody sword at the two priests, who were cowering in terror beside their wagon.

The churchmen looked blankly at him, but didn't reply.

"Answer me!" Will shouted, his face the bright red of his nickname.

The priests shook their heads.

"There better fucking not be," Scarlet growled. He turned and muttered to Allan-a-Dale next to him, "A handful of outlying scouts like the one I fell on could have really caused us bother."

Allan nodded agreement, his eyes warily scanning the forest, just in case the two priests were lying.

"Where were you going?" Robin demanded, as the outlaws gathered round their prey. "Everyone knows these woods belong to us. Why would you come through here in the middle of winter? What's so important?"

The elder priest, the one who had been extorting his guards to attack the outlaws, now sat silent, his face grey and slack.

The junior priest replied, his voice shaking with nerves. "We're on our way to Hathersage. To see Lord John de Bray."

"That bastard?" Will growled. "What you going to see him for?"

"We're from the Abbey of St Mary's. The abbot agreed to lend Lord de Bray some money after he was robbed in his own home by a gang of depraved outlaws."

"Hey! You watch who you're calling 'depraved'!" Little John cried with mock indignation, and the other outlaws roared with laughter.

"Well. This *is* a stroke of good fortune," Robin smiled thoughtfully. "I assume the money your abbot was sending to de Bray is in this chest here?" He nudged the great wooden box on the cart with the point of his sword.

The young priest looked away sullenly, without replying.

"Of course it is," Little John grunted, pulling himself onto the cart and smashing off the lock with a stone Allan-a-Dale passed up to him from the side of the path.

"How much is in there?" Will asked the priests.

Neither man replied, as Little John lifted the lid of the heavy box and hooted with delight.

The outlaws crowded round to see the great amount of silver held inside the chest.

"How much?" Will demanded again, grabbing the elder priest round the neck and hauling him to his feet.

"Two hundred pounds!" the clergyman shouted in fright. "The abbot is sending Lord de Bray two hundred pounds in silver!"

"Fuck me, we thought we were rich already," the teenager Gareth of Wrangbrook gasped, his eyes wide with shock. "What are we going to do with all that money?"

"Right now, we get it back to our camp," Robin replied decisively, sheathing his sword and motioning Little John to close the chest again. "Let's move. Allan, you can drive."

He looked at the priests. "You two can go," he told them.

"Go?" the elder replied. "What do you mean, 'go'? We have no escort thanks to you, and the road is teeming with wolf's heads!"

"Not my problem," Robin answered, dismissing the pair and heading off to check on Matilda.

"You!" the priest cried at Tuck as he walked past, joking with Gareth. "You're a Franciscan! How can you ally yourself with these brigands? Who are you? I'll see you excommunicated for this!"

Tuck shook his head pityingly at the priest. "Father, I have my own reasons for being part of this gang of outlaws, don't be too quick to judge me. Anyway, by the time you get back to St Mary's and your abbot chastises you for losing his two hundred pounds, well... *you* might wish you were still hiding out in this forest."

The two priests, pale and wan already, looked stricken as they realised Tuck was right. The abbot would be incensed with them when they returned. They stared at each other, eyes wide with fright.

Tuck shrugged his shoulders, told them how to reach the safety of the nearest village, and walked off.

The wagon groaned into life as Allan-a-Dale cracked the reins of the two carthorses, and the party headed back to their campsite.

Matilda, her initial shock and revulsion at the death and violence she had seen wearing off, allowed Robin to put an arm round her waist and the couple followed the creaking wagon along the hidden paths of Barnsdale forest in silence.

271

CHAPTER TWENTY-TWO

"The bastards have been killing, raping, pillaging our people for years – and you want us to parley with them?" Sir Richard-at-Lee glared at the Earl of Lancaster in disbelief, using his sleeve to wipe wine from his thick grey beard. "Are you mad?"

The earl raised a hand to placate the burly Hospitaller, shaking his head in consternation. "Think about it, Sir Richard! We are beset by foes from two sides – the Scots from the north and the Despensers from the south. Which threat is most immediate?"

Unlike the recent meetings where Sir Richard had met the powerful Earl of Lancaster, there was no one else present here today other than the two of them. The earl had arrived, unexpectedly, at Sir Richard's small castle an hour ago. Richard had told his steward to bring the earl and his small party in from the biting December winds before inviting Thomas into his hall where a great fire burned noisily and the table was set with mulled wine and sweetmeats.

The commander of Kirklees opened his mouth to reply, but Lancaster cut him off before he could begin. "Yes, I know what the Scots have done, they raided my lands too don't forget. But the king is moving against us now – will you stand and watch as he rides over me, as he and his toadies are about to ride over Mortimer, Hereford and the rest of the Marchers?"

Sir Richard shrugged uncomfortably. The Scots! How could they ally themselves to the hated old enemy?

"You do realise," Thomas continued, "that the Despensers banishment has been annulled by Archbishop Reynolds and the king's other cronies? The bastards will be back in England within the week!"

"What?" Richard hadn't heard this news. "Are you certain?"

"Yes, I'm certain. The king is ready to invite them home under his own personal protection. They laugh in our faces! And you were hoping the king would return the ransom money they extorted from you?" The earl laughed in disgust and Sir Richard felt his face flush in anger.

"Damn them! If this is true, my lord, I'm with you," the Hospitaller shouted before crossing himself and cursing. "I'd make parley with the Devil himself if it meant the destruction of that bastard Despenser."

"It's true, Sir Richard, believe me. And once the king has crushed the Marchers he'll be after the rest of us who oppose him. I've had copies of the petition we all signed at Doncaster sent to London to be circulated, so the people there can see for themselves what the king has brought on his head. I've also sent a messenger north to treat with the Black Douglas."

"Robert the Bruce eh?" Sir Richard grunted with a tight smile. "Well, if anyone hates Edward it's the Bruce."

"You're with me then?"

The Hospitaller nodded. "Aye, I'm with you."

"Good." Lancaster smiled in relief. He had hoped to gather an army large enough to crush the king's, but his efforts so far had been much less successful than he'd expected. "Raise your men. We must be prepared when they come."

"I will," Sir Richard replied thoughtfully. "And...I might even be able to enlist the help of a few extra longbow-men too..."

* * *

Sir Henry de Faucumberg, Sheriff of Nottingham and Yorkshire, was enjoying the brisk morning air. It was almost Christmas, and the snow lay thickly on the fields around Nottingham, the frost on the trees a pretty winter replacement for leaves. He was hunting with his favourite peregrine falcon, although there wasn't much prey to be had. Still, his servants carried wine and sweetmeats for him to snack on, and it was such a fine day he couldn't help having a fine time.

"My lord..." one of his retainers muttered, glancing over his shoulder towards the city.

"What is it, man?" the sheriff replied irritably, looking in the direction indicated. "Who the hell's that?"

Stumbling towards him through the snow was a small party of clergymen. De Faucumberg eventually recognised the man leading them.

"The abbot of St Mary's. What's brought him out of his warm abbey to come and see me?" he wondered.

He called his falcon back, and placed its hood over its head just as the abbot, red faced and puffing, finally reached him.

"Sheriff!" the churchman gasped.

"Abbot Ness!" de Faucumberg replied with a wicked grin, enjoying the abbot's wheezing discomfort. "Catch your breath, man, catch your breath. What brings you all this way?"

"That bastard Robin Hood, that's what brings me here!" the abbot grunted breathlessly. "Why aren't you doing anything about him? He's already ruined one nobleman, and he's near ruined me as well, while you spend your time out here hunting instead of bringing that wolf's head and his men to justice!"

"Calm down, abbot," the sheriff replied, still grinning. "Come, this is no place to discuss business, let's head back to the castle, where it's nice and warm."

Ness nodded irritably, his face falling even further when he turned and realised he'd have to make the long trek back the way he had just come. De Faucumberg read the abbot's thoughts but was wise enough not to laugh out loud as he strode off towards his Nottingham stronghold, the clergyman struggling along behind him, face scarlet against the crisp white of the winter snow.

On their walk back to the castle the abbot tried to engage the sheriff in conversation but de Faucumberg hushed him with a raised hand. "Not out here, with my servants around us, my lord abbot," he cautioned. "Robin Hood and his men are quite the folk heroes in Nottingham these days. I don't want what we say getting back to him, as unlikely as it may seem. We'll talk in private."

Half an hour later the pair sat in comfortable chairs in a small room in the castle, a log fire burning merrily in the hearth and cups of gently warmed red wine held in numb fingers. The servants had been sent away, and a thick oak door, complete with trusted guardsman outside, would deter anyone foolish enough to try and eavesdrop.

"Really, Sir Henry," the abbot chided. "Don't you think you're taking all this a bit too far? I mean, even if Hood has become something of a hero to the lower classes of the city, I hardly think your own servants would be so stupid as to carry gossip to him."

The sheriff nodded, taking a small sip of his wine, and sighing in contentment as it slowly warmed his whole being. "You're most likely right, abbot, but I don't want something overheard in our conversation finding its way into a local tavern, then growing legs and finding its way to the ears of the wolf's head. Whatever we decide to do about him will have more chance of success if he isn't forewarned about our discussion."

Ness shrugged irritably before draining his cup and letting himself relax in his seat with a contented sigh. "What do you mean these fugitives have become folk heroes anyway? The leader's just an arrogant boy."

"You know how it goes with the peasants," de Faucumberg grunted. "Local nobody rises up and deals a blow against us, the hated upper-class persecutors, peasants rejoice. The problem is – this *boy* has inherited one of the best-trained outlaw gangs in England. Adam Gurdon was a Templar Knight before he was outlawed: a natural leader of men and highly versed in the arts of war. He forged his rag-tag band of criminal scum into a lethal fighting force, apparently able to move, and act, unseen within the forests of Yorkshire. Robin Hood has taken control of Gurdon's gang."

"Where's this Gurdon then?" the abbot demanded. "Have him hunt these people down."

"Good idea, abbot!" de Faucumberg replied sarcastically. "I already tried that. Gurdon was killed by Hood and sent back to Nottingham with his own cock in his mouth, while the foresters I sent with him were routed."

Ness shuddered and shook his head in disbelief. "Well, *something* must be done. He's cost me a lot of money – and land too, if the rumours are true."

"What rumours?"

"The money Sir Richard-at-Lee owed me, remember? The man somehow managed to find it, which stopped me gaining ownership of the man's lands? You were there when he repaid the loan! Well, apparently it was loaned to him by Robin Hood, who stole it from the Lord of Hathersage's own manor house. Sir Richard was implicated, but nothing can be proven."

"Ah yes, I heard about that." The sheriff nodded thoughtfully. "A gang of outlaws, apparently with some inside knowledge of the building, was able to empty the place of valuables. I have to say, if the Lord of Hathersage" – he cocked an eyebrow at the abbot, who muttered, "John de Bray," in response -"yes, if John de Bray, can't defend his own house against a gang of outlaws, well, he deserves to be ruined."

"Maybe so," snapped the abbot. "It's hardly my fault the man let Robin Hood steal all his money, though, is it? But it was me that lost out on a very nice manor when Richard-at-Lee was able to repay the money I'd loaned him."

The sheriff shrugged. "I still don't understand why you're so upset. What's happened since I last saw you?"

Abbot Ness refilled his cup from the large wine jug on the table before continuing. The sheriff noticed the man's hands were shaking with rage as he poured the expensive liquid into his cup.

"Lord de Bray, like Richard-at-Lee before him, asked me for a loan, as the outlaws had ruined him. The man had no money to pay for the upkeep of his manor and, with Christmas almost here, he knew he would also have to pay for a feast for his villagers. I kindly agreed to lend him the money-"

De Faucumberg spat a mouthful of wine across the room. "Oh, how noble of you, abbot!" he roared with glee. "Interest free, was it, this loan, like the one you gave to Sir Richard-at-Lee? I thought that sort of thing was against the Church's laws, yet this is the second time you've spoken to me about loaning people money!"

"Never you mind the terms of our agreement," Ness retorted indignantly. "The fact is I agreed to give the man the money. I was doing him a favour, regardless of anything else."

"Let me guess," the sheriff smirked, holding the abbot's eye. "You agreed to loan the man some money, with an exorbitant interest rate, and if he failed to repay you within say…three years…he would forfeit his manor to you. Am I close?"

"You may mock, de Faucumberg," the abbot replied patiently. "But the Church is not made out of money. I made Lord de Bray a loan – if he chose to pay a little extra as a donation to the Church, that would be perfectly legal, as you well know."

"Save your sermon for the pulpit, abbot," the sheriff grinned, spilling wine down the sides of his lips as the alcohol started to take effect. "You wanted to line your own pockets – I'm sure you weren't planning on sending any of this 'donation' to the Pope. Get to the point, man. You agreed to loan this fool some money, yes? So what's the problem?"

"The problem, *sheriff*," the abbot spat out the word with sarcasm equal to de Faucumberg's own, "is that Robin Hood and his gang of wolf's heads waylaid the men I sent to Hathersage with the money! While you mess about with your falcons, or sit in this castle with your finger up your arse, Robin Hood is spending my two hundred pounds!"

De Faucumberg had leaned forward in his chair angrily as the abbot delivered his rant, but he sat back, open-mouthed, when he heard the amount of money Hood and his men had made off with.

There was silence for a time, the two men brooding into their expensive wine.

"No wonder this boy has become a folk hero," the sheriff finally grunted. "He's the king of outlaws. The man's rich!"

"Exactly!" Ness roared. "And it's all my money!"

The sheriff didn't even bother retorting. He was too stunned at what he was hearing. The more he thought about it the more he knew something had to be done, whether it was the middle of winter or not. King Edward would eventually hear of this. Abbot Ness had probably already sent a messenger to London with his complaints.

The king would expect his servant, Sir Henry de Faucumberg, Sheriff of Nottingham and Yorkshire, to do something about this. Or His Grace would find a replacement for the sheriff, just as he had a couple of years before when de Faucumberg had been charged with extortion . . .

"What is it, exactly, you want, abbot?" de Faucumberg asked, all trace of humour gone. "I've only just got my job back, and I'd like to keep it this time."

"I want that bastard Hood hunted down like the animal he is – his men too!" the abbot ranted. "And I want my money returned to me!"

The sheriff sat deep in thought for a while, while the abbot continued to throw wine down his neck in a black rage.

"It's about time for dinner, my lord abbot," de Faucumberg finally said to his guest. "Let me think on this for a time. I'll come up with something."

In truth, the sheriff could see no way to track down such a well-trained gang of outlaws, in a forest they knew better than anyone, in the darkest depths of winter. It simply wasn't possible.

There was only one way Sir Henry de Faucumberg could think of to solve this problem…

* * *

The sun tried to force its way through the thick blanket of fog and snow shrouding Wakefield as the outlaws – Robin, Will, John, Matilda and Much, made their way through the uncharacteristically quiet streets. Frost lay thickly on window ledges, and the smell of wood smoke filled the air as the villagers tried to warm their homes with blazing fires.

The mist muffled the sounds of those people who were working – even the metallic sounds from the blacksmith's workshop seemed weirdly stunted as the man saw them and gave a small smile in greeting, the only person in the village sweating on such a cold day as his furnace continued to turn out horse shoes and arrow heads.

"Christ, the people look grim," Little John muttered, giving the blacksmith a wave in return.

"The people are starving," Will replied softly. He nodded towards the smith who had turned back to his anvil, his thick arms cording with muscle as he hammered a horse shoe into shape. "The big man's children are probably at home crying because their bellies are empty. You wouldn't be laughing either."

"Well their bellies will be filled today," Robin growled, dismayed at the sight of the people he'd grown up around suffering impotently, the effects of another poor harvest and spiralling food prices taking their toll on all but the wealthier people of England.

They trudged through the thick snow, their feet making dry crunching sounds, and every now and again one would slip as their sodden shoes lost grip on the hard-packed surface. John led a pair of docile horses, their harnesses jingling quietly but, apart from the occasional snort, they were nearly silent as the fully laden cart they pulled slid through the snow slowly, leaving deep tracks to mark their passage.

A small crowd began to form behind them, the villagers throwing on their thickest cloaks to brave the cold and see what was happening.

They arrived at the village green and stopped, John holding old apples up for the horses to eat as he grinned and stroked their manes, mumbling soft inanities to them. Robin couldn't help smiling at the sight of his giant friend – so terrifying when angered or in battle – yet so placid and gentle otherwise.

The young wolf's head blew on his hands and nimbly climbed on top of the wagon, careful not to lose his footing on the frost and dusting of snow that had covered it.

He waited as more villagers joined the chattering throng, smiling and waving as he saw his father, John, pushing his way through to the front of the villagers who deferentially moved aside, recognising him, then Robin raised his huge archer's arms.

"Friends!" he roared, looking around at the people with a smile. "How are you?"

"Fucking hungry!" someone shouted in reply and there were smiles and grim laughs at that.

Robin nodded as the crowd fell silent again, wondering what he would say. "I know your bellies are empty, while some of our 'betters' hoard food!"

There was a chorus of angry shouts at that.

"I won't waste time with a speech," Robin cried, shaking his head. "We've brought you a present, courtesy of Lord John de Bray of Hathersage." He leaned down and pulled off the blanket covering the wagon, making sure he tugged it hard as the frost had hardened it in place.

The wagon was filled with barrels and crates. "Smoked and salted fish and meat. Dried and honey preserved fruit. Vegetables in brine. Cheese!" Robin raised his voice, grinning as the gathered people started to chatter excitedly, their mouths watering, as he pointed at the containers on the cart.

"Henry!" he shouted towards the village headman who had also been allowed to push his way to the front of the gathering. "There's not enough here to see everyone through the winter with a belly like a priest," he paused to let the smiling people cheer at his joke, "but if you ration it, it will make life a lot easier – and tastier! – for everyone." He held his hands high in the air again as everyone cheered then, with a laugh, cried, "Enjoy!" and jumped to the snow beside the other outlaws.

The crowd surged forward as if they would ransack the wagon, but John, Much and Will Scarlet drew their swords menacingly and roared at them to get back, telling the people to be patient.

Henry organised a party of guards from the villagers to look after the wagon until the contents could be organised and doled out or stored, and the villagers began to chant. "Hood! Hood! Hood!"

The outlaws smiled happily, pleased at their day's work, and Robin felt a lump in his throat as the people he had grown up with chanted his name in grateful appreciation. His eyes welled up at the thought of these good people being so hungry that a wagon load of food would bring them so much happiness and he quickly pulled his proudly smiling father aside.

"Come on," he shouted over the chanting crowd. "Let's go home. I've got some things here special." He pulled a sack from the wagon over his shoulder and nodded to the other outlaws who waved or smiled in reply and moved off to carry out whatever tasks they had planned. Matilda, Will and Much hefted sacks of their own for friends and family, while John had arrows, bread, spices and other provisions to stock up on.

"How's Marjorie?" Robin asked his father as they left the happy crowd behind and headed for their own modest house a short way off.

John shook his head sadly. "She's weak," he admitted. "She always has been, ever since…" His voice tailed off. Even after all these years, the passing of his other daughter still hurt terribly – he thought of Rebekah every single day, wondering what she'd be like now, hating himself at times for not being able to provide food for his family, even though he knew it hadn't been his fault – no one had any food back then, it had been much worse than it was now. But the thought of Marjorie maybe going the same way – starving – devastated him.

Robin patted him on the back reassuringly. "She'll be fine. I've brought good food for her – food fit for a lord of Hathersage!"

They smiled and pushed on through the snow until they reached the family home and made their way inside gratefully, the cosy fire warming their exposed faces and hands.

Robin's mother smiled in surprise at the sight of her beloved son and gave him a tight hug as John began telling her about his performance on the wagon.

Marjorie lay in bed, which had been made up close to the fire. Robin was shocked at the sight of his little sister – always thin, but now she had nothing on her, skin stretched tightly over her small frame. He had learned how to act though – how to hide his emotions and appear tougher than he really way – during his time with the outlaws, and he smiled at the girl as if nothing was wrong.

"Look what I've got for you!" he grinned, dropping his heavy sack on the floor and pulling a jar of honeyed apples from it. "And that's not all!" He emptied the food onto the ground as his family laughed and gasped. "Here," Robin handed his sister a piece of cheese and her eyes lit up as she bit into it.

"It's wonderful!" she gasped, her hollow cheeks screwing up slightly at the bitter, but delicious taste.

Robin piled small pieces of food onto Marjorie's bed until his mother stopped him. "That's enough for now," she scolded. "Too much of this and she'll be sick or it'll run right through her – that won't do her any favours!"

Marjorie smiled at her mother's fussing, but they knew she was right, so most of the food was taken to be stored away in the darkest, coldest part of the house, in a hole in the ground. Normally it would be stored outside, where it was even colder and the food would last longer, but in these hard times even the best neighbours might steal another's provisions for their own family.

"You sit by the fire with your sister and da," Martha ordered imperiously.

Although Robin was by now used to telling men what to do, he still automatically followed his mother's hard stare and commanding tone, dropping with a smile into an old chair as his father poured him a mug of warm ale from a jug next to the fire.

"Now, I'll make us a nice meal from some of this salted pork you've brought," Martha nodded appreciatively, lifting some meat along with an apple and some spices. "And you can tell us how you managed to find all this food."

Robin took a long pull of his ale, grinning in satisfaction at his sister as the liquid warmed his belly and he began the tale of the raid on Lord John de Bray's manor house.

It was good to be home with his family, even if only for a short while.

CHAPTER TWENTY-THREE

It was dark in the greenwood. A cloudy night, so the temperature wasn't too low. The young outlaw leader and his wife were in their makeshift bed in the big cave the gang were using to sleep in during the coldest winter nights. Outside the cave the other outlaws were sitting round the great campfire enjoying a supper of venison they had caught that day. They were roasting cuts of the meat on arrows held by hand over the fire, drinking ale and telling ghost stories. Matilda had gone off to bed early, and, sensing her low mood, Robin had followed her into the dimly lit cave.

He lay down beside her on their pallet, and pulled their thick, cosy blankets over them both, cuddling her in tight, sharing their body heat in the bitter night.

"I can't live like this, Robin."

The young outlaw raised himself up on an elbow and shook his head at his wife, holding an arm out in despair, casting great twisted shadows on the walls in the dim light from the braziers they used to keep the cave from freezing during the nights.

"What are we to do, Matilda? We're both outlaws. We're lucky-"

"Lucky?" the girl cried. "How are we lucky? Hunted like animals, until the weather's too cold even for the foresters to come out in? The threat of arrest, imprisonment, death, always over us every day we wake up? And you call that 'lucky'?" Her voice, which had been rising in both pitch and volume tailed off into a strangled whisper, tears running down her cheeks.

Robin pulled her in close and they held each other tightly for a while.

"I miss my ma and da," Matilda sobbed.

"I know," Robin replied. "I miss my parents, too. And Will misses little Beth. But at least we all still have those people and we still see them when we visit Wakefield. Much'll never see his da again, after the bailiff killed him . . ."

Matilda didn't reply, so he forged on. "We *are* lucky. Most outlaws have no chance – either the law gets them or the weather or hunger does. We have a group of friends here to look after us, plenty of food, money, warm shelters and caves to sleep in...things could be a lot worse." He leaned away from her, his earnest face shadowed in the brazier's orange glow, and took her hands in his. "I know this isn't what you dreamed of when you thought of marriage but it'll get better one day, I swear it will."

His young wife wiped her face and smiled prettily. "At least we have each other," she said, squeezing his hands.

"Exactly!" Robin laughed and gave her a quick kiss, but his face fell as he saw her expression drop again.

"I just don't think I can live like this much longer," she told him. "I thought I was tough. I've seen my share of violence and cruelty – Christ, haven't we all? But that day we robbed the priests...the killing and violence...And I never even killed anyone! How will I feel when I do?"

Robin stayed silent. He was surprised at Matilda's despair though. He'd known her all his life. She had seen much death and hardship in Wakefield growing up. He knew she was a strong young woman and he'd expected her to deal with life in the greenwood a little better.

He looked closely at her, seeing the tears still streaming for her eyes. "What's really wrong, Matilda?" he asked gently.

The girl's face crumpled as she looked at him. "I'm so frightened Robin, I can't live in this forest forever... I'm pregnant."

Robin lay in stunned silence for a while, completely lost for words. He knew enough to understand Matilda was expecting a reaction though, so he gave her a grin and hugged her in close before she took his silence the wrong way.

She smiled through her tears and gently broke his embrace. "You're happy, then?"

"Of course, I am!" He smiled, but his face soon became solemn, and he nodded at his wife. "I understand why you're so worried now. The forest is no place to bring a baby into the world. Are you sure about it though? How can you tell, you don't look any bigger…"

"I know, Robin. You might not be able to see it, but women have ways of knowing. Here." She grasped his hand and pressed it against her right breast. "Feel it?"

He gave a gentle squeeze and nodded, before trying the other one. "They feel heavier," he said, pressing his body against his wife's without even thinking about it.

"Robin!" she laughed in mock indignation, pulling away from him and the slowly hardening bulge between his legs. "Not now!"

She had brightened considerably on sharing her secret, but Matilda grasped her husband's hand fretfully, and wondered what they were going to do.

"I don't know," Robin admitted. "But we'll think of something."

They smiled at each other and lay back, quietly, for a while, minds racing with thoughts of parenthood.

Eventually, the campfire burned low, the pork and apples, ale and ghost stories were done, and the rest of the outlaws came to bed. Only the sentries on the first watch – and a thoughtful Robin – remained awake in the freezing December forest.

* * *

"You're up at last, then!"

Henry de Faucumberg grimaced as the abbot's loud voice rang through the hall. He waved a dismissive hand at the smiling clergyman who seemed no worse the wear for the previous day's wine.

"You're in a good mood, Ness," the sheriff grunted, as he sat down for breakfast opposite his guest. "No hangover?" He reached for a piece of bread and forced down a mouthful, glaring at the abbot.

"Hangover?" The clergyman laughed. "I'm a devout Christian – all things in moderation. You should take a leaf from my book. Greed is a sin, especially when it comes to wine."

De Faucumberg leaned over and grabbed the cup from the abbot's hand. He took a sip and smirked at the furious abbot. "This is wine, you pious oaf. No wonder you're feeling so bright."

Ness snatched his cup back and took a mouthful. "Have you decided what to do about Robin Hood and his outlaw gang, yet?" he demanded, slamming down his cup and tearing off a great chunk of bread.

"I have." The sheriff, filling a cup with watered wine of his own, forced down a long pull and stuffed more of his bread into his wet mouth. "I don't see any way to hunt down the outlaws in the middle of winter." He held up a hand to silence the protesting abbot. "It's not possible, Ness, not with the men I have. I'd need an army to find and kill those outlaws, and, given what's been happening recently with the Earl of Lancaster and his friends, well – the king's not about to send me resources to waste on hunting down a handful of criminals, is he?"

"Are you just going to sit here stuffing your face then?" the abbot demanded, spitting crumbs on the table in front of himself in consternation.

"Yes, my lord abbot," de Faucumberg retorted, "at least for the next half an hour anyway, while I eat my breakfast. Although you seem to have eaten half the contents of my kitchen this morning already."

"Get to the point, sheriff! What are you going to do about the outlaws in Yorkshire?"

The weak wine de Faucumberg had forced down his gullet was beginning to take some effect, the warm glow rising through his body and into his brain. It made his plan seem slightly more palatable.

"Since we can't even find them, never mind kill them, here's what I suggest...."

* * *

"Matilda! Robin!"

Gareth of Wrangbrook was on lookout in a thick old yew tree when he heard the man shouting. The teenager leaned down for a better look and recognised the fletcher from Wakefield: Henry.

Matilda's father.

Gareth knew better than to reveal himself – it might be a trap after all. So the youngster silently shinned down his tree and ran back to the camp to alert the rest of the men.

"You're sure it's Henry?" Robin asked when he had delivered his report.

"Aye, I've seen him before when I've gone to Wakefield for supplies. It was him for sure."

Robin rubbed his chin thoughtfully.

"Oh come on, Robin," Will Scarlet laughed. "Henry would hardly lead us into a trap would he? Not with his own daughter here. Stop being so cautious."

"Will's got a point," Little John agreed. "Let's go and see what the man wants."

Robin smiled at his friends, his blue eyes sparkling cheerfully. "Fair enough. But I want Arthur, Allan and Matt to flank us, and keep out of sight. Just in case. I'll go on ahead with Will and John. Gareth, you better get back to your lookout post. "

Matilda grabbed Robin's arm. "I'm coming with you. He's my da!"

"He's mine too, now," Robin replied with a grin, as his wife slapped him hard on the shoulder.

"In the name of Christ, don't you two get enough of that in bed?" Scarlet grinned, bringing more laughs from the rest of the outlaws, and an outraged flush from Matilda.

"Very good, Will. Come on then," Robin laughed, pulling his wife to his side and leading the way in the direction they could now hear Henry calling from.

As they neared the fletcher, Robin became serious again, signalling the outlaws to a halt. The men took defensive positions without needing instruction, hiding behind trees and whatever other foliage was still available in the barren winter forest.

"Robin! Matilda! It's me, Henry!"

The fletcher stepped back in shock as Robin suddenly appeared in front of him without warning. "Hello, Henry," the outlaw leader smiled, his eyes warily scanning the forest behind their visitor.

"For fuck sake, lad, you nearly gave me a heart attack there!"

"Sorry about that, Henry," Robin replied, his hand on his sword hilt, still staring into the trees and undergrowth around them for signs of an ambush. "Are you alone?"

"Of course I am" – the fletcher began, then his face broke into a massive grin as Matilda, flanked by Little John and Will Scarlet, stepped out from behind a thick tree trunk and raced to her father for a hug.

"Da!" she cried, tears in her eyes. "Oh Da, I've missed you!"

Henry was oblivious to the outlaws watching as he cuddled his daughter fiercely, his own eyes wet. "I'm here now," he told her, his deep voice cracking with emotion. "And everything's going to be all right, like it used to be!"

Robin wanted to ask the fletcher more, but Little John intervened. "Not here, Robin. Even if the fletcher did come alone, that doesn't mean he hasn't been followed. We should get back to camp."

The young leader nodded in agreement with his giant friend and John waved everyone back towards their camp, the fletcher following them with his daughter.

Safely off the well-worn pathways through Barnsdale forest, the outlaws, lookouts back in their positions, settled down to hear why Henry had come looking for them.

"The sheriff is asking for a meeting with you Robin," the fletcher told his new son-in-law. "Word is the Abbot of St Mary's came to visit him, and complained about you stealing a lot of his money."

"So why's he want a meeting with us?" Will asked. "Is he expecting us to hand back the cash? Not likely."

"Aye, Will, he does want the money back." Henry raised a hand to silence the outlaws' laughter. "The sheriff has promised pardons for some of you in return for the abbot's money."

That silenced the gang, who looked at each other hopefully.

"*Some* of us, Henry?" Little John asked. "Who?"

The fletcher looked slightly flustered as he replied, "Well, just Matilda, really…" His voice tailed off in embarrassment, but he placed a protective arm around his daughter and met John's eyes defiantly.

"You must be mad, Fletcher!" stormed Matt Groves. "That money's ours now. There's no way we're giving it up just so your daughter can go back to her nice life while the rest of us struggle to stay alive in this fucking forest! You've got a cheek, you have!"

Some of the outlaws grunted their agreement of Groves's statement; others were unsure what to think.

When the noise had died down, everyone looked to Robin.

"Well, Robin?" Groves demanded. "You're our leader. Tell the fletcher to go back to Wakefield and let the sheriff know he can shove his pardon up his arse."

"Give it a rest, Matt." Robin looked over in surprise as Will stepped forward to speak.

"Henry's only trying to look after his daughter; you can't blame him for that. Any one of us would do the same in his place." The fletcher nodded approval as Scarlet continued. "We already had plenty of money to see us through the winter, from *Lord* John de Bray's house. It's not like we really need the rest of it. What can we do with it in the forest anyway? Climb around the trees in fine silks? Lie in the cave eating lark's tongues?"

"So you're saying we just give the abbot his money back?" Groves asked in disbelief.

"Aye, that's exactly what I'm saying," Will told the older man. "Being part of this gang isn't just about staying alive and stealing from people. It's about friendship and looking out for each other. Well, we have a chance to look out for Matilda. One day, maybe someone will do the same for you."

Matt shook his head angrily, clearly unconvinced by Will's logic, and stormed off into the trees.

"Robin?" the fletcher looked over to his son-in-law again. "What say you?"

Robin's heart had leapt into his mouth when Henry had mentioned a pardon for Matilda – it was the answer to their prayers!

"The thing I want more than anything," he replied, looking around at the men earnestly, "is for us all to be pardoned – to be free again. I think this is a start. One pardon is better than nothing and, like Will says, we don't need the money stuck here in the forests. Let Matilda go home, I say."

Matilda gently released herself from her father's embrace and came over to hold Robin's hands. "But we're married now," she whispered, tears in her eyes. "We should be together."

Robin smiled. "We will be, some day, I swear it. I don't know how, but one day we'll all be free men again. Then we can be together, like a proper married couple."

Little John gave a laugh. "All we have to do is keep stealing money from rich abbots and the sheriff will eventually have to pardon the lot of us!"

The outlaws cheered at that, and the fletcher began to relax, sensing his daughter's freedom becoming a reality.

"However," Robin raised his voice again, "we have plenty of silver, but that money isn't mine to do whatever I like with. Every one of us has a say in this. Like Will says: we're more than just a gang, we're friends as well. The abbot's chest held two hundred pounds. There's seventeen of us. That means we're each due a share of..." He looked over at Friar Tuck who screwed up his round face and thought for a few moments.

"About eleven pounds!"

"Eleven pounds each," Robin nodded. "Matilda's my wife, so I don't mind giving up that money to free her, but I can't tell anyone else to do the same. It's up to you."

At Friar Tuck's suggestion they all agreed on a vote by show of hands. It was carried unanimously, although a small handful of the men were reluctant at first. Robin told them he would personally repay their share of the money himself, even if it took him forever, but, eventually, the men agreed to hand back their own share of the abbot's money in return for Matilda's pardon.

All except Matt Groves, who seemed to have disappeared sometime after the fletcher's arrival.

"I don't know what to say," Matilda told the outlaws, humbled by their sacrifice for her.

"Well, don't say anything then, lass," Little John grinned. "You get off home to Wakefield with your da, and make the most of your freedom."

"Look out for my Beth, will you, until I can steal enough money to get my own pardon?" Will asked her with a grin.

"Of course I will," Matilda smiled. "I'll treat her like my own wee sister."

All the outlaws said their goodbyes to Matilda. Every one of them had grown fond of the girl, and would be sorry to see her go.

Especially Robin. He felt like he'd been kicked in the guts as it slowly sunk in that he'd be living apart from his new wife from now on.

"What now, Henry?" Little John asked the fletcher. "How do we go about this?"

Matilda's father told them the sheriff would be at the old stone bridge a mile outside Wooley two days from then, at midday. There, he would give Robin – or whomever the outlaws chose to send – the letter of pardon for Matilda, in exchange for the abbot's silver.

The outlaws were happy enough with this: Wooley wasn't far from their camp, only a few hours walk, and the chest with the money in it was sitting, intact, in the very back of their big cave. They still had the little cart and the two old horses to pull it, so everything should be fine.

"Right, that's sorted then," Robin nodded, "You won't be leaving for Wakefield until the morning though, Henry, will you?"

The fletcher looked at the sun, gauging the time, and shook his head. "No. To be honest, I was hoping you lads would let me spend the night here. The light won't last much longer and I don't want to get caught out here when the temperature starts to drop."

Robin nodded, "Of course you can stay the night with us. We'll have a feast to celebrate Matilda's pardon, if we have enough food stored away. I'm sure we've some ale around too."

Now that Matilda's fate had been decided, everyone felt buoyant, even the men who had originally been unsure about giving up such a huge amount of money to save her. They genuinely did like Matilda, and were pleased to know she would be free again. Their reticence had, Robin reflected, been completely understandable.

Eleven pounds! It was a huge sum of money – more than most workers in England would earn in their lifetime.

But, as Will had pointed out, what was the point in being rich if you couldn't enjoy it? Besides, they were all still quite wealthy from the money and valuables they'd taken from Lord John de Bray's house.

They may be outlaws, Robin thought proudly, but they're good men.

He put the issue of Matt Groves to the back of his mind and joined his friends in preparing the feast. If this was to be his second last night together with Matilda for a while, he was going to damn well enjoy it.

The ale was passed around, some salted meat was roasted and the outlaws, along with Henry, enjoyed a celebration. The snow fell in Barnsdale forest as they celebrated life round a roaring campfire – their life together as friends who looked out for each other; the life Matilda would have restored to her and, for Robin and his wife, the life that grew inside Matilda.

Outlaws they may have been, but they were happy and free together that night.

Matt Groves appeared a while later, shuffling into the dim light sullen as ever, but Robin took him aside and told him he could have his eleven pounds of silver. Matt brightened considerably after that and the party continued long into the winter night.

Robin and Matilda didn't make love that night. Matilda slapped his eager hands away when they went to bed. "Not with my da here!" she snapped. "He might see us!"

The cave was so dark, even with the braziers lit, that Robin thought there was little chance of the fletcher seeing them doing much, but he didn't protest. They fell asleep after a kiss and cuddle, holding tightly to each other.

* * *

Hushed voices woke him during the night; the anxious tones intruding on his subconscious until he opened his eyes and wondered who was still awake at this time of night.

Carefully, so as not to wake Matilda, he rose from the pallet and pulled a heavy sheepskin around his shoulders to keep off some of the cold. Pushing aside the animal skins covering the entrance to their cave he quietly made his way to the small, but merrily crackling campfire where Little John and Will Scarlet sat, deep in conversation.

Shivering, Robin blew on his hands and settled down on a log next to his companions. "What are you two doing out here? It's fucking freezing, even this close to the fire."

"We didn't want to wake everyone," John replied.

"We're worried about this deal with the sheriff," Will added, his face anxious in the flickering orange firelight. "You know he's not going to just hand over Matilda's pardon and let us all walk off, right?"

John nodded. "I've heard de Faucumberg is an honourable man, for a noble, but we're wolf's heads – there's nothing to stop him killing the lot of us and taking the silver."

The three men stared dully into the campfire, entranced by the hypnotic flickering flames and their problem.

"What can we do?" Robin finally dragged his gaze away and looked at his friends. "Try and hide the men in the trees, ready to fire if the sheriff double-crosses us?"

Will shook his head. "De Faucumberg will be expecting something like that – he'll bring more men than us and have them search the area before he even arrives. We're going to have to come up with something better than that."

"This is what we've been trying to figure out for the past hour," John agreed. "The sheriff's men have already had their arses handed to them by us more than once recently – they'll be well prepared for any tricks."

Again, silence descended on the camp, broken only by the gentle crackling of the fire, until a smile slowly spread across Robin's face and he softly clapped his hands together in satisfaction.

"Here's what we'll do…"

CHAPTER TWENTY-FOUR

"You're really going to pardon one of these outlaws?" Abbot Ness was furious at the idea. "It'd be better if you would just hunt them all down. You have enough soldiers."

Here we go again, thought Henry de Faucumberg. "I've already explained to you, it wouldn't matter if I had a thousand soldiers. Finding a handful of men in an area the size of Barnsdale Forest, in the winter, is like looking for a needle in a haystack."

"But there's nowhere for them to hide!" the abbot shouted indignantly. "Look!" He pointed at the trees as they rode past. "The leaves are all gone. Where can they hide in winter?"

"There are still some trees with their foliage, even in winter," the sheriff explained. "And apart from that, the snow and ice makes it almost impossible to travel within the forest."

"The outlaws seem to manage..." the abbot grumbled.

"Oh shut up, man!" de Faucumberg snapped. "You're getting your two hundred pounds back aren't you? Besides, do you think I'm about to let the outlaws just walk away?"

The abbot sat up straighter on his horse and looked at the sheriff conspiratorially. "What d'you mean?"

"I didn't bring forty soldiers along with me just to keep the peace. The outlaws have seventeen men, I've been told. Well, sixteen minus the girl. We outnumber them more than two to one. And I chose a meeting point that's out in the open, so the bastards can't swing away up into the trees like monkeys, the way they normally do."

Abbot Ness smiled wickedly, then his face fell. "You're putting my life in danger with this plan, de Faucumberg."

The sheriff grinned. "Hmm? Yes, I daresay I am. No matter, I'm sure God will watch over you."

They reached Wooley an hour before midday, so the sheriff told his men to eat lunch, but to remain alert.

It was a misty morning, with a white blanket of snow covering the ground and the sun a small dim circle hardly visible in the cloudy grey sky. De Faucumberg sat on a big boulder, eating a chunk of buttered bread. A robin landed beside him and he watched it contentedly until another appeared and they chased each other off.

"They're coming, my lord," one of his soldiers shouted, as the faint creak of a horse-drawn wagon reached them through the damp mist.

"Mount up!" the sheriff roared, his breath steaming. "Be alert!"

"What about me?" Abbot Ness asked plaintively.

"Get on your horse, man. Just wait beside me." The sheriff shook his head in disgust.

Eventually, through the mist, two horses appeared, pulling a small cart after them with a great wooden chest on it. As it came closer, three heavily armed figures came into view, beside the cart. More than a dozen shadowy figures followed a little way behind, shrouded in fog.

"Robin Hood, Will Scaflock and John Little, I presume?" the sheriff shouted into the chill, moist air, his voice barely carrying.

"Aye!" the one in the middle replied, with a confident grin. "Who the fuck are you?"

The three men laughed.

"Very amusing, Hood," the sheriff shouted in reply. "Where are the rest of your men?"

"Shagging your mum!" Little John shouted, his great voice somehow piercing the mist all around. Even the sheriff's own men laughed at that, although they tried to hide it when de Faucumberg glared at them.

"Where's my money?" Abbot Ness demanded, the thought of his two hundred pounds lending him courage.

"Right here," Robin replied, patting the chest on the cart. "All yours. Once we get the pardon for Matilda Fletcher of Wakefield." Technically, she was Matilda Hood now, but Robin saw no reason to mention that to his enemies.

"Check that chest!" de Faucumberg ordered some of the monks who had travelled with the abbot. "Make sure there's two hundred pounds in it."

"There's not. There's one hundred and eighty-nine pounds. I give you my word on that." Robin told the sheriff.

"Our agreement is for two hundred pounds, Hood".

"Yes, two hundred, wolf's head!" Abbot Ness shouted, spittle flecking his lips in anger.

Robin shrugged. "Take it or leave it. One of my men refused your deal, so we had to take his share out of your chest. Our friend – a friar – says two hundred pounds less eleven is one hundred and eighty-nine, so…that's what's in your box, abbot."

"That's not the deal!" Ness ranted, but the sheriff waved a hand at him.

"It's only eleven pounds, for God's sake man. Is it all there?"

One of the men he had ordered to check the chest nodded his head from atop the cart, his hands still digging through the huge mass of silver coins as his companions tried to count the total. "It looks like it, my lord sheriff!"

"Where's the girl's pardon?" Will growled.

"Pardon?" Henry de Faucumberg retorted in apparent confusion, one eyebrow raised. He waved his hands at his men. "Circle them!" he roared.

Little John and Will Scarlet drew their swords, both looking angrily at Robin.

"Come on then, you fuckers," Scarlet yelled, drawing his sword and holding it in front of himself defiantly.

Little John held his huge quarterstaff before himself confidently, but he looked at Robin questioningly. The sheriff's forty men outnumbered them almost two to one. "If your plan's going to work, it better happen soon," he growled, eyeing the sheriff's soldiers warily.

"You men are outlaws." The sheriff nodded towards them. "What made you think I would honour a bargain made with men such as yourselves, who are outside the law? I'm sorry to do this – for outlaws you seem like honourable enough men but I must see justice done," he shook his head as if genuinely sorrowful, but raised his voice and shouted to his men. "Advance! Kill them all."

De Faucumberg's men began to close in on the outlaws, who, regardless of the freezing air, were sweating freely.

"We're not getting out of this," John grunted bitterly. "But I'm going to do my best to make it to that bastard sheriff before I go down."

Robin, dismayed at the failure of his plans, murmured his assent. "On my word, then…"

"Hold!"

Despite the freezing mist, the powerful voice, full of authority, reached everyone in the clearing. No one moved, eyes straining warily to see who had shouted the command.

"Stand your men down, de Faucumberg!"

Robin heaved a huge sigh of relief and flashed a knowing grin at his tense friends as Sir Richard-at-Lee and his sergeant, Stephen, materialized through the haze, their black mantles and snow white crosses seeming almost ethereal in the cold light.

Another armoured noble rode beside Sir Richard, and, by the noises following them, they had brought a small army along.

The sheriff's face fell as he saw the newcomers approaching. He knew who Sir Richard and his noble companion were, as did Abbot Ness who cursed in surprise at the sight of the man he had sought to dispossess of his lands not so long before.

"Get your men back out of the road, de Faucumberg, now!" Sir Richard ordered.

The three outlaws heaved sighs of relief as the sheriff grudgingly waved his men back behind him.

"Sir Richard came then," Will smiled ruefully.

"Aye, and just in fucking time too," John laughed, starting to relax as the threat of imminent doom passed.

"You have a document, I believe?" Sir Richard demanded of the sheriff, who remained silent. "A pardon for the girl, Matilda of Wakefield?"

The sheriff still said nothing, even ignoring the confused and worried whispers of Abbot Ness.

"Well hand it over then, de Faucumberg!" Sir Richard roared. The soldiers behind him were plainly visible now, even through the thick mist. He had at least fifty men with him, all in chain or plate mail, including a dozen or so mounted knights.

In contrast, the sheriff's forty men had come lightly armoured, and on foot, to aid movement through the forest, since they had been expecting a possible fight with seventeen highly mobile outlaws through the greenwood.

A pitched battle in the clearing they found themselves in now would be a slaughter and the sheriff knew it. His precarious position became even more obvious as the rest of the outlaws, marshalled by Friar Tuck, moved closer to the clearing, the fog parting to reveal longbows trained on De Faucumberg's men. And him.

He reached into his saddlebag and lifted out a scroll.

"Here," he grunted, nudging his horse forward, then, when he was close enough, he tossed it at Robin's feet, his face scarlet with rage and humiliation.

"Let's see it, Robin," Sir Richard said, beckoning the outlaws to come towards him.

Little John and Will still had their weapons at the ready, and they followed their young leader as he moved towards the mounted Knight Hospitaller.

Richard unrolled the scroll and glanced over it. "Good, it's in order," he said, returning the document to Robin, warning him to keep it safe.

"Now you may go, de Faucumberg." The big knight waved a dismissive mailed hand at the raging sheriff.

Abbot Ness finally found his voice as he realised the sheriff was going to retreat. "What about my silver? That cart and its contents belong to St Mary's Abbey!" he cried, pointing desperately at his money. "That wolf's head stole it!"

"Get out of here, now, de Faucumberg, while you still can," Sir Richard said to the sheriff. "And take that grasping abbot with you before I remove the bastard's head – man of God or not."

Ness tried to protest but the sheriff knew he was beaten and roared at the abbot to forget it and follow as he turned back towards Nottingham.

"The king will hear of this, Hospitaller!" de Faucumberg shouted angrily over his shoulder.

For the first time Sir Richard's noble companion spoke, laughing coldly at the sheriff's retreating back. "King Edward will soon have more to worry about than your whining, de Faucumberg. Next time we meet, I won't let you run away with your tail between your legs. England has had enough of Edward, and his lackeys like you!"

The three outlaws looked at Sir Richard-at-Lee in surprise, expecting some reaction to his companion's treason. The knight sat stony-faced on his great warhorse though, watching the sheriff and his men disappear into the mist.

"You're Robin Hood, then," Sir Richard's noble companion turned his head with a smile, fixing the young outlaw leader with a commanding gaze. "I've heard a lot about you, lad."

Sir Richard laughed at the blank expression on Robin's face. "This is the Earl of Lancaster," the knight said to the outlaws. "We spoke of him when I first met you."

Robin, Will and John had no idea how to behave around an earl, so they did what seemed proper and dropped to one knee, heads bowed.

Sir Richard laughed again, but his words were indignant. "Get up you fools! You never knelt to me when we met. Quite the opposite!"

The three outlaws were not enjoying this at all. They had no idea why the Earl of Lancaster had helped save them from the sheriff.

Richard was amused to see the three tough men nervously scratching the backs of their necks and fidgeting like naughty children. "Relax, lads, you're in the company of friends now," he smiled reassuringly.

Robin warily got to his feet, John and Will following his lead, and looked at the earl, still somewhat overawed. "You wanted to meet us, my lord?"

Thomas, Earl of Lancaster jumped down from his horse and walked over to stand in front of the outlaws. "I did, Robin," he agreed, extending a hand which Robin shook. The man's grasp was firm, but his face was open and his eyes were smiling. "I've heard a lot about you, from Sir Richard here, and also from my tenants. You killed my bailiff in Wakefield – Henry."

Robin placed a hand on his sword hilt but the earl smiled reassuringly. "Don't worry, lad, you did me a favour. I never realised how much the villagers hated him – since I replaced him the people have been more productive, which is all a lord wants to hear from one of his holdings."

Richard-at-Lee had dismounted as well by now and gave the three outlaws friendly pats on the back, smiling the whole time.

"The earl has a proposition for you, boys," the Hospitaller told them. "Why don't we head for one of the nearby villages and we can discuss it?"

Robin shoved Matilda's pardon safely inside his cloak and shrugged. "Let's go then," he replied. "Wooley isn't far, and I could do with an ale or two after this afternoon."

"What about the money?" Little John wondered.

Robin was no fool. He knew Sir Richard was a friend, and the Earl of Lancaster – who was watching Robin intently from atop his horse – had come to help them as well for some reason. But near two hundred pounds was a lot of silver. Enough to strain any apparent friendship.

"Since the earl and Sir Richard saved our skins, why don't we give them half the money?" Robin decided, with a smile towards the two horsemen.

"I still owe you men £100 for the loan you gave me to pay off Abbott Ness," Sir Richard noted, raising an eyebrow at Robin's generosity.

"We can forget that," the young outlaw shrugged, laying a restraining hand on Will's arm as the fuming outlaw tried to protest. "We helped you, you've helped us, and we all," he glared at Scarlet, "come out of this much, much richer."

The noblemen broke into wide grins. Robin knew – from the way the earl had been gazing at him – if it had come down to it, the earl would have demanded all of the money. He had more than enough men to back up such a demand after all.

But Robin's offer was enough to placate the lord and everyone, even Will when he realised what had just happened, was happy with the idea.

Sir Richard and the earl each filled their men's horses' saddlebags with silver until there was roughly half of the original one hundred and eighty-nine pounds left in the chest.

"I'll take the cart back with the rest of the lads," Little John offered. "Scarlet has more experience dealing with nobles than I do – I'm just a simple village blacksmith!"

Robin nodded gratefully at his giant friend and handed him the document of pardon for Matilda. "If it comes to it, forget the money, John. Just make sure this letter gets safely back to Matilda."

The great bearded outlaw nodded solemnly and tucked the document inside his bearskin cloak.

"Ready, lads?" Sir Richard asked, wandering over and putting a brawny arm round the shoulders of Will and Robin.

"Aye," Robin laughed. "Let's go get a drink."

The young outlaw was in good spirits. His men still had near a hundred pounds of silver they didn't expect to have after today, they were still alive, and his pregnant wife was a free woman again. The day had worked out perfectly. The only thing that could make him happier, he thought with a wry smile, would be a pardon for him and the rest of his men.

CHAPTER TWENTY-FIVE

"A pardon? For all of us?" Robin gasped in disbelief.

The Earl of Lancaster nodded enthusiastically. "Yes, Robin. For you, and every one of your men."

Robin looked at Will, who shrugged his shoulders and took a drink of his ale.

A short time ago they had arrived in the small town of Wooley and found seats at a table in one of the local taverns, a neat looking place, with two hearths in the main room. The earl had sent most of his men home, but kept a handful of guards with him, in case of trouble. Those men waited discreetly by the front door. Well, as discreetly as was possible for half a dozen armoured men in a small-town inn with only a handful of tables in it.

Robin, Will, Sir Richard and the earl had a table of their own and, since it was only mid-afternoon, the inn was quiet, so they were fairly private.

Small fires were smouldering in the hearths when they walked in from the frozen winter streets, but a shout from Sir Richard had seen the landlord piling on a few logs. Soon enough the room was lit by a cosy orange glow from each end and the four men sat contentedly with their mugs of ale, feeling the warmth seeping into their bones, drying out the icy mists of Barnsdale forest.

"What do we have to do for this pardon?" Robin asked eventually, as the chill left his bones and the ale warmed his head enough to help him think straight.

The Earl of Lancaster drained his own mug and shouted for another round, fixing Robin with a stony gaze. "Join the rebellion," he said quietly.

Again, Robin and Will looked at each other, but neither man said anything.

"You know I asked the king to help my tenants after a few hard years?" Thomas asked. "Well, he promised aid, but never followed up on his promise. My

306

tenants are struggling to stay alive – that means people like your family in Wakefield, Robin. The king expects me to pay him the same rents I paid when harvests were good, which would mean me squeezing more money from my tenants. Money they simply don't have. If I take any more rent from them they'll die, or have to become outlaws…No offence, lads," he smiled, draining his ale, "but we have enough outlaws in Barnsdale already."

Robin had no idea how to deal with the situation. Although he was the leader of the outlaws' gang, he was still only eighteen. He looked at the more worldly wise Will hopefully.

Scarlet shrugged his wide shoulders. "I'd say it's a good deal," he told his young friend. "What other options do we have? The king's a bastard, just like his da. He'll squeeze the people until they've nothing left to give, to pay for his wars against the Scots and the Welsh and whoever else."

"You think the earl's a better option than the king?" Robin asked, not caring that the earl was sitting at the table with them. He knew Will would be honest no matter who sat with them.

"Aye, he is," Scarlet replied. "I'm sure he's expecting to take a lot of money and lands out of this rebellion. Even take the throne for himself." He glanced at the earl but the man just stared back, giving nothing away. "From what the people say though, and since Sir Richard's backing him…well, I think he's probably a decent enough man who genuinely wants to help the people."

"Can his rebellion succeed?"

Will shrugged. "I've been stuck in the greenwood with you lot, I don't know how the balance of power lies. I don't see how it matters though."

Robin looked at his friend quizzically.

"You don't pick sides based on who'll win, do you?" Will grunted. "You choose the side that has the same goals and ideals as you do yourself."

Robin was out of his depth. He finished his ale and gladly accepted another from the landlord who was hovering around refilling each man's mug as it was emptied.

"I don't know you," the young outlaw said eventually, after some other small talk, "but I trust Richard and I think Will knows which way the wind's blowing so I'll join your rebellion, in return for a pardon once we win."

Richard-at-Lee hadn't said much so far, but he reached forward and clasped Robin's forearm now. "You're a strong man," the knight told him earnestly. "Exactly the kind of man we need to make England great again."

Robin felt his face flush red in embarrassment. He was no fool though.

"We'll join your rebellion, assuming every one of us is pardoned, but what about our wages? And the chain of command?"

"If you join our army you take orders like everyone else," the earl replied.

"That's fine," Will replied, understanding where Robin was going with his question. "But it would make sense to keep us – all sixteen of us – as one company. There's no sense in assigning new captains to a group of soldiers who already fight as a unit."

Thomas looked thoughtful but Sir Richard nodded at him and agreed with Will.

Robin grinned at Scarlet. "He's right, Sir Thomas, we fight best with our own chain of command. If we join your rebellion you should let us fight the way we know how. It's to your advantage."

The Earl of Lancaster wasn't too bothered whether the outlaws joined him or not, if he was honest. He was trying to gather the biggest army he could, and Sir Richard-at-Lee had told him Hood's men would be a good addition to his fighting force. But they were only sixteen men. As good as they supposedly were they weren't critical to his plans. He drained his ale and slammed a fist down on the table with a laugh.

"Fine! Whatever, Robin! You can lead your own men under Sir Richard's Hospitaller banner. And when we win: a pardon for the lot of you!"

Robin grinned and looked at Will for advice.

"Can't say fairer than that," Scarlet smiled, draining his own ale mug. "One more thing…the Lord of Hathersage, John de Bray?"

"What about him?" the earl wondered, confused by Will's question.

"I ain't taking orders from that prick. Is he part of your rebellion?"

Sir Richard shook his head with a wolfish grin. "He was never one of us, you know that – he's a king's man. Besides, the bastard's been ruined, Will. He has no money left, his tenants have turned against him, and, as we speak, the king is sending a man to replace him as lord in Hathersage. He's nothing."

Robin clapped his friend on the back. "I told you we'd make him pay, Will."

Will drained his ale and set his mug on the table grimly. "Once we're done here, then, I have some business to deal with in Hathersage."

The earl had no idea what Will meant, but he didn't care either. He had to get moving, to try and add more men to his growing army.

He stood up, Sir Richard rising with him, hastily downing the last of his own ale.

"Take care of your business, then, lads." Thomas nodded to the outlaws. "Sort out whatever you have to sort, enjoy your Christmas. Then be ready to bring your men to Sir Richard's castle at Kirklees when we call on you in the next few weeks."

"After that," Richard smiled boldly, "all we have to do is destroy the king…"

309

CHAPTER TWENTY-SIX

"So – who feels like kicking King Edward's useless arse for him?" Robin demanded.

The outlaws cheered and raised their ale cups to the night sky jubilantly, the joyful sounds filling the forest. The young wolf's head had never seen the men so excited.

"I can't believe it," the youngster Gareth grasped his leader's shoulders happily. "I never thought I'd be a free man."

"Slow down," Robin laughed, tossing back a mouthful of ale. "We still have to defeat the king's army first!"

Gareth shrugged as if the task was trivial and, grinning widely, wandered off to join the rest of the men dancing and singing by the great campfire which had been banked high to stave off the bitter winter chill.

"You'd think we kill kings every other day," Robin shook his head ruefully, enjoying the outlaws' reaction to the earl's proposal, but fearing the raucous celebrations were premature.

"Let us have our fun," Friar Tuck advised. "No, it won't be easy to beat the king's soldiers. Quite possibly every one of us will die in the battle, even if the earl wins in the end." He shrugged. "But we finally have a goal – a purpose. Something to aim for, rather than just scratching an existence from one day to the next in this forest, hoping the law doesn't catch up with us."

Robin realised the friar was right. No wonder the men were so excited. "Alright then, Tuck, what are you waiting for? Let's see you dance!" With a whoop, he tossed his empty cup on the ground, grabbed the portly churchman by the wrists and dragged him round in a manic jig.

On Christmas day, the outlaws who had family or friends in nearby villages went to visit them. It had snowed sporadically for the past few days, and the roads were treacherous for unwary travellers. The law would not be out hunting for wolf's heads in such harsh weather, so the men made the most of it.

Little John went off smiling and whistling to Holderness to see his wife and son. Gareth went to see his poorly ma in Wrangbrook, and Arthur visited his parents in Bichill. Some of the outlaws, like Friar Tuck and Allan-a-Dale, were happy to stay at the camp, feasting, carolling, and playing drunken games like blind man's buff with each other. They had even gathered some ivy and holly, with many bright red berries, and decorated the cave with them.

Matilda had taken her pardon and, escorted by Robin, and Will, gone home to Wakefield, a free woman.

Robin had asked Much to come to the village with them, but, with his da murdered and a new miller living in the mill where he had grown up, Much had decided just to stay at the camp with Tuck and the others.

In Wakefield, Matilda's parents greeted her with joy, as little Beth wrapped herself around Scaflock's legs, screaming in delight.

The Fletchers' house, like the outlaws' camp, and all the other properties in the village, had been decorated with evergreen foliage, which stood out gaily against the frost and snow, and many villagers were singing carols.

Robin headed off to spend the day with his parents, and Scarlet, who had brought his own bedroll, stayed with the Fletchers, who gladly agreed to put him up for the evening.

Before they went to watch the mummers performing their festive play in the village green, Will took Beth for a walk down by the river, a huge grin on his face the entire time. He would never forget what

311

Robin had done for him by rescuing his daughter and bringing happiness back into his life. She was a wonderful little girl, despite her harsh three years in de Bray's house, and Will knew his wife, Elaine, had been a fine mother. He wished she could see Beth now, but pushed the bleak thoughts out of his mind, and just concentrated on enjoying the day with his daughter.

Since it was Christmas he had brought her a gift – a little carved wooden dog on wheels, and they laughed and ran together through the snow, pulling it jerkily along behind them. Will's heart was light, and he offered a silent prayer to God for his good fortune.

Robin visited his family, taking them a ready cooked goose and some pickled vegetables for their Christmas dinner. He also handed his father a bag of silver to make sure they enjoyed the season without worrying about money.

Martha piled plates for them all, and they enjoyed a meal as a family for the first time since Robin had been outlawed seven months earlier. After the main course, a big mince pie was produced and Marjorie, who was looking much better since Robin had seen her last, was allowed first bite and told to make the traditional wish.

The big outlaw's heart swelled to see his little sister grinning as she bit into the tasty meat savoury, and he made a wish of his own, that Marjorie would enjoy many more happy, healthy Christmases.

Although she was stronger, his sister was still too poorly to go into the freezing afternoon to see the mummers with Will, Beth and the Fletchers, so the Hoods stayed home, happy in their own company, as the sounds of revelry filled the village outside.

As the light faded outside, making the already dim, smoky room seem even darker, they sat around the fire drinking warm ale and Robin told them of his intention to join the earl's planned rebellion. They knew King Edward would call the villagers to fight for him against the Earl of Lancaster's forces. Robin didn't want to find himself on a battlefield facing his own father.

"Don't worry about that, son," John told him. "If it comes to that, I'll join the same side as you. The earl has tried to be a decent lord to Wakefield, while the king continues to persecute men like you. There's no way I'll fight for a king whose unjust laws made my son live in the forest like an animal!"

Robin was cheered by his father's support, and the talk soon drifted to happier subjects, including his marriage to Matilda, which his parents were more than happy about. They talked long into the night, a well-banked log fire chasing the worst of the winter chill from the air, bathing the small room in a cosy orange glow.

John and Martha finally went upstairs to the little loft to sleep, kissing their son and daughter good night as they stretched out on their own straw pallets beside the fire which Robin now placed the stone cover over.

"He's a good lad," Martha whispered proudly to her husband as they climbed into bed and pulled the thick blankets over themselves. "A good man."

"Aye, he is," John agreed. "And maybe if the Earl of Lancaster can defeat that worthless bastard Edward…"

"Our boy can come home."

They hugged each other close and, full of hope, slept better that night than they had for months.

In the morning, Will and Robin said their farewells to their families, hopeful they would see them again soon, as free men. Still, even Will had tears in his eyes as he said goodbye to his little daughter, cuddling her fiercely and telling her how much he loved her.

Robin had embraced his parents and Marjorie, promising to visit more often, then went to the Fletcher's house to say goodbye to Matilda.

313

The two of them walked alone, thick cloaks round their shoulders as a light but icy wind whipped about the trees on the village outskirts.

"Did you tell your ma and da about...?" Robin wondered, placing a tender hand on his wife's belly.

Matilda shook her head. "No, not yet. I'll wait a couple more weeks until I'm showing more then I'll say to them. I don't know how they'll take it – they still think of me as their own wee girl. And, with you still being an outlaw..."

They walked a little longer, feeling melancholy at their parting.

Robin was overjoyed at Matilda being pardoned, and being able to live in Wakefield with her parents again, where she could raise their child in a normal environment.

He felt sad that he might not be able to enjoy being a proper father to the baby though. He'd never thought about having a child until now, but he wanted to do things right.

"I promise you, Matilda," he told her, grasping her hands and looking in her eyes earnestly. "I'll be here for you and our baby. I'll fight for the earl, and win my pardon. Then we'll be a proper family together!"

They held each other tightly, neither wanting to let go, but eventually they made their way back to Matilda's home, where Robin and Will bade everyone a last farewell, and headed into the forest to return to their camp.

The day before, Robin had visited the Wakefield headman, Patrick, and given him a bag of silver, as a Christmas gift to the village. Patrick had been shocked at the amount, but had promised to put it to good, and fair, use during the bad weather. He also told Robin he would make sure the villagers knew exactly who had given them the money.

Matilda, Marjorie and Beth would be well looked after by the people of Wakefield.

The two outlaws reached the camp by late afternoon, despite the thick snow, which slowed them and tired their legs.

"Scarlet!" Allan-a-Dale shouted as he saw his friends approaching. "Good news!"

"What's up, Allan?" Will wondered.

The minstrel hurried over, eager to share the news.

"Wilfred the baker sent word from Hathersage! The new lord there turned up yesterday with a dozen soldiers. John de Bray's been sent packing. Him and his wife were seen on the road south, struggling to get their horse and cart moving through the snow. Probably heading to London."

"Just the two of them?" Robin wondered.

"Aye," John nodded. "He's got no money to hire guards, has he?"

Will nodded grimly. "I'm going after him. Finally…finally, I'll have my revenge . . ."

Robin grasped him by the shoulder. "Do what you have to do. Take one of the horses."

They still had the two horses that had pulled Abbot Ness's cart of silver, so it would make the journey much quicker if Will took one of them to hunt his quarry.

"D'you want me to come with you?" Robin asked his grim friend. "Or one of the others? It'd be safer if you aren't alone, there's more outlaws than just us around these parts."

Scarlet thought for a moment; then he shook his head. "No, I have to do this alone."

In truth, he would have been happy for one of the other men to go with him for company but the fact was, he didn't know how he would react when he finally came face to face with the man who had murdered his family and made a slave of his infant daughter.

He believed he might butcher John de Bray, and possibly his wife too if she got in his way, and he didn't want any of his friends to be there to see it.

He saddled the youngest of the two horses and headed south without a word to the rest of the men.

When he returned to camp late that evening no one asked him what had happened, they simply welcomed him home warmly.

He accepted a mug of ale from Robin and gave his friend a melancholy nod of thanks.

It was done. Will Scaflock could, at last, move on – the darkness in his soul had finally been cleansed.

Robin never found out whether his friend had killed de Bray and his wife or let them go. The pain in Will's green eyes – the anguish Robin had there since the day he had met him – was gone at last.

Friar Tuck believed Will, a new man since rediscovering his daughter, had done the Christian thing and let de Bray go, while Matt Groves muttered to the outlaws of how he imagined Will had butchered both de Bray and his wife.

It didn't matter. Will Scarlet was, finally, Will Scaflock again.

For now.

* * *

"Fucking bastards!"

The servants cowered as de Faucumberg raged in his great hall in Nottingham castle, smashing things left, right and centre. These outbursts had been happening regularly, since the sheriff had returned from his humiliating meeting with Robin and the Earl of Lancaster.

"Bastards, the lot of them!" he screamed, face almost purple with rage. "Treat me like a fucking peasant?" He kicked over a chamber pot, piss spilling all over the floor. Even though he had made the mess himself, it only made him angrier as he screamed at his servants to clean it up.

"My lord . . . ?" The steward crept surreptitiously into the hall, trying to remain as anonymous as possible as the sheriff stormed around the room. "You have a visitor."

"Unless it's Richard-at-Lee or the Earl of Lancaster crawling on their knees begging my aid, you can kick them out! I'm in no mood for visitors!" de Faucumberg roared, before he eventually calmed down and, with a sullen grunt, dropped into the high backed chair at the end of the room.

"Well?" the sheriff roared at the cowering steward. "Show them in then!"

A tall, black armoured knight strode confidently into the great hall when the door was opened. He had dark eyes and walked as if he owned the castle.

The sheriff disliked him straight away.

"Who are you and what the hell do you want?" de Faucumberg demanded, as the man stood in front of him confidently, his big arms clasped behind his back.

"I'm here to hunt your outlaws, sheriff," the man replied, his face expressionless as he removed his helmet, revealing hair as black as his armour.

De Faucumberg snorted. "Oh are you? Well, I've been hunting those men for months – years some of them – and had no luck. I hope you can do better than I've managed. Who sent you? "

The stranger stood stock still, but his eyes moved to fix the sheriff in his gaze. "Everyone in the north of England has heard of these outlaws, and your failure to bring them to justice."

De Faucumberg's face became even angrier, as he glared at the stranger who had walked into his own castle and insulted him in front of his own people.

"You can hold your tongue, sir!" the sheriff snapped. "If you must criticise me, do it in private, not in front of my own men."

The big stranger remained silent, eyes fixed on an invisible point on the wall in front of himself.

"Who are you, anyway, and who sent you to save us all from the mighty Robin Hood and his men?" the sheriff demanded, spittle flecking his lips.

The knight moved forward, graceful despite his size, left hand resting gently on the pommel of his sword. He stood in front of de Faucumberg and looked boldly into the sheriff's eyes.

"King Edward himself has sent me, to destroy these outlaws that plague you. And I will destroy them, you can be sure of it."

He leaned down and placed his hands confidently on the table as he gazed at de Faucumberg. "You may have heard of me, lord sheriff. My name is Sir Guy of Gisbourne."

Historical Note

Writing historical fiction throws up some interesting challenges, and it's not always easy deciding how to overcome them.

During the time period covered in this series there was more than one sheriff in the north of England, where the action takes place. Some readers might have liked me to write the novel with 100% historical accuracy, and used the correct names for each different year. However, I decided to pick one man to fill the role of sheriff, who readers could get to know, and stick with him for the entirety of the series rather than introducing a different character for each book, who would flit in and out of the story, before readers could get to know them.

Sir Henry de Faucumberg was Sheriff of Nottingham and Yorkshire from 1318-1319 and again from 1323-1325 – around the time I've set *Wolf's Head* and its sequels. If Robin Hood did operate around the time of the Lancastrian revolt, as I think likely, de Faucumberg would have been a major thorn in his side for much of his life. De Faucumberg is also an interesting character in his own right, being charged on three separate occasions between 1313 and 1315, for theft and contempt of court, before somehow finding his way in life and being named sheriff shortly after in 1318.

He hunted down the Lancastrian rebels – the "Contrariants", was sheriff when the king visited the area in 1323 and, before being appointed sheriff, lived in Wakefield, just like Robin. He also held an estate in Holderness, where Little John originates.

Sir Henry de Faucumberg, with all these (coincidental?) connections to our other characters and places in *Wolf's Head* is the ideal candidate for our sheriff, I hope you will agree. Or at least see my point in choosing him for the position.

The next book in the series will see Robin, Will Scarlet, Little John *et al* dealing with the aftermath of Thomas, Earl of Lancaster's revolt. Sir Guy of Gisbourne will also pose a new threat to Robin and his friends – a hunter more deadly than Adam Bell/Gurdon ever was…?

I hope you'll join me to find out!

Steven A. McKay,
Glasgow,
December 26th, 2012

If you have enjoyed *Wolf's Head*, please leave a review on the website of the seller you purchased it from. Good reviews are the lifeblood of self-published authors, so please take a few moments to let others know what you thought of the book.

Thank you for reading!

To find out what's happening with the author and the sequels to *Wolf's Head* point your browser to:

www.facebook.com/RobinHoodNovel

Made in the USA
Charleston, SC
01 June 2014